~ SAND IN THE WIND ~

AN AFRICAN NOVEL
BY
KEITH MEADOWS

ISBN 0-7974-1785-0

First published in Zimbabwe in 1997 by
Thorntree Press (Pvt) Ltd, P O Box 9243 Hillside,
Bulawayo Zimbabwe

Printed by National Printing & Packaging, Harare

Also by Keith Meadows
Fothergill – Bridging a Conservation Era

THORNTREE PRESS

"Tiko lingahva zvihari itiko lingafa"
"A land without wild animals is a dead land."

- *Old Shangaan saying.*

"We are not separate from our environments: each species we destroy and each habitat we ravage, whether by bulldozer or pesticides, represents one more bridge that we have burned in our own ultimate battle for survival."

- *Warden Harry Kenyon, in an address to a wildlife and environment symposium, Kariba, June 1978.*

For pressed flowers, baobabs and river music
Long may they endure.
And for Danny Carney, who had the faith, way
back.

AUTHOR'S NOTE

This is not a true story. It would, however, be silly to claim that it is purely the product of the writer's febrile imagination. Contact with people and places, with conversations and situations, with wild creatures and wild places, together with being a part of unfolding history, helped to transform the germ of an idea into a book.

I would assure those who seek identity as real people amongst my invented characters that they will be disappointed, for no specific character is based upon a specific person. There is no intent to duplicate or compromise in fiction the personality or actions of any living person. Certainly you will find the names of real people in this novel, names of public figures synonymous with the country, its wildlife, and with events in the history of the country, be it Rhodesia or Zimbabwe. Just as you once may have enjoyed a cold beer at the bar of The Blue Room, or listened to Jack Dent who played the piano at La Fontaine for over seventeen years, or paused at the lay-by on the Zambezi Escarpment to stare whimsically over the Valley. As for the events herein, some happened, some might have happened, some are happening as you read this. Geography has been purposely confused, and the mixture of imperial and metric units of measure encountered throughout the book is not due to editorial dereliction. As the time span of the story covers thirty years, various yardsticks are wont to change.

Once again I am grateful to Ian Henderson for his support and artwork. For me, no one portrays elephants or 'the singing heat' of the Zambezi Valley as he does. Many thanks are due to Janet Clarke who has worked so hard in transposing my neanderthalic ramblings from vintage manual typewriter to computer disk, and, again, to Vivien Mitchell, for reading the finished manuscript. Any errors are my responsibility. I am grateful, as ever, to Angie. She has always walked the extra mile. And then there is Mviri, late of the Mukwishe, gentleman, scholar and superb tracker of man and animal – who showed me the way, long ago.

Sit around a campfire in the African bush for long enough of an evening and, sooner or later, the 'elephant debate' surfaces; along with those other perennials, malaria and snakebite treatment. As elephants feature strongly in this book, I am throwing myself on the reader's indulgence to put forward my small case for the elephant.

The human animal continues to do three things well. These are to procreate, and, subsequently, to put immense pressure on the space and food sources of our planet. We are literally eating ourselves out of house and home. Then, what we don't devour or debase, we manage very competently to ruin or destroy. However, we are also very adroit at pointing fingers, and this is where the elephant comes in for more than its fair share of condemnation. Sadly, the very problems that the human species causes for itself are also visited upon the elephant populations of Africa. The animals retreat before an ever expanding human population invading their range, a population that is only too ready to cry 'foul' should elephants trespass upon their newly won territory in any way. In turn, the displaced elephants are compressed into a few small areas, 'islands' of protection that have been set aside for them. Here, in time, their breeding and feeding habits begin to outgrow their havens, and consideration has to be given to culling, population reduction. By humans. Then there is the ivory trade, with its networks all over the globe, with, really, little control over it. Because the numbers of elephants, overall, are diminishing. But still you will read, on occasion, that there are too many elephants. *Too many elephants?* I don't think so.
There are too many people.

Keith Meadows, Elephant Sands, Hwange, August 1997

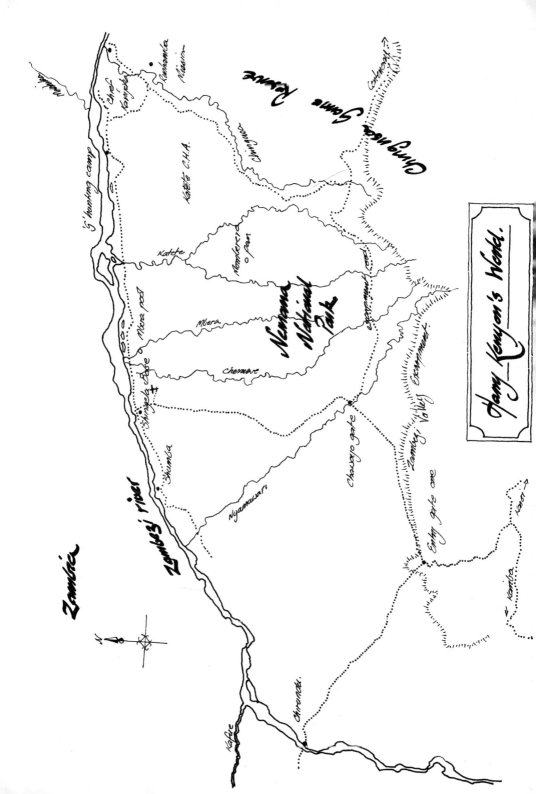

~ PART ONE ~

Summer, 1950s

MASTER OF THE CARAVAN, QUESTIONING A GROUP OF TRAVELLERS:

"But who are ye, in rags and rotten shoes,
You dirty-bearded, blocking up the way?"

ISHAK, MINSTREL TO THE CALIPH, ANSWERS:

"We are the pilgrims, master; we shall go
Always a little further."

(From **"HASSAN"** by J E Flecker. The reply is on the
SAS memorial at Hereford)

CHAPTER ONE

In the shallow black water off the sandbar the crocodile waited.

A shade over 17 feet long, the big saurian held station in the steady current that eddied around its great bulk, and it was as if the river chuckled and gurgled past some solid upthrust of rock. The alien muted drone that came from somewhere upcurrent, in the deeper river, tickling the animal's superb sensory system, registered automatically in the heavily protected brain. It caused no alarm. Here in the centre of its territory along this middle stretch of Zambezi River, there was no animal capable of harming this being, this leftover representative of a species that had survived for 170 million years. Its size and bulk, close to a ton, made it one of the superior living things in its territory. A killing machine. The perfect assassin. Depending upon the stimuli that flickered across its brain it would attack with devastating speed and power. Or simply disappear. With daylight, the only evidence of this 20th century dragon's presence would be the mute testimony of the splayed clawed feet and deeply indented body pattern on the nearby sandbanks. The crocodile was hungry. It had not eaten for a very long time. It waited as the vibration got louder.

In the searching stabbing beam of the hunting lamp the eyes gleamed like so many embers. The young white man at the prow of the small boat studied the eyes intently and then moved his right arm in a slight wave. The boat changed course, angling in out of the channel towards the bed of scattered glowing coals in the shallower water.

The man had picked his next target. Two sets of eyes away from the main concentration on the right. The crocs were at slight angles, showing only their nearside eyes to the lamp. He would take them first. Less disturbance there. And then traverse the beam across the remainder. With luck he would kill three, even four. Then they would call it a night.

1

They had taken six tonight. And that had taken longer than usual. The crocs were beginning to catch on, to wise up. He had not had to hunt so far downriver from his camp yet.

The eyes came closer, still angled.

He moved his left hand now, in a short chopping motion, and the growl of the outboard ceased. Without the motor noise the high-pitched aggressive whine of the mosquitoes reached a new level. Under a moonless sky the small dinghy drifted towards the crocodiles in a last thrust of momentum. The closest pair of the reptiles were less than ten paces off now, and the man was surprised that they had not turned fully to face the beam of light. Something cold skittered up his spine. He shook his head in the darkness and the Bulala lamp swung off target with the movement. No, he thought. It can't be ...

Dry mouthed he brought the beam back on to the red glowing eyes. They had drifted closer. Now he could see the water-silvery outline of the massive crocodile plainly. One animal! Not two. The thing looked like a submarine! His gaze stayed riveted on the huge ominous shadow, as mesmerised as the crocodile itself, unblinking in the beam. He felt the dinghy shift slightly as Kashili hefted the gaff, an indrawn hiss of shock breaking the silence. And he could feel his hands sweating on his rifle. Don't move, *ngwenya*, he intoned silently. Just stay put for three more seconds. At the same time he willed Kashili and the younger black man, Sehitwa, to stay still and not rock the boat. He could smell their acrid sweat of tension and fear. They, none of them, had ever seen such a monster in all their hunting.

The dinghy had slowed, almost stopped, and now the croc was just paces away, eyes malevolent and gleaming. The mesmerising orb of light shone down over the hunter's left eye and the butt of .306 was socketed up against his right biceps. In this fragmented fusion of time there was a flashback to the many crocodiles that had gone before. All hunted down in the same way, in the blackness of night, in the saurian's own territory.

At four paces he fired, the flat crack of the rifle rolling across the dark expanse of the big river. The soft-nosed bullet found the small brain, mushrooming and imploding on its way through the armour. The crocodile settled in the shallows soundlessly with a minute series of bubbles escaping from the bullet hole. The young man leaped out into the knee deep water, feeling the sand soft under his worn plimsolls. In awe he ran his hand along the knobbled back that still lay exposed out of the river. The natives joined him in the shallows, Sehitwa staring nervously around them in the darkness. This work, this night-time madness, was new for him. The young hunter grinned cheerfully at the tall finely muscled native.
"Come, Sehitwa, give me the rope. This one is too big for the boat. We will have to tow him back to camp."
As he spoke he looked at the crocodile, noting again the bullet hole placed a fraction higher than he had aimed. The hole looked small in the clear bright light of the shooting lamp. As he looked he saw the   tremor stir the massive reptile, wondered if the current washing silently past them had done it. As all this registered, and he shifted his grip on his rifle, more in sudden unease than anything else, the dead crocodile came to life.

It surged up on high, levering up off its rear legs, its mouth gaping, and a deafening hissing roar spewed into the night. The tail slashed one way, its great tree trunk head the other. In dinosauric savage spasm its jaw worked. Opening. Shutting. Repeatedly, again and again, the roars and the slamming jaws a cacophony of prehistoric rage. And in the mêlée of thrashing water, crocodile and men, Sehitwa was there suddenly in its jaws. Jaw snapping sounds changed, became sodden thuds as the native was broken between them. Blood sprayed with the water. Red and silver in the beam. He'd made no sound.

Kashili windmilled backwards, terror and the murderous scything tail giving him a speed that saved his life. The young croc hunter was on his feet, just, amidst the maelstrom. Over the sights of his rifle his horrified gaze took in the body of Sehitwa coming apart. The torso stayed fixed in the jaws, his lower trunk and legs churned away in the roiling water. As he lined up the ivory bead as best he could on the beast's ear region the whole savage action stopped as suddenly as it began. The crocodile settled again on the edge of the sandbar, now with Sehitwa's remains fixed in jagged clamped jaws. The water quietened.

Somewhere nearby a night bird cried.

Harry Kenyon, a few days short of his twenty-first birthday, stared back in the darkness. At the huge body twisting heavily in their wake. The outboard growled complainingly. It had been hard work getting the giant crocodile out of the cloying shallows into deeper water. He had put two more shots into the brain. Carefully. When things had quietened down. Insurance taken too late for Sehitwa, he mused bitterly now. The thing clamped in the croc's jaws at the end, what was left of Sehitwa, had broken off in the current and drifted away in the darkness. Nothing was left. He swore silently again. Kashili, looking back at him from the prow, felt rather than saw his companion's distress. The old tracker said nothing. There were always things to learn, some lessons higher priced than others. But now was not the time for it. He thought instead of the crocodile they had killed. It was the biggest either man had ever seen. Not in the gorge, upriver, where the crocodiles were generally bigger, nor in the river of his own birthplace, across the country, had such a monster been met. It was a shame about Sehitwa. But, the man was a volunteer, his own man. He had wanted to come and see the young *mukiwa's* prowess as a killer of crocodiles. Had laughed at any suggestion that such pastimes were different to following a honey guide to the bees' nest.

The sun came up from the middle depths of the Zambezi River. Slowly at first, oozing up out of the cold flat expanse of water. Then, as the sun shimmered free from the confines of the river, the early morning pewter changed swiftly. To molten silver. To the deep heart red of the wild plums that grew along its course, to mango, citron and tangerine. Shadows retreated into daylight. River music played.

Harry Kenyon walked up from the sandbank where they were skinning the crocodiles and paused to stare back out over the river. There was no breeze and the water was unruffled as it flowed smoothly in the main channel.
I love you, river.
He said this to himself, as he surveyed the expanse of the great eastward flowing waterway.

Here, ten miles below the border of Southern Rhodesia and Mocambique, and a couple of miles below the fly-blown outpost of Zumbo, the river was of great breadth. He loved it here as he loved it miles upstream where it passed through the lair of *Nyaminyami* into the restive swift turbulence of *Kariwa* gorge. And he loved the river in its questing snake pattern where it came near Shinde and could sense the end of its journey amongst the vast reeded mangroved delta on the Indian Ocean. Here, in the land of the two-toed Vadoma people, the river was a redolent big python, three-quarters of a mile across in the wet months; but now a mosaic of blinding white sandbanks, green-fringed islands, and a spider pattern of thin barely trickling veins that dribbled into the main channel of the river.

The dry season was far advanced now, in this year of 1950, with September sweating away into the heat haze of October. As another dry season had taken hold, the sun scorched the earth, sucking more and more moisture from air and land. The great unbroken sheet of water which the rains had fed into the Zambezi was shredded apart, torn into pieces by emerging islands and by smoothly sculpted upthrusting sandbars which lay scattered across the river like bleached bones in a shimmering mirage.

With the end of June, the green had gone from all but a narrow ribbon on either side of the Zambezi. Here only did the bush hold its verdant freshness and it was into this permanent greenery that the parched creatures of the bush regrouped. Elephant and zebra, kudu and impala, lion, rhino, leopard, buffalo and baboon ... their spoor patterns superimposed and forming a kaleidoscopic frieze along the river's edge in their quest for the life-sustaining river water.

Although, thought the young Harry Kenyon, staring out over the river, the game is not so evident now. Not much at all, here in Portuguese East Africa. The Portuguese have seen to that, over the years. Since the first white men with guns in the fifteen hundreds came up the river. The difference in the animal concentrations here and upriver in the Rhodesias is startling. Even the croc populations have dwindled.

"And, Kenyon ... ?"

He spoke aloud now, a trace of self mockery in his voice.

"... who's making a healthy contribution towards that? Hmm? You bloody hypocrite."

Harry cast a last glance at the river before turning and making his way through his camp to where the wide spreading mahogany shaded the sacks of salt and wooden barrels. A canvas bucksail covered the salt, whilst the barrels for the treated skins were stacked in neat array. There were over a hundred skins there now, six weeks hunting effort. Soon it would be time to put the word out once more to the villages along the river, and Harry would again head the small flotilla of dug-outs downriver to Chicoa. There, in the jumble of low white-washed and mud-daubed buildings that had coagulated on the Zambezi's southern shore, he would sell his skins to the oily, always sweating Portuguese store owner. Harry would spend as little time as possible in this pockmark of civilisation, restocking and paying his porters. Then he would make his slow return back up river to his base.

He would travel alone, against the flow, and the return journey would take several days. And he would use the occasion to look for a new camp. He had not moved base for two months, and he did not like staying in one place for too long. It wasn't a good habit, even in this peaceful remote area of the Zambezi Valley. It soon made for a predictable pattern of life which had, over the years, been something that Harry Kenyon tried to avoid.

The other consideration was the hunting. It had dropped off now, forcing him to hunt further afield at night. Using up time and precious petrol. He couldn't move upriver. Crocodile hunting had been made illegal earlier in the year in Southern Rhodesia, and the police post up in Miami, above the valley escarpment, was manned by a new member-in-charge. One Garnet Clayton was one of those energetic policemen who believed in having his men out and about almost permanently.

Harry had no qualms about hunting in their territory, and easily keeping a good amount of bush between them. But it was home ground. A big wild untamed vista of wilderness with which Harry shared a special bond, and which he had no desire to sully in a sneaking hunt and run affair with the authorities. Harry returned to where the carcasses lay in the heat of a new morning, his thoughts reluctant to return from that Eden he had come to know. There above the junction of the Luangwa with his beloved Zambezi.

Kashili's body gleamed with sweat as he worked on his last remaining crocodile. Harry squatted beside him, a critical eye watching the last knife movements separate the smooth supple underbelly skin, the colour of pale butter, from the rest of the animal. Without the help of Sehitwa, the skinning of an animal, normally taking about forty minutes, was taking a bit longer.
"You have not lost your touch."
He spoke in Shangaan, grinning fondly at the older man squatting splay-footed across from him.

Kashili grunted, jutting a jaw across at the last crocodile to be skinned. The giant.

"Your turn. I will watch you, little warrior, to see if you have forgotten any of the skills I have taught you. Of course, that animal is very big, and will be harder to skin. Do not be afraid to ask for my assistance."

He cast a sardonic eye at his white companion. Harry's grin broadened. You have taught me much, old man, he thought. Old friend, *my best friend*. You're the best teacher I've had. *Ever.*

He stood up and walked over to their last croc, taking the curved round-tipped skinning knife from its hide sheath. The crocodile lay on its back in the shallows, its creamy yellow belly glistening obscenely in the sunlight. Harry shook his head again at its massiveness and shivered suddenly as he thought about last night. I wonder what else you have in your belly, he mused. What history? He bent to his task. With swift flicking motions of his wrist he made deft strokes across the plated neck, the knife blade guided by the resisting shell of hide and taking the minimum flesh at each cut. The blood weeped only slightly for the skin was pale and fibrous. At the beginning of each new stroke of the knife, Harry carefully scraped away any flesh that still clung to the loosened skin. Swiftly and methodically, with the inner pleasure of a man performing an art, he worked his way down the carcass. The sweat dropped off him and he could feel the burn of the sun across his shoulders.

Already, in the heat, the crocodile was beginning to smell. From one of the reed thronged islands out in mid channel the softly raucous grunts of basking hippos echoed. In an hour the last inch of meat and hide was separated and Harry hefted the belly skin free from the carcass, dragging it over onto a patch of clean sand. Later they would hang the skins to drain, in shade, away from the beating rays. The final stage was salting and storing. He came back to the crocodile.

"Now, *ngwenya*," he murmured aloud. "Let's see what secrets you hold in your gut. What your tastes are. Methinks more than one local from these parts has ended up inside you."

Kashili hefted his panga and hacked deftly at the thick walled belly area. Both men stepped back when the panga punctured through into the stomach cavity, and Harry fought back his rising bile at the pungent rotting stench of the juices and decomposing contents. Gingerly he and Kashili used their knives to pick amongst the sludge in the stomach. Dominating the contents was the dissolving higher leg bone of a large antelope. Eland, judged Harry. I wonder how long it's been in there? Kashili manoeuvred out several stones, smooth worn, in company with some large tight packed balls of undigested hair that had coagulated from the game the old croc had taken. Peering down, Harry caught sight of a hard bright gleam amongst the ghoul's display. With his own knife he eased out a bangle of woven wire. Kashili grunted, and then he found another bangle, the size of a baby's wrist. The old man shook his head.

"Hau ... This devil has eaten well, and with little care."

Harry smiled bleakly.

"To him all meat is food, the same as *mhisi*, the hyena. Even you, old man, are food."

"Or even you, the little big hunter ..." Kashili chuckled grimly.

"... with your big gun, could find your way into the devil's belly. If you make another mistake on the river at night."

They found six more bangles. Harry glanced at Kashili.

"I must find out where Sehitwa's village is. To tell them."

Kashili shrugged, his voice noncommittal.

"He was not from here. And anyway, little warrior, men live, men die. In the towns as well as the bush. You have killed this crocodile, which has killed many other people. Do not feel bad with yourself. Last night it could have been you or me just as easily. Every person has a time. That is the way of things."

Way up on the hot thermals, under the high bright sun, a pair of vultures patrolled on feather-fingered wings.

"Come, little warrior," Kashili smiled at Harry. "The sun is high already. We have worked enough. Let us tow the bodies of the crocodiles out into the river, to their friends. Then let us eat."

He relaxed with a chipped enamel mug of sweet hot tea, up in the camp above the steep eroded river bank that was shaded by the valley evergreens. It was a good camp, well sited to catch the slightest breeze off the river. Campsites always had spirits, to Harry's mind, and this one had always been welcoming and cheerful. He looked around him now, from where he poured another mug of tea out of the travel worn kettle that nestled in the ring of fire-blackened stones.

On the edge of the grass-flattened clearing was his sleeping tent. It was a government issue green, and Harry had purchased it from a nomadic prospector on the Sabi river for one pound. It was a comfortable size and kept off the dew in the winter months, and the rain in the summer. Now Harry had positioned it so he could look down along his body out over the river bank, and he had pitched it so there was a good two feet between the tautly strung edges and the ground. Apart from sleep he spent no other time there. He washed, shaved, ate, read and relaxed in a larger cooler thatched shelter that Kashili had constructed. The tracker had a similar shelter of his own, thirty paces or so upstream. They shared the fire and the cooking duties.

A series of paths cut through the surrounding tawny bush grasses, connecting the various focal points of daily life. From Harry's living space to that of his companion, to the barrels and sacks of salt, to the two forty-four gallon drums of petrol and the bush worn army surplus jeep and trailer rig; and finally, from his camp down to the sandbank where the nightly haul of crocodiles were skinned and then dragged out to deep water where they were left to float on the current as food for their reptile brethren.

The trees around Kashili's hut were festooned with long strips of game meat. They ate very well on the river. Tiger fish, bream and chessa were plentiful, whilst the reed-fringed backwaters hosted various species of waterfowl. Harry didn't think things had changed that much from when Selous or Livingstone had tarried in the area.

They hunted that night again. And the next. And then another full moon had turned and the hunting was never so successful on these bright nights. Harry sent word to the bush villages that he was once again ready to transport more skins downriver. He knew that within two days there would be a dozen or more dug-out canoes bobbing gently in the shallows below his camp. The Chikunda tribesmen found such casual employment a break in the monotony of their bush lives, along with the fact that they knew the end of the journey would bring cloth and beads for their women-folk, spear heads, salt and seldom encountered luxuries.

Although Harry disliked the sun-drenched squalor of Chicoa, the time it took for his restocking and other sundry tasks gave him the opportunity to pick up the latest gossip of the region. From the two seedy bars, and over successive glasses of the thick transparent Anis, he would hear the official versions of current events from Tete to the western border, compliments of the reigning Chef Da Poste. Harry was a believer in the dictum that knowledge is strength. He had taken great pains to obtain the necessary licences, permits and signatures that the Portuguese governing society required, and, as custom required, had greased the relevant palms. Particularly those of the Chef Da Poste. And he made a point of monitoring unfolding events, wherever he happened to be hunting. It went a long way to helping a person keep a step ahead of the crowd, especially if you were a crocodile hunter on one of the wildest rivers in the world.

Under an almost full moon, the young man smiled in his sleep, in his camp on the edge of the Zambezi River.

CHAPTER TWO

Harry Kenyon nursed a beer at the heavy dark counter of The Corner Bar in the Grand Hotel and gazed out of the window as the first rains of the season bucketed down outside. It was mid November, and the pent up heat of the suicide month of October had been cleansed away by the new rains of the year. Outside in the bare thoroughfare of Speke Avenue the gutters flowed like high mountain streams and people moved hastily through the rain slashed afternoon.

He felt at ease here in the cool high-ceilinged dimness of the pub, with the malt smell of the beer mingling not unpleasantly with the tang of the freshly polished floor. He'd been in town for a little over a day, up out of the leaden heat of the Zambezi Valley three hundred miles to the north. The croc hunting season was now over, for this year, with the onset of the rains. He'd hunted hard and long on the big river, in Portuguese East Africa. Eight months. Several hundred skins, sold to that malaria-ridden trader at Chicoa, there on the southern curve of the Zambezi.

Now with the wet months upon him, he wondered again how he would spend his time. Most of the wild bush areas he knew would be inaccessible, even with the recent arrival in the colony of the new all terrain four wheel drive vehicles. The rivers would be in full spate, the tracks bottomless muddy traps, the game scattered. And living out under canvas in the rains for months on end was no picnic. He was, for the time being, quite wealthy. After squaring his accounts for the year's hunting; the salt, supplies, ammunition, bonus for Kashili, he still had three thousand pounds. That, his weapons and his hunting kit, was all he owned. And again he mused on how he would spend the rainy season. Vague tendrils of notions had crossed his mind. Perhaps he would head eastwards to Portuguese East Africa and find out about future elephant hunting opportunities. Or meander slowly southwards to the Union, the coastlands of Natal, or further to the fairest Cape. Maybe it would be an idea to head for the Cape and take one of the mail service liners up around Africa to England, and, whilst he had the money, visit Holland & Holland, or Rigbys or one of the other quality hunting weapon manufacturers and have a rifle made to his exact requirements. That idea appealed especially. But now it was coming on for winter in Europe. Cold rain, sleet, snow, bitter nights and short dull days. In the quiet homeliness of The Corner Bar, Harry Kenyon shivered. Outside, the rain hammered down over Salisbury, a grey swirling curtain of water washing the land clean. The young crocodile hunter ordered another drink.

On the window, white against the dullness of the rain-washed afternoon, a notice, neatly handwritten, drew his attention. He wandered across the room to read it. Perhaps it advertised a coming dance, where he might meet some girls, a rare occurrence. Or a farm auction where there was always bound to be hilarity and celebration of some kind. Where farmers and outdoor types of varying fortunes naturally gravitated, here in the blossoming new colony that was called Southern Rhodesia.

It proclaimed neither. The news it did impart was that, later in that day, at the Drill Hall out on Moffat Street, one Brigadier Michael Calvert would be waving the flag at a recruitment drive for volunteers to fight against communist terrorists in Malaya. Harry studied the poster. Outside of Africa his geography was sketchy. Malaya, if he remembered correctly, was somewhere out near China. Full of jungles and little known wild animals. That, he reflected, was new territory indeed. He wondered what the weather was like at this time of year out in Malaya. As he sipped reflectively at his beer, he noted that the time for the meeting was five that afternoon, a couple of hours away. A pleasant walk, if the rain stopped, along the purple-hued jacaranda lined streets.

The hall was crowded to capacity, the hum of many conversations drifting out into the rain-drenched afternoon. The downpour had stopped for a while, almost. A soft drizzle still wavered on the wind and Harry determinedly eased a way through the crowd until he could claim a space in the shelter of the back of the hall. Crowds gave him acute claustrophobia, especially when he was newly out of the bush, but the few beers on a stomach that was out of touch with alcohol, coupled with the charged air of excitement in the hall, caused him to look on the proceedings with a smile. The feeling of anticipation and electric restlessness in the hall was, he was sure, not just because some stranger would be inviting them to a war in some strange land. More, it was the rain. For the last two years there had been drought. And the country had suffered, had become dry and parched and died a little more with each passing day. The newly introduced tobacco crops and the life-supporting maize had withered and died; had been replanted and died again.

The cattle had died in their hundreds and the dust devils had swirled mockingly across the veld. And away in the wild places where Harry hunted and explored, those animals had died as well. Zebra, buffalo, wildebeest, warthog, kudu and other species had succumbed to the merciless heat, the grasses shrivelled and gone, the foliage on the trees devoured to utmost stretching height, the shade dissipated and the surface water further and much fewer between. Harry had seen baboons kill antelope to drink their blood. He had seen elephant carcasses, young and old, shrunken, grey, withered, around long dry waterholes. The scavengers had lived well, the hyenas and vultures were fat. The land was dying and the humans watched the skies. For they could be next.

Well into November there had been no sign of rain. Just the heat, thick and oppressive. Suffocating, oily, sweat pouring, a smothering hot blanket. Then there had been clouds. Not thick and black with rain, but light and puffy, balls of white flimsy cotton, scudding light-heartedly across the pale bleached sky. Teasing, irritating, maddening. Mocking. For days. And then they had built up. Roiled up against each other, thickening, darkening, swirling on the western horizon. From pale grey to charcoal to bruised black. And the first thunder had growled across the land from deep within the guts of the cloud massifs. And the rain had come. The thunder rumbled now, like some distant muttering monster, drowning the cacophony of talk in the hall. And it drowned the sharp staccato tattoo of the boots of the military men who now marched on to the wooden platforms.

The speech was good rousing stuff. The Brigadier knew men and how to appeal to men. He had the experience. In the aftermath of the latest world war he was a legend in military circles. Mad Mike Calvert was an original, one of the hard men. He fought hard and played hard, and his charismatic brand of idealism went over well with the rough and ready bunch who had come along out of mild interest to hear him. It was a simple pitch. In Malaya the communists were waging a war that was close to getting out of hand. Since its first major surge in 1948, hundreds of civilians, police and soldiers had been killed by communist terrorists. Calvert referred to them throughout the rest of his presentation as CTs. He gave the attentive men a little background, ironically pointing out that the CT Supremo, one Chin Peng, had been awarded the OBE in the Victory Honours in London just after the war, for his assistance against the hated Japanese.

Calvert did not dwell on such short-sightedness, but went on with the story of the embryonic war that was called an Emergency in Whitehall. The unfolding communist offensive, the support of the Min Yuen - the non combatant Chinese, for the terrorists, the philosophy of a long dead Chinese warrior, Sun Tzu, to 'kill one, frighten a thousand', the first deaths of European plantation owners, the executions, the Gurkha battalions already in Malaya fighting with minimal success, the jungle with miles after miles of slippery bamboo on the mountains, and the valleys and the swamps in between, with the trees reaching interminably to the sky, blotting out the daylight.

He told his audience of his plans and ideas for beating the terrorists, and of his desperate need for men on the ground. The Rhodesias were but one pause on his whistle stop tour, and in little over three weeks he would travel over 22 000 miles, determined to raise the manpower he needed for the Malayan Campaign. His closing address was simple, a man to man approval.

"Gentlemen, that is the situation. We have a new war in the Malayan Emergency, and we need more men to help fight it. Not just any kind of soldier will do for this job. We need men who can work independently of their command headquarters, men with a flair for the unorthodox, men who can stay out in those jungles for weeks and months. Men we can rely on to help beat the terrorists. Southern Rhodesia is my first port of call ... for a reason. When the Second World War broke out, yours was the first country amongst the colonies to get into gear and send men to join the fray. Your countrymen did a sterling job of work. You were known for the characteristics I've just outlined. We need you again!"

The Brigadier snapped his heels together, bowed slightly to the crammed hall, departed from the stage. It was good showmanship and brought suitable enthusiastic applause.

At the back of the hall Harry Kenyon looked thoughtful. He wondered if there were any tigers in Malaya.

Early in the new year of 1951, resulting from Brigadier Calvert's visit, a contingent of one hundred men from the Rhodesias set off for the blossoming conflict in Malaya. Making up C Squadron of the Malayan Scouts, commanded by Major Hugo Winters, they would join Calvert's initial group of A Squadron - veterans of Stirling's SAS, French Foreign

Legion, SOE, and the like, as well as the newly formed B Squadron from Britain - made up of Reservist and Territorial members of the wartime SAS. They would be the embryo of the new Special Air Service, which would evolve over the decades ahead to become one of the most effective military bodies in the world. To Calvert, who had commanded the SAS in the last phase of World War Two, and who had glumly overseen the disbandment of that unique body of specialists in November of 1945, the resurrection was particularly cheering. The one hundred men of the new C Squadron, Malayan Scouts, were entrained at Salisbury, travelling to the port of Durban in South Africa. From there a troop ship ferried them to the East. There was much joking and buffoonery amongst the men. It all seemed like great sport.

Harry Kenyon still had not ascertained whether there were in fact tigers in the Malayan jungles. Whatever the case, it was academic now. He was committed. He was in, boots and all. After the speech by Calvert in mid November he had strolled back to the hotel. The rain had stopped, although lightning flickered across the night sky and thunder rumbled threateningly. The officer's clarion call had stirred his emotions, had tugged at a not too deeply seated sense of chivalry. Sir Lancelot off to the wars. It would take care of his plans, or lack of plans, for the rainy season. It would be a change from the self induced solitary of night time crocodile hunting. A better idea than England in winter. And it would still be hunting. After a fashion. And he was good at that, despite his lack of years. He could arrange for his weapons to be cared for; sell his hunting gear. Old Kashili was back in his tribal lands, down where the Sabi and Lundi rivers joined. He was long overdue for a rest from the pressures of croc hunting out there in the inky blackness of the Zambezi at night. That monster they had killed, at the end, would be memory enough for a long time to come. Perhaps he would be allowed to take his rifle and shotgun with him to Malaya. They were very dear friends and would be invaluable. Maybe even Kashili would be able to come. It sounded like good fun, and the old boy was not that old that he would not enjoy a new kind of hunting.

And so young Harry Kenyon went to war. And it would be a while, more than a rainy season, before he returned to his own country.

*****

It was a whole new world. The initial basic training, light years away in Salisbury, was merely a tickler for the main event. At the Malayan Scouts base in Johore the new arrivals went to school all over again. Quite apart from the soldiering that would be required of them, the newcomers had a lot to learn about this country called Malaya. It was a long way from the Zambezi Valley and from the hot dry lowveld of his youth, with the sun yellow in a high bright sky and the stars at night cast bright and glittering across the soft velvet darkness.

Harry Kenyon thrived in his new role as soldier of the Queen. For a while, early on in his recruitment, he had found it difficult to adjust to the comradeship and gregariousness of military life. He had made his own way in life for too long, even though he was but twenty-two. But, soon a part of him responded to the all encompassing spirit of army life, and perhaps he had discovered a new kind of family that was a subconsciously welcome extension of the short, limited, albeit happy childhood in the African bush.

He adapted well. His natural flair for the unorthodox approach, his natural skill with weapons, his affinity with nature and the wild places, and his quiet steady-eyed assurance drew the attention of his instructors and officers. He came out of the jungle school with sergeant's stripes, a sharp keenness to join the jungle fray alongside the veteran A Squadron, and a fervent hope that he would get to see a tiger.

Always, there was the jungle. It dominated the life of every being in Malaya. The Malays, Chinese, British, the animist wild living tribes; all lived in the shadow of the jungle which hid the daily sun and which covered most of Malaya's 50 850 square miles. It was there rising around every kampong, it was there fringing every rubber plantation that for now occupied its earth, it moved swiftly to reclaim the scars made by the tin mines, it shrouded the twisting ribbons of tracks that wound through the wild fastness. And it was unlike any terrain the new soldiers had ever seen.

Always there was the jungle canopy. A hundred, two hundred feet above, blotting out the sun and the moon. And latticed between the giant boles of the trees were the creepers and the ferns and leaves and flowers and thick secondary growth that dipped and cascaded and hung to the forest floor. From the great mountain range that bisected the country from north to south, rearing to 7 000 feet, to the sucking marshes and mangroves at sea level, there was the jungle and the forest canopy.

In this green ethereal and dark shuttered world Harry and his comrades saw flying foxes and bears, small spotted deer, rainbow-hued parrots, long-limbed gibbons, crocodiles, and an insect world that boggled the mind. They discovered leeches, or rather, the reverse was true. Never were they free of these revolting black slimy blood sucking pests. They were always there, hanging in the dense overgrowth and in the fetid stinking waterways. Harry could handle the swarms of mosquitoes, the snakes, and the rest of the menagerie. The leeches were something else.

In this twilight zone a new game of war was played. A new battlefield had been drawn, a new game of hide and seek. Ambush and counter ambush. And first prize was beautiful and prosperous Malaya itself. For the next five years Harry Kenyon would be at war with the disciples of Mao Tse-tung, helping to turn, ever so slowly, the tide of the communist guerrilla offensive. The only time in modern warfare history when a counter insurgency campaign would be won. And he became very proficient at his newly learned trade, and, rather than seeing himself as one of the many cogs in the East - West jungle conflict, it became a personal thing. It was simply he, Harry Kenyon Esq, and friends, against the Enemy. And the jungle was the ring. This hunting of men was new adventure. And what's more, his chances of getting to see a tiger, regal in its natural state, were increasing.

*****

The heat, as usual, was killing them. An almost physical barrier that stood fast against them, weighing them down as they followed the tracks. And they were wet, as usual. If it wasn't the heat popping the sweat out of them, it was the rain. Usually both. Now the closeness of more rain sent the humidity soaring, sucking the body moisture from the skin, drying the lips and throat to rasping emery board.

It was the fifth day on the spoor. A lifetime. Time passing in the jungle was not measured in days or nights, certainly not hours. A twenty-four hour cycle had come and gone when you changed your map codes and frequencies. One day at a time, was how you took it. Today was all that mattered. Yesterday was finished and tomorrow would be a whole new ball game. So, making it through the day, this day, was the prime objective.

Five days, from the ambush position a few miles out of Ampang. Where the lads of the Guards Brigade, out of Hong Kong but a couple of weeks, had caught it. The point man had walked into a venus fly trap. Whilst his mates had been trying to lift his bloodied body out off the excreta-smeared bamboo teeth, the CTs opened up. Another two men down and much cordite in the damp close air.

Harry and his team had been half a grid square away, on some dirty business of their own. Special Branch intelligence had given them an arms cache. They'd just finished the

doctoring of the grenades and ammo when their Dyak tracker
had cocked his head. The not too distant fire-fight was but a
faint tremor to their ears, muffled by the jungle. Harry nodded
at Scratch Peters.
"See what you can pick up. We might be useful to someone."
The tall wiry Rhodesian fiddled with the set, searching
through the atmospherics. He found the channel, with the
communication unreadable. Harry shook his head as he
strained to pick up the dialogue.
"No go ... usual story. Let's take a look."
They led off, the four of them. Harry followed the little
tracker, with Scratch and Jack Mackie behind him.
They found the Guard's patrol, with four down out of
eight men. They helped with the first aid and then cast around
for the ambush position. The attackers had long since melted
into the jungle. Ever since the Dyaks had been with the
troops, Harry had spent as much time as he could with the
small lithe tribesmen. They were ideal for this type of combat.
Superb trackers, they were cheerfully shy, and their skill with
their long blow-pipes was positively scary. Harry warmed to
their spontaneity and bush skills from the start, and despite his
own fair skill at tracking, he learned a lot more.
Now, as they searched for signs, the little head-hunter,
Anak, called to him softly in his characteristic high reedy voice.
When Harry joined him, he jutted a chin at the barely
discernible ambush position. There had been five terrorists.
Now only a few scattered cartridge cases gleamed dully
amongst the greenery.
That had been five days ago. Yesterday the tracks had
split up. Three and two. The trackers held a short council of
war. Stay with one set or split up? Dividing your forces was
not recommended at jungle school. They split up, Harry and
Scratch staying with the three sets of footprints, Anak and Jack
going after the others. They agreed to give the pursuit another
forty-eight hours before giving it up and meeting back where
the spoor had split.

Midday now, according to their watches. No other way of knowing. The heat had intensified. Rain was close. The first in a few days. When it came they would lose the tracks. The faint almost invisible thread that linked hunters to hunted would be washed away. Bang. Five days of blood, sweat and leeches down the drain. Harry grimaced and gently cleaned the rivulets of sweat off the breech of his shotgun. Then he patted it lovingly. He much preferred this weapon to the recently issued Patchett carbine, and his skill with his shotgun was becoming legend in the SAS world.

They eased forward. The terrain was dropping away, in all probably down towards one of the hundreds of brown sluggish rivers that snaked through the jungle. Harry thought about this with mixed feelings. Rivers brought even more leeches. It was also where the odds increased slightly on your finding a CT base. The two SAS men moved on, ever more warily. Five days. And nights. Something had to give sometime.

It was Scratch who spotted the sentry, his gaze probing the jungle ahead as Harry concentrated on the tracking. At his soft hiss Harry sank to the ground. Scratch wormed silently across to him, putting his mouth close to his companion's ear. Briefly he gave Harry the information and the direction of the enemy. Even so it took Harry long seconds to find the sentry, and he marvelled at Scratch's eyesight. The terrorist was all but invisible. Both soldiers studied the area closely. No other sign of enemy. Just the one in the dark clothes perched amongst the creepers. He would be hard to get close to. Harry looked for a way to get up on him. Bloody difficult. The best bet at this stage, he reflected, is to move across at an angle. It won't bring us much closer but it will give another view of the situation. Pick up another sentry maybe, or a track, or any bloody thing. He whispered his thoughts to Scratch.

They eased their way painstakingly through the jumbled forest floor tangle. Sweat poured, a combination of new exertion and adrenalin surge. Thirty or so paces. An hour. Harry knelt up through the riotous undergrowth and searched again for their sentry. More difficult to see, now they'd moved, but it worked both ways. Aha! And now they had something else. Another part of the jigsaw fell hot damp sweatingly into place. He could see a hut. Or rather, a part of one. The human plaited greenery snagged his attention, down there amongst the plantain leaves.

He grinned. Okay. Alright then. That brings us a little closer to the party. What now? A bit of a stalemate, really. That sentry is in a very smart position, sod him. But we'll have to get rid of him before we do much else. He absently fingered the dagger that hung, handle downwards, from his shoulder webbing.

A soft breath of air feathered his cheek and he glanced upwards. The forest canopy stirred sluggishly and for a brief moment he caught sight of dark swollen clouds. Any minute now, he thought. More bloody water down our necks. He paused then, in his study of the scene ahead, and an eyebrow arched in a new direction of thought. Just how hardy and well trained is our comrade over there, he mused. I wonder how much he and his mates enjoy the rain down their necks? No more than us, I'll wager. Let's wait a little, me hearties. Softlee, softlee, catchee monkey. *Perlahan laman.* Let us use the bleeding rain for once. He lowered himself silently down and murmured his idea to Scratch. His friend shrugged and grinned wryly.

It came without warning. Another tropical squall. Hammering through the evergreen ceiling of the forest, soaking all beneath. Above the hissing sluicing of the downpour Harry could now actually talk softly.
"Just what the doctor ordered, hey? Let's go and sort these bastards out. Hope they haven't had too many of their little friends join them, or it could get a touch hairy. The sentry

certainly didn't waste time getting out of the wet, did he? So much for Uncle Mao's battle indoctrination. You all set, Scratch?"

"Yup. Ready, willing and able, as the lady said. Your shotty-gun all nice and clean and not going to jam on us? I've heard these new repeaters do, you know."

He grinned askance at Harry, water dripping from the end of his hawk nose. He scratched absently at the small of his back. It was an unconscious tight-nerved habit, which gave him his name. No one knew what Scratch's given Christian name was. The rain-sodden bush clutched silently at them as they moved in on the hut.

There was only the one hut, and a small opensided lean-to with dead ashes in a cooking hole. They went in fast. Harry left, Scratch right. A short savage explosion of sound as the shotgun and the Patchett gun did their work. Total surprise. No return fire. Bodies falling, limbs entangled. The smell of cordite strong in the confines of the hut. Blue smoke following them back out into the rain, swirling, dissipating. Scratch lit a cigarette, the first in days. Harry took out more cartridges.

"A few more off to the great rice paddy in the sky. Now the walk back. It doesn't quite balance does it? Five days of dragging our backsides through the *ulus*, and the end game over in less than a minute. Wouldn't it be nice if we could call in a chopper for uplift. Wonder how the other lads are doing?"

Scratch Peters grunted through a deep pull at the cigarette.

"I don't mind admitting, chum, that I'd have called this off at the end of the third day. I wouldn't have bet sixpence on us staying on the spoor for as long as we did. We were lucky with the rain. Bloody good show, Harry."

Harry bowed theatrically.

"Thank you, *sahib*. That's what we forget sometimes. The luck thing. It's always there, good or bad. You've just got to try and do everything else right, and hope the luck part of it is good." He jerked his head back at the hut.

"I wonder who these guys are? Anyone interesting? We'd better take the hands back for the Branch chappies to fingerprint." He loosened the dagger.

"Give me a hand, will you. And ignore the pun."

*****

Harry Kenyon was happily, unreservedly drunk. In the SAS bar in the Johore Barracks he leaned against the counter, elbows propped as he focused on the revelry. His company had just returned from R & R, a two week break from the jungle. Harry had gone to Singapore, was still in a daze. To a country bumpkin the delights of the bustling cheerful city had been revelation indeed. A far cry, Harry had mused one steamy afternoon as he lay on his back watching the girl's head bobbing over him, from the fumblings outside the Nurses Home in North Avenue.

He had returned from leave to a hero's welcome. It seemed that one of the bandits that he and Scratch had scribbled at the end of the five day marathon had been high up in the CT hierarchy. The fingerprints of one of the severed hands they had brought back matched those in the police files of one Shorty Kuk - so named because of his diminutive four feet nine inches. What he lacked in size, the hard core communist made up for in experience and ruthlessness. He had fought the Japanese alongside Chin Peng, was now one of the charismatic Peng's most trusted lieutenants. Amongst the Intelligence and Counter Insurgency types, it had long been said that Shorty Kuk would be one of the hard bastards to take down. The fingerprints made him one more name scratched off the List. The powers that be were very pleased with Harry Kenyon, and there was even talk of medals for him and Scratch Peters.

Harry saw the Commanding Officer enter the bar and pause to survey the scene. His gaze rested on Harry and he worked his way through the crowd.

"Harry, hello. How was your leave?"

"Fine, sir, thanks. The usual goings on in Singapore. Wonderful therapy. Now I just have to keep an eye on the vital parts and hope no rash appears." He added, "it's good to be back."

The major ordered two stengahs and turned back to watch the room.

"Well done on your last operation. I haven't had a chance to speak to you. Quite apart from the name you took out, it was a damn fine piece of work. Five days tracking is a hard grind in anybody's language."

Harry shrugged, and made a determined effort to remove any slur from his speech.

"Yeah ... well, these guys can for sure show you how it's done. And I'm lucky that I'd done quite a bit of serious tracking before I came over here. The bush is different, but the principles are pretty much the same. Game's different, of course. Crocodiles and elephants will be a little tame, when I get back."

Harry took a small pull at the newly arrived drink.

"Speaking of which, sir, any idea when we do go back? We've been here nearly three years, which was the contract for us newcomers."

The young-faced major chuckled.

"Good question. It's actually been a point of discussion with the new OC, Colonel Brooks. He's arrived within the last fortnight, so you won't have met him yet ..."

Hugo Winters paused for a long while. Then.

"I'd say, Harry, that you can forget about the Zambezi Valley for a while still. Like at least another year. Unless you get a really good dose of malaria, which is a chargeable offence, or get wounded. Or worse." The officer cocked an enquiring eye at the sergeant.

"The jungle getting you down, Harry?"

"No, sir. Not yet, anyhow. Apart from the bloody leeches. Time does seem to fly by here. Never a dull moment. Doesn't seem like three years."

Major Winters let his gaze roam over the bar, pausing again. When he next spoke his voice was contemplative.

"Well, things are changing a bit. Looks like the Briggs plan is working. Special Branch tell us that the CTs have pulled back, deeper into the jungle. Which gives us a new set of problems. And which ..."

He turned from the room to face Harry with a wry smile.

"... in the light of General Sir Gerald Templar's recent oft quoted remarks about winning the hearts and minds of the people, suggests that you and your muckers will be getting to know the *ulus* even better. The CT's are now seriously harassing the deep jungle tribespeople. Especially the Seman and Sekai. Taking their food, making them plant crops for them ... generally subverting them.

"The tasks for the SAS, whilst the regular troops carry on in the towns and plantations, harrying, will involve deep penetration stuff. To link up with the tribes, live with them, remove the current CT menace. As the General says ...win their hearts and minds."

Harry scratched at an old leech bite. The ministrations of the sweet massage parlour girls seemed a long way away, suddenly. He knew the major was keeping the information pretty general and downbeat. Nothing that base scuttlebut wasn't already saying. He had a feeling though, that between the lines there was a brand new story.

"I rather thought, sir, that we were getting pretty deep into the jungles already. I mean, how deep is deep?"

Major Winters chuckled.

"Like by parachute. Or chopper. For a month, two months. Staying in with minimal resupply. Hell, who knows, Harry. You may even get to see your tiger!"

The officer was grinning widely now.

"By the way, I trust your kit is up to scratch. Your deployment is tomorrow night. Briefing at fifteen hundred hours. You'd better get your men sorted out with the necessary tomorrow morning. Letters home to mum and the girlfriend. There won't be much opportunity out there. And, in case you hadn't heard, your names have been put forward for gongs. It went through today. The brass are tickled with your recent achievement, as am I, naturally."

The sergeant blinked. The major's voice sounded as if it were coming from a long way away. He drew a deep breath and took the officer's outstretched hand. The senior man continued to smile. He said softly.

"Maybe they think it will spur you on to greater heights. Whatever, very well done. Perhaps we'll persuade you to become a regular."

CHAPTER THREE

And so, in the new year of 1954, Harry Kenyon went native. Living amongst the naked little people of the jungle tribes he became attuned, more than ever, to the wild. The jungle acquired new dimensions. It remained the battleground, and the seek and destroy missions were conducted unendingly. But the jungle became home, and the cheerful uncomplicated little folk of the Sekai became family. And Harry came to feel a great responsibility for his new charges, and, as they revealed the secrets of the deep jungle for him, so did his commitment to their security increase. Together with the menfolk of the scattered tribe, he and his small band of soldiers turned the tables on the terrorist menace.

In weeks he had removed all but a transitory presence of the bandits. He introduced basic engineering aids, ram pumps and grinding mills. He became the bush doctor for a large area of the wild, animal loving tribespeople. In months he had built up an intelligence network that let him know within eighteen hours if communist insurgents had entered his vast area of operations. And, came the time when scheduled Rest and Recreation withdrawals were due, he requested that he be able to remain in the jungle. His request was allowed and he settled in for a further ten week spell. As this period drew to a close it became obvious to his headquarters that he was well on the way to being 'bushed'. A Royal Air Force request to SAS field operators to refrain from calling for bombing support on Sundays, to allow aircrews to rest, brought a short response from Harry's call sign. *With absolute pleasure. Please advise when it is Sunday* prompted the powers-that-be back at base to ensure that Harry was pulled out on the next rota.

After a month's absence from the jungle - three weeks in Penang and a week at Johore barracks lecturing on jungle survival - Harry was fretting to get back. He missed the stark simplicity of jungle living and was impatient to get back to the fortunes of his adopted tribe.

The chief medical officer kept a concerned eye on the young soldier. The months of deep jungle living had given Harry a sallow jaundiced look and he was much thinner now. Yet he seemed satisfactorily alert and rational, and certainly the results from his area of operations were commendable. Still, the CMO was uneasy about the SAS sergeant. Did he see there in the soldier's eye the gleam of the convert? Had not Kenyon perhaps gone a touch overboard in his new role as protector of the poor? Were they seeing the emergence of another Wingate, or Lawrence?

Captain Braithwaite took his unease reluctantly to Major Winters.

"Well ..."

The major rubbed his jaw reflectively.

"Have you had a thorough look at Kenyon? Had a chat with him? I can't say he looks the zealot to me, the little I've seen of him recently."

The captain shook his head.

"He's had a recent medical. And, yes, I've had a chat with him, when he came to see me for a resupply of medical stores to take back into the jungle with him. I must admit he seems fine, to all outside intents and purposes. A quiet, very self-assured young man. Very. That's the rub, though. It strikes me that perhaps he's a little too quiet. He gets that far away look when you're talking to him. The next planet along, sort of thing. A sort of hundred yard stare, when you're actually a couple of feet away. All very vague, I know. I wish it were a little more concrete ..."

Hugo Winters eyed his CMO intently.

"Are you saying he shouldn't be sent back to the jungle?"

Braithwaite returned the look with a wry grimace.

"The buck stops here ... right?"

He paused, stepping to the window that opened out over the parade ground.

"No, I wouldn't say that. There's nothing to indicate that the man is no longer capable of doing a good job of work."

His last sentence he left unspoken in his mind. *I wonder though, what the final price shall be? In terms of adaptation, returning to normal life. Whenever the hell that happens.*

Sergeant Harry Kenyon was back in the jungle for little over a week when two things happened. He was ambushed. And he saw his first tiger.

With two of the Sekai, he was three days out of their village, patrolling the boundary of their given operational area. Radio communications from the SAS team in their southern neighbouring sector had told him that there was bandit movement through their common boundary area. So Harry and two of his tribesmen moved in quietly, keeping to his side of the Ipoh River, which SAS Command had designated as being his extreme operational limit. There had been no sign of an enemy presence so far. No spoor patterns, no signs of night camps, no river crossing points. No human evidence at all.

Which made the ambush murderously successful. Simple. One prolonged burst of fire, reverberating amongst the bamboo. Straight out of the training manual. Harry and his men never saw their attackers. Indeed, Ahoi, shot through the head, never heard the ambush. The second tribesman, Petin, lived two seconds longer, hit mortally in the chest. Harry was shot in the stomach. His SAS training, and his position at the time of the ambush, third in line stalking the jungle trails, kept immediate death at bay. As the first micro-seconds of the ambush flashed by, he was reacting, his automatic shotgun pumping out retaliation in the direction of the attack. The ventriloquil effect of the dense jungle made the attackers' position confusing, but Harry directed his fire to the left front. In the jungle closeness the enemy could not have been more than eight paces from him. Face to face personalised combat, yet no eye contact there amidst the thick bush.

Harry realised that he was down and, worse still, he had dropped the shotgun. He was in the undergrowth beside the vague trail, lying alongside the bulk of a long dead forest ebony. He could see the shotgun, two paces away, and he saw the blood covering it. His blood. He looked down at himself and saw the hit. The front of his body was saturated red. Still he worried about the shotgun, and moved towards it in a crabbing crawling thrust.

A renewed burst of fire greeted the effort. Twigs and other bits of shrubbery peppered him and he saw fountains of brown forest earth erupt where bullets reached for him. Reflex action and gut-fluttering fear sent him across the moss and lichen covered tree trunk, away from unseen death. He knew it was short-lived sanctuary. They'd flush him out, or, more likely, wait him out. Blood loss would make him weak, cause him to slow down, faint. Then he'd be child's play to finish off. Maybe they'd just shoot through the tree trunk. It was huge and thick, but probably soft with age, its sanctuary false. Grenades? Not likely. One consolation. The jungle was too thick to start chucking grenades around. The thrower stood a good chance of getting it back in his lap.

So, thought Sergeant Harry Kenyon, I guess we wait. He was aware that his thought patterns were very clear. As were the colours of the jungle surrounding him. Decided to take that as a good sign ...

He felt for the grenade on his webbing. His only grenade. His fingers brushed across the strap of the radio that was on his back and he became aware of its hard shape digging into him. He unshrugged it and the accompanying small pack from his back and felt for the knobs. A new jagged hole told him that a bullet had hit the set. He cursed soundlessly. He scrunched himself into a lower profile position, half leaning, half lying against the trunk. He could see his intestines, pinky grey amidst the blood, the earth beneath him slippery wet from the bleeding. He unlimbered the grenade from the chest strap. With fingers now clumsy and ill-disciplined he closed the split pin and eased it partly through the twin holes on the shoulder ridge of the grenade. Then, judging it finely, he placed the Mills on the ground close beside him. He did this without taking his eyes away from the surrounding jungle.

Now he gave his attention to the wound, feeling it out with his left hand, keeping his right for the grenade. Two holes. In. Through. And out again. Across the stomach lining, he judged. Unzipped me a little. Where are they? Why haven't they moved in to finish it off? He opened his mouth wide, helping the ear canal, straining his senses for noise. With his left hand he pushed the intestines back through the hole, the right hole, more ragged than the entrance wound. His fingers were slipping in the blood. He brought his hand away from the wound, up across his chest, to wipe it on the dry cloth of his right shoulder. He wiped carefully, methodically, willing himself to keep his thinking logical. He got rid of the blood, from his palm at least. Then he sent his hand on its next task. Down his body to the pocket of his trousers, the broad baggy pocket on the side of his thigh, where the field dressings were. Dressings, field, for the use of, a refracted part of his mind sang. Ears still straining, eyes scanning the bush around him, he made his fingers fumble open the button.

He brought both dressings out and ripped at the first one with his teeth, tugging it away from the sealed covering. Then he brought it down to the exit hole. For the first time he flicked his eyes downwards to evaluate his progress. Pretty, he mused. White and red. Just like the Red Cross. Where are they when I need them? Not much white left though. Already. Just red again. He brought his eyes back to the jungle, and worked at the second dressing, one-handed still. He realised that he was panting and made an effort to control it. But it was difficult, with his mouth open, trying to listen. He got the second dressing down onto the wound, checking the blood flow quickly again, and seeing the pristine white bandages redden fast. Then he unsnagged the syrette of morphine that hung around his neck.

He heard movement in the bamboo and picked up the grenade with his right hand. Eyes searching his area of view, he raised the grenade to his lips and removed the delicately balanced pin with his teeth. Okay, you bastards, he thought. Come on! Come and play. He waited, right hand fast around the grenade, keeping the lever down. He felt faint now, and he thought he could feel his insides sloshing around when he moved. Come on, you bastards. He hoped he would at least be able to kill one of them before he died.

Dimness. Obscurity. Filtered green and yellow jungle light, dark now. Harry Kenyon wondered if he were dead. He lay unmoving, eyes staring, the pain in his gut deep and constant. Is this how it is, he wondered. Is this what we mean when we say 'Lights Out'? Sliding over the edge, light to dark. Blackness. Nothingness ... He widened his eyes, kept them from closing. From surrendering. He moved his head slightly and even that exploratory move caused a new spasm in his gut. So, I must be alive, he reasoned. He looked at his right hand, clawed around the serrated dark green steel of the grenade. In the last twilight the blood on his front was black now. He saw the pin, lying where he had dropped it when he'd pulled it from the Mills, in the folds of his blood-soaked uniform. Slowly, with great concentration, he replaced the pin. His right hand remained clawed rigid around the grenade. He used his left hand to pry loose the fixed grip. Put the grenade back on the ground beside him.

Why, he thought. Why didn't they come and finish it? We were hit in the middle of the day. It will be dark soon. What stopped them doing a proper job? He stared around him in the last light and mentally inspected his body mechanisms. Feet, still there at the end of the legs. Toes moving in my boots. Legs, okay. Bloody stiff and numb, but okay. He reached down to his groin, probing. Crown jewels still there. Fine. Gut area? *Fucked. Well and truly.* You know that , don't dwell on it. Chest, working well. Breathing properly ... in, out. In, out. Lungs still A One, so no drowning in your own blood. Arms and hands, stiff, but working. Sure, they looked after the grenade okay. Head? The brain's still operating, so that's cause for celebration. That just leaves your gut, and the bleeding. Just? It's enough. Plenty to keep you occupied. It sure as hell made your eyes water. We would have made the daily radio sked by now, all things being well. Which they are not. *Shaddup.* Don't whine. Positive thinking, old son, has got to be the order of the day. So, alright then ... The medic pack? Who was carrying it today? Today? Seems like years ago. It was Petin's turn. He was Number Two. And you still have another morphine syrette.

Harry marshalled his strength, using his back and his legs against the trunk for leverage. He was very stiff and the wound pain exploded out of its deep-rooted ache into savage spasms. The blood had dried on his uniform and it was heavy, starched, stiff. He kept the momentum of movement going, thinking he would pass out again from the new pain, seeing new blood soak through the field dressings. It took a lifetime to crawl up on to the tree trunk. From there he let himself fall down the far side onto the trail. He fainted.

When he regained consciousness it was full dark. He felt it before he opened his eyes. The change in temperature. The different sound of the jungle. A change in its metabolism. He started moving again. He found the blood patch where he was hit. No shotgun. They had taken it. He moved on along the trail, worming along on his side, trying to keep his movements economical and soft. To keep the blood escape down. A foot at a time. A yard. Long minutes. Years. He found Petin. He had died where he had fallen. Harry felt over the body, and then around it. Both his weapons were gone. The blowpipe and the issue carbine. So was the first aid pack. Harry Kenyon lay panting on the jungle trail and wondered what the hell he was going to do next.

For a long while he lay beside the body of the aborigine. A slight rain began to fall, seeping through the jungle canopy. It revived him a little and he forced his brain back to work. He had two immediate objectives, he thought. Stop the bleeding properly. And stop the infection. That was enough to keep him busy. Give that your full attention and forget anything else. Forget about how you're going to get out of here. Alive. In one piece. He stripped Petin of his sarong. You're lucky, he persuaded himself. The river is only a few yards away. They must have been in it when they hit us. You can clean yourself. And there's the powder. Your extra personal supply in the radio pack. The radio might be useless, but the powder is there. Doctor Kenyon's special remedy. The stuff to cure all ills. It sure as hell helps the village people, let's hope it helps you. It's back over the tree trunk. With the grenade. Jesus. The two most important things in your life, a fucking tree trunk away. Bloody miles. A fragmented part of his mind noted again the swear words, words he seldom used. Reaction, he supposed, well set in. Okay then. Do it. Go and get them. There's your spare shirt in your pack, as well. More material for the wound. So let's go, old son. I wonder what they're doing about the missed radio call? There's nothing they can do at night. And they're three days away, normal patrol speed. Without tracking time. Harry crawled back up the trail towards the tree trunk, bunching his dead companion's sarong tight against the bullet holes.

Daylight found Harry with his immediate objectives achieved. It had taken him several hours to get back across the tree trunk, staunch the new flow of blood caused by the exertion, rest, in a twilight world of semi-consciousness, check the radio again for any sign of life, remove the small flat tin of sulphur powder from the radio pack, get his spare bush shirt from his personal pack, check the pin in the grenade, and then haul himself painfully across the bole of the fallen tree into the blood-washed trail. This task caused him to lie in the trail regaining his strength and fighting off the deep urge to drift off to sleep. After an hour he forced himself to leave the trail, crawling doggedly across it into the frieze of bamboo thicket that separated the jungle path from the stream they had been following. It took him more deep pain-spasmed hours to force his way through the bamboo. A night's work to cover little more than a fit man's twenty paces, and consolidate his position as best he could.

Now, with daylight diffusing hesitantly through the jungle canopy, the soldier lay sprawled against a moss-covered boulder at the edge of the stream. He had cleaned the wound as best he could and very carefully packed all the sulphur powder into the jagged holes. He tried not to think about the maggots. He had found his wound crawling with them, had gagged trying to brush them off. Gave up eventually, not happy with the knowledge that there were many still in him. Working away. *You're up to maggots, Harry*. Shaddup. *What's it like being eaten alive?* Fugoff. A part of his mind wanted to go out and play. Did not want to be here anymore. He tried to ignore it. Along with the maggots. *If you go down to the woods today ...* *Go away, I said.* The sarong and shirt he had cut apart using them as wads to hold clamped over the wounds. For now the bleeding had stopped. But the pain was still there, deep-seated and constant. As long as he remained still, the wound did not leak and the gut pain didn't explode into new agony.

Which is fine, he reflected, staring down the partial clearing of the stream course. If you don't especially want to go anywhere. Which I do. I would dearly love to get my arse out of here. And if you still had your shotgun. Which I don't. We won't think about the morphine in the medic pack. Or about the enemy possibly coming back. So we just sit here and get stiff, and contemplate our navel. Three navels now, thank you very much. It's going to be a hell of a waiting game. He glanced instinctively at the grenade. It stood in squat comforting splendour on the stream bank, well within reach of his right hand. Once again the pin was finely eased out to minimum safety distance. It would take a second to grasp and arm it. And then, thought the SAS man. What then? Hmmm? Whatever, at least I'll go with a bang. Rather that than a whimper. And it's always just there, if things get too bad. He looked back at the cheerfully gurgling jungle stream, listening to the chatter of newly awakened pea fowl. A colony of black gibbons jabbered in the upper foliage and he heard the squeaky sharp bark of a flying fox. He could hear himself breathing. The high shrill alarm call of a mouse deer, close by in the undergrowth, echoed loudly over the stream course.

How long the tiger had been watching him, he wasn't sure. The mouse deer had seen it, or smelt it, and called a warning to the jungle. That was a while earlier. He wasn't sure how much earlier, he was losing track of time. But the day was still brightening and it had been cooler when the deer had called. Not long after that the hairs on Harry's neck had started to prickle. His searching gaze quartered the area again. It had happened often before, the rising hackles. It was an old and trusted defence mechanism, first experienced as a child. The day the two mating black mambas had dropped out of the tree ahead of him while he paused, wondering at the strange prickling sensation that had crept over the back of his neck. Kashili had recognised this special magic in the young boy, and, over the years, both men had benefited from the danger warning sign.

Yet he could still see nothing. He brought his visual sweep back across to his side of the stream and started again. The grenade was in his hand, pin out. He couldn't remember picking it up. He felt sweat trickle. The jungle silent now. Eye search. Foreground. Left to right. Look through the bush, not at it. Remember the rules of counter ambush. Middle ground. Foreground. Background. Systematic eye sweeps. Full jungle daylight now. Light reflecting off the water. Off the ripples. Ripples? No current here. Sluggish brown-green stream. *Ripples? Movement?* Harry's glance came back, and he smiled then. *There!*

Harry Kenyon, with his gut shot to hell, alone on a stream in the Malayan jungle, smiled at his first tiger. The huge cat was in the stream, chest deep amongst the reeds and trailing water grasses. Now that he had found him, Harry could still see why he had struggled to locate him. The big amber and white striped animal blended perfectly with the background. Only once the soldier had picked up the ripples and channelled his attention at that area, did the fringe of white that led from the ruff under the chin down along the underside of the tiger's body into the water, materialise. The tiger was on his side of the stream.

For a long time man and beast stared at each other, no more than fifteen paces apart. As their eyes made contact Harry could see the tiger's frame stiffen. He waited. A flock of babblers flew over them, raucously busy. Still the tiger stayed motionless in the stream. *God, but you're beautiful.* Royal is the only word for you, marvelled Harry. King. More so than our lions. So, boy, what next? Where do we go from here? Are you one of Jim Corbett's associates, or are you on your way about honest business? The grenade will be messy for us both. A fine fellow like you doesn't deserve that. It might only wound you. Make your life a misery. Blind you, perhaps, or immobilise a limb. Let's not do that. I'm half way there already. Shot up and leaking like a sieve. Not much good to man or beast. Harry chuckled at that and he saw the tiger's eyes narrow at the noise. Where's your tail, my lord tiger? Can't see it, with you in the water. It's a pity. If I could see your tail I could get an idea of what you make of this. Getting the twitches? Getting in the mood, maybe? Hmm?

Without breaking eye contact, Harry put the pin back across the lever of the grenade, thumbing it firmly into place. Okay, tiger. The ball's in your court. Harry chuckled again, unaware of the higher pitch making it a giggle. I ain't going to fight it, pal. This is bigger than both of us. He giggled again, and leaned back against the cool rock and watched the tiger. He felt as though some part of himself had detached itself from the rest of him, and was way high aloft looking down on the encounter. Tiger, striped, powerfully beautiful in the jungle stream. Man, ragged, weak, lying at its edge. A frozen tableau.

The tiger moved. Slowly, turning slightly, it began to wade across the stream. Diagonally, across from Harry, it narrowed the gap whilst angling away to the farther stream bank. Harry watched the muscles rippling beneath the striated wet-sleek orange and white hide. The big cat flicked one last sideways look at the human before flowing up out of the stream to disappear amongst the ferns and grass-clumped bamboo. There was no shaking of foliage or rustle of bushes. No disturbed undergrowth marked its passage. It as was if the tiger had dissipated like striped smoke into thin air. For a long time Harry watched the patch of bush into which the tiger had moved. The jungle sounds resumed around him.

He felt lonely.

Later that day, when the sun was directly overhead and the jungle lay in dappled torpor, they found him. Not his own team, but the SAS section from his southern boundary sector. Luck had played a leading role in his discovery. The team had been working on their western operational boundary, carrying out their own search for the transiting Malayan Communist Party terrorists. They had met up with a small band of aborigines, hunting, who had heard, dimly distant, a brief burst of firing. They had linked up with the SAS team and quartered the suspect area. A combination of chance and jungle intuition had led them to the ambush site. The bodies and signs told the story. For a long while they had crouched soundlessly by the bodies and blood patch left by Harry. Finally, Corporal Jack Mackie had nodded at the faint trail left by Harry into the riverside bamboo.

Harry Kenyon, barely conscious, heard the movement towards him through the jungle growth. Humans, of that he was sure. No other animal would make that much noise. He waited, grenade yet again at the ready. He was conscious that it was more of an effort to hold down the strike lever. He took a deep breath, wincing at the surge of pain. Fuck it, he thought. We'll go with a bang. He saw foliage shake. Not like a tiger, he mused. No movement with him. No noise. Like smoke. Not like these noisy bastards. *Come on, come on.* Let's get it over with. Come one, come all ... He caught a glimpse of drab green tunic, a dirty white hand grasping a sten gun. And then the full figure of Jack Mackie emerged into the stream clearing.

Harry grinned and shook his head. No, he said silently. Not again. I don't think I'll get that pin back in. A bit bloody shaky now. He held up his hands, the grenade in his right, the pin in his left, dangling from the third finger. Noisy bastards, he thought. Not like smoke. *Not like the tiger ...*
Jack Mackie moved swiftly forward to grab the grenade.

The jungle clearing was silent again, the helicopter gone. The bamboo and undergrowth that had been hacked aside to allow the helicopter in lay strewn around. Jack Mackie put his compass away and glanced around at his men.

"Jacko ..."

He raised his eyebrow at his softy-spoken name. John Johnson, short, square and solid, with the permanent boyish grin, gestured at the sky and the departed aircraft..

"What was Harry babbling about when you got to him?"

The corporal shrugged and shook his head.

"Buggered if I know. He was over the edge. Don't know how he was still alive. And I was more interested in getting hold of his bloody grenade before it went off in my face. Something about tigers ..."

~ PART TWO ~

Winter / Spring 1972-1975

"We few, we happy few,
we band of brothers.
For he today that sheds his blood with me
shall be my brother;"

HENRY V : Shakespeare

CHAPTER FOUR

The herd milled nervously. The elephants had become restless. There on the side of the mopane-scrub covered hill, with the air fresh and the stream close by, the bush still tasty and damp from the cool winter's night, they were starting to bunch protectively. Minutes earlier they had been feeding peacefully, browsing away from the small tributary that meandered down from the escarpment towards the Zambezi. Heading for the thick bush that would give them shade from the midday heat. Now they were alarmed. Why? How? Perhaps it was the plane, circling way up, its muted buzzing drone sounding like a persistent fly. The plane waited patiently, like the vultures spiralling on the thermals. It had done its work. It had found the herd, radioed its location to the team on the ground. Maybe the old female, the tuskless matriarch, felt the danger. Perhaps it was there in her system, deep rooted, from time immemorial, from the first time that early elephant had encountered its only enemy. Man. The tuskless cows were always more alert than their tusked counterparts, always more aggressive and more ready to react.

Certainly everything was just right for the kill. The breeze, wafting gently from the east, was perfect. Straight over the herd on to the killing team. The men could smell the pleasantly acrid-sweet scent of their droppings and the musty thick elephant smell. So, no warning there. And the stalk was textbook stuff. No noise. Plenty of cover amidst the scrub-mopane, still out of the elephants' sight despite the scant twenty paces separating the three men and their quarry.

Yet she was worried. The old cow wasn't happy. The herd was silent now. No more elephant talk throat-rumbling quietly. And the calves were gone, out of sight, tucked away beneath and behind the adults who formed the phalanx that now bunched shoulder to shoulder against some unseen foe. Trunks weaved sinuously, a nest of grey pythons, searching the breeze for sign. They know, thought the warden. Christ alone knows how, but they know. Poor bastards. In a second they're going to break and run. The flanks should be in position by now so let's go and get it over with. Before it's too late and things get messy.

He eased forward through the dry brown winter's grass, straightening out of his crouch and snugging the smooth-worn comforting stock of the Winchester Magnum into his right cheek. The matriarch picked up his deliberate movement immediately and wheeled to meet him. Standing tall, raggedy bush-torn ears sail-like, trunk questing, she loomed dark and huge across the front of his rifle. She charged. In the instant she started her attack he was firing, unconscious of the report and feeling the recoil only mildly as the adrenalin now surged through his system.

And the sounds of the rifle fire, his and the weapons on his flanks, blended into the cacophony of the terrified screaming, growling, trumpeting beasts that were dying a few paces away. He had killed the lead cow at seven paces, aiming straight up her trunk for that invisible mark just below the level of her eyes. He had seen the dust splash off the wrinkled grey hide and he had felt, just as much as seen, her stop dead in her tracks. Flinching from the blow of the 500 grain bullet, her back legs already collapsing. Folding up, falling, whilst her great head lifted back and she went down, on to her chest, front legs splayed out ahead, four tons of dead power. He had darted in and put another bullet into her for insurance and was already turning and lining up the ivory bead of the foresight ahead of the shallow vee'd rearsight on the next elephant that surged alongside the dead herd leader. Again he felt, rather than heard, the .458 do its work and part of him watched the elephant collapse across the dead cow whilst another part of his brain searched for a new target and yet he was still evaluating how the overall cull was progressing.

Seven seconds had elapsed. There were more elephants down than standing and he could see dust spattering off the surviving beasts as the bullets took their toll. He put down another animal, his brain automatically recording that it was his fourth, last, bullet, reaching behind him immediately for the back-up FN that Kashili held, and as he dispatched two more elephants he was already surveying the remnants of the herd for calves. They were harder to see in the mêlée, down there amongst the corpses that littered the veld, most still in death, some twitching, there one half drunkenly rearing, hit with a poor shot. Harry fired across the throng, putting the young cow out of her misery and automatically filed away his thought that at that angle it must have been young Munroe's shot ... and he had muffed it, and he'd better bloody well jack himself up and pull himself together, that was the second time in two day's work because *I will not tolerate sloppy killing* whatever the hell it is, and if he was going to get anywhere in the department he'd better look to it and I'll have a chat to the lad later, but in the meantime there's a young calf, a young male and he's a touch more than the required forty inches at the shoulder for the zoo, so let's put the poor little bastard out of his misery and check the rest of the calf crop, there he goes, down, and there's another youngster and there's no doubt that that little fellow is zoo material, female and well under the forty inch stipulation and the poor little bugger doesn't know *what's* happened to her, where's the scout with the dart gun, *oh damnanblast it, not the zoo for the rest of its life* ... and he carefully shot the calf through her left ear, seeing the blood geyser, and then he was looking across the downed herd that looked like so many lumps of grey putty jutting up out of the sere brittle grass.

Harry Kenyon checked his watch. Fifteen seconds. Nineteen elephants down. A clean cull. No foul ups or complications. No break outs. Straight in and wham, all down in a nice neat bunch. He grimaced and walked away from the slaughter and the noise and gaggle of the rest of the ground team that had now come up to the killing ground. It was always now, after a cull, that he wished he smoked, was tempted to call for a cigarette from one of the team. Just to give his hands something to do, and to get rid of the copper taste of fear and reaction, the dry ashes of adrenalin surge, that filled his mouth. That, and the other thing. The acrid bile that threatened to flood up from the pit of his stomach and swamp him, drown him, suffocate him with remorse to his own death.

It was always the same, whenever he was involved in cullings. Hippo, buffalo, impala, elephant, especially elephant. His Lady Macbeth syndrome, old Garnet Clayton, the chief warden, called it. The washing of the hands. And maybe he was right. For it was murder, organised murder, no matter what euphemisms the boffins thought up. Population reduction, control, culling, population management, whatever the hell else they used to label the killing, it was plain murder. And the problem was caused by humans and their rabbit-like procreation. And it was resolved by humans, with their graphs and scientific data, computers and office bound directors, and, finally, with the humans and their high power rifles. And it did not help the conscience at all that it was the only way out, the only thing that could be done. Cull. Kill to be kind.

Harry took three long measured breaths, drawing the air deep into his lungs, careful to keep his back to the others. It was his problem, his own private hell. He unlimbered the radio from his back. When he spoke his voice was controlled, measured, showing no sign of his internal turmoil.

"Kilo One, this is Harry. How do you read? Over."

The Cessna was circling lower now, ready to track any animals that might have broken out of the killing ground, or to monitor the progress of any calves that had been darted and that had got away, running hell for leather away from the madness that had descended upon them, before the effects of the immobilising drug began to work. Nigel Taylor, the pilot overseeing this culling operation, responded.

"Got you strength five, Harry. Nice work. No hassles. What do you want to do now?"

Harry scribbled in a battered notebook. Then he turned and looked back across the morning's work. The first of the contract labourers was arriving on the scene, jubilant as ever at the carnage in the bush. Sweat shining, raucous, they clambered amongst the fallen elephants, and their laughter and bright yellow overalls seemed obscene to Harry, there amongst the dignified, no chance in hell death of the elephants. From over the ridge he could hear the harsh alien growling of the trucks that were slugging their way into the cull site. The heavy meshing of gears and revving of heavy duty motors rose and fell as the column of contract vehicles encountered new obstacles in their cross country journey.

By late afternoon the fifty-odd labourers would have removed the main weight of meat, hides, feet, ears and tails from the carcasses, the trucks lugging their booty back to the main contractor's base camp. The meat would be hacked into strips and spread over acres of chicken-mesh wire, covering rough bush tables, to dry in the sun, to be eventually distributed as biltong to the protein starved bush natives in the area. The tourist trade would get to benefit from the rest of the plunder, in the form of wallets, briefcases, elephant-foot waste paper bins, trinkets, shoes and various other trivia.

The Game Department would keep the tusks, which, along with ivory from other culling operations around the country, and other miscellaneous tusks, would be sold at a department-controlled auction later in the year. Before the contract labourers began hacking at the bodies, department staff would inspect every elephant, tabulating as much information as possible from the dead animals. Age, sex, size, any unusual markings or deformities, old scars, bullet wounds, placental scarring, all would be noted. Tusks would be measured and marked, the very first task, and chalk lines made where the hacking of the tusks from their sockets were to be commenced. The heads would be chopped free from their bodies, and, along with the ivory, the jawbones would be removed with care, for boiling and cleaning, to aid future deeper research into ageing and feeding patterns by the biologists and ecologists. At the end of the day, the rest, the remains of the giant cadavers, would be left, bloody hulks upon the veld. And the wild bush scavengers would take over from their human counterparts.

Warden Kenyon checked his watch again. It was barely nine o'clock. This mornings' cull brought the season's total to 211 beasts. Which left a round figure of forty yet to cull, for their final allocated figure of 250 for the year. There was time enough to locate another herd today, and carry out a second cull. Maybe we can finish the operation this week, he reflected. Which will mean the end of the killing, in this area at least, for another year. We've been lucky, contacting the herds up here in the escarpment. It's bloody rough country and there's still enough scattered water to keep them wandering all over the place. The end of the week will see the end of July, so we've taken a little over a month to get our quota. Fair going when we've got to drop the herds where the contractors can get in to them. Thank Christ we've only got a target of 250. Only! Jesus. But over in Wankie they're taking off six hundred, and at Chizarira another five hundred. Progress. The magic word ... Okay, now cut that crap, boy, and just do your job. Cut out the bleeding heart stuff, and be thankful that the killing will be finished soon. For the time being, at least.

"Kilo One ... Harry. It's early in the day. Take a look and see if there are any herds in the workable vicinity. Look for units of twenty plus. It'll give the butcher teams something to bitch about. Maybe concentrate on the north, that way any new culls will be on the way back to base."

"Roger that. Been keeping an eye out whilst I've been circling. There was another herd, but they hightailed it when the shooting started. I'll see if I can pick them up. Out."

On the ground Harry grunted and made his way back to the corpses. The first vultures had already spiralled down out of a clear blue sky. They waited patiently, the surrounding trees filling with them.

CHAPTER FIVE

Peta Holt hung suspended in the infinite blueness of the San José Gulf. With quickening heart beats she checked the setting of her underwater camera. Around her the ocean stretched away to nothingness, and the world that had been silent just a few seconds before, now took on a vibrant new pulse.

She heard them first. The sonar clicks and squeaky-door creaks and their other vocalisations, and she turned in the water to face the open ocean of San Matias. And then she saw them. Indistinct blurs at first. Two, three, eight, a dozen, more, many more as they torpedoed up out of the depths. The noise level increased and then the ocean was full of dolphins. She guessed bemusedly that there must be well over a hundred of the sleek smooth animals arrowing towards her. She focused the Nikon and consciously made an effort to control her breathing, seeing from the erratic spiral of bubbles drifting past her face that yet again she was unable to control her excitement.

The dolphins were around her now, surrounding her, cavorting past and around in a maelstrom of shiny gunmetal greys. She held her breath as a quartet of the Dusky dolphins streaked straight at her, like a pack of homing torpedoes, veering off past her at the last split moment. She could feel the water surge from their fluid power, and knew that she had not wheeled nearly fast enough to follow their game through with the motor drive. Peering around her now she became aware that most of the activity was above her. The Duskies were breaching, twenty feet up past her, and the bubbled explosions of their leaping and diving mingled in a kaleidoscopic frieze with their twisting darting bodies.

She was about to fin upwards to join the fray when she felt the presence, close to her. Peta turned and he was there, within arms length, motionless, regarding her. She returned the appraisal, spellbound. Human and dolphin hung suspended in the clear blue ocean absorbed in mutual contemplation. Peta felt hypnotised by the unblinking dolphin stare and dolphin smile. Gingerly she reached out her hand and touched the slim grey snout, and then, gently, she ventured her hand further and stroked the smooth rubbery brow. His eyes narrowed, but the dolphin held steady, and she felt that for him too, this was a deeply moving experience. Then his mouth opened and there was the feeling of invitation, an invitation to match this tenuous trust. Peta clasped his lower jaw, feeling the rows of hard, sharp teeth. The mouth closed to hold her hand lightly, yet firmly, and across her mind flickered a memory of a retriever puppy gently mouthing a young girl's arm in backyard fun. For more long moments, a lifetime, the dolphin and the young woman hung there in strange communion. Then he released her hand. He backed off, as if with reluctance, and his flukes thrust strongly and she saw the muscles ripple along his flank as he swam up past her, faster with each tail thrust, and she saw him erupt skywards out of the sea into daylight. From below, through the mirror surface of the ocean, she followed the flickering refracted progress of his airborne leap, and then he exploded back though the surface and she lost him amongst the rest of the cavorting school.

Peta swam bemusedly up to the surface, her senses struggling with the enormity of the encounter. A wild, free roving animal of the ocean had, of its own accord, made contact with her, a human. Her mind reeled and she loved the dolphins more than ever. Around her, at the surface, the school was still at play, and she was very conscious of the raw power that seemed to charge the ocean with boundless vibrancy. They surrounded her and mesmerised her with their twisting, arrowing, turning, flowing formations. Her mind reeled at the commotion of their underwater vocalisations.

When she surfaced, she gasped. A few minutes ago the ocean had been unruffled, gently wind tickled, her grey inflatable held on solitary station by the drogue anchor. Now there were dolphins everywhere, roiling the ocean top with their boisterous aerial acrobatics. They look, thought Peta, feeling water seep beneath her mask as her wide smile broke the seal, as if they're jumping for joy. She focused the Nikon and shot until the spool was finished, went on to use the back-up camera. When she had used up that film she continued to watch, staring happily at the dolphins.

They departed as suddenly as they appeared. In seconds the ocean was empty. The turmoil subsided and the explosions of bubbles and clicks and squeaks and the powerful vibrancy their presence brought, was gone. Peta Holt felt the leaving as a wrench. All that life, all that magnificent expression of joy, upon her in seconds, literally buffeting her with its infectious free spirit, gone. It happened every time. She had swum with dolphins and whales several times over the last months, and their leaving saddened her every time. And more so today. Today had been extra special. Slowly she finned across the empty bay to the Zodiac.

From the pebbled alcove beneath the yellow wind-scoured cliff on which perched the expedition camp, she saw the skiff put out into the bay. Shielding her eyes against the sun-bounce off the now quiet ocean, she could make out the team's electrical genius, Al Henson, at the tiller. She unharnessed her aqualung and hefted it gently to the bottom of the inflatable. She left her yellow diving suit zippered against the crisp Patagonian cold but eased back the neoprene head unit. Shaking out her tawny mane of hair she towelled it, rubbing distractedly. She could still see the dolphins in her mind's eye, and she re-lived the encounter as she watched the wooden skiff approach. A wistful smile played across her face.

Al Henson could feel her contained excitement and her smile generated a chuckle from him as he manoeuvred the skiff alongside the Zodiac. He wore a sleeveless diving vest with his wetsuit pants and his normally unruly mop of dark tangled curls were hidden by a red knitted cap. His teeth were very white in the deep tan of his face and he'd trimmed the shaggy beard. The bare finely muscled arms added to the picture of health, and Peta Holt thought, as she had done often during her stay here on this remote windswept reach of the Argentinean coast, that he was beautiful. And that is the right choice of word, she mused now, as the dolphin images floated in her mind. Not handsome, or rugged, or macho, or whatever else is the fashion these days. Just pure uncomplicated magazine advertisement All American Boy very self-assured beautiful. And he certainly had made the long wind-howling Patagonian nights unlonely. And I will miss him when I leave soon. For at least a week or so ...

She shook her head again, unlimbering the tangled tresses her towelling had created, and she saw his eyes watch the movement. He leaned across and held the two boats steady.

"Beautiful! Goddamed beautiful! I was watching through the telescope. Musta bin two hunnred Duskies there!"

She nodded and her smile broadened.

"At least. God, yes, weren't they beautiful!"

Beautiful, she reflected. The magic word again, Peta girl. Everything is beautiful today, it would seem. But they really were, *he* was ... Indescribably, magnificently beautiful. And I don't want to spoil it by talking about it too soon.

Al pointed out behind her and spoke quietly.

"Well, looks like the show ain't over yet. The next act on the bill is about to start ..."

Peta turned to look back over the gulf and gasped. Lying off, no more than a cable's length, a pod of Right Whales gambolled. As she watched, a geyser of spray plumed skywards, pearly-white silver against the blue turquoise ocean. She thought she could make out six great bodies. A moment later the sea erupted in a shower of spray and thirty tons of black, wet, gleaming whale breached ponderously from the ocean. Up, up it went, the water cascading down its length as if down some mighty waterfall and the whale was a huge, stark silhouette against the deep blue of the ocean and then it was falling back, pulled back to the water by its own gigantic mass, and the explosion of the whale smashing back into the ocean boomed across the water. In moments, a second whale breached, looming mightily, spray-shiny, up into the sunlight, and for a heartbeat there was a miniature rainbow caught in the spray around its body. Then it too exploded back into the sea, and the ocean churned as the action spread to the rest of the pod playing upon the ocean surface.

"Peta, into the skiff!"

Al was breathless. His voice broke the spell and Peta blinked, struck with awe. She glanced bemusedly across at him and he motioned her impatiently into the wooden boat.

"Come on! Let's get over there! The skiff's faster, and won't puncture on the barnacles. Move it, girl."

Peta clambered across and Al gunned the motor. One hand on the tiller, he wrestled briefly with the craft's radio microphone and Peta could see his lips moving, the words whipped away into the wind of their passage.

She looked ahead to the whales. They had stopped leaping. Now they lay quietly on the surface, their huge bulks floating serenely. It's as if they're waiting for us, she thought. It's as if they breached to show us they were here, to attract us. Like, Hey, you guys! Here we are. Come on over! Al had finished his contact with base. Now he slowed the skiff, the outboard's aggressive growl dropping to a gentle murmur. They were less than fifty yards off the pod. They could hear the water lapping against the great bodies, and a gusty whoosh of a sigh, sounding like a wind blowing over an open pipe, as one of the whales exhaled. They drifted closer.

"Looks like Alpha's group," Al said wonderingly. His gaze was intent as he searched the whale group for familiar signs. They were almost in amongst them now. An adult, over seventy feet long, drifted slightly apart from the rest of the pod. As they watched, it rolled over onto its back and they saw the calf. The mother clasped her baby to her piebald underside with her large arm-like flippers, as if calming the offspring after the recent excitement. Peta gazed in awe, hearing her companion's exclamation as if from afar.

"It is Alpha! With a new calf! It can't be more than a few weeks old, it's only about fifteen feet long. We haven't seen her for a year. But it's her all right. I recognise her belly markings. And she's got that big chunk out of her right flipper. Probably caused by a killer whale when she was much younger. Man, this is terrific! Gotta get hold of base and give them the good news!

The whales stayed in the gulf for a week. And they gave Peta Holt the perfect finale to her sojourn in Patagonia. She dived continually amongst them with the expedition biologists, with Leroy Holmes and his team, and she flew with Chuck Montgomery in their Cassna 150 and filmed aerial views of the whole whale action, and, through the underwater microphones suspended from the huge triangle of the three orange transmitters, she eavesdropped on the whale talk. At night, up in the clustered warmth of the operations hut, she was an avid follower of the team's evaluations and observations of each day's events.

A half moon hung cheesy-yellow over the sea as she slipped away from the farewell revelry of her last night. From the cliff top base she followed the worn path down into the cove. Firelight bounced liquidly off the sand and scrub, from the blaze that was kept alight by the member who was on night monitoring duty. Tonight it was Al. He lay stretched atop a thick quilted sleeping bag beside the fire. Behind him a dish antenna on a three-legged stand faced out over the bay. His right hand fussed gently with the dials and knobs of a battery-powered recorder, and the connecting earphones made him unaware of her presence until she moved across the firelight into his line of vision. He grinned when he saw her and put his finger to his lips. Then he motioned her down beside him, and, when she was settled, passed her the earphones. She lay back and closed her eyes, and it was as if she was out there in the ocean with the whales as she listened to their breathing and out of water sounds, the sighs and moans and reedy trumpet calls. And when Al made love to her later, out there under the stars,

she kept the earphones on, and her own moans mingled with
the sighs and moans of the whales.

The next day the expedition plane circled once over the
cobalt water of the gulf and she caught her last glimpse of the
whales, and the skiff was there amongst them.   She saw the
colour splash of the red woollen cap and the brief wave before
the Cessna banked north for Bahia Blanca, and the commercial
flight that would take her to Beunos Aires. She felt the tears
prickle her eyes and wondered when she would play amongst
the whales and dolphins again.

CHAPTER SIX

Harry whistled tunelessly as he guided the Landrover along
the rough bush track. They were travelling slowly and
there was only the smallest disturbance of dust to smudge
the perfect valley morning. The warden was in good humour.
The cull was over. They had taken off the required 250
elephants, without complications. He had just made an early
morning visit to the cull contractor's base camp, having
breakfast with Van Deventer. The drying and salting operations
were almost completed. Soon, in the next three days, they
would vacate their base up there in the first low folds of the
escarpment, and Van Deventer and his crew would move across
the country to the next culling operation. Harry was pleased
about that. He would be glad when they were out of his Park,
signifying that the cull was well and truly over. For this year
anyhow. He had nothing against Basil Van Deventer and his
crew; they were good enough folk, and someone had to do the
undertaking work. Rather than have the dead elephants left to
rot in the bush.   The Game Department's frugal budget
certainly did not allow for the processing of the culling victims.
It was just that Harry found their presence in the National Park
unsettling, even if he had tucked them away in the foothills,

isolated from the rest of the sanctuary. A little like having some skeleton in your closet unearthed for public scrutiny. Like, say, having one of the red light ladies show up at your nice respectable wedding, Harry mused idly. Perhaps I'm being a little harsh. A little touchy.

He eased the Landrover to a halt, peering ahead over the bonnet at the spoor pattern that traversed the road. The large crêped lily pad tracks of an elephant, a large bull, showed where the animal had crossed, heading down on to the flood plain. The bull's spoor was over the tyre tracks that Harry's vehicle had made earlier on the way up to the cull camp.
"Looks like Chiruwe's spoor," murmured Harry. "What do you think, Kashili?"
Beside him the old, wrinkled black man was carefully measuring a pinch of snuff from a grysbuck horn that hung from a thong around his neck. The regulation bush uniform looked incongruous on his wiry, thin frame, the khaki shirt too large and fluttering like a jib sail. He nodded, following the trail with his eyes where the old bull had passed through the scattered jesse scrub. They both knew the elephant's tracks well. He was named for the river whose area he most frequented, a tributary of the Zambezi which flowed a dozen miles away, and he was one of their special treasures. For he carried big ivory. Ivory of the size that was seldom seen any more. Of the size that once was seen regularly before the hunters' guns had taken their toll across the African continent, but which now served as a reminder of better days. Chiruwe's tusks were almost perfectly matched at 107 pounds a side, thick, creamy logs, curving inwards in evenly balanced symmetry. Harry knew of only three other bulls still surviving that carried similar tusks, throughout the whole middle region of the valley. They were living history. He kept a close eye on their movements, and spoke about them to very few people.

When the African replied, he spoke in the Shangaan language of the south east lowveld of Rhodesia, as Harry had addressed him.

"Yes, but he is out of his usual territory. Perhaps the shooting of these last weeks has made him afraid."

He took a judicious sniff at the coarse, brown snuff that capped a calloused smaller finger. Right nostril. Left nostril. He worked his jaw a couple of times, taking it deep into his system, and offered the horn to the warden. Harry grinned and shook his head. He had never yet managed to hold back the sneeze for the polite minutes that custom dictated. As was the correct thing to do. Not since Kashili, as a much younger man, had first offered him snuff, before Harry himself had reached his teens. And that, thought Harry, was an awfully long time ago. A lot of water has flowed down the Zambezi River since Warden Harry Kenyon was a lad. Absolutely. He's right about Chiruwe. The old chap is a little far east of his usual range. Maybe the culling did upset him and he's taking a vacation from his own patch of turf. When we get the collaring and radio tracking whiz kids down here next month to try out their latest ideas, old Chiruwe will have to be one of the first candidates. He's the closest tusker of our 'Big Four' to the tourist areas, and sooner or later somebody is going to decide that his ivory is wasted on its rightful owner. And with the increased amount of government sponsored entertainment, the VIP hunts that are taking place more often nowadays, next door in the Chirora Hunting Area, I'd hate to have old Chiruwe wander across the Park's boundary and get shot. With a collar he'll be safe. A 'scientific experiment'. Hooray for science. Thank Christ the cull's done. Over. I think we'll declare today a holiday. This evening, anyway. There's been no time off for anyone on the station for the last couple of months, and everyone has worked hard. The fortnightly ration run has just come back, so we've plenty of the necessary. A few extra beers, some meat on the coals, and people can let their hair down a little.

Putting the vehicle in gear, he glanced across at Kashili and cuffed him fondly on a bony shoulder.

"What do you think, father? Should we make today a holiday and take some beers?:

56

The old man grinned, exposing a motley, snaggled mouthful of teeth.

"Heh-hey. Why not? It would be a civilised thing to do! We never seem to take such pleasure any more."

Harry laughed aloud, the laughter staying with them as they followed the track down on to the flood plain. The warden let his gaze sweep over the landscape, and, as ever, he felt the tug at his heartstrings.

Nemana National Park. This was his parish. Almost 900 square miles of Zambezi Valley unspoiled wilderness. From the high hot barren escarpment forming the southern boundary down to the Garden of Eden flood plains which fringed the great eastward-flowing river that served as the northern border of Rhodesia. The western boundary was the wide, sandy, acacia-studded Nyamawari River. It was always shady cool in the river bed, cool and cathedral quiet, with the canopies of the valley evergreens meeting often to form a vaulted canopy high above, where movement and silence merged. The convoluted river course led down off the escarpment and across the valley floor to the Zambezi. Inland, just off the low, hard foothills of the escarpment, a low level concrete structured bridge had recently been built. On the river bank near the bridge was Chawoyo Gate, the western entrance to the Park. A pair of stone and thatched huts and a black and yellow striped boom barriered the main dirt road into the National Park. On the other side of the river was designated hunting area, where any wild animals crossing out of the sanctuary of Nemana were legal targets for visiting sportsmen whose penchant in life was the hunt.

The same situation existed across on the eastern boundary of the Park. Here, the Katete River, almost a twin of its western sister, came down off the escarpment to join the Zambezi. Over the Katete and Zumbu rivers was the Katete Safari Area. Apart from transient patrols there was no permanent government presence in the Hunting Areas. They, each the size of Nemana, came under Harry's umbrella of operations. Professional hunters bringing clients into either safari region liaised with the warden's office in Nemana. Harry allocated National Parks' staff to the hunting teams who served as the required government chaperones of the safaris. On occasion, if government guests or VIPs warranted the warden's personal attention, Harry would himself be designated for the chaperone work. It was not a task he relished, this nursemaiding. In the main, the professional hunters operating in the concessions were an honest reliable lot, just as concerned with the ethics and conservation policies as Harry and his contemporaries. Certainly they were more polished at the public relations inherent in the safari game, than was Harry. Could undoubtedly handle the whisky side of it better than he. Nevertheless, when necessary, it was all part of the job, and, as he often mused, being a warden was a trifle more than looking after the bunnies and roses. The human factor was just as time consuming, and more often a pain in the you know where.

They motored slowly across the flood plain, and Harry, as he always did, no matter how many times he cast his eye over this part of the valley floor, despite his three years of officiating here, and his countless sojourns in the valley long ago as a footloose young hunter, marvelled at the beauty of the place. The timelessness. As the Landrover lurched up out of a grass filled gully, his gaze quartered the area.

Ahead of the vehicle a flock of helmeted guinea fowl, a hundred or so of the metallic bluey-purple birds, scratched and scurried across the track, making way distractedly for the car and closing ranks again after its passage. Herds of impala, tarnished gold, young rams kicking up black tufted heels, were spread abundantly amongst the trees. Family groups of warthogs rooted busily. A quartet of buffalo bulls, old worn-bossed bachelors, sat rump to rump in a sunny patch, relaxing their dark hours vigilance. A zebra stallion, keeping close to his mares and foals, trotted away from the Landrover, ever wary but stopping often to peer back. Beyond them, over their rumps, Harry could see a rhino cow and calf, and he recognised them too as old friends. On a tall upthrusting termite mound, nibbling at a creeper, three kudu cows turned funnelled ears in their direction, only momentarily distracted. Various troops of baboons slouched across the plain, grubbing, youngsters cavorting noisily, dominant males swaggering. And, as always, there were the elephants. In his present field of vision Harry could see ten of them, all solitary bulls, going about their business as they had been doing since the earth first coalesced.

And it was but mid year. The last days of July. Late winter, with the animal populations still scattered across the valley and up in the remote watered pockets of the escarpment. Where the grass was still green and surface water still available and the game dispersed far and wide. It was months away from the start of the great concentrations. Before the springs and pans and waterholes dried up beneath the merciless summer sun, and the grasses died and the tree foliage was devoured as high as the antelope and rhino necks could stretch and the earth was hot, dusty, barren with the dust devils dancing like pale-coloured djinns through the wavering mirages.

In September it would start. The animals would begin to congregate. Moving out of the mauve-brown heat-hazed dry country, dominated by the baobabs and jesse thickets. Leaving the waterholes that had been, still had to be, the focus of their survival. But baked clay now, hard as rock, cracked, preserving the lunar landscape of footprints until the new season's rains. Retreating to the river. In the shimmering heat haze of summer, it was hard to see where the valley ended and the sky began, over the vast brooding African silence.

By October the heat was intense, a physical thing. The evergreens, the great green spreading mahoganies and ebonies, the figs, the pendulous fruit-hanging sausage trees, the tamarinds, and the ubiquitous apple-ring acacias that followed the course of the big river, made oases of cooling shade. In October, suicide month in this part of Africa, the great wide Zambezi became the epicentre of life, and death. Buffalo moved in herds of a thousand animals, dust palls hanging over their massed black hides a hundred feet high. The elephant family units, the cows and calves and pre-puberty bulls, the culling targets, would converge on the river's greenery, with the matriarchs more testy than ever. The antelope; impala, kudu, eland, waterbuck, nyala, bushbuck and sable, along with zebra and all the smaller creatures, would leave their tracks intermingled in an ever changing mosaic at the water's edge. Here, they lived, and here too they died.

For the predators were there also, following the game. The big cats, lion and leopard, had an easy time of it. So did cheetah, wild dog and hyena. And at the end of the food chain, the scavengers, the jackals and vultures and marabou storks lived in a time of plenty.

In these last dry months there is a great tension in the valley. The food is becoming scarcer, and the erosion caused by the thousands of hooves causes the dust to hang forever in the air. And there is no safety in numbers from the killers who are everywhere, on the fringes of the herds, in the wings, waiting. And the heat is a suffocating blanket. The humidity builds, with no sign of rain. As October melts into November there is still no rain, and even when the first bruise-coloured clouds gather over the massifs of the escarpment, there is little cause for hope. The clouds build up slowly, roiling, lightning flashing, crackling blue-white amongst the dark swollen clouds, thunder warning, growling across the heavens. For days. Weeks. Taunting. Maybe in the last days of November, more likely December, the first rains come. Behind a bullying gusting wind, they arrive. Sluicing, warm, fat, wet drops, becoming a solid grey curtain. Cleansing. Life giving. Dust-flattening, grass-reviving, pan-filling. But sometimes the rains do not come, and then a lot of animals die. The natural cycle, nature's own management programme.

And yet, reflected Harry, as he slowed for a pair of elephant bulls making their leisurely way across the track ahead, we humans still have to play God. We still have to cull. To reduce. While we go on breeding like rabbits. And the boundaries around the game reserves and national parks become siege lines, not so inviolate now, and the humans get more and more hungry. Greedy.

Up ahead he could see the dry, grey thatch of the Park's headquarters.

Shingela Camp was the nerve centre of Nemana National Park, hugging the southern bank of the Zambezi River. The administration centre and living quarters of the department's staff were only finely separated from the tourist camp, a few hundred yards downstream. The focal point was the L-shaped admin block, situated in the almost permanent shade of a trio of tall thick-boled acacias. Shingela Camp was an orderly collection of white-washed buildings, grass thatched, and sited, wherever possible, close to big shade trees. Harry managed a permanent complement of three game rangers, who took it in turns to fill the role of tourist officer during the dry months of the tourist season, a research officer, sixteen game scouts, and a crew of a dozen general staff whose task it was to service the tourist facilities. The game scouts and general camp staff were black Africans, most of them with families. Thus they resided in their own camp, a few minutes walk from the office block. Nemana was otherwise a bachelor post station, and the assigned rangers and research officer lived in a series of small bungalows in a shaded tree line leading off from the office block, facing out over the river. The senior staff accommodation, that being the warden's house, was behind the admin block, in splendid isolation on a short promontory, looking out over the Zambezi. There were no fences. The tourist facilities, also, were open to the wild, and this was a part of what made Nemana Park different to every other wild life preserve in the country.

The Park had the status of a Wilderness Area. And here the tourist was a part of nature, living and roaming almost at will amongst the wild animals of the Zambezi Valley. It was common for big game, elephant and buffalo especially, to roam through the camp. Lions made kills within its confines, regularly. Antelope were more wary, and kept to the fringes of the camp area by day, whilst darkness saw a gravitation towards the camp, as if they saw refuge there amongst the human animals. The old solitary buffalo bulls in particular showed a fondness for the camp at night. Hyenas and jackals, and the lesser cats, were regular nightly visitors. Honey badgers muttered and grumbled their nocturnal way around the dustbins. Hippos left their daytime watery retreats to crop the rich grasses of the shoreline. By day, baboons and monkeys patrolled the camp sites, searching for titbits amongst their human counterparts' belongings. But it was the elephants that were the main feature of the Shingela tourist camp. Seldom were they not passing through, feeding unconcernedly amongst the tents and vehicles, shaking the *Acacia albidas* for their pods, dozing the day's middle hot hours away in the shade of the evergreens, or splashing in the waters of the river.

The facilities were spartan. Strategic communal shower and toilet blocks were the only buildings to blemish the river bank. Each camp area, sixty in all, was sited beneath one of the valley evergreens, and a low concrete grill with a site number marked each site. The tourist brought everything else with him, be it a groundsheet with the bare camping essentials, or a home away from home caravan. A hundred miles of dusty, teeth-jarring dirt road, leading off the main northern tar road, helped ensure that only the more serious wildlife enthusiasts visited Nemana. There were few rules to hamstring the visitor. They were guests in the valley. The wildlife was always right. Vehicles had to stay on the maze of maintained bush roads that traversed the Park. Humans, on foot, at their own risk, could wander where they liked. The hours were simple. Remain in camp during the hours of darkness; much safer that way, and plenty of wild life on your doorstep anyway. From first light to sunset, the valley paradise awaited you.

The very presence of the game, wall-to-wall animals, had ensured over the years that few tourists had come to grief. The animals were there, before one's wondering gaze, all the time. The vultures squabbling over the remains of the lion kill of the previous night; the squealing ear-flapping mock threat display of a pair of young bull elephants disturbed around a leafy bend in the track; the leopard, dozing, indolent, tail hanging, rosettes blending perfectly with the filter of sunlight through the branches of the acacia on the edges of the vlei; all were positive reminders that the visitor had best abide by the rules of nature. Treading carefully. Aware. Seek and ye shall find, oh yes, but make sure that what is on the other side of the patch of bush is not a whole lot of bad news.

In November, before the isolation of the rainy season set in, the Park closed to tourists. It would not reopen to the public until April, depending upon the persistence of the season's rains, which could delay the opening of Nemana. For the roads would have to be rebuilt, a yearly task. It gave the animals remaining on the waterlogged flood plain a six month respite from the human interlopers. And for the staff remaining in Nemana National Park, every rainy season presented new tests for ingenuity. Because the Park still had to function. Patrols still had to go out, ecology still had to be monitored, the remaining game, a skeleton cross-section of the drier months' inhabitants, studied: and vehicles, pumps, radio equipment, still had to be kept in working order. Even if the whole region was waterlogged. No matter that the shortest of vehicle journeys had to be slugged through in four-wheel drive. Despite the fact that aircraft could no longer land on the Park's bush strip, and that the hundred mile trip to the nearest tar road could, and usually did, take anything up to eight hours.

Even though the game dispersed, Harry enjoyed the closed season. Time was slightly more his own. He could actually plan ahead. It kept the visitors out of his hair. Not just the tourists, who were seldom a problem in these early days, and whose visits he enjoyed, but the rest of the circus. The head office types, whose treatment of Nemana varied between a Shangri-la away from department traumas, and a giant laboratory where it was acceptable to play with all sorts of weird and wonderful projects. With little warning, they always expected Harry to drop whatever he was doing. Anti poaching operations, game counts, field surveys, tourist management, road repair, capture work; all were expected to take a back seat when the Salisbury-based hierarchy arrived on the scene. During the rains the Zambezi Valley became a no-man's land. And, reflected the warden, as he parked the Landrover in a patch of shade outside the admin block, long may it last.

"Good morning, Harry."

"Hi, Desmond. How's the day panning out?"

Harry's gaze flicked appraisingly over the young cadet ranger. Small, shorter than the warden's hard five feet seven, and fair-haired, he had been at Nemana for nine months. His first station. So far he had performed well, as far as Harry was concerned, and he was starting to delegate more responsible tasks to the lad. Once again Harry made a determined effort not to smile at the peach-fuzz growth of a moustache that the cadet ranger was cultivating in emulation of the warden's own clipped military-looking growth.

"Fine. There are several radio messages on your desk. It looks like we're about to be invaded. Mr Parker is looking for you, he didn't indicate why. We have two game scout reports. One concerns hippo. A bull, hurt severely. Close to the Shumba game viewing platform. Corporal Kapesa was camped there last night, after his first day's area patrol. He cycled back this morning to report it. He says that there was a fairly major punch-up between two bulls during the night. I don't think he got much sleep. However, the loser, the younger bull, is looking very sorry for itself this morning, all torn and tattered. It's taken itself off away from the rest of the school and is sulking in a mud wallow just below the platform. There's a chance it might cause complications with any tourists visiting the platform. I sent Kapesa back to warn people away from there and to wait for further instructions."

The younger man paused.

"Go on."

"The second report is from the scouts at Chawoyo Gate. The lions were back again last night. Killed another beast from the tsetse test herd, which they've eaten, and hung around their camp for most of the night. They say one of the lions tried to force its way into a hut and that if you would care to visit them, you'll see the spoor all over the place."

Harry frowned and cocked his head.

"That's the fourth time they've gate crashed the test herd. You can bet on some more radio messages from Research and Veterinary HQ before the day is out. Old Doc Canby will lose his sense of humour if this becomes a habit. I wonder why the hell the cats are paying the herd so much attention now? Those cows have been down here for almost three months with no hassle. There's plenty of natural prey around. From the spoor patterns I've seen so far, I don't think it's the same lions every time. Youngsters, maybe? Not making the grade out on their own?"

Harry grunted.

"Whatever, we'll have to sort it out. It looks as if they're getting bolder, which is not good news. There's nothing that's bolder than lion or leopard at night, in normal circumstances, without them going to extremes. Right! What next?"

Desmond Taylor grinned.

"That's the bad news sorted out. All the dramatic stuff. There's also a tourist report. People called Jameson. On their evening drive yesterday, up on the Katete track, they saw a large pack of wild dog. They counted thirty-six of them. They reported it because they thought we may be interested in a pack that size. That's about it, Harry."

Harry nodded, his eyes scanning the large wall map of the Park that occupied one wall of the reception office.

"Invaded? By who?"

"Head office, and others."

The warden rolled his eyes.

"Must have heard the fishing's improved. When?"

"Tomorrow. Their ETA is eight o'clock."

Harry stroked his moustache thoughtfully.

"Great stuff. Bloody super ... Okay, Des, thank you. I would also like to see Charlie Parker. The hippo I'll go and see a little later. Isaiah Kapesa is capable enough to hold the fort there for a while and keep any tourists from getting eaten. The lions had better come first, while the spoor is fresh. As soon as I've checked the messages I'll go up to Chawoyo. If you have located Charlie by the time I go, he can come with me. What camp site are the Jamesons occupying? I'll go and see them and thank them myself for their interest. So tell Ranger Munroe, if he's got it logged to visit them, that I'll take care of it. He has still got the tourist officer duty, has he?"

"He has. For another week. The Jamesons are in forty-six."

Harry waved as he started out of reception for his office at the end of the short L of the verandah. Then he paused.

"What about petrol? What's the latest on our bulk fuel delivery?"

The cadet ranger came back with alacrity.

"Day after tomorrow. Friday. I radioed the police at Karoi, who phoned the depot for me. I checked our stats this morning and we're fine until then."

Harry gave him the thumbs up and headed for his office. Okay, he thought, so we've got everything under control. The lad's trying. That's good. And we haven't got any special dramas in our laps at the moment, which is also good. Maybe the lions will change that. We'll see. Let's see what the latest tracks tell us. Then we can decide whether we've got some habitual trouble-makers on our hands, or plain juvenile delinquents. Or whatever the hell else. The cull's over, which is very good. And it's turned into yet another really marvellous late winter's valley day. Superb! Which reminds me. I must put the word out that there will be some drinks and food at my place this evening. Harry entered his office, nose recording the smell of fresh polish, and made for the pile of radio messages on his desk.

The message from Garnet Clayton changed his mood. He re-read the chief warden's information, brow now furrowed. It certainly doesn't look like a fishing trip. Garnet and the director, fair enough. But army and police representatives? What the hell do they want? And all bright and early. If their ETA here is eight, they'll have to take off from Salisbury at six. And the director isn't known for his early rising habits. Reading between old Garnet's lines it's a top hat and tails affair. Extra best behaviour. What a nice way to spoil the week ...

The breaking of a heavy branch outside, cracking across the peaceful morning, interrupted his thoughts. He crossed to the doorway and peered out. An elephant was in the act of stepping back from one of the acacias under which Harry's Landrover was parked. A shower of leaves, twigs, and other leafy debris scattered over both elephant and vehicle. The elephant looked positively pleased with itself. Its vigorous shaking of the tree had not only splintered a large drooping branch, but had had the much desired effect of dislodging a lot of the apple ring shaped pods which all elephants enjoy. Harry recognised the animal as Chacadama, a prime bull with average tusks, whose range included Shingela Camp. He was a frequent visitor, and the game-cropped lawn outside the office block was already decorated with several cannon ball piles of his droppings. Harry had seen him once already today. As he had departed for the culling camp before sunrise, he'd had to pause along the track whilst the bull had relaxedly made his wrinkled baggy-trousered way ahead of them. The warden smiled now, even as he mentally berated the destructive habits of his favourite animals.

*****

"It looks as if we are dealing with eight of them. Made up of four distinct groups."

Harry yawned and kicked gently at the mopane log that jutted from the fire. He nodding in agreement. From behind him, in the river, came the contented old man's-club-chortle of hippo, and, along the bank, closer, he could hear the splashings of buffalo as they crossed to an island. The lion calling from the north bank had stopped now, but the hyena chorus from the direction of the tourist camp had intensified. Must have discovered some especially juicy garbage thrown out by a camper, he mused.

"From the spoor patterns over the last few weeks, and from what the scouts tell us, it seems to be the case. Single territorial males on either side of the Nyamawasi, with the river bed being their respective edges of territory, a pair of adult lionesses, maybe mother and daughter, and four other females. I still can't figure out why they've started giving us trouble."

"You can never tell with lions. They're like women. Totally unpredictable."

Laughter greeting this observation. Tall, elegant and ebullient, Charlie Parker was known in the department as a ladies' man. Some people wondered how he survived down in the valley in the wet months, when there were no lady tourists around to charm. His regular reconnaissance visits to the tourist camp in the season were a source of never-ending amusement. And jealousy, when female laughter echoed from his bungalow at the end of the row, somehow extra loud in the Zambezi Valley darkness.

"What plans have you got to stop them, Harry?"

Gordon Munroe, the station's court jester, balanced a fifth brown, empty beer bottle atop its predecessor. He asked the question without taking his eyes from his challenge, continuing, "Bait them? Trap guns? Or follow them up? Their pattern of attack is too erratic for trap guns, isn't it?"

The pile of bottles wavered. The ranger held his palms wide outstretched on either side of his balancing act, glaring at the bottles, willing them to stay in place.

Harry held his glass up against the firelight. It was still two-thirds full. Pink gin, with a little water, plenty of pink, molten red now in the glow of the fire.

"I'm going to catch them. Move them somewhere else. Away from temptation."

The bottles collapsed. Gordon Munroe was looking at him now, curiously, eyebrows raised. The others looked at him as well, in expectation. He grinned at them.

"Why not? Why should we always shoot animals that get a touch out of hand?"

"Because, Harry ..."

Charlie Parker's voice was studiedly casual.

"... no one has ever captured lions in this country to date."

Harry's reply was mild.

"Twaddle, absolute. At Kariba, during Operation Noah, we trapped lions on the islands. And even a couple of years after the rescue was finished, I remember Rupert was called back to catch a couple of lionesses on one island, and a leopard on another."

The research officer was unimpressed.

"Exactly. They were on islands. They didn't have the whole Zambezi Valley in which to play hide and seek."

Harry shrugged and the grin still played across his features.

"Well, we'll see. Never say never, I sometimes tell myself."

It was his favourite expression. His companions didn't push him. He took another sip at his drink. I think this had better be the last one for tonight, he reflected. Can't go meeting tomorrow's circus all woolly-headed and sponge-mouthed. That would never do. Dr Drummond would not approve. The director would be most put out. Even if I have seen him a little worse for wear on more than one occasion. Now, leave that alone, Harry. You sound positively bitchy. Menopausal? Hah! And why not? At 44 you're entitled to be. Harry smiled wider and shook his head. That was also a bad sign, the increasing one-sided conversations.

Desmond Taylor returned to the fire from the lip of the high river bank where he had been watching the dark blobs of the buffalo cross the moon-splashed water.

"Harry ..." He paused, as if assembling the right words.

"Do you think anything will ever come of these rumours of a dam being built across this stretch of the Zambezi? Another Kariba?"

Harry leaned back in the canvas camp chair, balancing himself with a foot on the log jutting from the fire. He pursed his lips, shaking his head.

"Who knows. I can't see it myself. We have Kariba now, for better or for worse, ecologically speaking, and Caborra Basa is well under way downriver in Mozambique ..."

He broke off as the hacking territorial cough of a patrolling leopard cut through the conversation. Immediately following its sawing came the shrieking, barking mayhem of baboons as they jostled for higher sanctuary in nearby trees. Harry took another sip, looking at his companions over the rim of the glass. He noticed that Wally Conway, the most recent transfer of the station, still had a smudge of engine oil on his elbow from that day's delvings into the innards of one of their five-tonners. He resumed the conversation, his voice contemplative.

"Dams. Tar roads. Radio masts. We really are girding our loins for the 21st Century. It will be diamond and oil fields next. The wild places dying. The elephants with no place to go."

Harry grunted and waved an arm out at the night-cloaked valley. "Hell, we think it's wild now. Imagine what it was like before Kariba. Even as early as 70 years ago. The slavers were still coming up the Zambezi, even at the turn of the century. There were cannibals in this region, across the river."

The warden finished his drink in a gulp and stood up.

"I'm sorry," he apologised. "Went off the subject a little. A dam? Another one, on this river?"

He shook his head.

"God forbid. I don't believe it will happen. I do remember that there were other potential dam sites that were surveyed along with the research on Kariba Gorge. That was in the late 1920s. Two sites were below the Victoria Falls, and upriver from Kariba. Batoka and Devil's Gorge. The other site surveyed was downriver from us, at Mupata Gorge. Kariba was started in 1955, about ten years after the first permanent geological camp was established below Kariba Gorge."

Harry was silent for a while. When he spoke again his voice was softer, wistful.

"I turned 21 in this valley. Kashili and I had been croc hunting for two years. We hunted for another year down here, without a break. 1948 to 1950. Before I went to Malaya. When I came back, in early '55, Kariba was the main news. The big venture. Cementing bonds between Northern and Southern Rhodesia, conveniently forgetting the politicking over the choice of the Kafue or the Zambezi as dam sites. The valley had changed. Horribly. People everywhere. New roads all over the place. Poaching, much worse, the game scattered to the four winds. Noise ... "

Harry grimaced.

"The start of the rot, Kariba. The valley has never recovered, despite what the pundits say. The river is slowly dying. And if they build new dams ... "

Harry shook his head almost savagely.

"It can't happen. It cannot be allowed to happen!"

Charlie Parker drew in a deep breath.

"Wishful thinking, Harry. Progress is the magic word these days. And dams are progress. Kariba. Caborra Bassa. Bright modern projects in deep, dark Africa. Hydro-electric power, bright lights for all. Great illumination. In case our coal resources run out. They won't let a few animals get in the way."

Charlie's voice was the voice of reason. He had on the research officer's cap now, planted firmly. The scientific approach left no room for emotion. Harry grinned dryly, ignoring the bait.

"Maybe, Charlie. Maybe. But public opinion can help. Kariba proved that as well. And the conservation cause has come a long way since Noah. You remember the publicity the game rescue operation received? All those journalists and TV crews and writers and goodness knows who else climbing on the bandwagon? Even royalty, Lord Mountbatten, came out and pottered around the lake, getting in everybody's way. You were a kid then, but you must have seen the newsreels and read about it. Who could ever forget those pictures of old Rupert Fothergill belting the rhino with his bush hat! The world got to know more about the poor little animals being saved on Kariba than they knew, or cared, about the shiny new dam itself."

The young research officer grinned.

"Okay, you do have a point. But you can't fight City Hall. You cannot stop progress. Not even with public opinion."

He shrugged dismissively.

"Hell, what are we getting excited about? It's all hypothetical mumbo jumbo anyway. There's nothing in circulation about a dam being built. That sort of project would surface pretty darn quickly. Let's drop it."

"Sure, Harry, relax."

Wally Conway had seen the oil smear, was rubbing ineffectively at it. He grinned across the dying embers at the warden.

"You were on Operation Noah for almost the whole rescue, weren't you?"

Harry nodded silently. It was time for bed, he thought. A burst of laughter from the direction of married quarters told him that the party spirit, compliments of the extra beer issue, would carry on for some time. He looked up at the night sky, searching for the Southern Cross; finding it and judging the time from its level against the horizon. He checked his watch in the fire glow.

Young Des Taylor gave the warden another prompt.

"Didn't the rescue start as soon as the dam wall was plugged, Harry? The waters came up very quickly, I read somewhere."

"I see you remember your local history, Desmond, so your schooldays couldn't have been all rugby and cricket."

Harry stroked his moustache as he remembered, and chuckled.

"Yes, I arrived on the scene there early on, as the rescue was being cobbled together by Rupert, Archie Fraser, and a couple of other chaps. Greg Gregory and Frank Junor. Kashili was there as well. We had hunted that region before the dam. He could not believe the change, all the hullabaloo. He was absolutely convinced that *Nyaminyami* would come up out of the gorge and smash down the wall. He was very dubious about the whole thing.

"Four and a half years later, at the end of Noah, in June 1963, with hundreds, thousands, of animals hauled off the islands, and the Zambezi now a ruddy great lake nearly 200 miles long and the northern bank not visible to the naked eye, he was still muttering predilections about the River God, that he would appear any minute and do us all in. I think the old boy's faith took a severe battering when nothing ever came of the River God prophecy. He was pretty much of a wild chap then, and I think he was looking forward to a little mayhem."

Harry yawned again.

"Well, I'll let you guys carry on and sort out the world's ills. I'm going to bed. I had best be bright and breezy in the morning. So had you all, by the way."

His yawn started the others off and the group split up. Gordon Munroe swept his torch beam across the area between the warden's cottage and the rest of the bungalows. A few pairs of eyes shone back in the wash of light. Waterbuck grazing, a few impala. He swung the torch in a wider arc. More gleams. Nightbirds, a genet on the prowl, a hyena shuffling past. He grunted with satisfaction. It was the right time to move. No elephants wandering around at the moment. Or buffalo, or lion.

The camp lay in darkness. The moon was over the half form. The river shimmered, molten silver, rent by the black mass of the island. Harry Kenyon lay on his back, hands clasped in a pillow behind his head. His bed was out on the open gauze-meshed verandah. Despite his keenness to end the evening and go to bed, he could not sleep. So he lay and listened to the night sounds of the valley. The evening's drifting conversations trickled through his mind, and he thought about the days when he was twenty years younger, when he and Kashili were hunting crocodiles and elephants along the big river. He thought about the monster croc, the one that had killed Sehitwa, towards the end, when he was growing weary of the killing. As sleep eventually claimed him, the lion on the north bank began roaring again. He smiled.

CHAPTER SEVEN

The aircraft raced it's shadow across the valley floor. Sunlight flashed off its windscreen as it banked and then steadied for its finals into the bush strip. Harry leaned against his Landrover, enjoying the day's first winter warmth. At the end of the gravel strip a trio of young elephant bulls browsed amongst the bush that crowded the airstrip. The impala that he had shepherded off the grass verge just before the plane arrived were now moving away to quieter haunts. A pair of hornbills looped over the cleared patch of bush, their wallowing top heavy flight taking them over him. The Cessna landed, small bursts of dust from the wheel impact swirling away. Now, without the dazzle of the glass, Harry could see Garnet Clayton in the left-hand pilot's seat. Beside him was Alistair Drummond. Two people, strangers, in the back. Harry caught a glimpse of camouflage uniform. He wondered, fleetingly, if it would be anyone from the old days. From Malaya, or the incursions in the late sixties.

The aircraft taxied across the gravel and on to the grass. Garnet Clayton cut the motor and the blur of the propeller slowed and died.   Harry came forward as they emerged, stretching cramped limbs, the director hamming it up a little and then striding across to meet the warden.

"Good morning, Harry! How's tricks?"

Big smile, great enthusiasm. Tall and languidly elegant, charm matching his good looks.   It almost works, thought Harry. Anyone who didn't know him would think he means it. The campaign smile. Harry shook hands. He'd left his beret in the vehicle, which took care of the saluting bullshit. Harry Kenyon was not sure he'd be able to keep the disdain from showing if he had to salute Dr Alistair Drummond.   He couldn't remember when he had last worn the green department beret. The badge, the silver waterbuck ram, was, in any case, attached to his worn floppy bush hat. And that was in his office.

"Fine, sir. Things are fine."

Garnet Clayton came around the front of the Cessna. He was a little taller than Harry, a little older.   The grey was much in evidence and Harry could see new strain lines around his mouth and eyes. That's what head office does to you, thought Harry, as he returned the chief warden's grin. Poor old Garnet. He's not cut out for department politics and the hassles of running the whole show. He should be in the bush. He's certainly aged since the Kariba days. And the days before that, when he was still police, and I was poaching. Something of Harry's thoughts must have been evident to the chief warden, for his welcoming grin turned wry.

"Hello, Harry. You're looking damn well. You never age. Must be the life you lead."

Harry chuckled.

"Garnet. Good to see you. You haven't been down here in ages. You should. It's the valley that keeps you young."

Garnet Clayton nodded, the wry smile staying on his features. Old Harry, he thought fondly. He's maybe got the right idea about life. Keep the hell away from the towns, especially head office, and drift with the tide. Look after your patch of bush, and the animals in it, and never the twain shall meet. He doesn't look forty, let alone forty ... what is it now, four? He's hardly changed over the years. It won't go on forever, though. He's warden now. It won't be long before he's due for promotion. Provincial warden. Desk work. Reports. And if he doesn't take it, the department will get awkward. Especially with Alistair Drummond at the helm. Harry is not his blue-eyed boy. Never has been, not since Kariba when Drummond was still new, with an even newer doctorate, and very superior.

The chief warden turned to the two remaining passengers, leading Harry the three paces across to where they waited.

"Harry, may I introduce Captain Peters, of the School of Infantry; and Superintendent Ryan, Officer Commanding Lomagundi District. Gentlemen, this is Warden Harry Kenyon, whose responsibility this stretch of the Zambezi happens to be."

"Superintendent."

Harry nodded at the khaki tunicked policeman. The handshake was brief, business-like. Then he returned the grin of the army officer and shook hands casually.

"Hello, Scratch. Didn't recognise you in the plane. How the hell are you?"

The camouflage uniform, faded and less distinct in its age, fitted the hard lithe form well. The blue parachute wings complimented the captain's pips. Clear blue eyes above a hawk nose regarded the warden with frank curiosity.

"Harry. Long time no see. Two and a half years? I've been thinking about you. Wondered where you'd got to. How long have you been down here?"

Harry's grin broadened.

"Two years and some. Virtually since I last saw you. In Matabeleland ..."

"Gentlemen ... "

The director cleared his throat purposefully.

"I think we should proceed to camp. We've quite a lot to talk about. The sooner we start the better."

He beamed benevolently at the group. Harry nodded at the soldier and moved over to his Landrover. A game scout detached himself from the vehicle. The warden spoke to him briefly.

"Have you got water and food, in case you have to be here all day?"

"Yes, sir."

It would be the scout's task to discourage any elephant or rhino from trying to use the aircraft as a convenient new rubbing post. Or hyenas from chewing the tyres. Harry waved a hand at the Landrover.

"Ready when you are, folks. Perhaps you would like to stand up on the back, sir? See more game from there."

The director nodded. Harry breathed a sigh of relief, catching Garnet Clayton's ironic glance. Okay, Garnet, he thought. You're dead right. Put him in the back, out of my hair, and see what advance information you can give me. Let's try and stay ahead of the crowd.

The cottage blended into the landscape. Sand-coloured walls and thatch-roofed, with the front verandah wide and the length of the building, green mosquito gauzed against the insects' constant offensive. Off the verandah, leading right up to the lip of the high river bank, was thick green grass, kept permanently cropped by the buck and hippo. A patio of water-smooth river pebbles, sunk into concrete, was beside the bungalow, sharing the shade of the Natal mahogany whose branches spread above. Rebellious bougainvillaea twisted amongst the greenery, its riotous colours cheerfully punctuating the deep shaded green of the foliage. A long wooden dugout canoe lay near the solitary concrete table beside which was a solitary chair, Harry's, where he would watch the sunset over the Zambezi. Today, several others had been brought across from the office block. The men sat quietly, making desultory conversation whilst a staff member removed tea cups. Wonder why he didn't want to use the office, mused Harry, staring out over the river to the blue-hazed escarpment of Zambia. Not like him. He likes taking over an office and playing centre stage. His gaze swept the northern bank, buff coloured, eroded, capped by a fringe of deep green riverine bush. No movement over there. Animal or otherwise. And the army? Scratch Peters? A captain now. And with the School. Out of the Special Air Service. Where does he fit in? Harry's gaze shifted closer, to the stretch of island in mid river, reed-fringed, with sandbanks bright white in the sun, a miniature sand storm eddying across its surface. The buffalo were still on the island, the ones that had crossed last night whilst they were having a few beers. Large, for a Nemana bachelor herd. Fourteen buffalo, black, heavy bossed, amongst the reeds. There were elephant as well, grazing the lush growth around the edge of the island. A pair of Egyptian geese scolded each other hoarsely on a sand bar. A Goliath heron stood solitary vigil in the shallows, unminding of the crocodiles basking nearby. Hippo chorus chortled over the river and Harry watched a fish eagle throw its neck back to cast its own voice across the valley morning.

Alistair Drummond's voice cut through his reverie.

"Well, chaps; I think we should get the major business of the visit over with first. That is, the police and army business. Then Garnet and Harry can concentrate on department affairs. At that stage, Harry, perhaps you would be kind enough to put a vehicle at our disposal, with one of your staff. I will show our visitors some of the Nemana Park."

Harry nodded.

"Fine, sir. No problem at all."

Anything to keep you happy, sport, thought the warden. It suits me for you to wander off on a little joy ride. Although it would be nice if you spared the time to visit the office, even for five minutes. The staff would think then that you actually thought about them, occasionally. Good for morale. After all, you haven't been down here to Nemana for at least as long as I've been in charge. Harry waited impatiently for the meeting to unfold.

"Superintendent ..."

The director nodded to the policeman.

"I'll leave it to you to carry on."

Ryan cleared his throat and crossed one blue and khaki-socked leg over the other.

"Mr Kenyon, my presence here is really only political. The Lomagundi District ends above the escarpment, with your area of jurisdiction falling under our North Border Control. However, any incursions through your area will very likely concern me."

He paused as Harry glanced at the army officer, then at the chief warden. *Incursions?* What incursions, wondered the warden. *What's going on here?*

"The farming areas of the Lomagundi District are amongst the most fertile in the country. And so any disruption of farming programmes in these areas would do our economy a lot of harm. And they are my particular responsibility. I'll let Captain Peters take over from here."

Yes, do, thought Harry. Maybe he'll get to the point and make some sense. He noted the vague sardonic smile that ghosted across the military man's features and guessed that he was no more impressed with the meeting's progress than he was. Scratch Peters made his briefing in a quiet conversational tone.

"There are signs, Harry, that we can expect incursions across the Zambezi by Nkomo's men. Nothing concrete yet, but there's something in the air. Special Branch's external sources are picking up bits and pieces of intelligence. They've used the valley before; I don't have to tell you that." He paused briefly to bestow an ironic grin on Harry. Then went on.

"The first incursions in 1966 culminated in our eliminating their units in April of that year, near Sinoia. So, from step one, it looks as if the Lomagundi District was a priority target for their offensives. In July 1967 we had the combined SAANC and

ZAPU infiltration near Victoria Falls. Your part of the world, Harry. Wankie National Park became the main contact area. We sorted that lot out. In 1968 they used this area again to try and infiltrate through into Rhodesia. That gave us a brand new war. Operation *Cauldron*. Your predecessor, Dave Scammell, was the first person to find sign of their presence. He found tracks, plenty of them, down near the Chewore's confluence with the Zambezi, and got the ball rolling. And that gave us a new ball game. The bastards had been in for six months. Base camps right across the valley and the first probes up over the escarpment into the commercial farming areas ... "

The officer grinned at Harry's impatient expression.

"Old history, I know. Bear with me, Harry, and I'll start to make sense ... "

He paused and gazed out over the river, and when he continued his voice was reflective.

"Well, we sorted out those ones as well. Although it took us a while, early March through until the end of April. We lost our first SAS guy in action on *Cauldron*, along with RLI and RAR men. It was a new dedication we were up against. The nationalists were better trained. Better motivated. Still, we killed fifty-five of that group, and captured a whole lot more. The valley was quiet for the rest of that year. Their second attempt at thrusting through it for the Lomagundi area had failed. There was a lot of speculation as to where they'd try next. This part of the valley again? Or back up above the Falls? Or somewhere new?"

Scratch Peters nodded at Harry.

"This is where you come back into the picture, Harry. You were still stationed in Wankie. December 1969 saw the start of a new operation. *Teak*, we called it, after the Kavira Forest where the latest insurgency evidence was discovered. Can't remember exactly how we found out about them. Harry?"

Harry answered, his glance sweeping across the visitors and on across the river. Some of the buffalo were in the water now,

lying in the mud of the shallows. The Goliath heron hadn't
moved. He remembered it clearly, as well the army man knew.
"There'd been a sighting in the forest area. The usual thing. A
stranger with a pack and what looked like a weapon. They
choppered the Tracker Combat Unit in to check it out. My
section had the duty. All National Parks guys. Paul Cantrell,
Tom Ormond, Robin Hughes, myself. We found the tracks of
twenty-two CTs and followed them for two days. Lost them
through anti tracking. But it got the ball rolling. Joint
Operations Command was moved from Deka to Lupane, closer
to the suspect area. Nothing happened for a couple of days.
Not a dickey bird.
Then they hit Victoria Falls airport and attacked the South
African Police Camp at Chisuma. They also blew the railway
lines. Plenty of spoor after that. The JOC was moved again, to
the airport this time. We had the first kills of the Operation.
On Christmas day. By the end of it, in January '70, twenty of
the CTs had been nailed."
Harry's gaze came back to the four men and he grinned
suddenly at Peters.
"That was the last time our paths crossed."
        The captain returned the game warden's grin with a
shrewd stare. That's right, Harry, he mused. When the
helicopter that dropped my section to reinforce yours took off,
you were on it. I helped put you in the chopper and I didn't
think you were going to make it. You had two bullets in you.
And you got another gong for your efforts. You left that part
out just now. Your tracker team caught up with the insurgents,
twenty of them. Five zoo keepers against twenty. It's strange
how your section, that Parks team, always got the best results.
Some people were jealous of that. Whatever, you nailed three
of them, and collected all their packs and spare ammunition,
grenades, and so on. Which made things easier for the lads
chasing them later. But not before you caught it. Two slugs.
One through your left shoulder, the other deflected off your

rifle across your chest. Two new additions to your Malayan wound.

Captain Scratch Peters drew a deep breath.

"Right, that's the background. Since then, through 1970, 1971, until now, there have been no major incursions. Small isolated incidents only. Enough to keep us ferreting around. Now, with the intelligence that's coming in, it looks as if there's a new game about to start. The question is, where? It would appear, if we are to believe our Special Branch colleagues, that the eastern valley will be the focus of any new activity. Not so much here, further downstream is more likely. Towards Kanyemba and Mozambique. Those areas are not as desolate as your wilderness areas here, and, if the nationalists can subvert the local population in those areas, it would provide a good logistical route into the north-east commercial farming areas. We do not think that will happen, but who knows? They've not penetrated the Lomagundi District with much success. Perhaps they'll pick new target areas. The north-east is equally important to our economy, agriculturally. Time will tell."

He held Harry's look of reflection.

"So, Harry. Hence our visit. To advise you, and ask for opinions in return. It will be everybody's war. Other army and police representatives are visiting your neighbouring areas, doing the same as we are. Any comment?"

Harry lifted his shoulders in an exaggerated shrug.

"Not really. We've seen nothing out of the ordinary. I have patrols out in the Park continually. There's been nothing dramatic to report. We're always on the look out for human spoor, because of the poaching implications. There's been nothing. I often monitor the northern bank, checking on game movements. There are a couple of fishing villages, upstream a little way, and even they have been deserted for several weeks now. Two months ago my scouts reported hearing a few shots across the river. Not automatic fire, single shots. They were up on patrol near our western boundary. They also saw what must have been a flare, a red one, early one evening. But that's all."

The captain wrote for a minute in a green-covered notebook.

"The shots and the flare. Did you report them to anyone?"

"Sure. There's mention of it in my monthly reports, which go to Salisbury. Also the fishing villages being deserted."

The army man glanced across at Garnet Clayton.

"Would that come to your office?"

The chief warden nodded.

"And what would you do with the information?"

Garnet Clayton shrugged.

"It would go on file. There's nothing unduly sinister about the information. If something came up later that might connect with those reports, we would re-evaluate it."

"And then?"

The chief warden inclined his head towards the director.

"It would go to Dr Drummond if it were considered significant."

Scratch Peters grunted.

"What *is* considered significant?"

Garnet Clayton bridled.

"That's an open-ended question. I would say that we treat as significant anything that relates to the safety and well-being of our wildlife, and the people who look after it. Does that answer your question, captain?"

Peters took a few seconds to answer. When he spoke, his voice was polite.

"Yes, Mr Clayton. I suppose it does. I can't fault your answer. I do wonder, though, if our interpretations of events in the future could not coincide a little better? It might make all of our jobs a little easier."

He sat back in his chair then, and placed both hands before him on the concrete table. He smiled around at the men.

"Gentlemen, that is my business taken care of. Superintendent, you?"

The policeman shook his head.

"Harry, anything you want to ask me?"

The warden gave a slight nod.

"What time span are we looking at, if your intelligence is correct? When does it all start happening?"

"Around Christmas, probably. With the start of the rains. Plenty of cover."

Scratch Peters favoured the warden with a wide grin.

"Why, Harry? Getting bored looking after the animals? Ready for a bit more soldiering? Get the old adrenalin flow back to form?"

Harry Kenyon grunted sourly.

"I get enough adrenalin flow, thanks. I'll leave the soldiering to you. I'm out of practice."

He stood up and walked across to the edge of the river bank. The river sparkled in the mid morning sun. The heron had caught a fish at last.

CHAPTER EIGHT

Garnet Clayton gazed at the single tusk that hung in solitary splendour on the main wall of Harry's office. The two men had moved across to the office block after the director and his visitors had left on their outing. Harry had given the task of chauffeur and chaperone to young Desmond Taylor, noting with wry amusement the youngster's nervousness. He had chuckled when the cadet ranger began stroking his embryonic moustache, eyes darting across to the waiting director.

"Relax, Des, he won't bite."

"Yes. Sure, Harry. But shouldn't someone more senior take the director out?"

"Hell, why?" I'm busy with the chief warden, and the rest of the station is busy. The buck stops at you. Good public relations practice for you. You'll find that Dr Drummond enjoys these rare opportunities he gets to meet new staff. If you go anywhere near Shumba viewing platform, keep an eye on that hippo. I had a good look at him yesterday. He's a little bruised and bent, but otherwise he'll be all right. I've seen worse. But, for a while, at least, we shall have to humour him. Let his ego recover. Gordon Munroe has been to each tourist in the camp and warned them, I trust?"

"Yes, Harry. We both did the rounds, yesterday evening, before we came over to your place."

"Good. Enjoy your game drive."

Harry chuckled now. The chief warden turned from the tusk.

"What a beauty. Every time I see that ivory I wonder what the bull looked like who owned it. What's so funny?"

Harry jerked his chin at the doorway.

"I gave the job of nursemaiding Drummond to young Taylor. I think he had a case of first night nerves."

He glanced at the tusk, his gaze sweeping it fondly.

"We'll never know. As I've told you before, I found it in a ravine, down on the Angwa River. On its own. All hundred and sixty pounds of it. Way back in 1947. When I was a pup. When you and I were both pups. You'd just come out from Blighty and joined the good old British South Africa Police. Your first station, wasn't it? I remember how the bush telegraph finally got to me down on the valley floor. There was a new *mukiwa*, a new white man, at the police station, and he was going to nail any and every bastard that was in the valley shooting elephants. Whether in the country, or across the river in Northern Rhodesia, or downriver in Portuguese East Africa."

Harry laughed and shook his head.

"You were hell on wheels, Garnet. You must have stayed as thin as a rake, chasing poachers all over the valley. I must say, though, that I was pretty damn surprised when I got word that you'd caught up with a couple of the hard core types. It couldn't have been a picnic. Ian Needham, for one, swore he'd nail your hide to the Chirundu Bridge."

Garnet Clayton smiled, eyeing the warden with patient irony.

"Never got you, you son of a gun. Never got anywhere near you. I still wonder about that tusk on the wall. Did you honestly find it? Lying there in the middle of the ruddy Zambezi Valley? No, don't tell me. I'd rather not know the truth. I'd rather believe you found it."

Harry spoke sombrely.

"It's the truth. There was no sign of the animal. No signs of a fight. No carcass remains. It was eerie. There was this tusk, big, and clean, creamy-white, lying a few yards from the Angwa. Kashili took it as an omen of sorts. I was getting sick of hunting elephant. I hadn't shot many in my young life then. Perhaps eighty. I called it a day when I found that tusk. Never shot another one. Until I joined the Game Department. Ironic, isn't it ...?"

Harry's smile was a little twisted.

"I've killed more elephants since I joined the department, in the cause of progress, than I ever did when I was a poacher. Something a little haywire there, hey, Garnet. Don't you think?"

Garnet Clayton sighed and sat down across the desk from the warden.

"Christ, don't let's start a moralising session, Harry. I have enough of that at head office. I don't need you on my back as well."

Harry let his chair drop forward with an unrestrained crash from his position leaning back against the wall. He leaned on his desk and looked steadily across it at his visitor.

"Speaking of that, you won't mind if I tell you that you look bloody awful? It's a few months since I've seen you and you're getting old, fast. Why, Garnet?"

The chief warden shrugged, returning Harry's steady gaze.

"Who knows? It's just because the department is getting bigger, and the chief warden's post gets busier with it. That's all. The price of promotion!"

"But it's killing you, man! No job is worth that."

Garnet smiled at his friend's bluntness.

"It will level out in time. I'm having to handle a lot of the director's day to day work. He's very busy. Rhodesia is slowly becoming the Mecca for wildlife that Kenya was, before they became independent, and Mama Ngee got her dirty little fingers into the poaching racket. Drummond has a lot on his plate."

Harry smiled but there was no lightness on his face. The smile was more of a grimace.

"It sounds as if you've become the patsy for the director. He's so bloody busy playing governmental politics he's not doing his proper job. He's a political animal, Garnet. He cares not a whit for the men under him. Christ!"

Harry stood up and kicked the chair away. For a second he stood glaring down at Garnet Clayton and then he shook himself brusquely and strode across to the doorway. He stared out over the camp to the river. The chief warden eased his chair sideways and stretched out his legs. From this new angle he could see Harry standing at the open doorway, back rigid, hands thrust deep into his trouser pockets. He smiled at the warden's back, a tight rueful twist of the lips. He waited silently.

Finally, Harry turned reluctantly from the view and returned to the desk. His voice was painstakingly light when he spoke.

"I'm sorry, Garnet. It's not often I lose my sense of humour. Can I order you some tea?"

Garnet Clayton watched Harry with a long thoughtful stare, unmoving. Then he shook his head.

"No tea, thanks."

A pause. Then, mildly.

"What's with you and Alistair Drummond? Why is it that the two of you bristle whenever you lay eyes on each other? You're like a couple of village curs eyeing each other, waiting for a chance to bite."

Harry laughed then, his mirth washing away the tension that had built in the office. He shook his head.

"Nothing. I suppose we just grate on each other's nerves. I'll have to mind my P's and Q's. I didn't realise it was so obvious."

"Well, it is. It's one of the department mysteries. The Kenyon-director feud. And don't give me that crap. I was at Kariba when he first arrived to join the rescue operation. Remember? The first few weeks were okay. There were no problems between you. Then something happened. All of a sudden one morning, you were at each other's throats. What happened, Harry?"

Harry smiled and showed his palms in mock innocence.

"Nothing at all. Really. I get a little impatient with our research types, once in a while. That's all. They can get so bloody condescending and scientific. And he was that, all right. Still is. And it gets to me occasionally. My apologies, Mr Clayton, Sir. 'Tis wrong to criticise one's superiors like this. Consider me reprimanded and arse kicked. Now..."

Harry rubbed his hands in gleeful, schoolboy imitation.

"What have you got for me, from HQ?"

Okay, thought Garnet Clayton, I won't push that one. He's not giving out anything on that score. I won't even mention the woman. The one that was there with the politician husband and daughter. Forgotten her name now. Monica, was it? Monica Hutton. Perhaps it would be pushing things too far. The chief warden tapped the closed diary in front of him on the desk. He didn't need to open it. He knew well enough what was on the agenda.

"I've had the Veterinary Department on to me. Doc Canby himself. Wants to know what you're going to do about the lions that are killing off his test herd."

"Tell him that I'll sort them out this week. I've already made a plan."

The chief warden's eyebrows made the next question. Harry grinned.

"I'll catch them and move them to another location, where they won't be a nuisance."

This time a verbal query accompanied the raised eyebrows.

"How?"

Harry's grin broadened.

"Drugs. I'm going to dart them. Knock them out. Then move them. Not too far. Probably close to the Chingusa River. About twenty five miles. I'm guessing that will be just far enough for them not to retrace their steps back to the Chawoyo Gate area. I've picked the release area already. Plenty of game. And water. A few resident lions there already. But not too many. I don't think there will be too much territorial argument, whilst at the same time the displacement factor shouldn't be too severe. They won't be that far from their original territory. We'll have to see. It's all pretty new. I can't ..."

Harry stopped. Garnet held up a hand, had been holding it up for the last few sentences. When he spoke it was slow and precise.

"What the fuck are you talking about? Drugs? What drugs? Since when have you been drugging lions? I'm not talking about Kariba, with trap cages on islands. I'm talking about now!"

"This will be the first time."

Garnet nodded, waiting.

"I'm sure it will work."

Garnet kept nodding. Exaggerated patience. Harry sighed.

"Okay, Garnet. Relax. I thought I'd carry out the operation first. And then let you know. Otherwise all the research boffins will want to be down here on the act, and we'd have a bloody circus on our hands. It's what usually happens."

Harry paused, found no change in the chief warden's expression, so continued.

"I've been having long and interesting correspondence with the South African Council for Scientific and Industrial Research. Remember Tony Hartman? He came down from Makerere University in Uganda to help us with early drug darting on Noah? Well, he's now with the CSIR and he's specialising in chemical capture of wild game. He and I have kept in touch since we first met at Kariba. They have been working with a new drug that the Americans put them onto. Ketamine. It's a derivative of Sernylan, and it's a lot more effective than that drug, or Scoline, or Succinylcholine chloride, or any of the others we've all played with. Tony is very confident that Ketamine will be the new wonder drug, especially where the big cats are concerned. Far more stable than the other drugs."

Harry paused again. Garnet's expression had changed. Forced patience had given way to restrained interest.

"To cut a long story short, I've got some Ketamine. Plus the necessary sized darts. They'll hold the required ten milligrams. And I've converted a shotgun, 20 gauge, to be used as the delivery weapon. Rather than use a crossbow. And this week ..."

Harry's voice was very firm.

" ... I plan to see if everything works as it should. What I was saying, when you so crudely interrupted me, was that I can't translocate the lions too far away. I'll use Landrovers, perhaps a five tonner, to move them. There's no antidote for Ketamine. It wears off after approximately two hours. Which, to be safe, gives me an hour and a half, maximum, to get them moved. Whilst they're still in dreamland. So, Garnet, tell John Canby that I'll have his lion problem sorted out this week."

Harry sat back in his chair and waited. The look of restrained interest on Garnet's face had been replaced now by wry amusement. The fingers of his right hand drummed on the desk.

"How long have you had this planned?"

"Only since yesterday morning, really. After I checked out their latest kill. I had rather hoped that their first attack was a random kill, and that it wouldn't become a habit. In case it did, I asked Tony Hartman to send me some Ketamine. There are several different lions involved. I have a fairly good idea which ones are causing the trouble. I know most of the cats in that area. We'll see. What do you think, Garnet?"

The chief warden blew a long breath through pursed lips.

"I wish you would let me know about your plans, Harry. I am your bloody boss, aren't I?"

"Come on, Garnet ..."

Harry chuckled.

"I'm a big boy now. Don't you think I can sort it out?"

"That's not the issue!"

Garnet Clayton's voice was flat.

"And you damn well know it. Hence all the cloak and dagger. It's the job of the research people in the department to initiate and oversee any darting and translocation work. You know that. You're treading on toes. Again. I know perfectly well that you can handle it before breakfast. That is not the point. Once research hears that you're carrying out your own projects with CSIR, and darting game on your own, they'll yell blue murder."

Harry kept his voice mild. Garnet was right.

"It's no big deal. It's not a major operation. And the whole thing is taking place in my Park. Right? The lions will be darted and moved a mere twenty or so miles to another part of Nemana. End of story. Come on, Garent, you're over-reacting."

"I am not. And you know I'm not. Research will be very annoyed."

"Fuck Research."

It was a strong invective for Harry. He continued.

"Why haven't they come up with the goods? How many letters have I copied to you, requesting them to keep field staff informed of new drug developments? How many replies do I get? Precious few. Research can go jump."

Garnet Clayton pointed a brown sun-spotted finger at Harry.

"You forget things, Harry. Like, for example, Alistair Drummond has a Dr in front of his name. And he is research. And, being research, Harry, he's going to be the main person screaming for your head."

"Fuck Drummond as well."

"Very easily said. You forget, very bloody conveniently you forget, Harry, that Drummond is my boss as well as yours! And, once again, Harry, you've put me in the middle. Who do you think is covering your arse up at head office? Who do you think keeps Drummond off your back when you start doing things your way? Who...? Me! That's who ..."

The chief warden had been shout whispering across the desk at Harry, his voice ragged and harsh. His eyes bored into Harry's. The warden returned the stare steadily.

"You may be a good warden, Harry. You may be one of the best wildlife men this country's ever seen. You might be a bit of a legend amongst the field personnel. You're Rupert Fothergill's protégé. But Alistair Drummond does not like you. And he is God, as far as we are concerned. And he is research. So why, Harry ..."

Garnet's voice ended in a sigh.

" ... do you make things so bloody difficult for me?"

Harry stood up slowly, and walked over to the tusk. For a long minute he looked at it, rubbing his fingers along the hardness of it, remembering when he and Kashili had found it out in the wild fastness of the valley. He'd been nineteen then, and Kashili in his late forties, heading for the end of his prime. He had decided, there and then, that he would never sell the tusk, no matter what he was offered. He would keep it. As a totem, as a reminder of all the elephants that had gone before. And of the ones that would surely follow. He turned abruptly from the great curve of ivory, and went back to the desk. He grinned ruefully at Garnet and held his hand up in the peace sign.

"Garnet, I'm sorry. Truly. When Drummond gets back from his joy ride, I'll put him in the picture. Then he can have words with me directly. Okay?"

The chief warden gave him a fleeting dry grin, and shook his head.

"No, I'll handle it. It's better if I inform him. Later, at some opportune moment."

He hesitated.

"You know, Harry. You won't always be in the valley. Sooner or later you must come up for promotion. Provincial warden is the next step. Old John de Beer is getting a little long in the tooth, which means that the Northern Matabeleland post will be vacant in the next couple of years. That could be your next rung up the ladder. Sometime, you'll have to end up at head office. It's evolution."

It was Harry's turn to shake his head and his answer was very soft, as if to contemplate such a fate aloud would be blasphemy.

"God forbid that I ever end up driving a desk in that madhouse. There's no way it will happen."

He nodded at the chief warden.

"Look at you. You're a bloody wreck. Ever since you left the field to go to head office. Look at old Ted Davison, the poor bastard. Thirty four years in Wankie National Park. Since 1928. He developed that Park from scratch. There was nothing there, not even any written history. He had to pick up what information there was from the writings of Baines and Selous, and learn the area from the bushmen. And what did they do to him? The department? Head office? With five years left to retirement? Peace and quiet for his last years? Growing old with Wankie? No. They move him to a desk at head office. Four walls. Slow death."

Harry's voice turned sour.

"I don't know how I'm going to beat that evolution you talk of, Garnet. But I will. I'll have to. I'll die if you stick me in the city."

For a long while there was silence in the office. From out over the river came the long mournful yelp of a fish eagle. Hippo talk, mellifluous with distance, blended with closer irritated trumpeting of elephants. Garnet Clayton glanced across at Harry and then to the tusk. He's right, mused the chief warden. Head office would kill him. Especially with office politics as they are these days. He's a relic now, amongst all the shiny new fast development. He's just as much an endangered species as some of his animals. When he spoke again, the chief warden's voice was gruff.

"Let's get rid of the rest of our work, Harry. Maybe we can get it over by midday, and you can take me for an hour's fishing."

"Sure. What else do you want to discuss?"

"Firstly, there is to be a wildlife conference at Kariba in the first week of September. A variety of people will be speaking and presenting papers. We'd like you to attend. Any problem with that?"

Harry shook his head.

"Shouldn't be, depending on what's happening here. Anybody interesting giving a chat?"

"Local people mostly. There'll be an update on elephant collaring and radio tracking. We've invited people up from South Africa, and we're hoping to get the Principal of the Frankfurt Zoo out.

Speaking of elephants, research have commented on the dearth of elephant calves taken from your culling exercises. Only ten came from Nemana."

The chief warden glanced enquiringly at Harry.

"Any special reason for that? Apart from the one I think I know about?"

"No. I destroyed most of the calves. It's kinder than having the poor wretches locked away in zoos for the rest of their lives. You know my feelings on that, Garnet."

"I do, and perhaps you're right. It nevertheless evokes comment by research. Are the breeding patterns of the valley elephants changing? Or is Harry Kenyon playing judge, jury and executioner, again? Not to mention the value of the lost calves. Four hundred dollars a calf, now."

Harry remained silent. Garnet Clayton swept an appraising glance over him before continuing.

"Leave, Harry."

"What?"

"Leave. Administration tells me that you've got eighty-six days accumulated. You haven't taken leave since you were transferred to the valley two and a half years ago. You must be ready for a break."

Harry laughed.

"I don't need leave, Garnet. Living down here. In paradise. Why the hell should I leave the valley and go on leave? Where would I go?"

The laughter petered out to a dry chuckle. He pointed a broad broken-nailed finger across the desk.

"You're the one who needs leave, chum. Remember your words to me, earlier today? I haven't aged, you said. Why don't you take a few weeks off and bring the wife down here? Poor Jessica must worry like hell about you. You can have my house. I'll camp out."

Garnet shrugged.

"Okay. At least I've discussed it with you. I told Admin that you wouldn't be interested. Remember, though, that you can't accumulate more than a hundred days. You forfeit anything over that. And, thanks, I might take up your offer. Jessica could certainly do with a break from Salisbury. She misses the bush as much as I do. I've only one more thing for you, Harry. Alex Gant."

The warden's eyes narrowed.

"What about him?"

"He's back in the country. He's been across in Botswana. It seems that things have got a little warm for him there, so he's back here."

"Doing what? Where?"

"He's at Victoria Falls at the moment. Doing nothing. Relaxing at the hotels. Spending money. Charming the tourist girls. Hasn't made a move out of the town."

"I'll bet."

Harry's voice was dubious.

"Are we watching the son of a bitch? Who's up there these days?"

"Tom Poulson. Yes, he's being watched. If he puts a foot wrong, we'll pull him in."

Harry grunted sourly.

"We've done that before, and the bastard got away. He's another poacher you never managed to nail, Garnet, way back when you were still police. And not many others have either. I managed to get him to court once, after three years work. Three years of watching and waiting, tracking him, following him all over the country. And they let him off on a technicality. He walked out, free as a bird. Laughing his head off. The bastard. I hope we're watching him carefully, Garnet. Because as sure as night follows day, he'll be up to no good. Do you remember? He was shooting pregnant cow elephants, removing the foetuses and getting them to China. He's bad, Garnet."

The chief warden rubbed his jaw reflectively.

"I'll keep you posted. Poulson is a good warden. He'll keep a keen eye on Gant."

Harry nodded.

"As long as he stays out of my Park. If I catch him, he won't make court."

Garnet Clayton smiled.

"Perhaps that's a good idea. Maybe I should have a message passed on to friend Gant. Quietly. Tell him there's good pickings down at Nemana. Harry Kenyon's patch of turf. We might get some interesting results. Set a poacher, a reformed poacher, I should say, to catch a poacher. What do you think, Harry?"

"Thank you, no. I'd rather have him out of my hair. Let him stay at the other end of the valley, and give someone else headaches. I don't need Alex Gant in my life."

Harry stood up and stretched, restless now.

"Come on, Garnet. Let's get some fresh air. One last question, by the way. How was my feasibility study on the tree lodges received? My idea for two or three luxury lodges up along the river?"

Garnet Clayton grinned.

"For once, Harry, your ideas have not fallen on stony ground. Everyone, the director included, thinks it's a sound idea. Aim at a different income bracket of people. The idle rich. Anything to help spread the wildlife gospel. They want to talk to you about it at a later date. And do something positive. Drummond will probably have a chat to you later today about it. Well done, Harry."

"Hallelujah, brother. I'm glad I make sense to you head office people occasionally."

Mid afternoon. The shade cast by the tall mopane trees on the edge of the airstrip gave patchy respite from the last waning heat of the sun as it dropped to the northern escarpment. Captain Scratch Peters paused and turned to Harry before climbing into the aircraft, putting his back to the others.

"Nice seeing you again, Harry."

His clear blue eyes scrutinised the warden's face.

"Ever thought of re-joining the army? Or at least the Tracker Combat Unit, even on a part time basis? We could use you. And I have a strong gut feeling that tells me we'll be needing your talents in the not too distant future."

Harry returned the officer's gaze, yellow-brown eyes meeting blue. He shook his head softly.

"No. I've had my share of the action. Malaya for five years, with a slug in me for my trouble. Then the TCU operations back here, with two more bullets in me. Disability pension awarded. There are plenty of others for you to call on. I'm getting too old to play soldiers. Besides, Samson and I never saw eye to eye, right from the start of the unit. When we had our first training exercises at Chitove Falls, across on the Lundi River. He's a first rate bushman, but he's an awkward type. No thanks."

Harry was conscious of the others waiting. Scratch Peters tried again.

"Alan Samson has left the unit. Two months ago. He's gone into politics. The unit has been taken over by the School of Infantry. I'm the new unit commander. I've been transferred across from the SAS to upgrade the unit and strengthen it. I could use you, Harry. We worked well together in Malaya. Most of the old school are still active. Hughes, Coleman, Cantrell, Williams, Whispering Jim Lannigan ... all the Parks men are still there. Later this year we'll be liaising with the SAS Tracking Wing and developing a permanent bush base on the edge of the lake. Why don't you give the zoo keeper lark a break? You're never too old for our kind of work. I know you. You're not the type to let a couple of bullet holes slow you down."

Harry shook his head again.

"Thanks, Scratch, but no thanks. Nemana is just fine. Give my regards to any of the lads you see."

Harry stepped back, breaking contact. The captain shrugged and climbed up into the Cessna. The door clicked shut behind him. Garnet Clayton was checking co-ordinates in the far side pilot's seat. Harry walked around the propeller to his window, and tapped on the perspex. Garnet flicked the window open.

"Sorry, Garnet. With the various topics we covered today, something slipped my mind."

Harry's look went past the chief warden to the director. He watched Drummond whilst he directed his question at Garnet Clayton.

"Is there any new thinking about a dam being built? Here, along the Zambezi?"

Both answering expressions were quizzical, the director's mixed with impatience. The chief warden shook his head.

"Hell, Harry. They'll never dam this portion of the valley. Kariba is still not being used to its full extent, power-wise. And they'll pick the sites above Kariba, if a new dam does come about. It can't happen."

Harry lifted his hand in a half salute and stepped back from the aircraft. The engine sputtered into life, and the smell of aviation fuel was strong and alien on the warm valley air.

Molten silver. The gentle symmetry of beaten pewter. Out of this the island climbed, a liquid dark mirage. Out of the river that flowed eastwards, away from the last heat of the sun which had dripped its fiery strength to bed behind the massifs of the northern escarpment. The long broken row of the mountains was blurred now, moving from the day's blue haze through mauve into the brief stark silhouette that preceded darkness. From away behind the camp came the last roosting squabbles of guinea fowl as they jostled for branches. Their harsh clamour joined with the strident chatter of francolin seeking their night-time retreats in the shrubbery that clothed the many anthills on the plain. Harry sat with Kashili in the early evening darkness, listening to the first of the night sounds. The birds, he thought. They give us the background to the nightly orchestra. The nightjars and the dikkops out on the sand banks. Then we'll soon have the little owls, making their contribution. The hippos are the bass, and they'll snort and chortle through the whole piece. And, any time now, the hyenas will be yodelling their way up and down the scale, and when *mhisi* starts, the jackals will come in with their wailing yelps. And all of this is just the prelude of course, to the main performer. The king himself, old yellow eyes. It won't be long before he's on the prowl, and letting everyone know it. Roar? I always wonder about that word, roar. It's awfully seldom one hears the real thing, à la MGM. Mostly he's giving out that series of long groaning growl grunts, that slowly die away into echoes. To start again. I suppose roar is as good a way as any to describe *nkhala's* contribution to our nightly orchestra. Tomorrow evening, I think, we will see if we can catch us a few lions.
"Kashili."
"Eh, young one. *Ute yini?*"

"Tomorrow we will go and catch those lions that are killing the tsetse test herd. We will try at night, first. It will be easier to find them when they are on the move, I think."

"Hau. Lions at night? That is worse madness than crocodiles at night. I am getting too old for such games. It is all right for you. You are young still."

Harry grinned in the darkness. A bat swooped between them at the speed of an eye blink.

That's what Scratch Peters thinks, as well. He reckons there's life in this old dog yet. Perhaps I should have invited him out on the lion catching operation. See if he still thinks being a zoo keeper is a touch mundane. A long way from Malaya, perhaps. But still very good for the adrenalin flow. Almost as good as tigers and getting shot.

Malaya came back to him later, as sleep claimed him. He saw the tiger again, standing in the stream, and he felt the pain of the bullet wounds.

CHAPTER NINE

The lion stared fixedly at the man crouched less than three paces away. He was a large male, in his prime, with a handsome dark mane. A lifetime of territorial skirmishing and survival in the valley had left a network of healed scars across his face. There were new lacerations from this night's encounter, but the man did not think they were serious. Antibiotics and some sulphur powder will fix them, thought the warden, as he slowly moved an upright finger from left to right across the lion's line of vision. The animal's gaze followed it dully. In the lights of the vehicles and spot lamps the shadows of lion and man merged fluidly into some mythic monster. Harry stood up and moved carefully around behind the lion's shaggy head, out of the animal's vision. The lion remained motionless. The dart in his shoulder gleamed softly in the wash of light. Harry waved at the vague shapes still on the vehicles.

"He's out. Corneal and eyelid reflexes are still there, but he's fully immobilised. Let's get him loaded. I'll treat his wounds when he's in the Landrover. We've been damn lucky getting both males tonight."

From the Landrovers in the darkness floated a voice.

"Harree. Stay zere, if you please. On your own for but a few seconds. Zat is a marvellos picture And smile, please, Harree."

The French accent seemed no less incongruous now, in the night of the Zambezi Valley, than it had been when the film crew had arrived the day before. Harry sighed quietly, smiled graciously.

"Okay, gentlemen. Shoot away. But quickly, please. Time is not on our side. In a couple of hours both of these chaps are going to be waking up, and wondering what the hell has happened to them ..."

Harry's grin broadened. He could hear the cameras whirring.

"And, I might add, one of the lions will be travelling in the back of the Landrover that you folks are using. If he comes around while we're still on the move to the release area, it could become a little crowded."

Harry was very pleased. The capture operation, so far, had gone well. Like clockwork. And now he was glad that the French crew were here. When he had first received the radio message from head office that they had been granted permission to film in Nemana, and, if at all feasible, accompany Harry and his team on the capture exercise, he had cursed violently. A circus, he had silently fumed. Another bloody circus! Showing off the treasures of Nemana was a task Harry usually welcomed, particularly when it involved foreign media. He would happily jump through hoops to bring the valley paradise to outsiders. But not right now, he thought. I don't need an audience at the moment. There's enough to worry about, without having to say cheese every ten minutes, and be taking extra care that no visiting picture-taker gets chewed up by an insufficiently drugged lion. I'm surprised that the head office research wallahs aren't here in force, with collective tongues in cheeks. Climbing in on the act. There hasn't been a peep out of them. Just a message to Charles Parker to make sure every area in his sphere of jurisdiction is covered. Perhaps Garnet can still work miracles up there. Or maybe it's very opportune that the film crew happen to be at Nemana now. I didn't know they were even in the country doing a wild life documentary, and I usually get word of such visits in advance. Nemana is always a prime department publicity area. They'll get good footage, however the capture operation turns out. Whether it's successful, or whether someone gets chewed up in a fiasco. Which it's not, so far. Harry chuckled.

"Kashili. Bring a cloth, or something, to cover the lion's eyes. If there are too many people moving around, it will disturb him."

The warden switched to English.

"Keep the noise down, please. The lion still has all auditory and visual faculties, even though he can't move. I don't want to upset him too much. Charlie, once the eyes are covered, bring the Landrover around behind us here. We'll load him first. Desmond, how is the other cat?"

In the outer fringe of light the cadet ranger was crouched silently beside a recumbent sandy form. Desmond Taylor's voice was guarded.

"He's fine, Harry. Although he came off worst in the fight. He's clawed quite badly on the shoulders. His breathing is good and regular."

Harry nodded.

"Perfect. I'll come and doctor him now, whilst this fellow is being loaded. Kashili."

The old man looked up from where he had arranged a bush jacket carefully across the lion's eyes. He nodded at the animal.

"He is very big. And his teeth and claws are very long. How long will your medicine keep him asleep?"

"Long enough for us to be out of reach, when he wakes up. Come, night warrior, you who hunt crocodiles and lions in the darkness. Help me patch up the wounds of the other male."

Harry grinned fondly at the old wrinkled native. Kashili bobbed his head softly and clicked his tongue.

"Hau. I keep telling you. I am getting too old for this night work. A man of my years should be home asleep with a warm woman. It is all right for you. You are still young. I will get the medicine bag."

The Landrover had been edged close to the hindquarters of the lion. Charlie and Wally Conway spread out a wide-spaced nylon net across the rump of the animal. Shadows flickered erratically as the film crew manoeuvred for the best photo angles in the glare of the lights. Harry left them to it and joined Desmond at the first lion they had darted.

Ten minutes, he judged, then we must be on the move. To have enough time to get these beauties across to the ChingusaRiver. With time to spare, in case we're held up in any way. Elephant on the road. Or a rhino that decides to argue the right of way. He squatted down beside the lion. Not as big as the other one, he noted. More scruffy, too. Not much mane. Hell, we were damn lucky to get these two with so little fuss. Let's hope the females are as easy. Kashili joined the two men, passing the canvas medic pack to Harry. The warden ran his fingers gently over the scratches on the lion's neck and shoulders, exploring the damage caused by the bigger animal. It's not that bad, he decided. He'll be a touch stiff, but he'll manage. I'll dose him with antibiotics as well. We'd better release them a fair distance apart from each other or they'll be having a replay. It was sure as hell an interesting demonstration of territorial behaviour and lion psychology. I hope the film boys got it all.

The drama had started while it was still light, in the late afternoon. Harry and his capture team, in three Landrovers, waited beside the sandy shaded expanse of the Nyamawari River. The four-man film crew was taking scenic pictures of the game men, the river bed, and the lone elephant digging out a water-hole at the curve of the river. Earlier in the day, against the background of the flood plain, Harry had explained to the camera lens what their objectives were. A tendril of blue smoke drifted up from the cooking fire of the Chawoyo Gate scouts. Their duties for the day were over. Tourists weren't allowed to leave for the tar road after three in the afternoon. The same rule applied to tourists entering the Park. They were not allowed through the first National Parks barrier at the junction of the dirt road with the main tar road. Thus the nuisance and danger of tourists stranded in broken down vehicles at night in the valley was avoided. Harry could see the claw marks scarring the wooden door of the hut the lions had attacked two nights earlier. He looked up at the lowering sun and then checked the lengths of the trees' shadows along the ground. It would be dark in an hour.

The roaring started on the opposite side of the river, slightly downstream from the waiting men. A shattering reverberating call, followed by the succession of long deep grunts. The camera team returned quickly to the vehicles,

staring nervously back across the sand river. Harry listened to
the grunts fading away and glanced enquiringly at Kashili.
"Close," said the tracker.
Harry nodded silently, waiting for the next call. A gentle breeze
stirred the butterfly leaves of the mopane trees. The lion called
again, the primeval roar louder in the late afternoon stillness.
"He is coming to the river. If he keeps moving this way he
must pick up the scent of the bait."
Kashili's voice was soft and matter of fact. Harry nodded
silently again, and his gaze swept over the dart gun, the
converted shotgun, in the weapon's clamp. Three thick darts
lay on a bed of felt in the metal dashboard recess of the
Landrover. Between Kashili's knees rested the Holland and
Holland .375. His glance flicked around at the rest of the team.

Charlie Parker and Des Taylor were in one vehicle, with
half a dozen game scouts on the back. Wally Conway drove the
third Landrover, with the film crew clinging to the roll bars
behind the cab. Gordon Munroe, with an SSG loaded shotgun,
accompanied the visitors. As the warden's glance passed over
him, he winked at Harry. He was enjoying the role of
bodyguard. And it gave him a chance to make up for the nervy
shooting on the cull. Harry had discussed the poor
performance with the ranger. It wasn't a major issue. No cull
was ever technically the same, and anyone could have an off
day. Harry had simply wanted to assure himself that the ranger
had his nerves under control, on this, his second year on culling
operations. His allocation of film crew protection duty to
Gordon was deliberate. He wanted the ranger to know that he
had his confidence.

The lion roared again, considerably closer now. Good,
thought Harry. He's on his way. He must have picked up the
impala. We dragged the carcass around for long enough, and it
must be nice and ripe by now. I'm surprised though. Would
have thought that the cat on this eastern side of the river would
have picked up the smell first. Never mind. It's time we eased
the vehicles downstream to the bait and to see if we can make

contact with Leo over there. He seems to be hot footing ... Hello! And now? A new bout of roaring had commenced from the valley bush behind the waiting capture team, crashing, rolling, echoing across the darkening landscape. This second lion was closer. Harry heard a muttered Gaelic curse. He glanced at Kashili beside him. The old man grinned askance back at the warden, scratching his grey woollen head thoughtfully.

"And now, my child? Are you going to catch two lions at one time? One in each hand? As an old man I am greatly interested in such feats!"

Harry grunted. The coughing end of the roar died away. In a second an answering roar from across the river filled the air. It began a chorus of lion sounds that Harry had not experienced before. Each animal's roar generated a new round of ear-splitting, air-buffeting, earth-trembling challenge. The vocal warfare increased as the lions drew closer to each other. The first lion, Harry was certain, had crossed the Nyamawari now, which put him in the later vocaliser's territory. Which, reflected the warden, should make things interesting. We certainly don't have the problem of locating these lads. I hope the film makers have got their sound recorders going. Christ, what a noise! I swear my Landrover is vibrating. He leaned over and nudged Kashili.

"Let us go and catch these noise makers, old man. I will show you how."

He had to pitch his voice loud, even within the confines of the half-doored cab, to be heard above the roaring. Kashili shrugged nonchalantly, maintaining the show. Harry leaned out of the Landrover and shouted above the tumult.

"Right! Let's move. Charlie, slot in behind me. Wally, you bring up the rear, until we've made contact."

He flicked a thumbs up sign at the Frenchmen and grinned at their determinedly casual response. Gordon Munroe broke the shotgun and checked the loads. He made the operation suitably efficiently theatrical and Harry watched one of the crew capture the action with a stills camera. He led the small convoy off through the now dark bush. He switched on the headlights, staring intently along the beam.

The roaring stopped suddenly, leaving an echoing silence that was eerie. As Harry wondered at this new development, guiding the Landrover along the track, he saw the lion. The animal was on the edge of the track and stared, green eyes shining, at the approaching vehicle. It showed no signs of fear, merely staring levelly back at the twin orbs of the headlights. He eased the Landrover closer. Kashili, as soon as they had started moving, had loaded the drug-filled darts into the barrels, followed by the adaptors and .22 blanks that would propel the darts. Now he handed the weapon to Harry. Converted shotgun in hand, the warden cautiously guided the vehicle closer. When he judged he was well within twenty paces of the lion he stopped the Landrover and leaned out over the door with the shotgun. The lion remained still at the edge of the track, profiled to Harry. Beautiful, he thought. Just perfect. He took a deep breath, let it out, mentally crossed fingers and squeezed the trigger. An angry rasping snarl erupted from the lion as the dart thudded into his shoulder. Growling in surprised indignation at this sudden attack, the lion whirled around, searching for his assailant. For a long second the big tawny cat stood poised, muscles rippling, one paw raised to strike, as it sought its adversary. Then in one fluid leap, it disappeared out of the light into the undergrowth. Okay, thought the warden, now we start earning our money.

They searched for the lion for thirty minutes, the three Landrovers weaving slowly amongst the bush hoping to pick up his motionless drugged form, or the reflection of his eyes in the probing beams of the hand-held spot lights and the headlights. The search was fruitless and Harry decided to get back to the track and move to their original destination, the hanging impala bait. Almost as soon as they regained the road, Kashili pointed over the door of the Landrover.

"There is his spoor. See how it is crooked, as if he is starting to get drunk."

They followed the tracks along the sandy dirt road. With Kashili's attention on the spoor it was Harry who picked up the movement further ahead, at the extremity of the headlight beams.

"There he is!"

He was relieved. He hated the idea of the lion lying comatose in the bush somewhere. The lion had strolled out of the roadside bush and now stood looking at the approaching Landrover. Harry frowned as the lights playing over the lion became stronger with their approach. The lion looked totally unaffected by the drug. Harry studied the animal closely.

"This is a new lion," he murmured to Kashili. "See, his mane is dark, and he is bigger. The first one had a thin mane, and was a less impressive animal. Who is who, I wonder? Which is the intruder from across the river? Is the dart gun ready, my friend?"

"Yes. Here. You can stop, I think. This one is coming to meet us."

Which indeed seemed the case. Head low, the lion walked up the beam of the light towards them. He was a magnificent animal. Over the purr of the stationary Landrover Harry could hear each low grunt that came with the lion's padding gait. For the first time he noticed fresh wounds on the lion's face. He wondered if the film unit had a decent view of the nearing big cat. Once again he leaned over the half Landrover door, and took aim at the approaching lion. At ten paces, holding his aim on the animal's forequarters, he fired, ducking quickly back into the cab. He knew the lion had picked up the silhouette and movement of his leaning out of the cab, and that the animal might easily charge when the dart impacted. With a furious spitting snarl the lion reared up, for a split second becoming the heraldic rampant lion incarnate. Harry was dimly aware of Kashili's muttered exclamation of awe. Then the lion whirled and, reversing direction, loped back up the road in very determined fashion. Harry rapidly put the car into gear and followed in pursuit, watching the spurts of dust explode beneath the lion's paws as it ran. It was the reaction he had least expected. He had guessed the lion, once darted, would leap into the tree line on the edge of the track, or break into a run in the direction it was facing. Straight at them. It was this latter reaction that had concerned him. Now he changed up to second gear in their pursuit of the darted animal. He didn't want to lose this one as well. The lion veered suddenly, at a right angle, off the track. Out of the light. Harry brought the vehicle to a stop. The lion could still be heard. The angry snarling and growling, and the violent shaking of the shadowy bush seemed very, very close.

"The rifle," whispered Harry. "The .375 might be useful if we end up with a lap full of annoyed lion. He's certainly giving it a full go. Not happy with life at all."

He manoeuvred the Landrover off the track, dodging the trees and undergrowth. Almost immediately they could see the disturbance of bush, and caught glimpses of tawny hide. The paroxysm of fury continued unabated, awfully loud in the night. Harry eased the Landrover closer, straining for a clear glimpse of the enraged lion. It looked as though it was attacking something on the ground. Harry checked the luminous dial of his watch. Three minutes had elapsed since darting. Another four, or perhaps five minutes, depending on the rage and adrenalin flow through the lion, should see him calm down, judged the warden. What the hell is he giving so much attention to?

The lion's rage slowly died. The snarling, growling fury subsided until the Zambezi Valley night was quiet. Away in the darkness a jackal yammered. The lilting gentle quaver of a nightjar seemed particularly soothing after the preceding mayhem.

Harry edged the Landrover closer and closer, until the front of the vehicle was no more than a few feet away from the battered undergrowth and the recumbent patch of tawny hide. Cautiously he eased himself out from behind the steering wheel, senses vibratingly alert for the first sign of movement from the lion. He could hear the humming of the camera from the crew's vehicle that Wally Conway had manoeuvred round at an angle to Harry's. He hoped young Munroe was wide awake with the shotgun. Felt very vulnerable the further he moved from the doubtful security of the cab, closer to what minutes ago had been a raging lion. Finally he stood peering down at the animal, and his eyes widened. There were two lions lying at his feet, eyes fixed staring up at him. The body of the second lion covered the first animal, where it had finally collapsed as the Ketamine took effect. Blood from the claw and bite marks glistened crimson-wet in the light. Harry knelt gingerly and passed a hand across both lions' vision. The stares of both somnolent animals followed his hand sluggishly. The warden stood up and moved out of the headlights' glare. When he spoke he was quietly jubilant.

"Let's get moving, folks! We have ourselves two drugged lions. A little tattered, but otherwise in perfect working order. Bring the net, please. We'll have to separate them. Then we can check the extent of their wounds properly, and treat them accordingly. Then we can load them into separate Landrovers."

Harry checked his watch for the hundredth time since they had left the capture area. The Landrover convoy lurched through the night to the release point he had selected weeks earlier. Twenty minutes, he estimated. We're cutting it fine, but we should make it on time. We might not have time to unload them. Leave them in the back of their respective vehicles to come round and depart. Better keep them decently apart. We lost time looking for the first cat. We were lucky the second fellow found him for us. Quite a night. First time out and two lions in one exercise. I hope the rest of the operation goes as smoothly. Up ahead, the dark spotted shape of a civet ghosted across the track. Harry leaned over and punched Kashili lightly on the shoulder.

"So, old man. Now you know how to catch two lions, one in each hand. Do you need further instruction? Next time I will leave the task to you. In your older wisdom."

Kashili hawked and spat over the side of the door into the darkness.

"Perhaps the young cock crows before it is light. Tonight has surely been a good experiment. But we walked on the edge for a time. That lion behaviour was not usual."

Harry snorted.

"What lion behaviour is usual? Especially at night? Look what happened to Len Harvey and Willie de Beer at Wankie in April. Both very good bush men, and look what one lioness did to them. As Charlie Parker says : lions are like women. Not too easy to out-think."

His companion chuckled evilly. Women were always a favourite topic.

"Perhaps Parker has more knowledge of such matters. He is always hunting those creatures. Forever smelling them out. Unlike you ..."

The old man glanced sideways at the warden. Harry let it ride. It was a recurring theme with the old native. Kashili pursued the line of his conversation.

"The time is long past when you should have taken a wife. I say that you are young ... you are much younger than me. But, in fact, you are becoming old. You are irresponsible in not acquiring a permanent woman. If your parents were alive they would be greatly disappointed that you are still alone. By now you should have many children. I should be teaching them the ways of the wild. As I taught you. And your father before you. Soon I will be too old to teach. And you will be too old to take a wife, and have children. It is all very well for you to say that the bush is your wife. But you are evading your responsibilities as a man."

Kashili flicked a quick oblique glance at Harry. The warden stared ahead, watching the old man's reflection in the windscreen. He kept his face expressionless. They drove in silence for a while. Harry checked his watch again. A nightjar dipped and glided ahead of them. Harry let the silence build. Finally Kashili coughed his impatience.

"Are you deaf now? Is old age capturing you faster then I thought? Do you not give your elders the courtesy of an answer?"

Harry kept the grin from his face.

"When did you last see your wives, *bava*? Or your children? When did you last visit the home of your forefathers?"

In the dim dash lit reflection Harry could see the old man glower.

"We are not talking about my family. They are well cared for by my brothers. We are discussing your, your ..."

Kashili paused, his arm out before him, making a snaking motion.

" ... your lack of direction."

He looked pleased with his accusation.

"Five years? Six?"

The black man stayed silent. The white man gave him a long look.

"That is a long time to have not visited your family. And yet you tell me that I should marry, and put more children on this already crowded continent, and become responsible ..."

Harry paused now, and shook his head in exaggerated consternation.

"I do not understand such thinking."

Kashili hawked savagely again and spat his disgust out into the night.

"We are talking about you, and why you have not yet found yourself a woman. Not the fortunes of my family. You talk like a politician. In circles. Changing the subject."

He lapsed into irritated silence. Harry checked his watch again. Good, nearly there. No hold-ups on the road, thank goodness.

The lions must have met up after we made contact with the first one, and had a quick skirmish. While we were searching for the darted cat. Then we found the second one and darted him, and he must have associated the dart impact with their encounter, and gone back in high dudgeon for a second round. Even though the first chap was down under the drug, he still went for him hammer and tongs. Tomorrow we'll come back to the capture area and see if we can substantiate that from the tracks. He looked at Kashili, who stared stonily ahead. The old boy's getting a little cranky in his old age, he mused. I haven't had a sermon in ages, but he really got himself wound up then. Perhaps he's right about late nights spent running around the valley. Maybe he really does think I'm past redemption. Left on the shelf. Harry smiled wryly to himself. Maybe he's right, in more ways than one. But we caught the lions well. I'd like to see the reaction at head office when the radio message goes through. And we'll catch the rest of them, the two groups of females, as well. In the beam of the lights he could see the big shadowy mahogany that dominated the bush-track on this side of the Chingusa River. We've arrived, he thought. With lions and humans intact. Hallelujah!

CHAPTER TEN

The oysters in their ridged shells were delicious, finely cold and having the taste of the sea. Peta Holt drank the liquid from the cup of the fluted shell and put it amongst the empty shells to the one side of her plate. For some seconds she savoured the taste and then compounded the pleasure by taking a sip of cold smoky white wine. Outside the bar, which was called La Grenouille Verte, autumn rain blew against the windows. She could feel the gusts of damp air whenever the door opened. The place was starting to fill. She nodded to some people she knew. This was her local bar, five minutes from her apartment off La Place Furstenberg, and coming here was always a kind of celebration for her. Peta had been back in Paris from Patagonia for two weeks. She had received a cable from *Life* that they wanted to buy her dolphin pictures, and *National Geographic* were looking at her killer whale sequences. Which is cause enough for minor celebration, she mused, silently toasting her own reflection in the rain patterned window. The bar was warm and friendly, and she used its hospitality with respect, enjoying her own company here as she did nowhere else in Paris. The Rum Batistes before the oysters had created a warm fire in the pit of her stomach. The drinks, her mood, the healthy glow of her skin from the outdoor months on assignment, made an already striking Peta Holt look, and feel, especially ravishing on this autumn evening. She hummed an early Eartha Kitt number as she half watched the flickering television up on a shelf behind the heavy wooden bar.

I could do with a man, she reflected. Perhaps it's the rain and the oysters. A stranger would be fine. Tall and dark, or short and fair. A one night stand. Someone magnificently sensual. She surveyed the patrons in the bar, thoughtfully sipping her wine. She could see no-one that especially attracted her. Sighed. I can feel it already, she thought. I'm getting tired of the city already. Imagine that, tired of Paris. And it would be the same if it were London or Washington or Johannesburg. It's all briefly stimulating to catch up with the arts, and friends and business contacts, but the wild places tug more and more. A sea change, dear? No, not really so. It's always been there. Where to next? The Arctic? The deserts? Africa? Who knows? She sighed again. Well, my girl, you've had your oysters and the rums, and the wine, and you are now mellow. And you are sitting here killing time, like one of the local *poules* waiting for the evening trade to pick up, and that wasn't meant to be a pun. Why don't you go home, the rain will stimulate your creative bent, and catch up on six months of neglected chores. Her gaze swept the bar again.

The only light in the room that served as her lounge and studio came from the small table lamp and the flickering colours of the muted television. Peta had forced her way through two letters, one to Al in Patagonia and one to her father in Hong Kong. She had taken a long leisurely bath and made herself some coffee. Now she lay in an elegant sprawl and idly watched television. She got up and walked across to the hallway mirror and stood surveying herself, unzipping the yellow caftan and holding it away from her naked body. Steady smoky blue eyes flicked over her mane of wind and sun bleached tawny hair. She turned herself one way and then the other, inspecting both profiles, checking the firmness of her breasts and the tightness of her thighs. Then she leaned in close to the mirror to examine her face. Critically she inspected the high cheekbones that accentuated the curved planes of her face and the sweeping curve of her neck. She looked for lines around her eyes, expecting to find some after the months along the Argentinean coastline, and she searched the area around her wide mouth, pouting at herself, and then smiling. There were no lines, but she nevertheless returned to the sofa dissatisfied and restless. Perhaps I have a case of advanced menopausal jitters, she wondered. Could that be the case, at tender twenty seven? No, I think not. You've got the hots and you're particularly restless, is all. A swim in a cold ocean amongst the dolphins would be good therapy. God, but they were beautiful! She stood up again and went into the kitchen for more coffee.

Despite the low volume of the television the roaring filled the flat and made things vibrate. The sound gave her immediate goose bumps and she returned quickly to the lounge, turned up the volume, and then sat cross-legged on the floor in front of it. The paroxysm of roaring continued unabated while the camera panned across a wide blue river scattered with clumps of basking hippo, while herons and other waterbirds waded in the shallows amongst the mottled yellowy logs that were crocodiles. Still with the lion sounds the camera moved away from the river, across a never-ending vista of African plain, studded liberally with huge shade-pooled trees, and fading away into the blue haze of the horizon. On the plain-herds of impala, zebra, waterbuck and eland went about their daily business, and the camera kept moving and there were buffalo and elephant and the roaring faded into a silent soundtrack. Peta wondered where the film had been taken. It didn't look like typical Kenya bush, or anywhere else in East Africa. At first she thought the river was the Nile and that the film would move on to the Murchison Falls, but the character of the big river was different. Botswana, she wondered. Rhodesia? A Landrover appeared on the screen, sand-coloured, bush-battered, the cab with only half doors, open-backed behind the cab. On the far side of the Landrover, away from it, his back to it staring out over the flood plain, a man stood with binoculars to his eyes. He was not tall, but his shoulders were very wide, tapering to a trim boyish waist. The much washed sun-bleached khaki uniform fitted his hard lithe form with a natural elegance. His hands on the binoculars were big, thick fingered and square knuckled. The long drawn out call of a fish eagle broke the silence of the sound track, floating over the stillness. Peta felt a tremor of recognition. There was something about the man and Landrover that tickled her memory. The camera moved around at right angles to the man, following him as he turned and walked back to lean easily against the vehicle. The Landrover had started the feeling. Somehow it looked familiar. Why, or how, she couldn't begin to fathom. It was something deep-rooted and forgotten. The camera zoomed in on the man and he turned to face the lens. Peta saw the man's face and the connection triggered, and she stared.

Harry Kenyon was talking easily to the camera and she thought, My God, he hasn't changed a bit. And it's, what ...? Ten years, twelve? And he looks the same! She moved closer to the television. We could be brother and sister, she thought. Except for his eyes. Those damn cat's eyes, yellowy-brown. Always watching. He was like a cat, a beautiful cat; he moved like one, with that same smooth feline grace, like water on glass.

And mother, bless her soul, did double somersaults over him. He really got to her. I'd never seen her act like that, before or after Kariba. Just as well daddy was being the perfect Foreign Office politico over on the northern bank. Which was half the problem anyway. Harry's words were barely audible behind the French soundtrack explaining the programme, but Peta watched his lips moving and imagined his voice talking. The roaring of the lion began again, swelling behind the soundtrack, and Peta felt her excitement build with it.

The camera followed the trio of Landrovers moving through the African bush, past herds of game, a lowering blood red sun, dust hanging in the air. The next frames focused on the vehicles and their occupants parked on a high barren river bank, an elephant digging in the sand of the dry river bed in the background. Faces drifted in and out of the camera's focus, young, fit, sunburned, some unmindful of the lens's intrusion, others self-conscious. Harry again, sitting relaxed in the Landrover, one bare muscled leg dangling over the door, sockless suede-booted foot swinging indolently. Harry laughing now, soundlessly behind the lion chorus, the face still younger in its mirth, no sign of grey in the tawny thatch of hair. And the face of an old African, much wrinkled, grey-headed, thin and finely featured, came into focus beside that of the laughing white man. Him too, thought the young woman. Kashili, I'm sure, was his right-hand man. He was middle-aged then, so he must be ancient now. On the screen there was new movement. Harry was leaning out of the Landrover, silently giving orders behind the French commentary, relaxed attitude still there but tempered with a new tension. Peta Holt watched the unfolding drama with rapt attention, and for a frustratingly short while she was back in the Zambezi Valley of her youth, and the clean sun-washed bush smell of wild Africa was strong in her nostrils.

*****

Blue. Never ending. Water and sky. Water where, since the earth had hissed and heaved, there had been none but the east flowing river, now spreading, relentlessly, implacably, to merge with the heat haze of the ever fading horizon. So that, to those in the small boats, it was if water and sky stretched away interminably, one becoming the other, with no respite from either. Sun, scorching; water spreading. Islands, once high ground, peaks of hills and mountains thrusting up out of the thick sullen heat of the valley trough, pimpled the surface of this new man-created inland sea. And to the islands the wild animals retreated. But the islands were only blemishes, temporary respite from the rising flood waters, and they were devoured by the waters very quickly, and they disappeared. And, unless the men in the small boats reached them in time to rescue them, the animals drowned.

The humans were gone. Fifty seven thousand wild living tribespeople had long ago been moved off the threatened land. With great reluctance, to be sure, for the Batonka people did not understand this magic word called Progress; but nevertheless they were taken to new lands. The elders fought against this great upheaval. Chief Sampakaruma fought against this madness. In vain. Fought against this wild tale of a great brick wall that would block the mighty Zambezi and create a vast new ocean, bigger than any floods that had been before. It surely was madness, this white man's tale. But the *mukiwas*, the white men, kept coming into the valley, and they became many, there by the neck of the river the tribespeople called *Kariwa*. And the wall did rise, and the serpent-like River god, *Nyaminyami*, who lived in the deep swift-flowing turbulence of *Kariwa*, also fought in vain against this monster that grew daily and throttled the river. *Nyaminyami* brought floods, the like of which had never before been experienced. For two successive years the River God wrought havoc upon the people building the dam, and many people drowned. But in the end the dam won. And the Zambezi River turned on itself, like the grey scorpion trapped in a ring of fire, and reversed its flow to the

Indian Ocean, surging back against its own massive strength, stopped by this new barrier. And for the first time since the earth had formed, the Zambezi flowed upriver.

The tiger ran strong and swift, and the line sang shrilly across the peaceful waters of the tree-shrouded bay. Then the fish leaped. Once, twice, flashing dark striped silver in the sun, jaws snapping as it tried to throw the hook. It splashed, twisting, back into the water, going deep, and ran again. For ten more minutes the tiger fish fought, and then it was exhausted and the woman balanced on the rear of the boat slowly reeled the fish in towards the waiting gaff. In the clear water of the embryonic lake she marvelled at the savage beautiful lines of the tiger fish as it struggled beside the craft.

The white craft, called the *ELIZABETH*, lay serenely at anchor, its reflection clear and sharp beside it on the surface of the backwater. The frenetic world of the dam site was a morning's cruise away. On the afterdeck, the small knot of people admired the newly caught fighting fish, whose colours, not yet dulled by death, still retained their deep striking hue. The Honourable Courteney Hutton smiled at his wife's endeavours. It pleased him to see her relaxed and smiling. The British Foreign Office official and his wife and daughter were guests aboard the yacht. Forward, in the spacious day cabin, the big slope-shouldered man who was their host, sat reading through a batch of radio messages. The Federal Prime Minister escaped to the still spreading Lake Kariba whenever his work load allowed. It provided rare and essential therapy from the task of managing the vast spaces of the three colonial territories. The usual bluff genial expression of the Prime Minister was clouded now as he contemplated the latest news from his northern border. He knew that the tranquillity of this quiet Sunday, in July of 1960, was over. For the last twenty-four hours reports of the Congo revolt had been channelled through to him. Events just across the northern boundary of the Federation of Rhodesia and Nyasaland were steamrollering to new savage excesses hourly. The Katanga Province was in bloody turmoil, with the revolting army on the rampage, deaths mounting horrifically, and the Belgian administration collapsed. At Kasumbalesa border post the barriers had been lifted and the refugees from the Belgian colony were pouring through to the sanctuary of the Rhodesias.

Sir Roy Welensky finished reading the last of the radio communications and spoke quietly to his secretary.

"Michael, ask our guest to join me, would you please. And then have us head back for Kariba at best possible speed."

While he waited for Hutton to join him the ex prize fighter sighed. The Belgian Congo, he was sure, was but a continuing part of the malaise of the whole new pattern of emerging Africa. The riots in Nyasaland, his own back garden, the previous year were another symptom. Banda and Chipembere were becoming synonymous with Nyasaland, despite last year's clamp down. Now, he reflected, we have the Congo chaos, and the epidemic spreads. Lumumba is a bright new star, moving to centre stage, stealing the limelight from Kasavubu; and this latest message from Moise Tshombe in Katanga adds to the brew. He turned and observed the elegantly safari-suited visitor climb down the steps into the cabin and was conscious that his khaki trousers and rumpled sleeve-rolled white shirt fared poorly in the sartorial match. He handed the sheaf of messages to the Foreign Office representative.

"Sorry, Courteney, but we'll obviously have to cut the fishing short. It looks as if this Congo business is way out of hand, already. With every chance that it could spill over into Northern Rhodesia. There's an airforce Dakota on the way to collect me, and you, now. It will be waiting at Kariba for us by the time we get back. The sooner I can get back to Salisbury the better. You will no doubt want to liaise as closely as possible with your Consul in Elizabethville, who so far at least, seems to be weathering the storm."

The Prime Minister paused, feeling the motors of the boat throb into life and the craft get under way.

"I have ordered the mobilisation of our Northern Rhodesian
Territorial Forces, and the First Battalion are leaving today for
the border. Tshombe has asked me for assistance, which I will
discuss with the Cabinet this afternoon."
The Honourable Courteney Hutton glanced speculatively at the
Federal premier.
"Surely you aren't considering committing any of your forces to
an external conflict? I'm not sure London would approve.
Certainly not at this early stage."
Sir Roy smiled without humour.
"At this early stage? Murder, mayhem, refugees by the
hundreds, communications virtually blacked out? I would say
that it's getting late in the day, Courteney. I haven't said that I
will assist Moise Tshombe, but I certainly will consider the
option, along with any others that seem realistic. When we
return to Salisbury, and have improved communications, I'm
sure we can plan whatever is necessary with London."
He nodded at the woman and the girl, visible through the front
windows, sitting braced on the prow of the launch.
"Will you bring Monica and young Peta back to Salisbury? I
can arrange transport for them at that end, if you like."
The Englishman frowned slightly.
"I suppose so. They were looking forward to this break on
Kariba. So was I. We haven't seen much of each other lately,
with the Office keeping me on the hop. Peta was especially
looking forward to the visit to the game rescue base. The girl's
mad about animals. Perhaps, Sir Roy, you would be kind
enough to arrange another trip for them in the future? I would
appreciate it."
The bulldog expression of concern caused by the Congo events
momentarily lifted, returning the open-faced geniality to the
Prime Minister's face.
"Perhaps we can do better than that. The *ELIZABETH* is
berthed at the Game Department base near the dam wall. I
know that the chief game officer is down from Salisbury visiting
the operation. If Archie Fraser is available, and it can be

arranged without too much complication, I'll see if he can help. Operation Noah is just as much history as the dam itself. Your family should see it."

CHAPTER ELEVEN

He had been born in the Zambezi Valley. Had lived for most of his life within the sphere of that river. He had travelled widely in his 52 years, had made great elephant journeys across Africa, and there were periods when he was away from the valley for years at a time. He had been far, far away north, following the water systems of the Great Rift Depression up through the land of the Nyasas to the immense plains beyond in East Africa. He had mingled with the thousands of wildebeest in their yearly migration across the Serengeti. He had bathed his weary travel-worn body in the water of Lake Victoria, travelling westwards into Rwanda and the Belgian Congo. Amidst the brooding forest fringes he had seen the greatest of the man-apes, and he had swung back down the continent, picking up the embryonic Congo River, eventually, following it through and on into the Rhodesias. Southwards still, to the inhospitable desert wastes of German West Africa, not liking the region at all, detouring with the smell of good water getting stronger as his trunk tested the winds. Into the vast inland delta of the Okavango, where he stayed for a while in its furthest reaches, before making his leisurely way down the edge of the Kalahari wasteland. In the river-bed pools of the Crocodile and Shashi rivers he replayed childhood games and cooled himself from the hot African sun. Eastwards then, into Portuguese territory, tasting the warm salt waters of the Indian Ocean, playing in the sea alongside dugongs and turtles. Returning inland, away from the coastal belt, he had stayed on the Save River, following unknowingly the paths of the slave traders. To its confluence with the Lundi. And for a few seasons he had stayed in this region that was dominated by the great red sandstone cliffs on the southern bank of the Lundi River

This hot low-lying region reminded him sometimes of the valley where he was born. The great brooding silence, the heat, the wide river vista, the endless assaults of the tsetse fly. He browsed amongst the ironwood forests atop the jagged Nyamatongwe Plateau, and, unknowing of its history, rubbed itching flanks against the rubbled ruins of the Lost White City of the Lundi. In the timeless green-gladed expanse of the wide Tamboharta Pan in the crook of the confluence of the two big rivers he had met with other bulls, a midnight great clan gathering of three hundred animals, and here he had respectfully greeted *Dhlulamithi*, the king, whose tusks ploughed the earth, and who lived despite the attentions of the man animals that pursued him.

In time he moved on. Away from the cliffs whose steep eroded red-earthed sides were like hills of blood in the dying rays of the afternoon sun. He kept to the river systems, the Lundi, Nuanetsi, Umzingwani, Gwayi and Lukosi; westwards, trekking back across the fringe of the Kalahari, traversing the Caprivi Strip and upwards into Angola. Then came the time when some deep-rooted yearning urged a return to the place of his birth. And he followed the Zambezi home. From the birth place of that river, where it is but a small clear pool bubbling up out of the earth, there by Kalene Hill, in the north-western corner of Northern Rhodesia, close alongside Angola, he followed the young Zambezi on its own odyssey. Back through Angola into Barotseland, where, during the rains, the Kalahari sand plains are covered by a vast lake which feeds and nourishes the lower and middle reaches of the Zambezi. South, touching Bechuanaland, and then eastwards across the Caprivi towards the wide sandy expanses above the spray-soaring, tumbling Victoria Falls. His journey took him along the ridges of the tortuous gorge systems that flanked the river after the Falls, until the gentler shores were reached, and he followed the

Zambezi's course through a region which one day would be drowned when the largest man-made lake on earth was constructed. This part of the valley, close to where the Sanyati River joined the Zambezi, was well known territory, and from Kariba Gorge downriver to his birth place near the Mupata Gorge it was only a scant hundred miles or so, which was nothing compared to the many, many miles he had journeyed. He travelled this region in good spirits.

He had been born close to the river, near to the entrance of this tumbling barren gorge which the local humans called Mupata. Under a wide spreading fig tree that grew out of a red-earthed anthill, his mother had stood splay-legged, alone in her privacy, away from the herd bathing in the river, and given birth to this second of her offspring that she had carried within her for almost two years. An elephant birth is an event of consequence, and, after his mother had cleaned him and examined him, gentle trunk probing and feeling over his new-born bulk, she had led him, stumble-walking back to her herd. The vultures that had been attracted, first by her seeming helplessness, and then by the debris of the afterbirth, dropped down from the surrounding trees where they had kept patient vigil, and squabbled as they cleared up after the birth. There were several bulls, breaking their solitary wanderings, passing time with the family unit. During the time of the cow's absence they had fidgeted and fussed like so many expectant fathers, whilst the rest of the herd, cows, calves, youngsters and pre-puberty bulls, had dozed the middle day heat away. They were aware of the cow's return to the herd, before she emerged from the surrounding bush, tiny calf tottering drunkenly, trunk loose floppy dangling, enmeshing between its front legs, along behind her. The visiting bulls met her first, coming to her, slowly, respectfully, trunks outstretched, congratulatory, entwining gently in turn with hers. When this greeting was over, the mother reached back with her trunk behind her swaying bulk, and delicately she led her new offspring forward. The bulls, tall above the baby, played their trunks over the calf, not actually touching the small animal, smelling, evaluating, acquainting themselves with the new-born elephant. There was much whooshing and loud sighing and soft throat rumbling as they went about this christening, and then the bulls led mother and calf back to the main herd, where the cows greeted her fondly and inspected their new member.

For the first year the young elephant never strayed more than a trunk's length from his mother, and the herd was always to be found near the Zambezi.

With the rainy season the herd could move further afield, making use of the scattered surface water and the seasonal rivers and seeps. There were other young elephants of varying ages amongst the family unit and their wandering was very much dictated by the available water. Because an elephant has much to learn, it has the longest childhood of any animal, except man. The young calf will suckle for up to six years, and, when adult, it will have a food intake of a good 300 pounds a day. In its lifetime it can traverse a range of many hundreds of miles, man animals permitting. There is much a growing elephant can absorb from its clan : much more than if it were to branch out in solitary learning. Where to find water, when different food plants come into season, where there is always food and water, even in the driest times, the ancient elephant trails that linked the fast disappearing wild haunts across the continent, and, of more and more consequence, how to avoid their only predator, man. An elephant childhood will last for fifteen or sixteen years. If the animal is a female, she will stay with the herd, and become, in time, a mother herself. Unless she is barren, in which case she will still play an important role in the life of the herd, playing aunt, nursemaid, defender or perhaps even devoting her full time and energies to leading the herd. Young bulls, reaching this milestone in elephant life, are destined by nature to leave the family unit and fend for themselves. If he shows reluctance, the adult cows will tusk him from their midst. In this way there are less mouths to feed during the dry months, and, with the young bull now sexually mature, it prevents inbreeding. The following years will be the independent young bull's testing period, for, whilst he may have reached sexual maturity, his size, experience, and strength will have to grow before he can joust successfully with the other socially mature bulls in competition for the cows in heat. Bulls do not form permanent units, but rather tend towards loose assemblies and liaisons with other individual bulls, with no long term social commitments. They are the pioneers, searching out new territories and preceding the family units into new areas, where there are untapped food supplies. Bull elephants are born to wander. And once, sometimes twice a year, they are prone to go a little crazy. When the testosterone level is high, and they are in a state of musth. And their tusks are growing always, from the time they are born. Until they die.

He had not left the valley for a long time now, as he looked down the hill to old age. The man predators were everywhere, and that meant destruction. His last long journey had been back to the ocean, and even then he stayed on the Zambezi, following it through to the deltaic channels feeding into the Indian Ocean. He had collected one of his bullet wounds on this journey. The valley itself had changed. Whilst still in his early adulthood he had seen the man animals come more frequently to the valley. And there, below the gorges of Kariba, he had seen the steel latticework of the Chirundu bridge begin to crawl over the river, spanning the Zambezi fully two years later. It was as big as the hard steel bridge that crossed the river amidst the spray of the Victoria Falls, which had been there before his entry into the world. And there near this new bridge, great noisy, evil-smelling monsters ripped the valley bush apart so that the earth lay naked and exposed. And a new growth of vegetation evolved here, which was deliciously, addictively sweet when it matured. But the man animals were very protective of their sugar cane, and many elephants were killed in the cane fields. This was human progress, and with it came more of the man animals, and roads and tracks spider-webbed further and further into the hitherto unsullied valley fastness. He would come to carry three bullets in his body from them. But there were still places, secret places, in the valley, where elephants could go and find peace, and he learned very well which haunts were the safest. Where man hesitated to go. There were hidden pockets in the escarpment, to which the valley elephants migrated, and they tarried there, unmolested, until the water gave out before the start of the rains, and they were forced to return to the great river.

And then there came a wide sheet of river, ever spreading; hourly, daily, by the week. Yearly. And the rich verdant vegetation at the edge of the river was gone, and it became impossible to swim to the far side of the water, to old haunts. Some elephants tried, and they drowned, lost amidst the maze of drowning vegetation, the land smell in their nostrils, confused by this new phenomenon, panic setting in as they swam in circles, getting nowhere. And more humans came to the valley, man animals smelling strangely of far haunts, quite unlike the familiar sweetly acrid smoky scent of the humans who had lived always in parts of the valley. And now, above the Kariba Gorge, there was a great concentration of humans, and, to the bull, who was in his prime, it was evident that the man animals were responsible for this new desert of water.

So he moved to quieter territory. Downriver from this new mayhem, past the new shiny steel bridge, and the sugar estates. To the endless serenity of the vast floodplains between the Nyakasanga River and the Mupata Gorge. This journey was not without peril, for it was the time of the tsetse slaughter, which, although the elephant could not know this, was a continuing phase of the man animals' progress. For as long as there had been elephants in the wilderness, there had been the tsetse fly. And, for a long time, this white hot probing biter of an insect had been the saviour of the remote haunts and the animals that lived there. For humans did not relish the attentions of the tsetse fly. It brought illness, and occasional death, to them, and sure death to their livestock, which did not have the natural immunity of wild game. Yet progress reversed this protection factor, as the ever increasing humans hungered for more land; and embarked on a great slaughter, the like of which had been unseen in this part of the world. As host animals the wild game was charged and decreed guilty, and quickly sentenced. And they died. In their hundreds of thousands, they died. And the guns of the Tsetse Department echoed across the Rhodesias.

Yet his move back to the quieter reaches of the valley, away from the turmoil of the new inland lake, was uneventful. He journeyed carefully, under the mantle of darkness, and up in the high hot barrenness of the escarpment, away from the lower country that attracted the man animals. So, for a very long time now, he had lived in the region of the valley that was known as the Zambezi Wilderness and Safari Area, of which Nemana National Park was a part. His sixth, last, set of molars were still new. Once they were finished, worn down, he would die slowly of starvation. He was happy in his ageing isolation. His lifetime of accumulated wisdom was vast, and the young bulls still came to him for counsel, and there were still the regular old men's gatherings, with the throat-rumbling nostalgia of far away haunts, in quieter safer days. He had not mounted a cow elephant for a while now; that seething urgency had dissipated with his advancing years. He remembered the times when the heat in his loins had matched and blended with the needs of the cows in heat, and the tentative girlish touchings of their trunks had been a preamble to their great couplings. It was an awfully long time since he had deviated from the straight and narrow, and laid waste the occasional native village, or gone on a marula binge. But the memories were pleasant, and there were no regrets. Now, whilst his teeth lasted, he could feed well, and the Zambezi was always there, and the man animals could still be avoided. Even if the weather patterns had gone a little crazy, and the droughts seemed longer, and came with more frequency, and the rainy seasons were erratic, not flooding the valley plains as they used to, bringing tons of new alluvial soil to give the animals fresh strong food. There had been no floods since the wall blocked the gorge.

To the man animals that knew him he was called Kabakwe. In the Shangaan language of Kashili, this meant The Big One. Kashili had christened him thus, many years ago, before he and Harry Kenyon had joined the Game Department. In the footloose days of their own bush travels. When they too had wandered freely across the Zambezi Valley fastness. Kabakwe's tusks, perfectly matched, weighed a little over 120 pounds a side, and he was the king of their 'Big Four' tuskers in the Nemana National Park. The warden and the old tracker followed the bull's fortunes closely, for he was a symbol to them, like the tusk in the office, of the past and the present. And, for Harry Kenyon, the big tusker was an uneasy reminder of how tenuous the future could be, for all of them.

*****

"This is Nemana Base. Kenyon on set. Go ahead with your message : Over"
Harry leaned a hip against the desk and wondered why head office wanted him. It was seldom good news, with messages that came out of routine schedules. Garnet Clayton's voice echoed nasally from the set.
"Hello, Harry. How's the lion capture going?"
"Well, Garnet. The two males are settling down in their new areas. We've kept a close eye on them. As have the female and the grown daughter. I'm hoping we'll get the remaining four suspect females before the week's out. The film unit left today. I reckon they've got some good footage, Garnet. How about a little extra warning with the next visitors you send me? I presume it was your doing?"
Garnet Clayton's voice was studiously neutral.

"Affirmative on that. With the director's and research's initiative. It was thought that the French team would serve as an ideal monitor of the capture. Non partisan, so to speak."

Harry grunted sourly. He paused for a significant count of five seconds. Then.

"What can I do for you today, Garnet?"

He could hear the wryness in the chief warden's voice when he replied.

"If I said this was purely a courtesy call from head office to see how things are down at Nemana, would you believe me? Okay, probably not. So, here we go. Two things, Harry. First, the wildlife seminar I mentioned to you a few days ago. A slight change of plan there. Hope you can help out. We've had a couple of let downs, so we've had to restructure the seminar a little. We would appreciate it very much if you could now attend as a guest speaker, instead of straightforward Parks management. We'd like you to deliver a paper. Nothing too long and involved. Perhaps an hour or so. Any comment, Harry?"

Harry grunted. Unimpressed.

"What exactly would you like me to spout on about? This kind of thing really isn't my forte, Garnet. I don't mind local wildlife talks, or in-department sessions, but not this high pressure stuff. And it's pretty short notice. You must have access to better suited people, surely?"

"No, I don't. What I had in mind, was for you to give a chat on game capture. You're one of the leading lights in the field. A lecture on the evolution of capture in this country to date would be of great interest. You could start with the trials and errors of Operation Noah, bringing us through the years to your present lion capture work. Your rhino capture experience, on its own, makes a subject. On Noah, and the following Sengwa rhino captures, with Rupert; and the later operations of the Umfurudzi/Gona re Zhou translocations with Paul Cantrell and Roy Thorson, you must have caught nearly a hundred rhino. With only one small scratch to show for your efforts! I think that this subject, presented by you, alongside a similar talk by Roscoe Daniels on the elephant collaring and telemetry, would make an ideal afternoon's presentation. There's no one better qualified than you two chaps, in the capture field, to present the whole story."

Harry scowled at the radio. Spare me, he intoned. Save the Dale Carnegie stuff for the head office sessions. He searched his mind for a plausible excuse to give the chief warden. He thought that, face to face, he could extricate himself from the order that was beautifully sheathed as a request. But not over the Parks network. The conference was two weeks away, at the beginning of September. Bloody hell, he must have some task scheduled for that period. It was time he carried out another patrol in the eastern sector of the Park. He hadn't checked on Kabakwe since the cull. And it was time the other tuskers were visited, as well. He was about to raise this point when Garnet's voice floated disembodied again from the radio set.

"Incidentally, Harry. I forgot to mention that we'll be using this occasion to celebrate Rupert's retirement from the department. We've invited him up to the lake and there'll be a presentation and drinks at the end of the seminar. I know you wouldn't miss that. And Rupert would be awfully pleased to see you again."

Harry glared at the radio. You son of a bitch, he thought. You saved that for the last on purpose. Just when I thought I had you beat. Old Rupert! Retiring at last, just to die of boredom. But he's right. I wouldn't miss Rupert's end of service party. He lifted the handset.

"Okay, Garnet. You've got yourself a speaker. I'll get cracking and put something together. Do you want pictures?"

"They'd be useful. I know you've got some good 35 mill stuff, and we have some fair black and white coverage in the library. If you could select some suitable slides and get them up to Karoi in the very near future, I'll have them collected from there and organise some decent prints."

"Sure. Will do. Where is Roscoe working at the moment?"

"He's at Chirisa, Harry. Working at the new research complex. It's early days yet, but I've a feeling he'll pull the rabbit out of the hat with these new radio transmitters."

Harry nodded thoughtfully. That's good, he reflected. Excellent news. Because I think it's time we kept closer tabs on our 'Big Four'.

"Roger that, Garnet. There's nothing more from my side."

"Just one more thing, Harry. I have a letter here from some photographer, requesting permission to visit the more remote parts of the valley, especially Nemana, to obtain good feature wildlife stuff. He seems a good one. Articles in *Life*, *National Geographic*, the *East African Journal*. He'll be here in a week or so, and we can use some good prestigious coverage, so I thought about inviting him to Kariba for the conference. Depending on how he comes across we could plan things from there. If he fits the bill perhaps he could return with you to Nemana?"

"Well, there's no harm in checking him out. If he looks sympathetic to our particular cause, by all means, let's show him our animals. Anything to spread the gospel. Name?"

"Peter Holt. When he gets here I'll have him in to my office for a preliminary chat, see if he fits the bill, and, if so, I'll arrange the conference side of things."

"Fine, Garnet. Where will the conference be held? And what date, please?"

"We've decided to have it across the lake, at the safari lodge. The hotel is still new and could do with a boost. We've booked the whole place for the two days, everyone arriving the evening before the seminar starts. That will be fifty people, spending three nights and two working days. The dates are Thursday and Friday, the 5th and 6th of September, with you preferably being there on the evening of the 4th."

Harry waited until a fish eagle, perched in the acacia grove shading the office block, stopped called.

"Roger that. Thanks, Garnet. See you at Kariba. I presume you'll let me know if any new plans develop?"

"Sure, Harry. Out to you."

CHAPTER TWELVE

❝...thus, ladies and gentlemen, has game capture, particularly
chemical capture, evolved over the last twelve years. Since
our first frenetic drug-darting attempts during the early days
of Operation Noah. And it would be remiss of me to not pay
tribute to a couple of gentlemen who are amongst you at this
seminar, who in fact should be up here now, as they taught me
all they knew about game capture ...”

Harry threw a half salute at the back of the hall, where Rupert
Fothergill and Doc Canby were sitting unobtrusively. He
chuckled as both men shifted uncomfortably in their seats,
uneasy under the scrutiny of the turning heads. Harry went on
swiftly, removing the pressure, noting with inward amusement
the look of relief on both the game veterans’ faces.

“Mechanical capture, using funnel traps, plastic sheet bomas,
and drop nets, with shepherds in the form of helicopters,
ideally, or vehicles, or horses, or human beaters, failing all else,
driving the game into the trap areas, has its fundamental
problems. Although helicopters are the most efficient means
for capturing large numbers of animals in the shortest space of
time, their cost makes their use virtually prohibitive, to us at
least. As we all know, our department seems forever doomed
to sucking the hind tit, or rather, teat, when budgets are
allocated ...”

Harry paused for a moment as a low groundswell of rueful
laughter rippled through his audience. He could feel, without
having to look, the director’s disapproval at his irreverency.
And sod you, he thought. If the cap fits, wear it. His glance
once again drifted back to the young woman in the crisp white
linen suit, sitting at the end of a middle row closest to the centre
aisle. Smoky blue eyes looked steadily back at him. Full lips
parted easily in the ghost of a smile. Harry felt his breathing go
haywire, and for an instant of time he was back in a sunny
classroom, and the prettiest girl in the school was smiling
demurely at him from the other side of the room. Like the

colour of the valley horizon when the seasons first bushfires start, he thought. At least she finds it amusing, unlike friend Drummond.

Who is she? Sitting there on her own as if she owns the place. She's bloody marvellous. And I don't think I've been in the bush that long. He was aware that he was still looking at her, and that the audience was over its amusement and waiting for him to continue. There was something about her that nudged at his memory. Since he had first seen her amongst the throng that morning there had been a niggle in his mind that wouldn't go away. Now, as he forced his attention back to the lecture, she crossed long tanned legs beneath the severe cut of her white skirt. Further laying waste his hold on his concentration. Oh dear, he thought. He flicked a swift glance down to Garnet Clayton, sitting beside the director in the VIP seats of the front row, and noted a sardonic smile playing across his features. Okay, he remonstrated with himself, get a grip on yourself, Kenyon. *A grip? On who? Oh no, cut that out.*

His voice was over serious when he resumed his lecture, as he struggled to recall his last words.

"As a matter of fact, ladies and gentlemen, as I stand up here at this moment and contemplate ... ah, the, er, cost of such a seminar, I cannot help wondering how much aviation fuel we could have purchased; or how many hours flying time, we could have paid for."

Harry smiled disarmingly.

"However ..."

An eyebrow arched magnificently over an enquiring blue eye. Wide, wide eyebrows, he thought. Like her mouth ...

" ... department economics are not part of my ecological niche. In that field there are far better qualified people present."

He bowed slightly to the VIP seats of the front row, noting the fixed polite expressions of the director and their principal guest, the Minister of Environmental Affairs. Garnet Clayton looked resigned. Harry moved on into safer territory.

"I believe that the third method of capture, the type that we are all driven to use on occasion, that being physical capture, will eventually phase out. It is dangerous to animals and humans alike and has limited applications. For the capture of a few animals, such as impala, at night with spotlights, and the young of certain other species, it may continue to be a useful capture method. But I believe that drugs, chemical capture, will continue to develop and specialise to the extent that catching animals by hand, or lasso, or throw nets, will become outdated." Harry paused briefly, and kept his eyes determinedly away from the girl.

"I should say, at this point, that despite our self congratulatory excitement at drug capture development, this is not a new spectrum. Drugs have been used for many decades to immobilise game. The Bushmen have used a coagulant made from the *Acokanthera* plant on their arrows to kill wild animals.

"Since time immemorial they have done this. As do the Wata in Kenya. Poison extracts from other wild plants, such as the desert rose, *Adenium obesium*, and from one of the euphorbia family, *Euphorbia tennuispinosa*, are added to their brews. Most of these wild plant poisons affect the cardiac system of their prey animals. From elephants to bushbuck. A lethal dose for a human would be in the region of only 0,0002 of a gram. The Orinoco Indians in South America use curare for the same purpose. So we, in our brave new world of advanced knowledge, are only carrying out variations of a theme. It is an expensive field. Animal immobilisation is not a cheap operation. M99, which we are using widely now, after its introduction in the country in 1964, costs four dollars a milligram. That is 4 million dollars a kilogram. The drug is yet another derivative from morphine, and thus is very potent. As an example, 3 milligrams of M99 will put a rhino to sleep for an hour."

Slim tanned legs uncrossing, calf muscles finely taut. A flash of shadowed thigh above the knee, deliciously disturbingly brief. One elegant hand, long nails delicately pink, no rings, tugging softly unconcerned at the hem. Harry turned away and indicated the series of photographs on display behind him, using the moment to glance surreptitiously at his watch. Good, he thought. A little over the allotted time, with no scratching for words. Bloody good show.

"Behind me there is a brief photographic history of game capture operations in Rhodesia. Early Wankie days, Operation Noah, Operation Rhino, and so on, until our recent lion capture in Nemana, which I've already mentioned. Please feel free to come up and have a look, and I'll answer any questions you might have."

Harry flashed a grin at the audience.

"Thank you, ladies and gentlemen, for your time."

He left the rostrum to pick up his beret and jacket from the seat, acknowledging the clapping with a polite wave.

Peta Holt watched him talking to an older man in national parks uniform, wondering how long it would take for his glance to return to her. He's very nice, she mused. Not beautiful, like Al. Just nice. And he really hasn't changed that much, even to a grown woman of twenty-seven. Who was a teenager the last time she saw him. No grey in his hair, even though he must be in his forties. And he still looks hard and fit, flat gut. And those hands! They still look like coal shovels. An involuntary shiver rippled through her as a long past scene videoed through her mind, and she could feel those hands, and the bare blade of the knife, on her naked body. *Whoa, girl!* She silently reprimanded herself. You're a grown up lady now, not a moonstruck kid. Get hold of yourself. Ah, yes indeed. Perhaps that would do the trick. That, or take a long cold shower. You've no oysters to blame this on, Peta my girl. Just behave yourself and listen to all these animal men, oh God, it gets worse, and think about the fantastic game shots you're hoping to get.

People were up and moving around now, stretching cramped limbs, looking at the photograph display behind the small wooden rostrum. She could see Harry still immersed in deep conversation with various men. She got up and went to look at the display, her eyes scanning the varied cross-section of animals in different stages of capture. He's good, she thought. Damn good. There's a good feeling in all of those pictures. There were warthog, various antelope, from small duikers to masked sweeping horned sable, hyenas, baboons, rhinos, plenty of rhinos, elephants, and, of course, the lions. She went back along the line of photographs, engrossed in their story.

Harry was talking to Roscoe Daniels, Roy Thorson and the Cantrell brothers. He had been on capture operations with all of them, at one time or other. Elephant with Roscoe, rhino with Roy, and the final months of Operation Noah with the Cantrells. Plus the Umfurudzi rhino captures last year. They had all shared many camp fires together. Harry was pleased his part of the show was over. Roscoe, big, shambling, genial, blonde shaggy-bearded, would be up there next, giving his talk on elephants. That's good, thought Harry. Now I can relax a little, and ride the rest of the conference through. This afternoon and tomorrow. Then back across the lake with Roy, and back to Nemana. Presuming of course, that I can find Kashili amongst the women and the beer halls. Lucky bastard. I wonder where this photography chap is? I'd better check with Garnet. I suppose I should have got here last night, along with everyone else. And been properly introduced to the mob. But two nights here are plenty.

Harry had driven up out of the valley, across the escarpment near Makuti, and back down into the valley to Kariba. He had spent the night at Roy Thorson's house, after dropping Kashili in the township with stern instructions not to make too much of a dent in civilisation. Ron's house, on the piece of department land called The Point, had been their base camp during Noah, a motley collection of tin quonset huts and scrounged tents perched precariously on bare stony ground far above the rising water line. Now Roy was warden in charge of the Kariba basin, and The Point was very different, darkly tree shaded, thickly lawned, the house nestling almost unseen amongst the greenery. They had sat up late on the open concrete verandah, staring out into the darkness of the lake, drinking gin and beer and reliving old adventures. In the calm of the early lake morning they had flown across the safari lodge in Roy's Super Cub.

Harry's glance swept the room, searching for a person who might be the photographer. His eyes came to rest on the girl studying his photographs, and he grunted. If you'd got here last night you would have met the lady, he thought. He nodded at the slim white-suited figure.

"Who's the beauty over there?"

Roscoe shrugged. The Cantrells shook their heads, Paul answering.

"Good question. She only arrived this morning, just before you boys. Came over on the float plane. Quite something, Harry?"

"Yeah, you bum ..."

Roscoe chuckled evilly.

"I saw you choking on your words up there just now. Trying to look up her dress. Time you got out of the valley, boyo, and found yourself some permanent female company."

Harry smiled.

"Funny you should say that. Old Kashili's been nagging me to do the same thing. He reckons I've been left on the shelf! You're all like a bunch of old women. Excuse me, chaps. I think I should explain some of my pictures to the lady."

As he approached her the perfume reached him. Soft, subtle, a faint essence floating on the lake breeze, mingling with the clean soap smell. She was taller than he had first judged, taller than him. He found himself pausing momentarily, looking at the silky sheen of her tawny hair. To his surprise, his breathing had gone shallow, shot to hell, in fact, and he could feel his heart thumping against his rib cage. Just like when you were going into the thick stuff after a wounded cat, he thought.

"That's a rhino ..."

She turned slowly and looked at him. Steady appraising stare, blue eyes ... smoky blue eyes, like the haze over the valley after the first fires of the year, he thought again. A smile forming. White teeth. Wide full lips. The perfume stronger.

"Really?"

Harry grinned, aware of his own stare, nodding. Getting his breathing sorted out.

"Black. Male. About eight years old."

He waved out through the windows of the hall towards the blue expanse of the lake.

"We caught him very near here. On that island you can see from the balcony of the lodge. Starvation Island we call it. He was one of the last rhinos we caught on Noah, right at the end, in mid '63."

She raised an eyebrow. Harry thought she used the mannerism with great effect. They sweep beautifully, he reflected, curving magnificently across the blue. And over the long curling lashes. Which, if my past experiences mean anything, indicates the colour of her pubic hair. Tawny, also. The sudden detour of his thoughts startled him. Christ! You're acting like a damned juvenile. Eyes ... pubic hair. *Pull yourself together, Kenyon.* He kept his voice normal with a struggle.

"Enjoying the conference so far?"

Smile widening, spontaneously. Eyes lighting.

"Oh, yes. I'm really glad I was able to make it."

"How did you actually come ..."

Harry's sentence was interrupted by the insistent banging of a stone on the table beside the rostrum.

Alistair Drummond had taken charge of the proceedings.

"Thank you, ladies and gentlemen. Thank you. Please take your seats, so that I can introduce our next speaker to you."

Harry turned to finish his question, but he stopped when he saw the girl studying the director. He couldn't interpret the expression, but there was a restrained intensity that surprised him.

"You know him? The director?"

She glanced quizzically at Harry, her gaze searching his face.

"Yes. We have met."

Harry cocked his head thoughtfully. Her gaze had switched back to Drummond. The rows of seats were filling quickly. She smiled fleetingly at Harry.

"I'd better get back to my seat. It was nice meeting you. Thank you for telling me about the rhino."

He watched her make her way back down the aisle to her chair. Long legged, relaxed, hip swinging walk. He looked down at Garnet Clayton, who was studying him. The chief warden grinned. Roscoe Daniels stood patiently by the rostrum, waiting to be introduced by the director. Harry realised he was holding things up and moved on down past the elephant collaring expert to his own seat. Roscoe nudged him in the ribs and whispered hoarsely in his ear.

"Like I said, boyo, you've been down in that valley too long."

CHAPTER THIRTEEN

"Full moon, in a couple of nights."

Rupert nodded silently, leaning on the balcony rail beside him. His pipe was cradled, unlit, in his cupped hands. The sun had gone down, behind the landmass across the lake. On the fading silver sheet of the lake's surface the island stood in dark sober silhouette, thick bush crowding the serrated shoreline. Black ink on a silver scroll. Way down below the lodge indistinct forms moved through the rapidly deepening dusk.

"Elephant. And buff," said Harry.

Rupert nodded again, with a soft grunt of acknowledgement. He continued to stare silently out across the darkening lake. Harry took a swig from his glass, savouring the first drink of the day, feeling the gin dominated mix take hold in his gut. Behind them, across the long balcony that perched out over the steep cliff face, in the dim lights of the bar, Roscoe, Roy, the Cantrells and several other Parks men talked and laughed. Harry could hear Denis Cantle's high schoolboy voice amidst the early evening revelry. Rupert grunted again, staring at the island now.

It's funny, thought Harry, how much one grunts in the bush. It becomes a habit, a major form of communication. The longer you live in the bush, the more you grunt. You grunt to attract attention, or to show displeasure; in disbelief or appreciation; in bass or falsetto; scepticism or enthusiasm; agreement or no. A grunt for every occasion. A grunt for all seasons. Old Rupert grunted with memory just now. Looking out at Starvation. And I reckon I know exactly what's going through his mind. Because I've been thinking the same thing.

"Whoever would have thought, Harry, that one day we'd be sitting up here on our backsides like damn movie stars, in a fancy new hotel, drinking expensive booze, looking at that bloody island."

Rupert shook his head in the darkness. The tinkling of ice in drinks echoed from the bar. His gruff slow voice was reflective. "It's just as well that island came at the end of Noah. I think I might have given up in despair if we'd had the problems Starvation had given us right at the start of the rescue. You'd never think that island stank of death, once upon a time."

Harry grunted now. It was true. They had given the island its name, way back when the end of the game rescue was in sight. When the lake waters had backed up and spread to almost their final capacity. After four and a half years. It was as if the island was a final supreme test of endurance. The rains had come late. Too late for some. And the game trapped on the island, the buffalo, kudu, sable, warthog and zebra had slowly starved to death. They had eaten all the greenery they could reach. The warthogs had rooted out all the tubers and underground food that was available. The elephants had, eventually, been driven off, or shot, when they continually disrupted the rescue. The lions, too, were eventually driven off this last island. Which left the rhinos, eleven of them, and the rest of the game herds to be saved. Before they starved to death. For some of them the rescue teams were too late. The warthogs retreated to their burrows and died. The buffalo, the older animals first, dropped behind the ever patrolling searching herds for new food, and died. A pall of dust hung permanently chokingly over the dry barren hoof-eroded dust bowl. And the island reeked of death. The rains did come, but they were very late. Too late to rejuvenate the bush so that the animals could feed again. Some animals were just too weak to save. The stress killed them. Drugs were fast running out, with no replacements coming from Salisbury. So, in the end, amidst the swirling dust, under a merciless sun, and with the ever present danger of the irritated hungry rhinos appearing in full charge, they resorted to running the animals down and catching them with their bare hands. When they were finally through with Starvation Island they left no animals on it. No live ones, anyway. It was strange, thought Harry now, finishing his drink, that no vultures ever came. It was almost as if the death was too much, even for them.

Rupert glanced sideways at him.

"For a crocodile poacher, and an ivory poacher, you shaped up all right. You were the only one to see the operation right through with me ..."

He chuckled softly.

"And now you're the big bwana in game capture here. Well done."

Harry grinned in the darkness, and reached out and gripped the old warden's shoulder.

"Thanks. Although you had your doubts, didn't you? At the start. When I was a newcomer to the other side of the coin, still carrying the blood of poached animals. You were very reticent about my joining the team, and you didn't make life particularly easy for me. Even though I was working unpaid, living off my ivory and skin profits earned before I went to Malaya."

Rupert chuckled again.

"You had a reputation, Harry. The Crocodile King. Apart from the ivory. A lot of people chased you around the valley, including me. It was hard to believe that you'd had a change of heart. I figured you must have an ulterior motive in wanting to give us a hand."

Harry grunted.

"I shot a lot of crocs, sure. All along the river. There were a hell of a lot of them, Rupert, before we started building dams and invading the valley. Elephants? You know, I was telling Garnet a few weeks ago, that I've shot more elephants, many many more, on department business, on culls and problem animal control, than I ever did ivory hunting. I shot 82 jumbo, across the country, and in neighbouring countries. All old bulls with big teeth. I was never indiscriminate. Never touched small tuskers, and walked miles around cows carrying ivory. Guilty? Yeah, I suppose I am. I regret it, now. The poor bloody jumbo are taking a pounding. But I hadn't seen the writing on the wall when I was seventeen. And even these days, it's not the actual hunting of the elephant that's going to be their downfall. It's their range restriction. Us bloody humans are breeding so fast we're eating ourselves out of house and home. And the poor bloody elephants."

Rupert nodded soberly in the darkness.

"Yah, Harry. Sometimes when I think of my retirement I get very depressed. You retire, and then what? You're out of the herd. Living on your memories, which are good ones. I'm lucky in that respect. What else? Do some prospecting. Fishing. Do a little part time work for the department, maybe. But still, you're winding down. You've outlived your usefulness. It's not a good feeling. Then I see how the department is changing. And I'm glad I'm getting out of it."

From out near the lodge's rubbish dump a hyena chittered, and it felt to Harry at that moment as if the scavenger were adding it's own sinister epitaph to the thoughts of the two men. When he spoke he made his voice light.

"Well, old friend, whenever you get too bored you know you've always got Nemana as a refuge. To get the cobwebs and the city smell out of your nostrils."

Rupert looked at him then, scrutinising the younger man's face in the night.

"You think they'll let you stay in the valley forever? Head office? Drummond? Even Garnet Clayton?"

Harry shrugged, without answering. Rupert went on.

"It can't happen, Harry. They will move you sooner or later. It's the system, and you can't buck it. Transfer, promotion, whatever; it has to happen. Even without Drummond in charge, it's the system. And if you're on the wrong side of Alastair Drummond, he and the system will beat you. And you sure as hell are on the wrong side of him. He's never forgiven you for that hiding you gave him, over that woman who was visiting the rescue operation."

It was Harry's turn to stare at his companion. When he answered the old roving warden, his voice was hushed.

"You know about that? How? I've never, ever, said a word to anyone about that night. And I doubt he did."

Rupert smiled and shook his head.

"I was away. Across the valley, remember? Sorting out that man-eater at Chirundu. That's why you got to play nursemaid to the woman and her daughter. Langton, my tracker, didn't come with me because he had malaria. I left him behind on whichever island it was that we were using as a base. He saw you haul Drummond out of the woman's tent ..."

Rupert paused and put the still unlit pipe away in his shirt pocket. His voice was dry when he continued.

"He also saw you go in the woman's tent the next night. And noted that there was not nearly as much opposition raised at your visitation."

He cocked an eyebrow.

"Some double standards there, don't you think, Harry."

Harry stared out over the lake, noting the faint wash of light on the horizon that was Kariba village. When he finally spoke his voice was mild.

"Perhaps you're right. It only happened once, and, looking back now, I'd say it was pretty much inevitable. From the

minute she stepped on that island there was something between us. It was strange, but it was there. Like an electric current. She was very beautiful. And lonely, and bored with her politician husband. Drummond acted like an idiot. He'd been sniffing after her from the start. It was a joke at first. Then it became embarrassing. Ask any of the lads who were there then ... Tommy, Graham, Boyd ... He became the laughing stock. Then, when he forced his way into her tent one night, late, after topping up on Dutch courage, he really blew it. She was trying to get rid of him without creating an incident, but he wasn't having it. I was making a last camp inspection and heard the trouble. And dragged him out of her tent. He went berserk, tried to take my head off with a rock. So, I had to deck him."
Harry sighed.
"And you're right, Rupert. I guess as long as he's director I'm walking on thin ice. Sometimes I'm surprised that he hasn't done more to make things awkward for me."
Rupert snorted.
"Only because he's been busy playing king maker and consolidating his position. Stay tuned, boy. Your time will come."
The revelry from the bar quietened suddenly and the two men turned to look back into the wan light. Garnet Clayton and the girl had joined the bar crowd, she shaking hands as the chief warden introduced her. She had changed after the seminar, whilst the men had gathered in the bar to swap news about their different territories. Now she wore a pair of snug fitting khaki slacks topped by a simple Chinese silk blouse of deep maroon. The sheerness of the material and the unfettered swing of her breasts made it obvious she wasn't wearing a bra. Harry grinned dryly at the unwavering attention she was getting, noting Roy Thorson's thoughtful expression. He nudged Rupert.
"You can see Roy's getting set to make some earth-shattering comment, as only he can do it."
Rupert chuckled.

"There's a lad who isn't too far behind you as far as chequered careers go. Roy preferred the lowveld though. Killed a lot of crocs. He's another good example of poacher turned gamekeeper. He's one of our best wardens. Maybe there's a moral there somewhere. When I see that people like you two, and the Cantrells, and Denis Cantle are still in the field, it gladdens my heart. There's no substitute for good field operators, no matter how indispensable the research types think they are."

Harry listened with only half an ear, watching from the darkness of the balcony as Garnet chaperoned the girl around, introducing her to conference guests. There was still something about her that tugged at his memory. Why, he silently wondered, is Garnet playing the attentive escort? Who is she? And he thought again, hell, but she's a beauty.

Amidst the bar noise he heard his name mentioned. Garnet's voice. Chas Cantrell was pointing out to the balcony. Harry watched as the chief warden took the girl's arm and guided her out of the fast crowding bar towards them. He could feel his pulses trip and took a deep breath, looking up above him at the night sky. The star studded canopy stretched over them with the sharp clarity of late winter and the night air tasted crisp and fresh. Yet it's September, he thought, one of the best months of the year for the valley. But the October heat is just around the corner.

"Harry. Rupert. So this is where you're hiding. Wool-gathering, I'll bet."

Rupert's soft chuckle of acknowledgement accompanied Harry's answer.

"Garnet, evening ..."

He nodded politely at the girl.

"Hello ..."

She grinned her reply. It was that, thought Harry. A grin, not a smile.

Garnet spoke again and Harry wondered at the mischievous quirk that slipped into his smile.

"I don't think you folks have properly met?"
Harry shook his head, aware of Rupert leaning back against the railing, effectively making him chief spokesman whilst he monitored events. From down below, near the edge of the lake, a shrill brief bout of trumpeting erupted.
"No, we haven't. Apart from a brief chat earlier today."
Steady unwavering gaze, eyes dark in the night. He caught the scent of her perfume. Garnet introduced them.
"Gentlemen, I'd like you to meet Miss Peta Holt. Peta ... Harry Kenyon, and Rupert Fothergill."
Her hand was warm, the shake friendly and firm. Peter. *Peter?* Holt? Harry stared at her, aware that he had held onto her hand for too long and that she had retrieved it casually and was now shaking hands with Rupert. *Peter?* She was speaking.
"How do you do. A pleasure to meet you both. I've heard a lot about you. I enjoyed your lecture today, Mister Kenyon."
Teeth white, wet glistening in the starlight. Perfume. Harry looked at her and then switched his attention to Garnet Clayton. Broad grin meeting questioning stare.
"Peter Holt? As in photographer?"
Garnet nodded.
"Photographer, yes. Peta spelt with an A. And, indeed the same person."
She laughed softly then. Harry felt his stomach tighten.
"It's not the first time my gender has got mixed up. Sometimes it can be an advantage, other times not. I hope the fact that I'm a she and not a he doesn't complicate matters."
She looked directly at Harry with the last sentence. He shook his head. Rupert had his pipe out again, this time making a positive attempt at getting it going. Harry could feel the elderly warden's amusement, even though he had not yet said a word.
"Not at all. I've been wondering all day who our photographer guest could be ..."
He grinned.
"Now I know. Welcome to Rhodesia, and ..."

He flicked a thumb over his shoulder at the night-shrouded lake.

"... the valley, or what's left of this part of it."

"Thank you. I have actually been here before. Way back. But it's terrific being here again."

Harry tried to locate the accent. English, certainly, and probably from a good expensive background. But there were other accents there too. Her consonants spoke of a Gallic affinity, but there was the drawl of America. Garnet was patting her on the shoulder.

"I'll leave you with Harry and Rupert. Then perhaps you can start making some sort of arrangements to visit Nemana, and whatever other areas of the valley interest you."

He raised an eyebrow at Harry.

"That all right with you, Harry?"

Mock serious. Solicitous. Bugger you, thought the warden. Who am I to argue?

"Sure. No sweat, Garnet. We'll make some plans."

The chief warden left. Rupert sucked attentively at his pipe, the tobacco mixing not unpleasantly with her perfume.

"I'm ..."

"Would you ..."

"... really looking ..."

"... like a drink?"

They stopped, smiling self consciously. She thrust her hands into her pockets.

"I'd love a drink. Scotch, please. A large one."

Rupert belatedly entered the conversation.

"I'll get them. Same again, Harry? Anything with the whiskey, Miss Holt?"

"Lots of ice, thanks. And it's Peta. With an A. Like in Liza, with a Z."

It escaped Rupert as he grunted gruffly, shy smile breaking across the craggy landscape of his face. She turned slightly to smile him on his way and Harry caught the silhouette of her breasts against the bar lights. He felt his mouth go dry. She turned back to face him and he shifted his attention guiltily to her face. The smile remained as she moved to lean against the railing beside him.

"So," she said, "at last I get to meet the famous Harry Kenyon." Harry frowned.

"Famous?"

"Sure. As in French television. Hauling lions out of the bush by the tail."

Harry laughed.

"Oh, that. Have they edited it already? On the silver screen so soon?"

"Yes, indeed. Philippe Dubois put a very good package together there. Gosh, I can still hear that soundtrack. The night I had those lions in my living room, back in Paris, I had goose bumps for hours. That programme did your wild animals, and your Zambezi Valley proud."

I won't, thought Peta Holt, add that you came across pretty well yourself.

"Pleased to hear it. It's all there, really. The valley, the bush, the river, and the animals. It's just got to be portrayed correctly. Which, one would think, is quite straightforward. But you can never tell with journalists, or film crews. Or photographers."

Her smile never faltered. Ouch, she thought. Take that! Not fair. Why pick on me, Mister Kenyon? She kept the retaliation back. Just. But she could not stop the frost from creeping into her voice.

"There is always that factor. The credibility gap. In my experience one is more inclined to encounter it in the hard news field. Not so much in the feature stuff, especially where wildlife is concerned. The people who are into that are usually supporters or converts to the cause."

She looked directly at him, and her voice was as crisp as the night air.

"I hope you won't be disappointed with my work on the valley. And I hope you don't tar all journalists and photographers with the same brush. I'll be very interested to see what you think of my portfolio."

How the heck did I start this, Harry wondered. What on earth made you stick that particular knife in? You're neurotic, Kenyon. Maybe Roscoe's right and I've been in the valley too long. He shook his head.

"I'm sorry. There was no offence intended. Really."

He held up his hands in mock surrender.

"I know you have a good reputation, and that your work is first class. Garnet wouldn't of let you come this far, otherwise. And ..."

He grinned. One of his best, out of the top drawer. One of those he usually reserved for head office management meetings, when he was getting off squashed toes.

"... I look forward to showing you Nemana. Or anywhere else in the valley."

"That's no idle boast, Miss Holt ... Peta. You'll be in good hands down in the valley. Harry knows it like the back of his hand."

Rupert had returned with the drinks, determinedly social. Harry watched her face as he passed her drink. The smile had returned. Crisis averted. She returned his look with exaggerated innocence and her voice was very sweet.

"I'm awfully glad to hear it."

Rupert picked up the innuendo in her tone but wasn't quite sure of its target. He glanced from one to the other appraisingly. Peta Holt decided it was time for a total truce. It's nerves, she thought.

"From what little I've heard of the valley it doesn't suffer fools."

Harry nodded, relieved. Rupert cleared his throat, and his voice was carefully neutral.

"Peta, Garnet has invited you to join the director and him for dinner. With the minister."

"My goodness. Right amongst the Special People. Thank you, Rupert, but I don't really think it's my cup of tea. Perhaps I could join you two gentlemen and start educating myself about the valley. That's if you don't mind, of course."

Rupert looked uncomfortable. Across the verandah, forming a separate island amongst the crowd, Harry could see Garnet, Alistair Drummond and the minister watching them. He felt a surge of resentment, and struggled to keep it out of his voice.

"It's the proper thing for you to do, I suppose. Perhaps we can have a drink later."

She shrugged. He was aware of the movement within her blouse.

"You are right of course. I shouldn't be selfish, or rude. Yes, thank you, I'll see you later."

She gave them her wide infectious grin and left them. Rupert glanced at Harry.

"You've been down in the valley for too long, Harry. Don't do anything stupid."

Harry watched her retreating form. The tailored slacks gave more life to her long-legged stride. He shook his head mildly.

"Me? Come on, Rupert. You know me better than that."

Rupert grunted.

*****

The safari lodge lay in darkness. The generator had been switched off at ten-thirty. Only in the bar was there a flickering light, a guttering candle throwing liquid shadows across the room whilst a last untired quartet of game men talked on into the night. Cicadas shrilled distantly. A bat swooped. From the vlei behind the lodge a zebra barked. On the low walled verandah of his cottage, Harry sat silently in an old wicker chair and listened to the night. He and Rupert had eaten dinner with Roscoe Daniels and Denis Cantle and then retired to the quarters they were sharing. They had left Roy Thorson talking to the young hotel receptionist. It looked as if Peta Holt had been monopolised for the evening. She had caught Harry's eye once and lifted her shoulders in a slight helpless shrug as the minister expertly kept the conversation flowing. Harry winked sympathetically. Peta was not the only woman at the wild life conference, but she was the youngest and certainly the most attractive, so it was predictable that she would be well attended. He smiled now in the darkness, as he recalled her comments on the pros and cons of being Peta or Peter. It certainly looked as if the advantages had stacked up for her this night. Everyone, from the honourable minister to the inscrutable Rupert, had paid her homage in their own ways.

On the periphery of his vision there was movement, shadow within shadow, and a sudden soft scraping of branches. As he watched, an elephant ambled slowly from the bush thickets bordering the lodge and made its way into the lodge complex. Harry studied the animal as it walked towards his cottage and could see in the forming moon that he was a prime bull, carrying short stubby ivory. The elephant paused at the corner of the cottage, blocking the end of the open fronted verandah with its great bulk, sampling the bougainvillaea that crowded down from the wooden eaves of the building. From behind Harry, in the bedroom, the rhythm of Rupert's breathing changed as he altered his sleeping position. He watched as the bull stripped a branch of the shrub with curled prehensile-tipped trunk and then tuck the bunch of leaves far back behind his whiskered mouth into his throat. There was a rumbling noise, quickly followed by the heavy plopping and sluicing flood as the elephant evacuated his bowels, and the elephant smell was very strong on the night air. The bull moved on past the verandah, four paces from Harry, and he craned his neck to look up at the great pachyderm as it passed. He was aware that he was still smiling, his thoughts of Peta transposing to the pleasure of watching his recent visitor. In the cottage Rupert mumbled in his sleep.

More movement, and for an instant he thought it must be more elephant. But it was the figure of a man following along the path of the bull, moving wraithlike across the grass through the shadows of the shrubbery and scattered cottages. He watched the form approach his verandah, still in the steps of the elephant, and he was wondering what was going on and readying himself for confrontation, and then he saw her mane of hair as she stepped out of a shadow. She hadn't seen him, seated deep within the verandah's own shadow, and he waited until she drew level with the pillared doorway before he spoke softly.

"You forgot your camera."

She jumped, with a startled rattle of breath, whirling to face the voice from the deep shadow. Harry chuckled quietly.

"Insomnia, Miss Holt? Following elephants around at night?"

She recognised his voice then and he could see the shine of her teeth, and watched the tension dissolve out of her tensed form.

"God ... you gave me a fright! I was so busy following him I was oblivious to anything else."

Her charged whisper sounded very loud in the still of the night.

"That's a dangerous habit to get into. You should always watch your back in the bush. There may have been others behind you both that you hadn't seen."

As Harry spoke there was a new muted disturbance of vegetation, and the grey shadowed bulk of another elephant followed the first visitor silently through the lodge complex. Peta moved on to the verandah and they watched the second elephant making its unhurried loose gaited way past. She was amazed at the big animal's silent passage. There was no sound, even though the elephant moved past them less than a few paces away. She sat on the low wall, feeling her heart thump. Elephant had always done that to her. And, she thought now, it's been a very long time since I've seen a wild elephant. Especially that close. From the direction of the lodge swimming pool came the unmistakable squirting sucking squishing sounds of elephants drinking. Harry laughed softly.

"Five star types, obviously. The lake's not good enough for them."

Peta felt the adrenalin flow weaken and subside to a mere flood.

"Ohhhh, God; but they're beautiful! So much bulk and power, yet so darn quiet! They're like great grey ghosts."

Harry could hear the tension still in her voice, in the whispered excitement. He could smell soap, the perfume gone. The effect was the same. A giant eagle owl grunt-hooted. A jackal yammered. He spoke softly.

"They've come to welcome you to the valley. It's a good introduction. Down at Nemana there will almost never be a time, by day or night, when you can't see an elephant somewhere in permanent sight. In the dry months, at least."

Peta Holt sighed and shifted to lean her back against the pillar, adjusting the wrap around cotton print material she had thrown on, before resting folded arms on drawn up knees. Rupert snored gently. Some small animal scuttled busily amongst the shrubbery.

"I can't tell you how good it feels to be back here. It's been such a long time. There's been other countries, other wild places; Kenya, Tanzania, Kruger, Gorongosa. But, somehow, I've never managed to get back here. To this country, or the Zambezi Valley. Not since I was a girl. Not since college."

She gave a soft rueful laugh.

"When I heard the lions, a few weeks ago, and saw the valley bush on the television screen, I was done for. On my way. Then when you appeared on the screen, Harry Kenyon, it was like a time warp ... And, here I am."

Harry studied her from his patch of shadow, wondering what on earth she was talking about. Seated there on the verandah wall he could see her plainly in the silvered wash of the overhead moon. One half of her face was in the shadow of her night-darkened hair as she turned to look at him, and he thought she resembled some modern surrealistic painting. Again, disturbingly, something flickered across his memory, like one of the night hunting bats that dipped and swooped over the lodge. He heard her, and examined her words, like stones, mentally turning them over and searching for hidden clues.

And all the while her gaze lay upon him. He shook his head, finally.

"Me? I don't understand, Peta."

She watched him, cat-like, and then she lifted her head and nodded out towards the lake.

"There. During the rescue operation. In 1960..."

He stared at her, still mystified. She turned her head back to him, face slashed by shadow.

"I was fifteen, then. And my surname wasn't Holt. My mother and I spent a week with you and your rescue team. Whilst my father was traipsing around counting refugees coming over the Congo border ..."

It began to form then, in his memory. As he looked anew at the high sculpted cheekbones and the eyes that were almost too wide set. In the night he could not see their colour, distant smoky blue, but the direct forthright gaze should have brought it back long ago.

"You probably don't remember me, Harry. A skinny knobbly-kneed fifteen year old. But I like to think that your remember her. Do you? Harry? Monica Hutton? Mrs? Wife of the Honourable, now Sir Courteney Hutton?"

She was watching his face intently, searching its shadowed contours, and she saw the realisation sweep across it. He ran one large hand through his hair. For a long time there was silence between them. A branch splinter-cracked somewhere in the lodge grounds as the nocturnal visitors browsed. His voice was reflective when he eventually responded.

"That was a long time back. How is your mother?"

"She's dead. She died a while ago, a couple of years after we left Rhodesia on one of Dad's transfers."

"I'm sorry."

She shrugged gently.

"It happens. You cannot believe that at the time; but it happens. The Big C. She was luckier than most. Three months from diagnosis, she was gone. God, I missed her. She was a real sport, you know. A real trouper. We were like sisters, rather than mother and daughter. We were friends. I suppose it was because we were always tagging around after Dad and his never ending assignments around the world, never really getting to know the people properly where we were stationed; before we moved on. So we got to know each other well. I'm not terribly religious, but I thank the Lord she was spared the long, long years that some cancer-struck people have taken to die. With all that clever soul and pride-destroying treatment meaning nothing."

Another jackal called down on the lake shore, to be answered immediately by another behind the lodge. Harry stood up, easing slowly out of the wicker chair so that it didn't creak. Rupert was best asleep. He carried enough secrets. He moved across to the wall and sat facing her, leaning back against the corner pillar. She was glad he had moved. She wanted to be able to see his face more clearly, unmasked by the shadow.

"Did she tell you?"

Peta nodded.

"Yes. But I knew. I saw you from where I was sleeping on the launch. Quite a revelation for a fifteen year old."

Harry returned her level look.

"Ships in the night. A very lovely lady, your mother. She was the most attractive woman I'd ever seen. And what happened, once, between us, was extra special."

He let his glance sweep over her face.

"When I first saw you, today in the conference, there was something about you that rang a bell. You have her eyes. The same. I just couldn't place it."

He smiled and rubbed at his jaw. She could hear the stubble rasp against his hand.

"So ... a full circle. We meet back at the lake. Your name? Holt?"

She ran splayed fingers through her hair, repeating the action so that it became a combing motion.

"Husband. William Holt, Junior. Never forget the 'Junior'. Real storybook romance stuff. A whirlwind affair. I'd known

156

him four months, before I married him. We had another six before he went out of my life."

Harry waited, watching the combing motion. An errant breeze rustled the bougainvillaea.

"I met Bill in Laos, in '69. I was in Vientiane, trying to put a story together on the shadow airlines the CIA were operating. He was with the Agency, running teams of Yau tribesmen in to Red China. His official cover was 'Air Operations Representative - Continental Air Shuttles', which fooled no-one of course. The Agency pretty much controlled the show then. To cut a long story short, he made one trip too many."

"Killed?"

She shook her head, loose finger-combed hair swirling.

"Nothing so simple. He was listed as MIA. Somehow, if your mind happens to work in the same convoluted fashion as the Agency, Missing In Action doesn't upset the statistics as openly as KIA. When he didn't come back he got a citation from Helms. I could never work out whether it was posthumous or not."

She smiled crookedly at Harry.

"It was a no-win situation, anyway. It didn't take me long to work that out. He was married to the CIA. A born insurrectionist, even at home. Which wasn't very often. It was a relief to get out of Laos. So, there you have it, Harry, the edited edition of how my name changed."

She changed the subject.

"You haven't changed."

Harry chuckled, quietly rueful.

"I don't know about that. I don't feel very much older than when I was on Kariba in those early days. Rupert and I were talking about that, earlier tonight. Did you know that tomorrow evening will be his retirement party? You'll be present for the end of an era. He was the first game ranger in the department. It's a different world now, with all the bright new ecologists and zoologists taking over the wildlife scene. Sorry ... I'm wandering. We were talking about Noah, the last rescues on

Starvation. That was twelve years ago. And I don't feel any older. Mind you ..."

He held up a broad finger.

"... at the tender age of, fifteen, did you say, I probably didn't look that young to you then. I was over thirty, and I'm told kids consider that as being geriatric. After Rupert and Len Harvey, I was the oldest on the team. If I still look that age it must be because of my clean living."

Her low chuckle blended with his. She shifted her position on the hard concrete of the wall, leaning towards him. There was no shadow across her face now, and in the light of the moon and stars he caught a glimpse of blue.

"Talking of clean living ... I don't know how old you were then, but do you know that you were the first man, and this includes my father, to see me stark naked? Not only see me; but touch me as well. All over."

Her voice was mock serious.

"Do you remember, Harry Kenyon?"

In the cottage Rupert snored. Or grunted. Harry wasn't sure which. He studied her in surprise, and then he did remember. The memory of the mother had transcended that of the young daughter. Now it all came back. The screams in the night, the visitors' second night on the island base, terrified, agonised. Harry had charged across the makeshift camp to their tent, tripping over guy ropes, stumbling over equipment, singeing himself as he rolled through the embers of the fireplace, his only weapon being his bush knife, snatched in haste. As he ran he wondered what could be attacking the woman and her daughter. They'd cleared the island. Perhaps a lion had returned. Or leopard. Snake? Harry charged on. It was ants. Matabele ants everywhere, flushed out of their homes, and now on the march. In the torchlight the ground swarmed with movement and their sibilant hissing was very loud as they attacked out of their formation. Harry grabbed both females and hauled them out of the tent, dragging them down to the water's edge. Both mother and daughter were in soft cotton pyjamas. He could feel the ants biting him now. The girl had the most ants over her, and she was bucking and twisting in agony.

"Strip!!" He shouted hoarsely at the mother. "Into the lake! Strip off your clothes!"

He struggled with the writhing girl, shoving the mother away to fall in the water, dragging the girl with him into the lake as well, hooking his fingers in her pyjamas and ripping them off, thrashing the water furiously, doing anything to cause turbulence and disturbance that would remove at least some of the red hot biting insects.

It partially worked, especially with the mother who had not taken the brunt of the attack, but there were still a lot of army ants with nippers stuck fast into the girl's skin. She was keening now, incoherent with shock and pain, still struggling frantically. He pulled her along the shoreline, away from the main concentration of ants building up along the edge of the water, into the shallows where he could see her pale body in the dim starlight, and gently and firmly clipped her alongside the jawline. Then, whilst she was dazed and her desperate struggles had quietened, he ran the razor sharp blade of his knife across her body, scraping away the ants, shaving them from her skin. With sweat-beading concentration he gradually rid her body of the tormentors, willing his hand not to slip or the girl not to heave suddenly out of her comatose state, for the blade was very keen.

Finally, from long-limbed shanks to slim graceful neck, from tight dimpled buttocks around to the soft fleece of early womanhood, he had rid her of the safari ants. When he eventually stood back, allowing the mother to take her full weight in her arms, from helping him steady her inert body, he saw that she had revived and had been watching him work. He sighed with relief. There wasn't a scratch on her. It was, he thought, the finest skinning job he'd ever done. After that young Peta would only sleep aboard one of the launches. And it was after that when Harry had hauled a drunkenly amorous

Alistair Drummond from the mother's tent. It was towards the end of their sojourn with the rescue team, with the fires fanning between the ranger and the diplomat's wife, that Harry Kenyon had finally succumbed, and himself gone to her in the night. And Monica Hutton had welcomed him with unleashed passion.

Later, on the occasions she allowed herself to indulge in the heated memories of that night, she blamed the moon, though there was no moon.

"I remember. You were a very brave girl. Soldier ants have been known to kill anything that gets in their way."

She giggled.

"Well, that was a real case of ants in the pants. It was horrible. Afterwards was even worse. When you'd got the ants off, and I was dazed, and the water was beginning to cool the bites; I looked up and there you were, carefully scraping the last ants off my breasts. Such as they were! I was mortified!"

She sighed theatrically.

"Do you realise just how much that sort of thing could affect a girl's outlook on life, Harry Kenyon?"

He squinted at her, letting her play it out. She took another deep breath and shook her head, the amusement, dry perhaps, still in her voice.

"You've quite a legacy. The first man ever to strip me; and the first to hit me. And you'd forgotten. Ah, well. Such is life."

She hung her head in mock resignation. Then she stood up.

"It's time I caught up on my beauty sleep. It wouldn't be good form to doze off during lectures tomorrow."

Harry stood with her.

"I'll walk you back to your cottage. Make sure you don't get carried away by some wild beastie."

Peta smiled inwardly. I could give you a smart aleck answer to that, she mused. But I won't. Even if you have seen me naked and defenceless. They stepped off the verandah, out under the open sky. A nightjar called tremulously. Beside him, she said.

"You know, you left your mark on my mother."

He stopped and surveyed her intently.

"Explain that, please."

"She never forgot that night with you. Later, when I was older, we talked about it, a little. She had never experienced the bush before, not the real wild bush. Operation Noah was a new world for her. And you were a new kind of man, quite unlike the types she was used to mixing with. Very different to my father. She cherished that week on the lake. That night. She wasn't promiscuous. That was her little detour off the straight and narrow. Her fling, away from the stuffed shirt protocol of the Foreign Office. I'm glad that you gave her that happiness."

He continued to watch her.

"You sound as if you're apologising for your mother's indiscretion. Don't. I'm not sure how much penance one is supposed to pay if one breaks the Eighth Commandment, and I don't care. And I'm very glad to hear that it was something special for her also."

He started them walking again. He felt her watching him.

"I'm glad, at least, that you never beat me the way you thrashed Drummond that night ..."

Harry grunted.

"He was a fool. And I was foolish. I took that beating too far, and he's never forgiven me for it. Although neither of us has ever mentioned it."

It's strange, he reflected, how the secrets have come out tonight. I thought Drummond and I were the only two who knew about the fight, apart from Monica. Then Rupert. And now, Peta. I wonder if Drummond knows who she is?

"And now he's your director? That can't be awfully satisfactory for either of you."

Harry grinned dryly.

"So far that hasn't affected me. He's only been in the big office for four years, and he's had a lot on his plate. Time will tell."

He led her off the subject.

"Where is your father now?"

"Hong Kong. Still with the Foreign Office. Still climbing up
the ladder, still playing diplomatic snakes and ladders. He's quite
a VIP now."
"See him often?"
She shrugged.
"Every two or three years we arrange for our paths to cross.
After mother died we somehow went our different ways."
She stopped in front of a cottage, and then moved on a pace
before turning to him.
"This is it. And I must admit I'm tired. At last. I wasn't earlier,
before the elephants paid us a visit. But the day's caught up
with me, especially casting back over twelve years."
Harry smiled, noting the distancing movement.
"Me too. Another full day inside tomorrow. Sitting in a room
always exhausts me. I'm sorry we didn't get a chance to talk
about Nemana. Tomorrow, some time." He flicked her a small
salute.
"Sleep tight."
She watched him walk back to his cottage. He stopped and half
turned back to her.
"You have, if I may say so, your mother's beauty, Peta Holt."
He turned away and she stood watching until the darkness
swallowed him up. Only then did she say softly.
"Thank you, sir. You're not so bad yourself, Harry Kenyon."

CHAPTER FOURTEEN

The float plane eased off the water in a shower of spray, its
red and white livery briefly flashing in the new day
sunlight. The small slim New Zealander at the controls
murmured into the radio microphone and then turned the pilot
to starboard to follow the shoreline of the lake. Harry had
asked the aircraft to follow the lake border of the Mutusiadona
National Park as far as the jagged slash of the Sanyati Gorge

before heading across the water for Kariba. In the right hand seat Peta sat poised, camera at the ready, watching bushveld and shoreline slip past.

The conference had been, so the head office hierarchy had said, a great success. It had brought under one roof a good cross-section of the department's experts, and, together with the South African visitors, and the good doctor from Frankfurt, a lot of knowledge and experience had been pooled. Harry had enjoyed meeting up with old friends and colleagues, and was especially pleased that Roscoe Daniels would be coming down to Nemana next week with his gear. They would be collaring the 'Big Four' tuskers. Furthermore, for the duration of his visit they would have the facilities of a chartered helicopter. Harry wondered if some of his barbs had gone in a little deep at the conference. Whatever gods had delivered unto him the helicopter, he devoutly thanked them and had made a long mental list of the things that could be done with the chopper, quite apart from the elephant locating for the collaring. There were areas high up in the hostile sun-parched escarpment that he wanted to inspect. Hidden remote valleys and ravines that would take him weeks to study on foot, but which could be done in a matter of days by helicopter. He also wanted to get down to Chief Kanyoka's area, where the Chingusa joined the Zambezi, and inspect the region from the air for any signs of increased poaching activity. To look for signs that would show that the subsistence hunting necessary for the local tribespeople to survive had mushroomed into commercial slaughter.

Kanyoka's people had lived on the Chingusa River for generations, long before the Nemana area had been declared a National Park. To some departmental policymakers it was paradoxical allowing the tribe to remain on the border of the newly proclaimed sanctuary. A conflict of interests was predicted, with the hunting habits of Kanyoka's people flying in the face of conservation efforts. However, there were also those amongst the department hierarchy, a lesser contingent, but just as vocal, who advocated that the locals remain. They had been there for years. So had the game. And, to date, the marriage had prospered, with wild man and wild animal living harmoniously. Twentieth century man and his trappings had not so far disrupted this remote patch of earth. And so Chief Kanyoka continued to govern his clan on the land of his ancestors. And, so far as Harry Kenyon was concerned, the tribe's presence alongside the game sanctuary was welcome. Through their far ranging bush wanderings he was kept informed of events unfolding in this part of the valley, soon learning of any abnormal ripple in the pattern of valley life. His planned aerial inspection of the area was extra insurance against being caught unawares by any man-initiated development.

The float plane tilted, and Peta was shooting through the open window. An old bull elephant, a one tusker, stood in the clear shallows. Ears flapping and trunk aloft he shook his great head and backed away from the noise of the aeroplane. Over the growl of the engine Harry heard the throaty alarmed squeal of the elephant. The sun flashed off the solitary tusk. It's the culling, he thought. I'm sure of it. I'm certain the elephants have come to associate aircraft noise with death and destruction. They circled the old bull once and then left him in peace. A flock of pelicans patrolled a reeded backwater, looking like a fleet of miniature galleons. Wonder where they're from, mused Harry. Don't see them on the lake often, the salinity doesn't suit them. The surface of the lake was glassy calm, a glinting jewelled mirror. The reflection of the plane raced them across its smooth serenity. Along the lush panicum shoreline a large herd of impala leaped, joyously, as if celebrating the survival of another predator filled night. Their hides gleamed like old copper pennies in the sunlight. A flock of sacred ibis ruffled the water of the shallows, taking off in wheeling erratic flight away from the path of the aircraft.

Harry let his thoughts return to Rupert's retirement bash the previous night. It had been, really, an anticlimax. Eighteen years of dedication ending with a clichéd speech from the director, a copper fire screen with an improbable elephant scene painted on it, a fishing rod, and Rupert shuffling, nervous and uncomfortable in the limelight. Harry's heart bled for the senior warden, and, not for the first time, he reminded Harry of the animals that held the stalwart's special affection. The black rhino, misunderstood, undaunted, an old soldier with not many victories to celebrate. After the usual back slapping and half-hearted promises to keep in touch, the party had broken up. Rupert, Harry, Roy Thorson and the Cantrells had sat out on the balcony overlooking the darkness of the lake, and talked about old times, each man aware that this would be their last time together at one time. Peta had sat with them for a while, but had, sensing their own intimacy, excused herself. She noted that there was no move made to encourage her to stay. Alistair Drummond had stopped at their group in the shadows, and had been jocular and gung-ho cheerful, but had moved on when responses were low-keyed and guarded. Poor old bastard, thought Harry now, and pushed the thoughts firmly away. For he could see the spectre of himself there, in Rupert's shadow. A bateleur slid past the float plane's right wing, gliding effortlessly on the day's rising thermals. Harry looked on and past the eagle to the distant bulk of the escarpment. Ah, yes, he mused. The valley is changing, and not so slowly. He remembered when he had returned from Malaya, eighteen years ago, and had seen the advance of progress then. Long after the steel bridges across the Zambezi, and the vast acres of the sugar estates. Before the lake called Kariba.

*****

He stood on the platform, alone amidst the welcoming mêlée, and watched the crowd. A chill night wind blew across the railway lines and an unseasonable shower pattered insistently against the wide domed perspex of the station roof. He shivered and wrinkled his nose at the cloying smell of the shunting yards. Beside him, his green issue kitbag rested against one of the steel pylons supporting the station roof. It was all he had, no fuller than when he had left for Malaya, almost five years before. He leaned against the pillar and watched one of the returning soldiers embracing a pretty girl with dark hair and a red ribbon. Her eyes were squeezed shut and tears glistened on her cheeks. Harry looked away, envious. He surveyed the milling throng on the platform for a while longer and then hefted the kitbag up on to his shoulder. He eased through the crowd to the far side of the platform, heading for the main station entrance on Railway Avenue. Someone gripped his shoulder. Scratch Peters grinned back at his enquiring stare.

"Hey, Harry! Where are you off to?"

Harry smiled at the excitement in the other's voice, and thought : I reckon I'd be fairly darned keyed up if I'd had a pretty girl waiting for my train. After five years ... The dark-haired girl clung to Scratch's arm, as if afraid she'd lose her man if she let him go again.

"Town. I'll put up at the Grand for a couple of days. See you back at barracks for muster."

"Isn't anyone meeting you?"

Harry shook his head.

"Hell, Harry. That's no damned good. Not after four and a half years away in the *ulus*. Come along with us. Let's celebrate."

Harry saw the cloud of disappointment slide across the girl's face. Scratch was tugging her forward to introduce her.

"Martine, this is Harry Kenyon. He's the guy I wrote about. Remember? We got our gongs together, after we'd, *he* had, tracked down those Commie bandits for five days. Harry ... meet the girl in the photographs you've been seeing for the past five years. I guess miracles still happen. She waited after all."

Harry nodded, and his voice was as cheerful as his friend's.

"Hi, Martine. Pleased to meet you for real. I feel I know you already. Scratch has kept us all pretty much up to date on your doings over the last few years. If he'd had his way he would have been here hours ago. We had to stop him getting off the train at the border and running ahead."

The girl laughed but he could see she was still preoccupied with the thought that she might have to share the first homecoming hours of her man's company with a stranger. He turned away.

"See you, folks. Meet you back at barracks in a couple of days, Scratch."

"We'll give you a lift to the Grand, Harry."

Harry shook his head.

"No, thanks all the same. It's ten minutes walk. After six weeks on troop ships and trains it will be a nice change to walk in a straight line."

He waved and pushed on through the crowd.

"Harry."

He turned back reluctantly.

"You still going to demob? Pack it in? Even with the promotion the major promised you?"

Harry grinned wryly.

"Yes. Absolutely! Five years of soldiering is plenty. I've seen my tiger. Time for a change of scenery. As my own boss."

He shoved into the crowd. The girl looked enquiringly at Scratch Peters.

"Tiger? What does he mean?"

Scratch shrugged, chuckling.

"Harry always reckoned that he joined the army to see a tiger. Nothing more, nothing less. No great call to arms, no solider of the Queen type patriotism. He just wanted to see a tiger. In its natural habitat. That's all. Quite a joke, really. Five years in the army, with a couple of bullet holes ... to see a tiger."

Salisbury had changed little in the time he had been away. A few extended streets, a new, second cinema, and the price of gin had crept up to fourteen shillings a bottle. Harry savoured the two days spent in the luxury of the Grand Hotel, revelling in the return to sleeping in a comfortable bed, on his own, without the barrack room chorus of the last years, or the leech infested wet steaminess of jungle bivouacs. He refused the commission that was offered him if he stayed on in the Special Air Service. His back pay from the Malayan commitment had been paid into his bank account, swelling his ivory and crocodile skin profits, which made Harry Kenyon, at twenty-seven, a young man of fairly independent means.

"You're a born soldier, Harry. There's a hell of a future for you with the SAS. What are you going to do now? Go on an almighty binge and spend all your jungle pay?"

Harry nursed his drink. It was his farewell party in the SAS mixed ranks mess. He had put fifty pounds behind the bar of The Winged Stagger and was determined to utilise the investment to the full. The speaker was a short barrel-chested man with hard grey eyes. Ronald Dalyrimple had served through the Squadron's Malayan Campaign as Sergeant-Major. Beside him John Johnson and Hugo Winters watched Harry as he took his time in replying.

"Haven't made up my mind yet. I'll buy myself a four-wheel drive vehicle and head for the bush. I've seen what there is to see of Salisbury. I think I'll head down south-east to the Lundi and see how Kashili is. Make the trip something of a pilgrimage. I haven't been back to the lowveld since my mother died after the war, ten years ago. I'll play it by ear. Maybe Kashili is well settled now, with plenty of wives, kids, and goats. Maybe he's been stamped on by an elephant, or chewed up by lions. If he's around, and keen, maybe we'll start hunting again. Down on the Lundi, or back to the valley. Who knows? I'll make a plan ... The army? I've had enough. It's been good fun, and I've met a fine bunch of blokes through the Squadron. But it's not my game, Ron. I'll leave it to you guys, the professionals."

Harry grinned around at the circle of faces.

"There's more than enough of you to start, or end, another war."

Hugo Winters grunted.

"The bush life is a short term thing. The way this colony is expanding, there will be precious little bush in a few years.

Look at the Zambezi Valley. Your second home. They've started building that dam on Kariba Gorge, which they say will be completed by the end of 1958, four years away. That will be over 150 miles of your valley drowned. Gone for ever. That's the future of the Zambezi Valley, one of the wildest, most inhospitable places in Africa. Imagine how quickly the rest of the more accessible bush areas will be flattened."

The commanding officer shook his head and rattled the ice in his empty glass at the duty barman.

"Forget it, Harry. Stay with us. The family. You'll get to see plenty of wild places in time. Remember the slogan of Johore? Join the Army. Visit exotic lands. Meet interesting new people ..."

"And kill them!"

The chorus from the surrounding soldiers drowned out the major's voice. Harry grinned dryly. He'd had enough of the Kenyon for Permanent Force campaign.

"Well, never say never, so who knows."

Kashili lived under kraalhead Murumbini, under Chief Ngwenyenye, down in the hot south-east of the country where the Lundi and Sabi Rivers met on the remote border with Portuguese East Africa. Their tribal lands were on both sides of the border and had been so long before the white man and his progress had nominated border lines and drawn them on maps. That the Europeans had drawn these lines did not worry the Shangaans at all. They continued to cultivate the rich alluvial soils along the Lundi's banks, growing maize, pumpkins, and sorghum, and their diet was supplemented with wild fruits and wild bush honey. Protein was plentiful. Fish from the river, the ubiquitous scratching native fowls, and the wild animals that were hunted in the timeless bush. No cattle or goats could live down there on the Lundi because of the tsetse fly. From the fruit of the marula tree and the distillate from the sap of the river side *mlala* palms they made *mkumbi*, and when they drank this liquor, the Shangaan drums echoed long into the night.

The hippo and elephant and baboons lived harmoniously with these remote people, seldom plundering their crops, and there was no domestic stock to attract the attentions of the big cats. The white people seldom braved the heat and desolation of this forgotten corner of the country, the nearest outpost being the dusty Portuguese border town of Malvernia, ninety miles away. All things considered, life treated Kashili's people well. After five years at war in a foreign land, Harry Kenyon was in good spirits as he guided his war surplus jeep along faded familiar bush tracks, detouring the many trees felled by the region's elephants, dodging antbear holes, skirting treacherous deep sand patches that would have him stuck for days. Until at last he caught the first glimpse of the river gleaming distantly amongst the bushveld. And there, along the wide gentle flowing Lundi, the kraal complex of Kashili's tribe hugged the tall tree-shaded banks.

"And you say this cat, this devil that moves like the smoke from a cooking fire, is bigger than the biggest lion we have ever seen? Hau! That is something! And its colour is that of the flickering fire itself ....?"
Kashili shook his head in wonderment.
"It is almost not to be believed."
Harry grinned across at his friend. They were sitting on a bank of high sculpted sand, far out from the tree edged shoreline of the main river course. The green depths of the Lundi swept past beside them, tugging at their fishing lines. Both men were clad only in ragged shorts and the sun had burned Harry's body so darkly that from the shoreline the two men looked to be of one colour. Harry had been down here for two weeks now, in the kraal of his friend which lay below the 300 metre contour, the lowest land in the country. The gusty wind-bullying month of August had given way to September and the early heat of the lowveld summer was in the air. Harry Kenyon still had difficulty in realising that five years in another country had gone by and that he was back in the heart of the African bush he

loved, alongside his oldest friend, who had not changed in the slightest. To Harry it was like a time warp.

"Do you not believe me? Are you saying that this is an old woman's ramblings?"

He made his voice indignant. Full of mock outrage. Kashili took a long drag at his cigarette, one out of the carton of Springbok that Harry had brought with him. The white paper was stark against the tribal cicatriced ebony of his face. He blew out a long stream of blue smoke, which swirled away in the breeze of the river. He studied the end of his cigarette with great deliberation.

"If you say it is so, then it is so. Who am I to doubt such stories as you have told me? Of great forests, with trees as tall as mountains. Of foxes that fly like birds between the trees. Of hunters that kill with reed pipes and needles. Of people jumping out of *ndeges*, out of the steel birds, and floating like leaves down to earth ..."

Kashili shook his head again, mock seriously.

"*Aizvona!* No, younger traveller of distant lands. Of course I believe you. For you *mukiwas*, you white men, are known to do strange things."

Harry grunted at the double-edged appreciation. His line jerked, once, twice, pulling tight across his fingers. He struck, feeling the hook take purchase, and struck again for security, and began hauling the fish in. As he pulled the line, coiling the retrieved nylon as the fish gave way, he wondered if the old man was settled now. If the wanderlust had weakened and village life had claimed him. As he guided the bream to him through the clean and glinting water of the shallows, he spoke casually.

"My time in your kraal is growing short. Soon I must continue on my journey. I have been away from the country for too long and my eyes are hungry to see how it is. My heart is impatient to return to the wild places that you and I discovered ..."

He paused as he took the fish from the river, removing the hook deftly. He glanced obliquely at Kashili, who stared impassively back at him.

"What about you, *bava*? Father? Are you happy here, with your people? Do you no longer have the hunger to seek out the places where the people are few?"

A flock of open-billed storks flew past them, up river. In the stillness of the day's heat the two men could hear the wind rush of their wing beats. Kashili grunted and shook his head, watching the birds until they were out of sight. When he answered, his voice was soft and held irony.

"*Uvulavula inge u chikosha che wasati.* Now you talk like an old crone. Whilst you have been away I have waited. I have done my duty here. My family lives well. My youngest wife is with child. The other children are growing strong. You have seen how my eldest, my son Shadrek, is as one with the bush. A good hunter already. We want for nothing. But I too hunger for the wild places. Before they are gone ... Before the time comes when a man cannot find a place where people have built their fires already ...!"

He paused, snuffing out the smoked cigarette between hard calloused fingers, and then tapping the little residue tobacco back into the box. With the tobacco of the last smoked cigarettes he would be able to roll at least another one of his own. He cocked an eye at the washed blue glare of the sky.

"It is almost the time of the whole moon, and it is also the time of the year for *sayela*, our fish drive. Before the first rains swell the river. I must help with this, even though the fish are fewer now, poisoned by the big new sugar farms farther up the river ... Then we can go."

They went back to the Nuanetsi first, to the overgrown mounds of earth behind the long closed weather scoured trading store that had once been the centre of Harry's life. The store had been his father's base, his citadel, manned uncomplainingly by his mother whilst Geoffrey Kenyon had forayed out on his hunting, prospecting and exploring

expeditions, returning for the short whirlwind breaks between
journeys. Here, along the wild river and amidst the never
ending expanse of featureless lowveld bush, Harry had grown
up, the only white child for a hundred miles. From his father
and the wild tribal scarred black man who was his constant
shadow he learned about the bush. His mother taught him to
read and write and his learning books were a far cry from the
boring works he would struggle through later at boarding
school. He walked from Cape to Cairo with Grogan, fought the
Matabele and Kikuyu with Boyes, and hunted with Karamoja
Bell, Sutherland and Selous. When his father had departed to
add his bit of mayhem to the Second World War it was just as
though he was off on another wild jaunt. Except that this time
eleven year old Harry wasn't allowed along. And Kenyon senior
never came back. The district priest from Fort Victoria brought
the letter bearing the news that Harry's mother was now a
widow, forwarded from Air Force Headquarters in Thornhill.
Geoffrey Kenyon's last adventure had ended in the blazing
cockpit of a Hurricane over the Bay of Biscay. Less than two
years later Harry's mother had died from a combination of tick
bite fever, solitude, and the debilitating strain of running a
remote trading store on her own. Then there had only been
Kashili.
It seemed, thought Harry Kenyon, as he looked down on the
lichen covered rocks that perched atop the graves, as if there
had always been Kashili.

Old haunts. Bechuanaland, the game swarming hinterland of
the Chobe and Okavango Rivers. Portuguese East Africa, the
Sena Plains, and herds of buffalo three thousand strong with
the snowstorms of cattle egrets whirling above. Elephants on
white Indian Ocean beaches. Back into the Rhodesias, along
the Zambezi, scarred now by the cancer of the great wall that
had spread resolutely across Kariba Gorge. Harry shot seldom,
just for the pot. It was as if the man hunting in Malaya had
served as a catharsis, purging out of him any want to slay. And

the tusk they had found, lying in solitary splendour there alongside the Angwa River, had truly seemed like an omen.

From up on the baking rock-strewn heights of the gorge, Harry had looked down sadly at the massive concrete wall below. It was October 1958 and the big news was out. The wall was ready. Progress had triumphed. Before the end of the year the wall would be totally sealed and the Zambezi would be trapped. Harry had sighed and stared westwards across the shimmering heat haze of the condemned valley, where the river flowed placidly. Gone, he thought. Hundreds of miles of wild Africa, gone forever. And what about the animals? What are they going to do? Who's told them about it all?

He'd heard that a skeleton team of Game Department men had a base of sorts down on the lower slopes of the escarpment hills fringing the Zambezi. More out of curiosity than anything else the ex-crocodile hunter, ivory poacher, soldier and bush wanderer had gone down there. His reputation had preceded him. Harry Kenyon's name and the valley were closely linked, along with ivory and crocodile skins. What the hell did he find of interest in a Game Department base camp? Harry left. He made a last pilgrimage upriver, past the Sanyati and Umi Rivers, walking the trails one last time before the lake started forming in a few weeks time. Drowning that part of the valley. The wild animals were plentiful, congregating along the Zambezi in those final parched weeks before the rains came. Harry noted the concentrations with mounting concern. How would they react to the flood that was imminent? How could they know how far and how fast the water would spread? How in God's name were a dozen or so Game Department men going to help them?

Harry and Kashili went back to Kariba. Back to the Game Department base. The final sealing of the dam wall was three days away. His reception was the same. Suspicion and dislike. The wolf among the shepherds, the flock vulnerable. He held the team leader's stare and braced himself for the violence he could see building behind his eyes. The ranger was older than him, but he was hard and leathery, his knuckles scarred. Harry was aware of his reputation too, stubborn and ready with his fists, a boxer of note, and a dedicated ranger. Harry motioned at his weapons in the jeep, moving his chin slightly, watching the ranger's eyes.

"I know what you're thinking. You're wrong about it. Keep my guns. Lock them away. I hardly use them these days ..."

Rupert Fothergill's eyes narrowed. He waited, remaining silent. Harry broke the eye contact, nodding past the ranger at the blue haze of the valley behind him.

"You're going to need every man you can get, if you're going to save any of those animals out there. I'm volunteering our services, mine and Kashili's. Free. No pay, we'll work for nothing. Just food."

Fothergill watched him, unmoving. Finally.

"For how long? Till you've worked out where the elephant are moving away to?"

His voice was harsh, angry. Harry sighed, and for an instant considered laying down the first punch. He saw Fothergill interpret the feeling and tense. To hell with it, he thought bitterly.

"Mister, I know you won't believe it, but that valley, and the game in it, means as much to me as it does to you. You're so damn sure I'm out to poach your animals, yet what proof have you got? What information has your department got about my doings over the last three years? Since I've been back in the country? Not a damned thing! Because I haven't touched one croc or one elephant. I haven't shot an elephant in over nine years!"

Harry paused and shook his head.

"Anyway, fuck you. Do it yourself."

He turned away, back to the jeep. He half expected an attack, was disappointed when it did not materialise. Angrily he climbed behind the steering wheel.

"Kenyon!"

He flicked a glance at Fothergill. He hadn't heard the ranger follow him. He stared at the man, seeing him sort out what he was about to say and knowing that the ranger was having difficulty in finding any middle ground. His tone was still uncompromising, but now there was the smallest hint of uncertainty.

"You're either very smart, or I'm dumb ... or both. But you're right. When that river starts to back up I'm going to need a lot more help than I've got. Or will get. So, if you're offering your services, I'll take them. But I'm warning you ..."

He stopped as Harry put up a hand.

"Save your breath, mister. Let time tell. I'll be on that new bloody lake long after you've gone home."

He cocked one eyebrow at the sombre-faced Game Department man.

"Look at it this way. At least you and your bunch will know where exactly I am, for a change."

Almost five years later, at the end of Operation Noah, when the vast new lake had stopped growing, putting a new mass of 177 thousand million tons on the earth's crust, backing up behind a wall that was the largest man-made construction since the pyramids, they were still there. Rupert Fothergill and Harry Kenyon were the longest serving members of the rescue team. In uneasy truce at first, the ex-poacher and senior game ranger sweated out the weeks and months. Harry's irritation at the rescue leader's stubborn mistrust was tempered by his admiration of the older man's dedication. Rupert's suspicions were gradually eroded by Harry's tireless rescue efforts.

One evening, six months after the start of the rescue operation, Harry arrived late back at their most recent base on the latest drowning hill top. Laid carefully atop his bedroll were his rifle and shotgun, gleaming dully, newly cleaned. Rupert was studiously writing up the day's log by the light of a hurricane lamp. Three months later Harry was elevated from unpaid volunteer to temporary ranger status. By the end of the first traumatic year of Noah he was placed on permanent staff. Ranger Harry Kenyon had been accepted into the fold. Kashili politely refused the offer to become a senior game scout. He had, he explained to the chief game officer who was visibly surprised at the refusal, enough on his hands looking after the young man Kenyon.

June 1963. The rescue operation was over. Over six thousand animals had been saved. The team had split up. The Cantrell brothers, Graham, Frank, Tinkey, Ron, Len, California, Langton, Kadigidigi ... all were scattered across the country in new posts. Rupert and Harry brewed a final cup of tea on The Point below the hulking mass of the dam wall. Rupert had been posted back to headquarters in Salisbury, to put some semblance of order into his five years of neglected paperwork. He was not happy about it. Paperwork was not his strong point and a headquarters posting didn't bear thinking about. Harry was due to leave that day for Wankie National Park, the great, hot, arid, sandy stretch of wasteland that only the bushmen had inhabited thirty five years ago when Ted Davison had been sent there with an annual budget of £500 to get the place developed. Neither man was happy about leaving the valley. Harry, at least, was grateful that he had got the Wankie posting. It was one of the wilder National Parks of the country, even as developed as it now was. He felt sorry for Rupert, going to join old Ted Davison who was spending his last years with the department dying a slow death behind a desk. With luck, Harry thought now, it's a temporary posting. He's too good a field man to keep at headquarters, and he's still younger than Davison. Once he's sorted ...

The grinding of gears of a vehicle as it struggled down the rough bush track to the remnants of the base interrupted his thoughts. Landrover, he thought. More than one ... two or more. The two rangers stood against the edge of the lake watching as three Landrovers ground up out of a ravine and emerged into the camp clearing. They were dark green, with Northern Rhodesian registration plates.

"Looks like a visitation from our opposite Game Department," Rupert murmured.

"Wonder what the occasion is?"

Harry watched wordlessly. There was something familiar about the man driving the leading vehicle. The small convoy halted. Harry caught the flash of a grin in the dim interior and waited as the door was thrust open. He recognised John Johnson immediately despite the eight year gap since he had last seen him. Which, he recalled now, as the short powerful man strode across to him, was at my SAS farewell. To what do I owe this honour ...?

"Don't look so bloody miserable, Harry. You look as though you've lost a lion and found a rabbit. What about a big smile for an old mate!"

Harry laughed, while he still wondered at the visit. He could see there were men filling the three Landrovers.

"Hello, John. it's good to see you. What brings the SAS to these peaceful parts?"

They shook hands. John Johnson chuckled, shaking his head.

"I'm out of the Squadron. Things are too bloody peaceful. A short spell up on the Congo border a couple of years ago, when Hammarskjold's plane crashed and blood pressures were up, and that's about it. A man could die of boredom ..."

"We're off up to join Mike Hoare in the Congo. He's recruiting mercenaries to fight for Tshombe. It's a good contract and we've been promised plenty of action."

He squinted at Harry in the bright morning sun.

"I heard you were finished down here, so I thought I'd look you up on the way north and see if you wanted to come along. There're still positions for senior NCO's and officers. We could use you up there, Harry."

He grinned and winked.

"Quite apart from the fact that I get paid a commission for every soldier I bring up there. How about it, Harry? Feel like doing a bit of soldiering again?"

Harry grinned, then laughed outright. John Johnson hadn't changed

"Thanks for the invite. But no thanks. I'm out of playing soldiers, John, since the Malayan campaign. I'm a game ranger now, and I'm happy as a sand boy in my patch of bush here ..."

He swirled the tea leaves at the bottom of his battered enamel mug and flicked them away.

"You go and enjoy your war. Mind you don't get caught by the Balubas!"

John Johnson shrugged and grinned amiably.

"Okay, sunshine. Just thought I'd give it a try. You're bloody wasted, nursemaiding animals."

He flicked a salute at the two men.

"Cheers, gentlemen. Keep watching the newspapers for the exploits of Five Commando. You'll know where to find us, Harry, if you change your mind."

Rupert and Harry watched as the vehicles drove out of the base. A fish eagle screamed, its call echoing across the new lake. Rupert glanced at his companion.

"No hankering at all, to get back into it?"

Harry shook his head gently.

"Each to his own. I enjoyed my days with the SAS. I'm fine where I am now. Leave the soldiering to the soldiers."

The float plane lurched as it hit a thermal, disturbing Harry's thoughts. He sighed, smiling wryly to himself. Easier said than done, old son. It seems as if fate has always tried to juggle me back into soldiering. Being a game ranger certainly didn't mean I was out of the war games. Because while I was at Wankie I was back into it. Back into action. Couldn't really stay out of it. Tracker Harry Kenyon. And, like Scratch Peters said a couple of weeks back, before he gave me the sales pitch about rejoining, we were sure busy. The Tracker Combat Unit covered a lot of ground, and we nailed the bastards. Of course, you were successful in picking up a couple more scars for your troubles, but by then the incursions were pretty much sorted out. So there was no more cowboys and indians when you came out of hospital. Peace and quiet again. And anyway, they gave you invalid status, with all the holes in you ... half your gut shot away. And a new posting. To the best game reserve in the country. Back to the valley. He sighed again, restless now. *I wonder what the hell are the ramifications surrounding Scratch Peters' visit?* The drone of the engine changed pitch and the float plane tilted. Up past the tawny swirl of the girl's windswept hair he could see Kariba village. He grinned suddenly. *Kenyon, he thought, what more could you want? The best posting in the department. Nemana, the most beautiful place on this earth. Just waiting to be shown to this awfully beautiful lady who wants nothing more than to take pictures of your beautiful animals for the rest of the world to see.*

*****

Harry eased the Landrover to a halt on the gravel verge of the road. Below them, to the right, the escarpment dropped away sharply to sweep down to the valley floor in a series of undulating brown-hued colours.

They had left Kariba in the soft dark of early morning, and now as they climbed out of the Landrover the sun was newly risen. The air was still clean and sharp, and the grey-green blur of the valley bush spreading as far as the eye could see was not yet distorted by the heat waves. Peta took a deep breath, savouring the smell of the early morning valley bushveld. She gazed wonderingly at the panorama, her eyes drinking in the space of it. There was nothing but bush stretching away endlessly, distinct and sharp to the eye in the near areas of the escarpment, fading away into the blur of distance. Away, away to the east was a brief sparkle of sunlight on water, and the darker hue of the vegetation must be where the Zambezi flowed, she thought.

Kashili cast about the ground, checking automatically for spoor patterns. He paused in his inspection to take some snuff from the grysbuck horn, his hands following the ritual whilst his eyes swept the valley below. Vultures spiralled gently on the first thermals, not high yet, still searching for the currents. A dog baboon barked hoarsely from a nearby thicket. Guinea fowl chattered. The distant scream of elephant floated up to them from the valley. Peta took another deep breath and sighed. Harry watched her, noting the peace on her face mingling with the exhilaration, and grinned.

"Welcome to the Zambezi Valley. Nemana is down there, about two hours drive away."

"It's too beautiful for words. I don't know why I waited so long."

There was a Landrover parked in front of the orange and black striped boom at Entry Gate One. Harry's glance swept the vehicle automatically as he parked beside it in the speckled shade of the great baobab that dominated the camp. There were two people in the front, their silhouettes hazy through the dazzle of the sun reflecting off the windows, but Harry could see that the person in the passenger's seat was a black man. A white man was signing the Arrivals books balanced on the steering wheel. Harry glanced at the registration plates, surprised to see the Botswana prefix. It was seldom that people from the neighbouring country, with its own impressive wild life sanctuaries, came as far afield as Nemana. He could see the outline of a ragged unkempt beard on the white man. The man turned to glance across at them when the game scout on duty saluted Harry. A wave of anger surged through the warden as recognition struck. He saw Alex Gant's eyes widen as he in turn recognised Harry.

"Wait here, please."

Harry's voice was tight. Peta watched as he left their Landrover and walked around to the driver's side of the other vehicle, wondering at the sudden change in him. Relaxed and happy he had been. Now she could see that he was coiled and tense, his expression bleak. Harry took the Visitors book from the game scout and scanned the page. Gant's scrawl was the first entry of the day. Despite the request in the book for visitors to print their details clearly, Gant's writing was illegible. Harry's anger mounted and he struggled to keep himself in check. He was aware of the other man's scrutiny. He looked up to meet his gaze, noting his dislike mirrored in Gant's eyes.

"What do you want at Nemana, Gant?"

Alex Gant shrugged, letting a sardonic smile ease on to his face. "The same as anyone else. I'm a tourist. I haven't seen this part of the world for years. So, me and old Jackson here thought we'd have a peek for old times sake. Is that a problem, Kenyon?"

The last sentence was wrapped in a sneer. Harry shook his head.

"For you, maybe. Not for me."

Harry took the stub of pencil from the game scout and wrote rapidly in the Visitors book. Then he gave the book to the scout and spoke to Gant again.

"You're not setting foot in this Park, Gant. You're banned from entering Nemana. If you're found within the boundaries you'll be arrested."

He saw the fury mottle Gant's face.

"Who the hell do you think you are, Kenyon? Jesus Christ? What makes you think you can call any shots here?"

Harry returned the savage stare.

"I'm warden of Nemana, Gant. And Nemana stretches from here through to the Chingusa. It's my territory. If I hear so much as a whisper that you're sneaking around, I'll have your balls."

Gant laughed hoarsely.

"Yes? Like before, Kenyon? Wasting the taxpayers' hard earned money trying to nail me in court. I can see you still think you're hot stuff. But are you? Do you reckon you, or anyone, can keep me out of Nemana if I want to operate in there?"

Harry took a deep breath, fighting the urge to reach through the vehicle window and seize the poacher by his beard and slam his head into the windscreen. Instead he spoke quietly to the game scout.

"Corporal, I think I can hear your call-sign being called up on the radio. You had better go and answer it."

When the man had left, after hesitating only slightly because he knew the radio could not be heard from the boom, Harry addressed Gant. His voice was soft, but ragged and intense.

"Hear me, Gant. If you come into this Park I will shoot you on sight. Do you understand me? I will hunt you down like the vermin you are and cull you. No arrests and court room theatre. Just a bullet in you."

Despite himself Gant recoiled at the vehemence in the warden's tone. Harry stepped back from the Landrover and altered his tone to a normal pitch.

"Now get out of here."

Alex Gant let his gaze sweep over the warden. Then he hawked and spat into the dust at Harry's feet.

"We'll see, Warden Kenyon. We'll see about that."

Harry stood and watched until the poacher's Landrover had disappeared from his sight. Then he took a deep breath, letting the air out slowly, trying to get some sort of control back. Great, he reflected. Bloody terrific. That's all I need. Alex Gant in Nemana. Why is that son of a bitch in this part of the world? Trying to get into my Park? The Big Four? Has he got wind of them? The bastard. Thank Christ the collaring team will be here in a few days. We're going to have to watch those tuskers like hawks if Gant's around. He took another deep breath, looking across at his Landrover. Kashili leaned against the back of the cab, indolently paring his nails with his bush knife. He glanced pointedly off in the direction that Gant had taken and then spat. Peta's eyes were big with concern as she regarded Harry. He grinned then. The beauty and the beast, he thought. No. The two beauties, in their own special ways. He thrust the feeling of premonition aside.

CHAPTER FIFTEEN

Today the buffalo was hidden beneath a fluttering squabbling mass of vultures. Their hissing, squalking arguments floated over the sun-beaten flood plain. Peta thought they looked like a massive dingy brown feather duster being shaken. Around the perimeter of the jostling vultures the marabou storks waited like bored funeral attendants, bald old man's testicles crops swinging emptily. Harry let the Landrover drift to a stop near the mêlée. More vultures rested heavily in the surrounding trees, already replete from their meal.

Yesterday they had seen the kill, just after first light. Harry had heard the communication grunts of the lions in the pre-dawn blackness, lying newly awake in the tent that had been pitched near his bungalow. Then had followed ominous silence. He had dressed and washed and called softly to Peta, bedded in his quarters. She too had been awake. They drove upriver from Shingela, aiming for the area of the last lion calls. The greyness of first light was rapidly giving way to the clarity of the sun's soon emergence in the east when they came upon the small herd of bachelor bulls grouped defensively. Pawing the ground and noses high as they quested for scent, they formed a dark knot on the edge of a grass rippling marsh. Harry felt a twinge of pity. He knew the animals well, had followed the fortunes of the old buffalo continually. There were seven; there had been ten at the start of the year. And now maybe six, he reflected, as he picked up the first of the cats. A lioness, she flowed sinuously through the marsh grass, eyes intent on the buffalo, only the occasional tense flicker of her rounded ears betraying her position. Harry searched for the others. A minute went by. Two. Dawn bled across the sky like a fresh wound. Francolin called stridently. Zebra stallions barked shrilly. Harry saw the dun blur of a second lion just as the buffalo lost their nerve and broke their formation to run. It was what the lions were counting on. While the bulls held their ground, standing in a phalanx, shoulder to shoulder with horns presented to the enemy, they offered a formidable target. When they were running, lumbering, muscle-bound, dark, heavy, away to safety, they were vulnerable. Harry and Peta saw the lions break cover, vague tawny forms emerging out of the ground in a shallow pincered attacking formation. Harry counted seven lionesses running, a male away off on the far side of the herd standing tensed. One of the bulls was dropping back, falling behind his companions. Harry recognised the broken blunted tip of the left horn, the massive boss covered with the green excrescence of age, the healed scars on one flank, legacy of past brushes with death, and his heart went out to the old bull. The buffalo lumbered desperately hump backed on but the lions were up to him now, had singled him out at the first sign of lagging. A young lioness, too keen and inexperienced, was sent tumbling by a flying rear hoof, but another was on the bull's back, fastened to the black hide, one massive paw hooking over across the buffalo's face and then both animals were down in an explosion of dust that glowed crimson in the fresh rays of the sun. The buffalo was covered by the tawny forms now and a long gurgling bellow issued from the mêlée. Harry let out the long breath he had been holding. He watched the cats swarming over their quarry, counting them again, noting age, sex, looking for signs of pregnancy or swollen teats that indicated cubs were around. Beside him Peta shivered.

Today, a day and a half later, the lions were gone, and the hyenas and smaller scavengers had already had their turn. Now the vultures were in full attendance. A big lappetfaced volplaned down on to the edge of the jostling hissing swarm and advanced threateningly on the birds, massive nine foot wing

span displayed, head thrust forward. As smaller vultures gave way the bird gained access to its chosen part of the carcass.
"Uggh."
Peta wrinkled her nose.
"They are horrible. Repulsive."
Harry raised his eyebrows.
"Why?"
"Well ... look at them. They're obscene the way they squabble over the buffalo."
Harry rubbed his jaw reflectively.
"Can't say I agree with you. I've seen humans perform with less finesse over the dead. Not to mention the wrangles that go on over deceased estates and wills. The birds are just eating, which we all do to stay alive. The buffalo eats grass, the lions eats the buffalo, the hyenas, jackals, vultures and ants have the remains. The cow eats grass, we eat the cow, but when we die we get stuck in a jar or a hole in the ground. Which is a bit of a waste really."
Peta shook her head firmly.
"It *is* horrible the way they swarm over the remains. Almost unnerving, in a way. It's a wonder they manage to eat anything the way they push and shove and curse each other."
Harry smiled at her, remembering that even in the previous dawn's unjust first light, hauled out into the day with little chance to perform a woman's various miracles with her looks, she still had looked bloody gorgeous. And so it was now, in the harsh unrelenting heat of midday.
"It looks much worse than it is. They argue a bit, sure. It's natural ..."
Harry's smile widened.
"Have you ever seen a supermarket on a crowded shopping day? That really brings out the best in humans ... everybody slamming and clanging with those damn trolleys that never go where they're aimed. Or a bunch of women at a choice sale? Then you see some squabbling and pushing and shoving ... makes these fellows quite genteel by comparison."

Peta giggled, shrugging her acceptance of his comparison. He felt unreasonably pleased that he'd made her laugh. He pointed out at the vultures.

"There's actually a remarkable degree of order there. Fighting is usually between vultures of the same species. On that kill now there are four types of vulture, and they have arrived in a sequence. Usually the smaller species arrive at the kill first, the white headed and the hooded, and they are the ones who check out the scene ... watching for predators that still may be around protecting the kill, checking to see if the carcass, if it's not a kill, is in fact dead. The next to arrive, normally, are the white backed. The biggest vulture, the lappetfaced ... like the big fellow who just came in, is usually the last one on the kill. Although when he does arrive, he takes over the show, pecking and shoving all his smaller cousins out the way."

Harry paused, as a flurry of feathers erupted out of the scrum. Peta watched them, wondering which of them was which.

"Why do they arrive in that order? What decides that one type of vulture gets on to a kill before another? It looks very much like first come first served to me."

"Flying patterns, mostly, I think. If you spend any amount of time in the bush you watch the birds a lot. The smaller vultures patrol a lower area of the sky, above the hawks and eagles, but below the large white backs and lappetfaced. It's my guess that the first level of vultures react to the eagles ... say the bateleur, who is a low cruiser, and so the chain reaction goes. One level of vultures watching the next and all reacting accordingly. It makes sense for the bigger vultures, with their wider wing spans, to be at the top of the umbrella. Certainly there seems to be a consistency in the arrival patterns, from my observations."

Harry paused, his hand on the door catch.

"It doesn't stop there. Each vulture species tends to eat off different parts of a carcass."

Peta frowned.

"But meat is meat, surely?"

"Well, yes ... but, like the cuts we buy from a butcher, there are lots of parts. And the different vultures go for different aspects of the kill."
Harry grinned at her, seeing her distaste for the birds now mingling with grudging interest.
"I'd like to see if there's anything worth retrieving off the bull. I.have a friend who would enjoy a few bits of meat. If you're still interested I'll carry on about vultures later."
Peta glanced enquiringly at him, making a small moue of distaste.
"I am. Is your friend that hungry?"
Harry chuckled, climbing out of the Landrover.
"Sure. Methuselah will eat anything. I'll introduce you this evening, if he's around."
They drove back to camp as the sun dropped and the day cooled, bringing the magic soft light of day's end. Ahead of the Landrover a herd of zebra stampeded across the track, their stripes creating a surrealistic frieze as they traversed the deep shadows of late afternoon. Hordes of purple-hued guinea fowl scratched across the soft earth of the flood plain and innumerable troops of baboons grubbed below the great dark evergreens. A small herd of sable, a majestic sweeping horned bull and his harem, trotted away from the vehicle's intrusion, whilst impala leaped and bounced along in tandem with their passage. There is, Peta thought, as she looked about her at the teeming wildlife, a different feeling in the air as sundown draws near. The animals are on the move and you can see so much more now and in early morning, but there's a tension in the air now that you can't feel in the morning. It's as though the animals know that darkness brings a new round of danger, a new battle for survival. They somehow look as if they're gearing themselves up for the latest attacks that must come in the night. In the mornings there is a different atmosphere, a feeling of relief almost. As if they're thankful at having made it through another tooth and claw filled night ... Oh dear, Peta Holt, she silently remonstrated herself. You are being

sentimental and silly. Anthropomorphic is the word Mister Kenyon would use. Putting words in the animals' mouths. Four days down here in paradise and you're talking for the animals. You are hooked, Peta my girl. Nemana has you by the heartstrings. Why, oh why, haven't you been back to the valley before? What a magnificent book a person could put together about this place, let alone a magazine feature. A year, two years ... just taking photographs of Nemana through the seasons. Two years of non-stop photographs of the wildlife here. With this man next to you to show you the animals and tell you all about them. Oh yes, what about that, Peta Holt? That crept up pretty damn smartly, did it not? I wonder how Harry would feel about your getting underfoot for two years? How about it, Warden Kenyon? Feel like a surrogate wife for a while, hmmm? Cut that out right now, girl! Four days in the valley and you're going loopy already. What will you be like in another week? And what would the man think of your ...

Peta felt her stomach contract as she saw the great grey bulk of an elephant materialise out of the shade of a trio of ebonies on to the track ahead. Harry stopped the Landrover, watching the animal, eyes sweeping automatically to check for any more elephants in the scrub alongside the track. The elephant turned and shook massive ragged ears at them and advanced purposefully along the track towards the vehicle. Peta felt her breath catch in her throat and her heart started banging against her ribcage. She glanced at Harry. He was watching the closing elephant with a half smile quirking his mouth. Feeling the weight of her look he winked and indicated the elephant with his chin.

"Young bull. Showing his oats. I'll give him a yard or so more to test his nerves before I back up and let him have the best of the day."

She brought her glance back to the animal, which now looked as big as a house. At a half dozen paces it stopped and shook its head again, ears wallop-slapping like distant thunder, dust flying. He stood tall, looking down his trunk at them. As quickly as it had come at them, it turned aside and made off, head and tasselled tail aloft in consternation.

Peta let out a long ragged breath. Harry grinned at her.

"You okay?"

She nodded.

"When elephant get that close I get a little weak at the knees. They're so damned big."

"That's good. As long as you keep a healthy respect for elephant you're less likely to land in trouble with them. It's the people who become casual with them who end up getting trodden on. By the way, the collaring team arrives tomorrow, so I'll be introducing you to our 'Big Four' soon."

She smiled, waiting for her stomach to unknot.

"That's terrific. I hope no one gets casual."

The sun teetered upon the distant mauve massifs of the northern escarpment, casting a molten crimson path across the fading pewter of the river. Smoke from the seasonal bush fires hung like blue mist over the far landscape, deepening the twilight prematurely. Harry stood at the edge of the indented shoreline that formed a backwater from the main channel and whistled again, a long lilting call that echoed across the still water. Out in midstream between shoreline and island a sudden swirl boiled the surface. Harry waited, watching the river. The surface swirled again as a heavy body twisted beneath it, and the spreading ripples and eddies were the colour of claret in the last of the sun's reflection. He whistled and hunkered down beside the water's edge, motioning Peta down beside him. A few paces out, in the shallower water, a shadow moved. Peta gasped as a great barrel-like shape had emerged and then sank back beneath the surface. The head, all whiskers and big bulbous eyes, had scrutinised them matter of factly. For a split second of horror she had thought it was a hippo, because of its very size, before reason told her that the shallows made it impossible to be so. Harry chuckled softly and tossed a lump of meat out on to the water. Immediately there was a gurgle and a mist of spray and the sucking sound of displaced water as the giant vundu swirled at the surface again and the cavernous mouth closed over the meat bobbing on the water. The soft evening light glinted off the brown mottled body as the fish lay motionless on the surface watching the humans. Its black dorsal fin swayed gently from side to side, high above the water.

Harry held out a second piece of meat, clasping it lightly so it dangled from his fingers. A flick of its fan-like tail surged the fish closer to the man and the offering, the wide mouth gaping as the man-sized fish twisted and took the meat, rolling lazily to submerge with the booty. Harry offered a chunk of the buffalo meat to Peta.

"Here, take it. It's the best way to Methusalah's heart. He's the biggest vundu I've ever seen, easily 200 pounds. Been living in this stretch of river for years. Kashili and I have been bringing him occasional snacks for a couple of years. It took a long time for him to accept us."

Peta took the meat gingerly.

"Hold it by that piece of sinew. Let it hang. Methuselah's not awfully fussy. He'd take your hand as well."

The vundu eased up out of the water again and she felt its power as it drew the meat into its maw. As it dropped back below the surface the water surged in a miniature whirlpool. The sun had gone completely now, leaving the last indigo miasma of final twilight. A lion roared from the far bank, the sound reverberating across the river.

They walked back to the house in companionable silence. Peta felt at peace with the world, marvelling that another day had slipped past so rapidly. It felt as if she had only just arrived in the country. But the wildlife conference, the preliminary meetings with Garnet Clayton at the headquarters, her first sight of the sere winter-brown countryside as the ageing Viscount droned into Salisbury, had happened over two weeks ago. Time had evaporated with the first days of the African summer. And yet, paradoxically, a part of her felt as if she'd been her forever. Her days down at Nemana had drifted into each other. Day into night into day. She couldn't remember looking at her watch once. She was awake with the dawn, shiver keen with anticipation for the day ahead, and almost before she knew it, the sun was sliding past the northern rim of the escarpment. The diary she had started on her arrival at Nemana, a habit she followed on all her travels, was already a dozen pages along, written complement to the pictures she was taking. She glanced askance at Harry walking beside her, seeing for the hundredth time the easy loose young boy's stride. She'd observed him enough by now to know that the relaxed aura about him didn't stop his audio-visual reflexes from working. Now his gaze was automatically sweeping the river frontage, the distant smoke from the married quarters fires, the track that led downstream to the tourist camp, the vague forms of the rangers sitting on his verandah. He grunted softly now, glancing at her, catching her scrutiny and nodding ahead.

"Charlie Parker, with young Taylor in support tonight. You've made a conquest there I'd say. I can't remember when I've had the pleasure of Charlie's company three evenings in succession."

Peta laughed softly.

"I've gathered he's the Lothario of your band of merrie men. He is a little obvious. I suppose I should be flattered. What do I do to back him off? I don't want to hurt any feelings down here. I don't want to upset the equilibrium of Shingela Base."

Harry shrugged.

"Tell him you've left your heart in San Francisco, or Paris, or wherever. I don't know. I'm sure you can handle it with the right style."

She glanced quizzically at him, looking for more signs of the sarcasm she thought she had heard, surprised at this new cynicism. It was something that had not surfaced before. He slowed his stride and reached out to put one large hand gently on her shoulder, turning slightly so he could see her clearly.

"That was a compliment, by the way. It wasn't meant as anything else."

He took a breath. She could feel the imprint of his hand, wide palm, fingers, pressing warmly through the soft cotton of her bush shirt.

"Now is as good a time as any to say that it's good having you down here. I did have my doubts originally ... the usual paranoia about journalists, especially lady ones, underfoot all the time; the ramifications of a woman down for any length of time on an all male station. The usual chauvinist stuff, I suppose you would say. But it's been a pleasure. You're not only beautiful, Miss Holt. You have style. Of that I'm sure all of my team will agree, not just Charlie. They're all a little hooked on you."

Her shoulder was burning where his hand rested, and she could feel her breathing deteriorate. Her stomach squeezed and did a series of somersaults, much in the way it had done with the elephant earlier in the day, and for an agonising instant she thought her knees would give way. Ohhh, she wailed silently, Harry Kenyon ... I think I'm done for. I guess mother passed it on to me. I have been trying to ignore it, right from day one, listening to you talk about all your animals. I've tried to ignore it. Because I don't want to complicate anyone's life, especially my own. But I'm not winning. And now, out of nowhere, we have this ... this ... This what, exactly, Peta? Hey? A casual compliment from the big bwana and you're looping the loop. 'They're all a little hooked on you, Miss Holt.' *Really! Is that so, Mister Kenyon?* That's nice. But how about you, Harry Kenyon? Any room amongst all the animals governing your heart for little old me? Because my heart isn't in San Francisco, or anybloodywhere else. Because it is very firmly down here in the Zambezi Valley.

An owl called from the darkened foliage above the bungalow. Bats swooped. A night ape screamed. Harry took his hand from her shoulder as they arrived at the gauzed verandah. She could still feel its warmth.

The forming moon cast a blue pallor over the valley. Stentorian hippo talk echoed back and forth over the river, shrill then deep. A leopard wood-sawed its way past camp. Harry lay awake staring up through the dark at the canvas. He had lain thus for two hours, listening to the night chorus, waiting for it to lull him to sleep. A fishing owl moaned. He got up and stood listening, testing the darkness. Hippo grazed behind the bungalow. He could hear the grass being cropped. He left the tent and paced the few yards to the high wind-scoured bank of the river, feeling an errant breeze whisper over his naked frame. Out on the moonlit sand a small herd of buffalo bulls trudged back from the river. There were six, and he thought it was the herd from yesterday. The shadows of a pair of plovers dipped and wheeled, clamouring as the buffalo passed close to their nest scrape. Fireflies danced over the water. He took a deep breath, savouring the smell of the river and the night air. At the edge of his vision something flickered, making him tense. A light, very low, was on in his, now Peta's bedroom. It flickered fluidly again as he looked, the erratic glow of a hurricane lamp. He was surprised he hadn't noticed it when he had first emerged from the tent. He wondered if Peta had fallen asleep with the lamp on. He watched for several minutes, wondering if she was asleep, or reading in its wan light, deciding whether to move closer and establish whether it needed to be put out. He waited another few minutes, without seeing any sign of movement. Both the lamp itself and the bed were just out of sight behind the low window sill. The windows were bare. He had never bothered with curtains. A breeze rustled the leaves of the mahogany beside the bungalow, and the light wavered erratically, throwing grotesque shadows across the room. He was sure she was asleep.

A hyena sniggered and chittered somewhere across the near office block. Harry padded silently across the grass to the rectangle of light. One of Peta's cameras came into view, hanging by its canvas strap from the back of a chair. He could see part of her inert form, shrouded by a single light sheet. Harry stopped, aware suddenly of his nakedness. For a moment he stood unsure, feeling a little foolish with his dithering, deciding that he'd better go and put on his shorts in case she woke up. The hyena giggled again, closer and louder, a banshee chorus up and down the scale. The legs beneath the sheet swept aside and suddenly Peta was standing at the window, peering out into the darkness. Harry stood frozen, mortified, transfixed as much by her sudden movement as by her total nakedness. The vision of sleep-tousled hair, huge eyes peering out at the night, at him, high upthrust breasts with peaked nipples reacting to the night air, the dark bush of hair below a firm sculpted belly stabbed through his senses and even as he wondered what the hell to do next, he felt his breathing go shallow and his throat constrict. And still he stood staring. She saw him then, as her eyes adjusted to the shadow of the mahogany canopied above. Harry saw her flinch, heard her gasp, and his mind reeled in his turmoil ... to run, get his mouth working to apologise, to drag his eyes from her nude form. He shook his head, trying to clear his brain. The hyena laughed again, as though in shrill mockery. Peta was staring open-mouthed at him, the first shock leaving her face, leaving an intensity Harry couldn't read. He prayed that the earth would swallow him up, that she wouldn't start having hysterics, that he had on some clothes ... And still he gaped. Peta moved closer to the open mosquito-gauzed window, and he could see her breasts tremble as she took a breath. She stood up against the screen and he could see her nipples pucker at the touch of the cold wire threads. Her eyes were sweeping over his nakedness. He wished he could move. Do something. His limbs felt leaden, and yet he was sure his legs would buckle if he did move. He realised that he was sweating, and he was aware of the heat in his groin. And still he stared at her, mesmerised. His breathing roared loud in his ears.

"Harry ..."

Her voice was choked. He could see a mercuric thread of saliva glisten between her lips, see the rise and fall of her breasts. As if from afar, from another planet, he saw himself move, crossing the space separating him from the window. He felt as if he had run a mile through sand. He shook his head again and put one hand up to the window, fingers splayed across the gauze, feeling the warmth from her breast, denied the touch, smelling the scent from her. Eyes inches apart, feeling the other's breath hot on their face, they stared at each other. Peta's hand came up between her body and the gauze, reaching his hand, flattening against it.

"This ... I ... you're ..."

Harry heard his voice croak. His breath rasped. His body felt as though it were engulfed in flames, and he knew the heat in his groin had stirred to full arousal. Peta placed her lips close to the gauze, eyes locked on his, and her voice was ragged.

"Harry, please. This is torture. I can't wait any longer ..."

He nodded, unable to talk. Hands shaking, fumbling with the screen, about to smash his way through it as it finally opened and he slid it up, reaching for her, hands grasping at him as he stumbled into the room, trembling, pale curves against the dark shadows. The light flickered violently and went out. A gasp, an intake of breath. The hyena giggled insanely, away in the distance now.

The helicopter, looking like some great bulbous-eyed insect, clattered up over the ridge line, hugging the contours of the lower escarpment. Sunlight bounced off the plexiglass bubble and the hammering chatter of the Bell 47's piston engine reached a new stridency as the aircraft flared and dropped gently on to the faint bush track. Debris peppered the waiting team and the mopane scrub whipped and lashed frenziedly in the air rush of the rotors. The tumult subsided as the motor died and the blur of the main blade gained definition with each slowing revolution. Inside the small helicopter the pilot and the warden inspected the tattered map attached to a clipboard resting on Harry's knees. The ground team saw the teeth flash of the warden's grin and saw an answering thumbs up sign from the pilot. The rotors came to a drooping halt and the two men clambered from the craft to join the small knot of people waiting near the Landrovers. Harry looked immensely pleased. "Okay, we've found number three. He's looking well. Marula is just over the ridge, about forty minutes walking time away. The Landrovers may as well stay here, the bush gets pretty thick further on. Everything set on your side, Roscoe?"

The big Parks scientist nodded amiably.

"Ready to roll, Harry. Just lead the way and we'll add Marula to the world of science. If his ivory is anything like the others I reckon you have the best tuskers in the country down here. I'd guess that bull Braystone found on the Lundi a few years back still had the biggest tusks we've ever heard of, but these jumbo of yours aren't far behind. And at least these are alive still, and their ivory isn't hanging on some embassy wall in Washington."

Harry nodded.

"I remember that old bull from my early days. Kashili and I stalked him often when we were down in the lowveld. I used to wonder if he was related to *Dhlulamithi*. He was magnificent. I could never bring myself to drop him. It's unforgivable that some bloody VIP was allowed to kill him. Pity collaring hadn't evolved then. Maybe he'd still be around."

Roscoe Daniels squinted at the sun.

"We'd better move before it gets any warmer. I reckon I could melt. I don't suppose you'd consider having the chopper ferry me across the ridge? In the interests of science, and my legs?"

Harry grinned. Roscoe was always good company, in or out of the bush. His unflagging ebullience was matched by his passion for elephants.

"I've got that chopper for another three days, is all, with a bloody miserable fuel allocation. With a hundred things to do still, when we've finished with our 'Four'. So the taxi service is out, I'm afraid. But I don't mind giving you a piggy back."

Roscoe sighed heavily.

"Ah, well, *c'est la guerre*. Perhaps all is not lost ..."

He beamed at Peta.

"Peta, are you coming along? Please say yes. I must have someone sensible to talk to."

She smiled widely and hefted her camera bag. Roscoe reminded her of a massive jovial Father Christmas.

"Oh, yes. I'm tagging along all right. Wild horses wouldn't keep me away. I want to get pics of the darting of all of the 'Big Four'. For posterity. I can't believe there are more elephants with tusks as huge as the first two we've darted and collared. Why Marula, incidentally?"

Harry watched a pair of red-billed hornbills dip and glide overhead.

"When he was first seen by national parks staff it was the marula season and he was stuffing himself fit to burst in a grove of marula trees. Chiruwe got his name from the area he frequents a lot ... along a tributary of the main river, the Chiruwe. The first bull we darted on this exercise, Katete, is also named after an area. He's our most southern ranging big bull, living mainly in the Katete petrified forest area down near the Chingusa."

Harry smiled at Peta.

"Kabakwe is the fellow we'll collar last. He carries the biggest tusks of the 'Four', and he's the hardest to keep track of. He still wanders over quite a large range, despite his age, and I worry about him the most. Thank God we have the chopper to get up and help locate him. Kashili gave him his name, way back when we were shooting crocodiles on the Zambezi. When Nemana was still known as the Urungwe Area. The name stuck. It means 'The Big One' in his Shangaan language."

He looked around for Kashili. The old tracker was squatting in the meagre shade of a mopane tree, quietly smoking. As Harry's glance found him he nodded his readiness, hooded eyes holding a hint of dry amusement. Harry grinned, noting the hunting spear stuck in the ground, water canteen slung. Waiting.

"After you, old one. I am sorry you have to wait for us. Lead the way. The elephant is over the ridge waiting for you."

Kashili grunted, easing himself upright.

"You are indecently happy ..."

The tracker spoke in his native Shangaan.

"Which is good to see. I hope that your night time hunting has not left you too tired to keep up with an old man like me. Do not worry, little hunter, I will go slowly so that you do not stumble."

So, thought Harry, as the small procession wound its way through the bush, it's that obvious. To Kashili at least. I wonder how observant the rest of them are? I actually thought I was doing a bloody good job of acting naturally with Peta. Being quite proper. But, really and truly, I couldn't give a damn. She's here, for as long as she likes, with me, now. And that's that! Tomorrow the tent comes down. No, today. So, anyone still with any doubts about territory need not surmise any longer. Christ, Peta Holt but you are bloody marvellous. Where have you been all my life? He turned and glanced back along the file of people snaking through the bush, and she met his glance from behind Roscoe and grinned and his heart lurched. He winked broadly and thought, hell Kenyon, but you're a lucky bastard. If she can cook as well as she takes photographs and makes love, I reckon you've hit the jackpot. Thank you, Monica Hutton. Thank you for that one night long ago, and for having a daughter like Peta. Harry Kenyon felt like whistling, but they were close to where the old elephant should be, and he didn't think Kashili would approve.

CHAPTER SIXTEEN

They found him dozing in the shade of a big ebony, trunk hanging limply askew over one inward curving tusk, ears fanning indolently as they provided a blood cooling breeze. It was a tranquil scene. Harry could imagine the old bull dreaming elephant dreams. He felt almost apologetic about the

SAND IN THE WIND

disruption they were about to cause. They stalked upwind to within twelve paces, Roscoe carrying the converted .500 delivery weapon, Harry providing insurance with a department .470. Peta completed the close quarters trio, toting her cameras, whilst the remainder of the team waited further back. Roscoe raised an eyebrow of enquiry at Harry. The warden nodded.

The smack of the dart carrying the seven milligrams of M99 into the wrinkled grey hide was drowned by the flat explosion of the .500. With a bubbling trumpeting scream Marula whirled in a flurry of panic, great pachyderm dreams shattered. Confused, myopic, wavering between flight and confrontation the old bull stood, shuffling this way and that. Searching for the source of this huge alien disturbance. Partially obscured by the thick bole of the ebony, the wind in their favour, the three stood immobile, hardly daring to breathe. Harry offered up a silent prayer. Please God, I know I really have no right to ask anything of you, because I'm an irreverent son of a bitch. But please make him clear off. Just move him on out of here while the drug does its job. Don't let him hear us, or let the wind change. No eyeball to eyeball stuff. I couldn't bear it if he came at us and I had to put him down. Just get him the hell out of here. *Please.*

Marula was backing away. Ears spread, trunk aloft questing for danger smell, he retreated. Head high, throat growling. With a final massive shake of his fanned ears he turned and made off at high speed. *Thanks, God.* Harry let out a great sigh of relief, snicking the safety catch back on. Behind him Peta was shooting with the zoom lens. In those frozen moments of time when the old bull had stood poised between flight and charge, she refrained from clicking the shutter and Harry was pleased with her discipline. Anything could have started the elephant on his earth shaking, steam rollering defence against attack charge.

"Let's go," he murmured, "Now we start earning our money. I hope the drug is sloshing merrily around his system. It could be a long run, otherwise."

200

The drug took twelve minutes to work. They found him down beside an anthill, big logs of tusks ploughed deep into the black loamy earth, twenty minutes later. Immobilised, he loomed peacefully above them as they worked. The pattern of bush sounds, silenced by the shot, had long since returned. Baboons argued, doves called, warthog grunted. It took half an hour to put on the bright coloured heavy plastic collar, take his measurements, examine him for old snare and bullet wounds and mark his tusks. Roscoe held up a hand as he noticed Peta focus her camera on the delicate marking exercise.

"If you don't mind, Peta. It would be better if we kept this part of the operation unrecorded. Much better that way. Hopefully the collar will protect him from safari hunters if he strays out into the concession areas. In the near future we'll be adding radio transmitters to the collars as part of a programme to monitor certain animals more thoroughly. But nothing, really, will deter the dedicated poacher from killing these big fellows. And if one does get shot, it's better if they don't know exactly how we have marked the ivory. The way we're doing it, the tusks can't be sold on the local market. They'd be quickly identified at any department monitored auction, and our undercover unit would soon hear of them if they were put on the market illegally. I'd hate any of your photographs to fall into the wrong hands, giving our little tricks away. Harry?"

He looked at the warden for confirmation. Harry nodded, shaking a palmful of large brown ticks into a battered brown envelope.

"Roscoe's right, Peta. Rather not have those particular shots for posterity. If you've taken any of the others being marked I'd appreciate it if you destroyed the shots involved. There's enough odds stacked against these chaps already."

Peta shook her head.

"Okay, you're preaching to the converted. No pictures."

Harry paused for a moment, looking at her, enjoying her presence here.

As the last of the marking was completed, Peta Holt ran a hand reverently over the wrinkled latticework of the bull's shoulder. May you see many, many more sunsets in your wild places, elephant, she intoned silently. And when the time comes when you are to die, may it be peacefully and in the place of your choosing. Roscoe held up a syringe of antidote, letting his glance sweep a last time over the recumbent bull. Harry motioned Peta and the rest of the team back, leading them to a respectful distance. The M285 would take two minutes to do its work and have Marula recovering. They watched as the burly scientist administered the injection into one of the prominent veins on the back of an ear, pat the elephant fondly once, and then move quickly across to join them. Harry counted off the seconds silently. At sixty-four the old bull's eyes opened, and for a few heart beats the animal remained motionless. Then it heaved upright in a surge of dust, the bright yellow of the collar incongruous against the grey hide. For a minute Marula stood swaying slightly as his trunk moved about, sifting the scents mingled on the ground around him. Then, with a great gusting sigh he moved off through the bush. They watched him until he disappeared. Roscoe grinned at Harry.

"Three down, one to go."

Harry slapped him on the back.

"The operation has gone damned well, Roscoe. No hiccups at all. You're a wizard. Once it's over, it will be my great pleasure to supply you with as much beer as you need to stay immobilised for a week. That's a promise. Kabakwe, here we come!"

Harry watched a kudu bull, trophy size, spiralled horns laid back over its rump, bound through the tangle of scrub below. The helicopter tilted, following the path of the jesse shrouded dry river bed beneath them, and the wide worn game trail that meandered beside it. A rhino, in solitary hulking repose beneath a tamarind tree, wheeled and jabbed its horn aloft at the sudden invasion of the noisy machine. Harry saw the oxpeckers fly off its back, and, though he couldn't hear a thing above the jack-hammering clatter of the engine, imagined he could hear the birds' chirring alarm call. He felt the vibration again, shuddering through the frame of the machine, jarring up into his body through the bucket seat. He flicked a glance at Gunther, noting the Austrian's eyes sweep over the instruments, a frown creasing his forehead. Feeling Harry's unspoken query, he grimaced. Harry switched his attention down past the right hand side of his body to the ground slipping past below. Thirty feet, he guessed.. Terrific. Bloody marvellous. Let's hope ...

There was a sudden ear-splitting shrieking noise, ripping through his senses. The helicopter bucked and lurched violently away to the right. There was a blur of grey thorn bush kaleidoscoping with a fleeting glimpse of clear blue sky as the choppers lurchlocked in to become a spin, and Harry was scrabbling to locate the release catch of the seat straps before they smashed into the ground, a part of his brain not believing what was happening, and then there was a bone-jarring crash as the rotor blade hit the ground, kicking the helicopter over, up into the air again, branches and foliage screeching against the metal of the cartwheeling aircraft, and a final smashing crash as the helicopter came to a last dust-erupting upside down halt. Harry could smell the aviation fuel strongly as he fought to release himself from the harness, the straps biting into his shoulders as he hung upside down. The catch snapped open, releasing him to fall in an untidy heap, half in and half out of the helicopter. He saw a jet of magenta coloured fuel spurt from a severed pipe, and kept the momentum of his action going, rolling free of the stricken machine and gaining his feet in a lurching, crabbing scramble away. No more than fifteen seconds had elapsed since the helicopter had first started to fall out of the sky. Harry heard his name called, looked back. Gunther was still strapped in the machine, fastened to it, hanging like a pendulous fruit within the buckled smashed bubble of the cockpit. He was struggling frantically, frenziedly with the straps. Harry sprinted back, his brain registering that the pungent smell of aviation fuel was much stronger now, seeing it splashing over Gunther, hearing the pilot cursing incoherently as he fumbled frantically to free himself. Harry slapped the man's scrabbling hands away from the release catch and punched the red-painted steel disc, reaching in and grabbing him, hauling him bodily from the wreck. There was a searing whoosh of flame, engulfing both men, a billowing inferno with them at its core. Harry heard the pilot scream and then he had him out, away from the blazing helicopter, running, carrying him as far as he could before the machine exploded. They had covered less then twenty paces when it went up, a fireball bursting skywards, spewing pieces of wreckage in all directions. Gunther was on fire, his clothes doused whilst he had been trapped. Harry rolled him on the ground, beating at the flames, smothering the fire with his own ripped off shirt. His own hands were raw, but he couldn't feel anything. At last the flames were out. Gunther was gasping in agony, clothes charred, skin raw red and peeling. Harry held him close, talking gently to him, trying to soothe him. The man's eyebrows and hair had been burnt off, and Harry gagged at the smell. He wondered how long it would take the ground team to find them, as he watched the surrounding bush. For a moment, in a weird telescoping of time, he was back on a jungle track in Malaya, his companions dead, his gut shot to hell, waiting for the enemy to close in and finish him off. It was very vivid. He shivered in the heat of the day, shaking his head to rid himself of the flashback. He could feel the pain in his hands now.

Harry Kenyon and Peta Holt lay naked in the sun on the clean whiteness of a sheltered sand bar. It was a Sunday, two days after the crash. Gunther Lachner was in Kariba hospital, recovering from first degree burns. The collaring operation had come to a temporary halt. It would not be difficult locating the last tusker, Kabakwe, without the use of the helicopter, but it would take longer. And it would have to wait, because, for the moment, Harry was walking wounded. He had come out of the crash lightly. Torn ligaments in one shoulder and burned hands, the latter damage making it impossible for him to properly grasp a rifle. After the Civil Aviation enquiry team had left, he and Peta had driven downriver, Peta chauffeuring the Landrover, until they were several miles past the nearest tourist track, until they had selected the private beauty of this spot. Roscoe Daniels had departed, with the helicopter wrecked, back to his new research block at Sengwa. He had left the dart gun and necessary drugs with Harry, to complete the collaring of the 'Big Four' as soon as he was able. It irked Harry that they had not managed to collar Kabakwe along with the other three bulls. Kabakwe roamed the most, had the largest range, and was thus harder to keep an eye on. Still, considered Harry now, we'll give it a couple more days, let the hands heal some more, and then go and find him. I want to do it myself. I'll be happier when there's a collar on him, and his tusks are marked ... with Alex Gant in the area.

He looked admiringly at Peta's outstretched body beside him, glistening with the heat of this new October day. And their recent love making. She had ridden astride him, looking down at him, holding on to his bandaged hands gently for support and then her grip slipping to his shoulders as she had bucked harder, approaching climax. Harry had ridden with her, gasping partly at the exquisite pleasure and partly from the damaged ligaments, eyes drinking in her beauty above him, breasts bouncing, hair whipping frenziedly across her face, eyes and luscious mouth widening in tandem as the sensation peaked. They came as a fish eagle called from the acacia on the bank behind them, their breathless gasps blending with the haunting sweet melody it its call. Peta dozed now in relaxed uninhibited satiation upon the sand, one elegant hand outflung to lie in the shallows. Harry felt his breathing quicken and shook his head in amused wonderment at her effect on him.

He gazed on past her over the wide vista of the river. It was wide here, perhaps half a mile across. The sand bars marking the shallow areas were clear, a foot or so below the surface. Around the shallows swirled the deeper swifter running channels, a maze of darker, greener currents of the river. A school of hippo dozed in one of the deeper channels, a hundred yards out, clumped together like massive pigs in a sty, dark and pink bodied in the clear water. Malachite kingfishers made iridescent arrows against the water and the bright white sand banks further out. The banks added their own character to the river, reed-fringed, with cool green game-cropped grass cloaking the inlets and channels. In some places the banks were high, scoured by wind and water so that they made shadowy, jagged precipices, ever changing in shape as they eroded and crumbled and slid into the river. In other places the sand banks sloped gently to meet the river, and here the clean white sand contrasted beautifully with the turquoise of the water and the emerald of the reeds. There were elephant on the islands today, always, in the hot months, silent shadowy bulks against the whiteness. Ahh, thought Harry, the river. Always the river. When I die, scatter my ashes over the river ...

"A penny for your thoughts, lover."

Harry brought his gaze down to her. Her eyes were closed against the sun, looking up at him from behind the shelter of long lashes. He smiled, drinking in her nakedness which was still new to him.

"I was thinking that the river and your legs have something in common. They both go on forever."

Her lips parted in a wide smile.

"Gad, a romantic, yet. I think I'll take that as a compliment. A girl can never have too many of those."

Harry leaned back on one elbow beside her, feeling the warmth emanating from her body. A butterfly, a tiny dancing artist's palette of smeared yellow and orange, landed on one nipple. For seconds it balanced upon the pink-tipped peak, wings fluttering, and Harry saw the nipple harden at the faint caress. Then it took off, forsaking the high ground for the sweat-beaded moistness at the edge of the dark forest below. It perched in the hair of her groin, a bright flower in a curling, rambling thicket. Harry stared in fascination, seeing the minute sliver of insect tongue flicking at the sweat droplets along the hair line. He shook his head wonderingly.

"Well, he sure know what he wants. No beating around the bush with that fellow!"

Peta smiled languorously, reaching for him, finding him hard.

"Me too, lover," she whispered. "How about you?"

"Oh, yes," Harry smiled, "please ..."

CHAPTER SEVENTEEN

The green Citroen gained some speed as the last of the buffalo herd crossed the track ahead, heading inland away from the Zambezi. The sighting of the herd, over four hundred animals, was a fitting finale to that morning's game viewing excursion. The Elliot family had left Shingela at sun-up. The early start had been worth it, for they had seen leopard, lion, elephant, rhino, and now buffalo ... all of the Big Five. A late breakfast back at camp, followed by some bream fishing for that night's dinner, was the next priority for their last day at Nemana.

The explosion that erupted out of the earth ripped the front of the car from the rest of the body, casting the engine block a dozen yards away. The legs of both adults in the front seats were slashed and shredded, and the rest of their bodies, and their two children, blasted and hacked by flying glass. A wheel, ripped from the axle, hung ensnared from the top of a tall leadwood, the tyre burning brightly. The smell of the burning rubber mingled with the pungent smell of explosive and scorched twisted metal. A child's scream of agony echoed across the flood plain. Blood dripped steadily from the ceiling upholstery inside the wreck.

The anti tank mine was a TM46, manufactured in the vast armaments factory at Kuybyshev in the USSR. The light brown steel casing contained twelve pounds of TNT as its main charge, which could be boosted according to the desired effects with another forty-four pounds of explosive. The whole deadly package weighed a fraction over nineteen pounds and could be fitted into a hole of little more than fifteen inches in diameter and four inches deep. A detonating pressure of 396 pounds would cause the detonator and striker mechanism to do their job and destruct. The landmine had lain in its secret place since midnight, ten hours previously. It had taken the guerrilla squad exactly forty-four minutes to lay the mine.

Harry cocked his head as the sound of the explosion reached them, echoing over the hot morning's silence, reverberating off the distant walls of the escarpment They were sitting, naked still, eating a brunch of tinned sardines and asparagus, scooping the contents from the tins with their fingers. A jossak of water hung from a piece of driftwood Harry had imbedded in the sand. Two bottles, gin and lime juice, and two enamel mugs, stood beside the driftwood. He frowned, pausing, reluctant to break the mood.

"That doesn't sound like good news. We had better make a move, Peta. I must check that out."

Peta nodded her agreement, licking the sardine oil from the fingers of one hand, whilst reaching for her discarded clothes with the other.

They saw the plume of dust of a racing Landrover as they approached Shingela. Harry told Peta to stop and they watched as the other vehicle closed and came to a halt in a cloud of dust beside them. Harry could see from the tight expression on Wally Conway's face that whatever had happened was bad.

As they returned to base he had gone through the alternatives that could have caused the explosion, and the most likely explanation he had arrived at was that one or more of their gas bottles had somehow gone up.

"Landmine, Harry. Back up the river road, about two miles."

208

Harry felt his gut tighten.

"Who? How bad?"

"Tourists. I don't know who, or how bad. Charlie and I went to investigate the sound and found them. Jesus, it's a bloody mess. Charlie stayed and sent me back to find you and radio Kariba for a doctor."

Harry cursed softly, evaluating the situation in his mind.

"Have you radioed?"

Wally nodded. Harry continued, speaking distinctly.

"Okay ... Go back to the office. Have all the staff there report to you. Everyone, understand? Have them on full alert, with weapons. We don't know what the hell else is about to happen. Stay at that radio, Wally. Send me Gordon Munroe. Keep Des with you and have him visit the tourist camp to prevent any people going out. Tell Gordon to bring a radio, and to collect my revolver from my house. I won't be much good with a rifle if anything starts happening. Tell him to say off the road when he comes to the scene. There may be more landmines ..."

Harry paused, sifting through the eventualities. No, he thought Don't tell me it's started again. What Scratch Peters came to talk about those few weeks ago. *Not here.*

"Peta ..."

She was watching him intently.

"You go back with Wally please. And stay with him at the office, to assist him."

She pointed at his bandaged hands.

"You can't drive with those. I'd better come with you."

"No. I'll handle it all right. I want you at base ..."

To Wally, he continued with instructions.

"Radio Kariba again. Get hold of the Tracker Combat Unit. I'll pick up whatever signs are around in the meantime. Perhaps they can come down with the doctor. Keep me posted on his ETA and whether he's travelling by fixed wing or chopper. The latter would be preferable. Have Kashili come with Gordon, with another medic pack. If it's a landmine, and they're still alive, they're going to need a lot of help."

The distant throbbing of the helicopter came to them as Harry found the tracks. He left Kashili at the spoor and returned to the wrecked car. The Elliot family were all still alive, although Harry did not think the father would make it. The blast had been on his side of the vehicle and although the engine block had absorbed the brunt of the explosion, he was still badly hurt. They lay wrapped in blankets and Charlie Parker had saline drips going into both adults. In the track, the blackened crater caused by the blast gaped obscenely. The smell of the explosive and burnt rubber still fouled the air. Gordon Munroe was speaking into the radio handset. He turned as Harry returned.
"They'll be with us in two minutes. There's a tracker team on board with the doc."
Harry looked at his watch.
"Damned good time. Just under an hour. Gordon, you and Charlie help with the casevac, will you. Kashili and I will get on the tracks."
The noise of the helicopter grew louder as the ranger guided the aircraft to them on the radio. The throbbing of the rotors changed pitch to a solid whacking sound and the jet whine screamed. It appeared through the gaps in the tree canopy, wheeling as the pilot looked for an open area in which to put the machine down. Harry could see a man in camouflage kit sitting braced in the open doorway of the Alouette, automatic rifle held casually. He recognised the tall gangling figure of Andre Franklin and grinned dryly to himself. Looks like they've sent the first team, he reflected. Good show. Although it's a waste of time. Because I know where those tracks will go. Straight to the river. By first light today the bastards who put that mine down were back in Zambia.

The three man tracker team, together with the two game department men, stood at the edge of the Zambezi River and stared at the northern bank. There was no sign of movement, no sign of any human presence across there. The tracks of the four men who had brought the landmine from the sanctuary of the neighbouring country had indeed ended at the river. There were the scuff marks of the canoe, the sharp indented feetmarks in the wetter earth where one of them had pushed the canoe off. Peter Rabie swore softly. Whispering Jim Lannigan, the third member of the army tracker team, let his binoculars drop and swing from their strap around his neck. He too swore savagely.

"Fucking bastards. Not a fucking thing moving over there. Not a dickey bird!"

Harry stood silently. What for, he wondered. What was the idea behind that? One random bloody landmine. Achieving what? And what else have they got up their sleeves? Who, precisely, is 'they'? He shook his head and glanced at Kashili.

"What do you make of this, old man?"

His friend shook his head also, and spat.

"I do not know. I do not understand the meaning of this madness ..."

He watched a fish eagle patrolling, high over the river.

"But I think it is trouble."

Shingela tourist camp lay quiet and deserted. Families of mongoose ranged through the area in companionship with the baboons who inspected the vacant camp sites. A pair of elephants browsed from the acacias near the ablution block. The tourists had been gone for a fortnight now. After the landmine incident National Parks headquarters had decided to close Nemana ahead of schedule, before the month end. More trackers had come in, along with a detachment of army engineers, and the main dirt road out of the Park had been swept for more mines. There were none. The remaining tourists departed in convoy. Nemana National Park was left to the animals and the staff of Shingela. Harry had increased his patrols through the Park and now had game scouts on observation duty, watching for any sign of movement over the river. There were no new developments. No sign of more infiltrations. No movement on the northern bank. The army patrols that operated in the Park, searching for any signs of further terrorism, came up with nothing, and were withdrawn. The tension slowly dissipated, as peace reclaimed Nemana. Harry Kenyon maintained the extra patrols and vigilance. But there were just so many precautions one could take. And work had to continue. Soon the worry over landmines would not be as acute, for when the rains came most of the tracks within the Park would again become unusable.

October, the suicide month, drew to a close.

"Come on, slowcoach. Move!"

Desmond Taylor revved the motor of the stationary Landrover, hoping the noise would help persuade the elephant wandering along the track ahead of them to move off it and let them pass. There was still another twenty miles to the boundary gate at Chawoyo, and then another hundred over the escarpment to Kariba. And it was getting late. Beside him, Corporal Joseph Chisambiko slumped miserably in the passenger seat, nursing his toothache-swollen jaw. Each bump of the bush road caused spasms of pain to rocket through his head. The young ranger glanced sympathetically at the game scout, his sympathy balanced accordingly with his anticipation of a night out in the relatively bright lights of the lakeside resort after he had taken the scout to the hospital. Ahead, the elephant flapped its ears and trumpeted suddenly, before swinging into a full run away from the road.

"Thank you kindly," said the ranger. "And about time too."

They were the last words the young man ever spoke. The rocket from the Russian made RPG 2 anti tank launcher exploded in the open cab of the Landrover, killing both men instantly. There was no need for the prolonged burst of machine gun and assault rifle fire that followed the rocket strike, raking vehicle and occupants. The crippled Landrover jerked to a halt, water from the bullet punctured radiator hissing into steam as it poured over the engine. A flock of parrots erupted

out of the upper branches of a baobab, screeching their fright at
the cacophony of sound shredding apart the late afternoon
peace.

Harry watched Game Scout Kapesa make his way across to his
bungalow from the administration block.   Peta continued to
concentrate on the aerial manoeuvres of the carmine bee eaters
in the waning evening light.   The first hippo chorus of the
evening had started, echoing over the quiet waters of the river.
He felt the twinge of unease cramp his stomach.
"Good evening, corporal."
He returned the scout's crisp salute.
"What's the problem?"
"Mr Taylor has not reached Chawoyo Gate yet, sir.   I have just
had their last radio schedule of the day, and they have not seen
him. He should have gone through there long before now, sir,"
the scout added superfluously.
Harry nodded in agreement, keeping his face open, feeling his
stomach twist even more.
"Okay, corporal, thank you ..."
He paused.
"Anything else from Chawoyo Gate?"
"No, sir."
Like what, thought Harry.   Like explosions heard, maybe?
You're over-reacting, boy.   He's broken down, or had to wait
while a rhino decided to take over the road.
To the corporal he said.
"Have Mr Parker and Mr Conway meet me at the office, please.
And have my Landrover fuelled, together with Mr Parker's.   I
would also like four game scouts to report to the office, on the
double.   I will issue weapons to them."
Okay, Harry, he thought, as the scout trotted back to carry out
his instructions.   Don't be such a bloody pessimist.   He
returned Peta's anxious look, making his voice light.
"I'd better go and see what young Desmond is up to.   Charlie
can follow me in his Landrover.   I'd rather you stay here with

Wally, on radio watch. I'll take backpacks with us, so we'll be in touch. The clot has probably run out of petrol."

"Why two vehicles?"

The question caught him, and he hesitated before replying.

"You think there's trouble, don't you?" she continued.

Harry shrugged and then leaned to kiss her, seeing her eyes wide and searching his face.

Full darkness had fallen by the time they saw the Landrover in the wash of their headlights. Even in the pale illumination Harry could see the extent of the rocket damage. He stopped his vehicle, feeling the hair on the back of his neck rise. Without taking his gaze from the scene ahead he spoke quietly to Kashili.

"Stay here. Out of the vehicle, and listen for any noise. I'll walk the rest of the way in."

The black man nodded wordlessly. Harry climbed out and walked back to the second Landrover. He caught the flash of starlight in the eyes of one of the game scouts in the back of the vehicle. Charlie Parker stared warily into the surrounding darkness.

"What's up?"

Harry watched the Landrover at the end of the tunnel of car lights for a moment before answering.

"Trouble. Of the worst kind. Cover me, whilst I go in and take a closer look. I can see one body in there. If anything starts, open up fast."

He collected the radio set, on the way past his Landrover, shrugging the straps over his shoulders. He walked out, away from the track and their vehicles. He didn't want to walk down the beam of light. After about twenty paces he stopped, listening. He hoped the game scouts on the Landrovers had noted his direction and didn't start shooting at shadows.

He waited for another two minutes, making himself count off the seconds steadily. There were no alien sounds breaking the night rhythm of the bush. Which, he thought sourly, could mean absolutely sweet fuck all, depending on how good the enemy was. He noted how quickly the situation had evolved to being him and the enemy. He started walking in the hundred paces to the ambushed Landrover. He carried his FN loosely, safety catch off, his senses screamingly alert. He walked slowly, watching the surrounding night shrouded bush, rather than the rocketed vehicle itself in the wash of light. A shape, shadowy, moved between himself and the vehicle, and he was down on his knee with the rifle at his cheek, finger tightening on the trigger when the hyena sniggered. He barely stopped the last of the trigger squeeze in time. For a moment longer he knelt where he was, controlling his breathing, feeling the adrenalin surging through his system. He took a lungful of fresh air. Go away, *mhisi*, he said silently. Not this time, you won't. We'll take this kill home with us. They're not for you. He stood up and went on. He could see the bullet scars now, as he got closer. And the shrapnel marks. At this distance the car lights winked and sparkled in the scattered shards of the windscreen. His pace slowed even more. He didn't want to see the rest. He didn't want to see the remains of his men.

There was nothing anyone could do for either Ranger Desmond Taylor or Game Scout Joseph Chisambiko, as Harry had known instinctively when they had first come across the mangled Landrover. He stood now and stared into the shadowed cab of the vehicle, glad of the softening effect of the far off headlights. Finally he closed his eyes and rubbed a hand savagely across his scalp, feeling the healed burn scabbing hurt anew. What now, he asked himself. Where do we go from here? As if in answer, a jackal howled into the night, to be answered by others. A hyena whooped his contribution to the chorus, the scavengers scenting new death on the air. Still Harry stood, staring at the bloodied shredded bodies. An expensive toothache, he reflected grimly. Two lives. And if they hadn't come along at this moment in time, offering a nice easy target, who else were they going to chop? What other nasty work did they have planned? What else have we got to look forward to? A nightjar called tremulously, its quavering refrain floating serenely on the night air. He unslung the radio. I suppose, he considered glumly, that it's time to get things moving. Why should I hog all the fun ...?

Captain Scratch Peters ran his hand over the soapy smoothness of the tusk once again before turning back to Harry. The warden had tipped his chair back from his desk to lean against the wall behind him. There was a three day growth of stubble on his face, and his uniform was wrinkled and sweat stained. The army man too looked bush worn. They had both spearheaded tracker teams in a combing search of the immediate hinterland of Shingela, covering over a hundred square miles of valley bush in their hunt for any further evidence of insurgents. The tracks of the eight man ambush had, again, ended at the river. The combat tracker teams, together with Harry and his best trackers, had then extended their search area and swept the bush for any sign of other infiltrators who may be laying up and biding their time. The search had been fruitless. The valley soil had been innocent of any alien spoor. The ambush had been another hit and run operation. Harry waited silently now, watching the army officer impassively.

"What we have here, old son, keeping it simple ... is a bag of shit."

Harry remained silent. Peters continued.

"We haven't a clue as to what their objectives are, hitting you. Tourism here is minimal, and mainly local, and the rains are about to put this National Park in mothballs. If these incidents were in Wankie National Park it would be a different story. There's nothing happening in the rest of the country. Just here! Is it a random terror campaign? The start of something major? Or isolated incidents that will dry up? Who knows? And, again, why here?"

He paused, giving the warden a chance to answer. Harry shrugged. There was nothing new in the captain's theorising. It was cold soup. Harry had lain awake for endless hours asking himself the same questions. Scratch Peters went on.

"Special Branch has no more than do our own people. Between you and I, the SAS are over the river now. Maybe they will come up with some leads. We'd better find out what these bastards are up to, sooner than later."

"And then what?"

There was only mild interest in Harry's voice. He had his own ideas on how the issue would evolve. He wondered how similar they were to those of the establishment. The army officer shrugged now.

"The best I can do is to establish a small base down here, reporting back to our main base at Kariba. I think a call sign strength of, say, ten men will do initially ..."

He paused and eyed Harry keenly, as if making up his mind about something. Then.

"The Tracker Combat Unit has just become obsolete. Remember when I last saw you? I mentioned that I had been tasked with establishing a new unit? Well, it's about completed. The unit will be called the Selous Scouts. We have the nucleus of men required to get the new unit going, and are recruiting more quietly. The tracking role will still be a major part of our work, but we will also be specialising in other special operations tasks. Pseudo work, for example. The hierarchy feel there will be need for pseudo operations in the future. The deployment of the men down here would serve a dual purpose. It would provide you with some backup and it would be their first exercise under the auspices of the new unit.

He paused again, still watching Harry closely.

"I'm telling you this, even though it is top secret, because we've known each other a long time. And because I'd like you to join us. With your background, and with your ability to speak the local languages, you would be very valuable to us. I know you are off the books, with your various wounds. You've already walked the extra mile. But I also know you're a tough son of a bitch. The Scouts are going to be one of the most élite and clandestine outfits in Africa, responsible only to God, or the Devil, depending on where one's loyalties are. Join us, Harry."

Harry stood up and left his desk to go and stand at the open door. For a long minute he gazed out over the river, noting vultures circling above the blue haze of the far bank. He took a deep breath and then came back and sat down.

"I appreciate your trust, and your offer. But no thank you. I'm not interested in soldiering any more, Scratch, even if it is unorthodox. I'm very happy doing what I'm doing. Looking after my animals. No more, no less. You have plenty of men to choose from, for your special new unit."

Now it was the turn of the warden to fix the officer with a long intense stare.

"I don't know what is going to happen next, with this new terrorism. But I'll lay you odds that it's not a passing squall. These incidents down here are probes, testing our reflexes for the big event. I would guess that we are looking down the gun barrel of a brand new war."

The captain returned his stare levelly.

"And so? Where will you be, Harry? Where does that leave you?"

Harry tapped the desk.

"I'll be right here, old son. Looking after my animals. Brushfire wars in Africa have never been very kind to the wildlife. So, whilst you and yours are busy with your own counter insurgency operations, I'll be minding the store here. Or wherever."

Scratch Peters grunted sourly and shook his head, standing up as Harry had done and striding across to the doorway to stare out. As his gaze swept the river frontage he saw the girl appear atop the bank, cameras and binoculars slung over her shoulders as she strode easily through the midday heat. For a few moments he watched her appreciatively. Then he turned back to the warden.

"You seem to have things pretty well mapped out. What about the girl? Where does she fit into the scheme of life?"

Harry Kenyon smiled briefly, softly.

"Peta? Good question. I'm not awfully sure yet. I've only just found her ... and I'd hate to lose her."

~ PART THREE ~

Autumn 1975

"Certainly there is no hunting like the hunting of man and those who have hunted armed men long enough and liked it, never really care for anything else thereafter. You will meet them doing various things with resolve, but their interest rarely holds because after the other thing ordinary life is flat as the taste of wine when the taste buds have been burned off your tongue."

ON THE BLUE WATER : A GULF STREAM LETTER
by *Ernest Hemingway*

CHAPTER EIGHTEEN

She had been dead for two days. The warden, guided by the vultures, found her deep in some thorn scrub. Lions and hyenas had had a field day with her, opening up her underparts for the vultures and smaller scavengers. He stood for a long while, studying her and the area around her. The movements of the animals had obliterated any signs of the killers' spoor. He wondered how quick it had been. Or how slow. Had the bullets been well placed, bringing her down quickly. Or wild and indiscriminate, leaving her to stagger through the bush, her life leaking from her, until she dropped. He could feel the rage building in him, swirling up. He walked around the swollen stinking remains, away from the butchery at her head, and his movement caused an explosion of vultures to erupt from where they were coagulated on more booty, a score paces away in the scrub. He threaded his way through the jesse tangle to the calf. There was little left of it. Its hide wasn't as thickly developed as its dam's, and once its mother was down the predators had taken it easily. Perhaps the humans had killed it along with its mother. Probably. Even though the front horn was but a nub. From the remains he guessed the calf was no more than six months old.

He swore savagely, silently, turning away, back to the mother. Back to the festering grey hulk of the rhino that tainted the valley air with decay. The raw places where her horns had been, gaped obscenely, maggots working industriously, and he felt a new surge of rage. Choking. Okay, he thought. That's it. That's enough. It's done. They got her. Now they are gone. So, get your act together and see what you can find. She is the first rhino that's been poached in your park for a long time, even with our new war. So see what you can establish, and take it from there. Kashili will be here in a while, once he has checked out what was underneath those other birds. Then we can make a plan. Maybe he's found something similar. In the meantime, see what you can do here.

Harry tied his old army issue face veil across the lower half of his face, adjusting his breathing so that he took short shallow breaths, and moved in close to the carcass. Minutely inspecting the grey armoured hide, he slowly worked his way along its rigormortised length, searching for bullet wounds amongst the lesions and wrinkles of the antediluvian armoured surface. With his bush knife he probed and scraped at old scars, scraping away the dried white mosaic of excretions of the vultures and marabous that had mounted sentinel atop the carcass, exploring the raw rubbing sores amidst the skin folds around the shoulder. All the while the flies buzzed angrily at his interruptions and the thick sweet smell threatened to suffocate him. He paused once as some unseen animal rattled the nearby thorn scrub in sudden flight.

He found no sign of bullet wounds. They would be, as per Sod's Law, on the side of the animal against the earth. And there was no way, without a Landrover and chains, he would be able to move her. He was disappointed. That leaves the spoor, he reflected. What's left of it, after a couple of days, and depending on exactly where they shot at her. He looked up at the sun. It was mid morning, the white shimmering orb inching its way to its zenith. He moved away from the carcass to stand in the shade of a gnarled fig tree, still smelling the rhino on his clothes and trapped in the hair of his nostrils. He wondered how much longer it would be before Kashili joined him. What had he found beneath the spiralling formations of vultures, a mile away? He moved out away from the cool shade of the fig tree, starting his first circle of the rhino and her calf. Slowly, methodically, he patrolled, searching the ground for any sign of spoor, picking up nothing on his first 360 degree sweep. Widening the search pattern. In this way he covered four revolutions of the carcass, moving slowly, silently, eyes roving for evidence of the poachers, whilst all other senses monitored the bush around him for anything out of rhythm. He found tracks, wind scoured and faint, almost obliterated by game spoor, several hundred paces from the rhino. He studied them intently, casting about for more signs in the immediate vicinity. There were the distinct figure-of-eight patterns that Rhodesian Army trackers had come to recognise as being on the footwear used by insurgents. Ubiquitous at first, and easy to identify, the tell-tale spoor patterns were encountered less now, in this third year of bush war, as the logistics personnel of the nationalists over the river in Zambia realised the vulnerability of such easy to place spoor patterns, and footwear became less type-cast. The tracks did not tell Harry Kenyon much, as faded and disturbed as they were. But now he knew that there was a nationalist terrorist presence in his Park, and that they had shot one of his rhino. He brooded about that, as he crouched beside the spoor under the orb of the noonday sun.

It was a new development. Since the first attacks in October 1972, there had been little disturbance in the lives of the staff running Nemana National Park. The landmine and the ambush had been isolated incidents, probes, distracting the attentions of the government forces whilst massive clandestine infiltrations had taken place many miles to the east of the Park. Erupting into a determined new phase of insurgent warfare at Christmas, with attacks on the establishment throughout the agriculturally rich north-east areas. National Parks headquarters had kept Nemana closed to the public, and the affairs of the Park and the neighbouring safari concession areas had continued to be run by Harry and a reduced staff. Young Desmond Taylor had not been replaced, and, with no tourists, Warden Kenyon very obviously did not need a tourist officer. So Gordon Munroe had been transferred across country to the Gona-re-Zhou. Leaving Harry with one research officer and one ranger, and his complement of game scouts. And an army base of thirty men established within the deserted tourist camp at Shingela. Harry Kenyon viewed this development with mixed feelings. Certainly, with only the wide smooth expanse of the Zambezi River separating Shingela from the nationalist base camps in Zambia, some sort of reinforced presence at Nemana was welcome. Especially with Peta Holt living there, a permanent fixture now as she built up the contents for the book she was putting together on the Zambezi Valley. Nevertheless, whenever Harry saw the bulldozed raw earth ramparts, and machine gun and mortar bunkers, and the bush hacked down providing for fields of fire, he winced. The fact that army patrols were afield throughout his Park, carrying weapons amongst his animals, also caused him concern. Human nature being what it was, added to the fact that there were soldiers who were not used to the numbers and proximity of game as it existed at Nemana, could cause over-reaction and have some of the game killed unnecessarily.

Yet, he had to admit, the situation was satisfactory. The army base was a permanent fixture in Nemana, a government force outpost firmly ensconced with flag flying on the country's threatened northern border. And there had been few complications. Right from the start Harry had gone to the captain in charge and explained his law of conduct to him. The warden realised that fresh meat was necessary to their ration requirements, and that eyes may be cast over the endless herds of game out on the plains. Venison would be a natural consideration. Therefore, along with his own fresh ration needs for his base, he would be happy to supply them with an animal a fortnight. Which he would shoot. There would be no reason for any army personnel to shoot any game in Nemana National Park. Not even in self defence. Until personnel became familiar with the game conditions in the Park he would be happy to allocate game scouts to patrols. This would lessen the chance of confrontations, real or imagined, and do away with the justification needed by soldiers to open up on any game.

And, to date, the arrangement had worked well. The army patrolled Nemana, adding to Harry's field strength, and he supplied them with the agreed fresh rations. To Harry, then, it had been a temporary measure, until the few months needed to clear up the incursions had passed. But the incursions had continued, and increased, with the white owned fertile farming areas over the escarpment badly subverted and in permanent conflict. And it did not look as if the army base in Harry Kenyon's game sanctuary would be withdrawing any time soon. Apart from isolated rocket and mortar bombardments from across the river, more dramatic than accurate, the nationalists' attentions focused elsewhere. It was evident that Nemana National Park and her neighbouring safari areas were being treated by the insurgents as transit routes. Harry's patrols, and those of the army, discovered crossing points and tracks of infiltrating groups. Always the paths led inland, into the heart of the country, leaving the valley peaceful. The nationalist hierarchy did not wish to draw too much attention to their infiltration points, for this was their downfall in their incursions during the sixties. So, life in Nemana had retained an almost peaceful normality. And Harry Kenyon and Peta Holt had fallen even more in love in their valley paradise, and the wildlife of Nemana went about its business undisturbed and unthreatened.

Until now, thought Harry. All of a sudden we've got this. Which means what? Why are the bastards poaching? I didn't expect to find their types of spoor. Anyone else, sure. This part of Nemana is pretty damn isolated. There's no way through this area that takes you up the escarpment, so it's not some random killing by some group moving inland. It looks like a straight poaching case. Why would they risk drawing attention to themselves, after all this time? And where ... The melodious lilting whistle of a guinea fowl echoed across the midday silence of the hot bush. Harry listened for a moment and then answered the call. He stood up with a final glance around him at the spoor and then moved off, back towards the carcass of the rhino. A grey loerie protested his presence, calling stridently from the top of a lightning struck acacia. Harry rubbed a hand across the four day stubble of beard, feeling the sweat running freely. He could still smell the death odour of the rhino, ingrained in the sweat and dust. He wondered how Peta was, back at Shingela, letting his thoughts stay with her as a luxury. Undoubtedly she would be working on the book. Putting the final presentation together. God, but she had some magnificent material. Over two years of photographs, through all the seasons, from the dry, parched winter barrenness to the first sweeping blue veils of the rains sluicing across the valley. And she had already sold the book. Had been paid a nice fat advance on the strength of her earlier work and her first introductory brilliant photographs. Her publishers were going to bring it out as a coffee table production. Plenty of glossy pictures with a flowing down-to-earth text that would take the reader through all the moods of the Zambezi Valley. And the animals within her portals. She had titled it, eventually, finally, after much nail biting, *'Valley Eden'*. Harry went along with the title. For it was that. Although, he mused now, a bleak smile twisting his features, we have a few snakes to snuff out. His gaze swept the surrounding maze of bush for a sign of Kashili's presence.

The old tracker whistled softly from the deep shade of a drooping *cordyla*. He had already found the rhino carcass and the remains of the calf, with the warden's spoor in attendance. Now he waited silently as Harry joined him, unlimbering the radio and bedroll. When the white man spoke he kept his voice barely above a murmur, as was their bush habit.

"So, *bava*. Father. You were a long time following up on *makhoti* the vultures. Which makes me think you found something bad. You have seen what I found here. I have found tracks, but they are old and the wind has hidden them. I cannot find the mark of the bullet in that upper side of the rhino. What did you discover?"

Kashili dug into the pockets of his worn bush jacket, taking from each, separated so that they did not rattle, a slim dull metallic cartridge case. He held them out to Harry. His companion looked at them, turning them over in the palm of one hand. They were from an AK47 Assault Rifle. Kashili held out his hand again and dropped something else into the warden's palm. The mangled bit of lead pinged dully against the cartridge case.

"They shot an elephant. A good bull. They have taken only the tusks and the tail. No meat. I dug that out of him. There were two other hits, but I did not take those as well. Like the *melembe*, the bull is about two days old. There is the spoor of eight men. Theirs is easier to see because they are carrying the ivory. I tracked them for a short way. They are aiming north, for the river."

Kashili stopped, waiting. Harry stared at the objects in his hand and took a deep breath. Well, he thought, there we go. A brand new ball game. A rhino and an elephant in two days. That we know of. No meat taken, just the horns and the ivory. Where does that leave us? Good question, Kenyon. Pity about the answers. Goddam. Goddam and blast! He sighed, a long ragged breath.

"Okay. I know where the tracks will end, just as you do. But let us go back anyway, to the bull, and follow them up. Who knows what we may find? Perhaps we will see something across the river from where they left the Park. We can then follow the river back upstream to Shingela. At least we'll have good water. It is already dry up here. The waterholes are not lasting well after the poor rains."

They followed the tracks of the nationalist poachers for two days. Down out of the grey uniformity of the thorn scrub that cloaked the ravines and hard ground of the lower reaches of the escarpment on to the vast lushness of the flood plains. The route of the marauders was positive, no detours that spoke of military duties, but a straight northward trek to the Zambezi and the sanctuary of the neighbouring country beyond. The two men stood at the river and stared across its mirrored expanse. The purple-blue haze of the distant bush lay under the awesome silence of the valley. To Harry Kenyon it was as though the vastness and the silence mocked him. He had never felt that before. The silence was a balm. The vastness had always served to shield him from the outside world, to cocoon him and the wildlife that survived there from the whims and idiosyncrasies of the brave new modern world. Now its silence shouted its mockery at him, telling him nothing. Now its vastness worked against him, allowing intruders into his world, unknown and unheralded. To kill wantonly, and leave at will. Harry grunted and turned upriver towards Shingela, another day away.

In the light of the guttering candle Peta Holt traced the cicatriced ridges of his old scars with soft touches, feeling his breathing slow to normal. Harry lay on his back, spent, breathing open-mouthed, watching her leaning up on one elbow beside him. Sweat glistened on her breasts, as it did on him, and her breathing too was ragged. They remained silent for a long while, and he shut his eyes, feeling her fingers caressing the old wounds with infinite gentleness. It was his first night back at Nemana base. He had returned dispirited and depressed from the patrol, late in the day. From the army encampment, two hundred yards downstream in the deserted tourist camp, had come erratic short bursts of automatic weapon fire as a practice session went under way. The shots, splitting apart the afternoon serenity, irritated him, worsening his mood. The accumulated paperwork in his office didn't help.

He found Peta in the bunker outside the front of the bungalow. She had taken it over, moving sandbags and readjusting the firing ports, tamping down the dirt floor with a layer of hard earth from a termite mound. Now the bunker had an added use to that as protection from rocket and mortar barrages. It was her dark room. All the photographs she had taken since she had been at Nemana had been processed here. She stood now, as he entered, studying a newly developed roll of film against the light of a pair of hurricane lamps. In the muted glow her features seemed stark and soft at the same time. Harry felt his spirits lift as soon as he had stepped quietly down into the bunker and eased aside the calico curtain. She turned at once, smile widening as one with her eyes as she came to him, hands reaching to rub across the stubble of his beard, going up to run through his hair as she rubbed her face tight against his, unmindful of the bristles. She held his face between her hands then, kissing him deeply, smelling the sweat and the strong bush smell on him and relishing it, wanting to be part of it. Finally she stepped back, her gaze sweeping over his face.

"Hello, lover."

He stared back at her, drinking her in.

"Hello you too."

"Hail the conquering hero."

He had grinned ruefully, and she saw the depression in him then.

"Not so much the conqueror, I'm afraid. We came, and we saw, but that's about all."

He changed the smile, working at thrusting aside the mood, running one hand through the mane of her hair, feeling its heavy smoothness, loving it. He made his voice light.

"All you need is a lamp post, and with this lighting you could be the first choice for a remake of *Irma La Douce*."

Her smile widened, her voice slipping into burlesque French.

"Thank you, monsieur. I'll take that as a compliment. And, talking of such things, does monsieur realise that he has been away for over a week? And does he know what such an absence can do to a girl? Does monsieur wish to shower now, this very minute? Or later?"

She paused and made her voice normal, running one finger down the side of his face.

"I can actually wait. A few minutes, anyway."

Harry laughed, feeling his depression erode.

"Shower, first. With a drink, a stiff one. And you scrubbing my back."

He opened his eyes now, in time to see a bauble of sweat shimmering from one nipple, trembling with her breathing, swelling, to drop on his chest. His heartbeat was almost back to normal. He ran a finger over a sweat-silvered nipple and then put his finger to his lips and licked it. She watched him, cat-like, luminous eyed in the dying candlelight. From the lawn out front they could hear the steady rhythmic cropping sounds of hippo. Peta broke their silence.

"What are you going to do, Harry? About the rhino and the elephant?"

He shrugged briefly, grimacing.

"I'm not sure yet. Tomorrow I'll have a chat with the army, after I've had a long look at the map. See if we can divert more patrols into that general area. Maybe those are the only two carcasses. Maybe there's more, scattered to hell over the remoter inland areas. The more I think about it the more uneasy I become. Those animals, killed there in an area that has not been infiltrated by insurgents before, can only have been deliberate poaching targets. And, if so, what other areas have been penetrated? And, if they have, what has prompted this new development?"

Harry shook his head.

"Plenty of questions, damn few answers. What I wouldn't give to have the use of a helicopter for a while."

Out in the blackness of the flood plain lions called.

He stood, patient and serene, in the cool shadow of the acacias that gave their midday shade to the administration block. Harry found him there, aloof from the comings and goings of the day's routine, when he returned from the army base. He was not a young man, although he had the poise of one. The short tuft of beard was more grey than black, and the wrinkled folds creasing an otherwise flat belly told of past fortunes and famines. From the waist up he was bare, the flesh spare and landscaped by old encounters with animal and bush. A pouch, of bushbuck hide, Harry noted, was slung on a thong of sinew from one shoulder. At his feet a small kaross of hyrax skins was rolled compactly. A slim-bladed hunting spear pegged the earth beside the kaross.

He's travelled light, reflected the warden. He knew the man as one of Chief Kanyoka's elders, and it would have taken him all of four days to walk from their village to Shingela. That he had done so, and that he, Ndende, had come, instead of a younger man, was of significance. Harry joined him in the dappled moving shade, his mind sifting through the ramifications of the visit as he went through the lengthy customary courtesies of greeting. In time they came to the main business at hand. The tribesman held Harry's gaze as he placed his words with care between them, arranging them with deliberation, as one would place stepping stones across a stream. Allowing the warden the time he needed to digest the information.

"The vultures feed well in the bush about our village."

Harry returned his gaze, selected his own words with as much care.

"The birds always feed well in this valley. The hunters and their prey are many, and so there is death often."

"This is true, and we are fortunate that this is so, that the animals are many. For without the animals we too would soon die. Our destinies are tied. But now there is more death than is normal. Death that is wasteful. The animals that are being killed are left to rot in the bush. They feed no-one but the scavengers."

Harry felt the knot start in his gut, and he did not want to ask the question.

"Which animals are dying?"

"Elephant. And the rhino."

Ndende regarded him impassively. Harry looked away, turned his head to stare out across the river. Seeing nothing. After a long while he brought his gaze back to his visitor.

"For how long has this killing been happening?"

"Since the time of the new moon."

The warden thought it out. A little over three weeks. He considered himself fortunate to have learned about it so soon. Time in the wilds slipped by rapidly. And he knew that, for Kanyoka and his elders, it had not been a simple decision to send word to the warden. Rather than await the next Game

Department patrol. There was much more to this. He sighed and said softly.

"I thank you for coming to see me ... Tell me about the killings."

Now it was the turn of Ndende to shift his gaze and stare out over the river that sparkled under the high noonday sun.

"We found the first kills a long way from our village. While our men were out collecting honey. In the place of the salt licks we found them. Elephants ..."

He held up one hand, five fingers splayed.

"They had been killed with guns. We did not understand this, for the only people with such weapons are your men, and now the soldiers who sometimes come into our area. And the elephants had been killed badly, with many bullets. Which is not your way. We did not know why you would be killing these animals that you so fiercely protect. Leaving the meat to rot. Taking only the tusks and the horns. We elders discussed this often, late into the darkness, for it worried us ... Only the leopard kills with such abandon, when the moon is high and the winds of the night are strong."

The tribesman looked briefly back at Harry, returning his attention to the river. A flock of storks wheeled above the calm mirrored surface, their reflections wheeling and gliding in tandem.

"Then one day, I was out hunting. I heard the sound of guns, not too far from me. For a while I waited, and then I went carefully to see what was happening. For we had decided, Kanyoka and we elders, that there was something wrong with this killing. It is as well that I went with stealth, for there were men who were acting as sentries, hidden in the bush. But it was obvious that they were not of the bush, for they were easy to see. Three elephants had been shot. There had been much gun noise for only three elephants. They were young bulls, and their ivory was not so big. Already they had begun to chop out the tusks ..."

Ndende paused, his gaze fixed on the circling storks. Harry waited.

"They slept that night near the elephants. I slept close by. It was not a peaceful night, for there were lions about, attracted by the blood. They, these hunters, were nervous of the darkness and the animals. They fired their guns several times. The next day they finished removing the tusks and departed. There were several of these men. Of my colour, but certainly of some very different tribe. I followed them to the river, with the tusks. They took *makoros* from the reeds, where they had been hidden, and went across the river. I watched them until they had gained the far bank. Since that day I have sometimes seen smoke from cooking fires across the river."

Harry watched a blister beetle weave its erratic way between them, the red spots on its shell bright against the dry earth. A dove called serenely from the branches above them. The knot in his gut was still there, tight bound, heavy. He felt nauseous.

"How many? How many kills have been found?"

The tribesman grunted.

"More than the fingers of three men. Mainly elephant. They are easier prey than the rhino living in the thick bush."

Harry's nausea increased. *Over thirty animals. In three weeks.* His mind whirled at the extent of the carnage. And that was in Kanyoka's territory alone. Apart from what he and Kashili had found. Apart from whatever other carcasses lay undiscovered out in the valley bush. He took a deep breath, struggling to steady himself. Ndende watched him in silence.

"Who are these people, Ndende? Why are they killing these animals? What are they doing with the tusks and horns?"

Harry could hear the raggedness of his voice. He could see his reflection in the dark eyes of the tribesman, tense, control slipping.

Ndende paused before replying.

"Long ago, when there was trouble, when there was war down here in our valley, when men came from over the river with guns, and there was much bloodshed, we saw people such as these. They are of the same kind. They carry the same kinds of guns, I do not know their proper name. They skulk like the hyena through the bush. They have visited our village under the cover of darkness, whilst we slept. We have seen their tracks. But they do not do us the courtesy of speaking with us. They do not want us to know their business. The elephant teeth are going over the river. This we know. But we do not know what happens after that. We can guess, as you can, but we do not know. Kanyoka is very afraid that this will bring more trouble. More bloodshed. We are all afraid. Up until this time we have not been a part of the troubles that are plaguing this country. We live our lives peacefully. We trouble no one. But it would seem that we must become a part of it, against our wishes. Chief Kanyoka knows that this news I bring to you will bring troubles to our people. He thinks you will send soldiers, and so blood will be spilt. Perhaps our blood will also flow. He asks that you meet with him and discuss this matter before you act. He reminds you that you have known each other a long time. Since you were a young man hunting crocodiles along this river, before you worked for the government. When you and Kashili were also simple hunters, like us. This, he asked me to tell you."

Harry smiled faintly, a wry twist of the features, acknowledging the message, returning the tribesman's frank stare. A shadow slid over them, a vulture in its ceaseless quartering search. The dove had stopped calling. The storks had moved on downriver. He sighed, drawing air deep into this lungs, expelling it through tight lips.

"Kanyoka is right. I must come to your area with game scouts as soon as possible. And perhaps the soldiers also. The poaching must be stopped. Already it has gone too far. And we must settle our accounts with these vermin from over the river. We will cause you no trouble. How can we? You have helped me. You have been my eyes in that distant part of my territory. You yourself have walked far to tell me of this evil that has been happening. I will not bring trouble to your people."

Ndende shook his head, a frown furrowing his broad forehead. "I hear you, as Kanyoka would hear you. But there will be trouble. The *nganga* has warned us. He has seen it in the bones. He says that we will be forced to leave our village. To abandon it. This is why Kanyoka requests that you speak with him. Alone. Before any soldiers come. Whilst we still govern our own lives. He asks you to return with me. In your motor, following the track inland, below the mountains, we could reach my village in a day. For your own safety we should not go all the way to the village. If the poachers have returned they may hear the motor. Perhaps they would run, or perhaps they would hunt you. I can go and fetch Kanyoka and the council elders, and return to meet you in the bush."

Harry studied the dark tribal scarred face before him, searching behind the muddied eyes for expression. Of course, there was none. The veil was down, keeping the outside world at bay. There was just his own reflection, peering back. He nodded, finally.

"Very well. We will return together, as you have said, and I will meet with Kanyoka. This courtesy I cannot ignore. We will leave whilst it is still dark tomorrow. You and I, and Kashili. Thank you again, Ndende, for journeying here with this news. Even if it is bad for both of us."

A fly, fat, blue-green, buzzed past the captain's nose at an angle, to crash land against the gauze of the tent window. Within the musty confines of the operations tent it was noisy. Irritatingly distracting. He stood up and swatted the insect savagely with a dog-eared codes book. Harry waited for the young officer to sit down again before he continued. From the vlei behind the army camp a baboon barked, the sound unnaturally loud in the late afternoon stillness.

"So, Jeremy. I will go into the area tomorrow, meet with Kanyoka and get a first-hand update on the situation. It certainly looks like a straight poaching operation as opposed to anything military oriented. Then perhaps you and I can plan some form of reaction."

Captain Jeremy Willis eyed the game warden sceptically.

"I don't like it. I think you're making a mistake, and we are approaching this problem in arse about face order. One, I smell a set-up. Into which you seem sublimely happy to walk. Two, any form of incursion is an army problem. To be resolved by the army, assisted if necessary by you and your men. Not the reverse, with you tiptoeing in and maybe stubbing your toe."

Harry smiled without humour. The lad was right. A little self-righteous perhaps, but correct. The military waved the big stick. But there was more to this than a straight seek and destroy operation. And it was his patch of turf. His animals getting killed. He wanted first crack.

"Jeremy, I'm not going to rock your boat. I owe it to old Kanyoka to meet with him. Before we press the panic button. If it wasn't for him we wouldn't even know about these bastards. Despite your patrols. So, please, do me a favour, will you? It's my neck. Let me snivel into the area and get an update. Give me a couple of days. I'll take an SSB along, so we'll have radio contact. And we can peel our brains and brawn accordingly. Treat this as an advance recce. Any new intelligence can only be an advantage. What we've got is nearly five days old. Okay?"

The young officer grunted without enthusiasm. He had no intention of being manipulated. Or intimidated. Especially by a bloody zoo keeper who was more interested in his animals than the terrorists pouring into the country. But he did make some sense. He knew the area like the back of his hand. And he knew the tribesmen. Or thought he did. If he was happy to walk in there and stick his neck out, it was his neck. Fresh information would be useful. Could save a lot of time and trouble. And lives.

"Okay, Harry. We'll do it your way, up to a point. I want a patrol to come with you. Half way. They can base up with their own vehicle somewhere over the half way point between Shingela and wherever you plan to meet the chief. If you have any problems, or establish that there's an immediate task for us, the reaction time will be that much faster. As you say, there will be radio contact. You've got your two days. After that we'll be coming in to take over."

Harry nodded. He couldn't ask for more. Two days was fine. He could do what he wanted to do in that time. With a little luck.

Late that night he lay listening to the calls of patrolling lions, feeling Peta's long smooth shanks close against him as she slept. He lay still, not wanting to wake her, thinking out the days ahead. Aware too, the thoughts intruding, that she would soon be leaving. The other world, the one outside the valley, would be reclaiming her for a while. For a few months whilst she put the book together in London with her editor. The thought of Nemana without her did not make him happy.

CHAPTER NINETEEN

The wild dogs had no interest in them. In moments their lithe, patchworked hides were swallowed up by the bush.

From the time they had materialised out of the mopane scrub, silent predatory wraiths in extended hunting line, paused to inspect the two humans crouched silently beneath the buffalo thorn, and moved on, no sound had been made. Yet their silent passing left an intensity in the air, a savage cleaving of the valley quiet. Harry shifted his position slightly so he could watch in the direction they had departed. Kashili remained motionless, listening to the rhythm of the bush surrounding them.

They had been thus for over five hours. Since Ndende had left them to go to the village, eight miles away. Their Landrover was half a dozen miles back on the track, wedged tightly obscure in the jesse thicket. The five man army patrol was half a day's drive further back, in waiting bivouac. Their radio would be permanently on to receive any contacts from Harry. Now it was mid afternoon and the valley lay in sun-hazed torpor. The mopane flies plagued them. Harry doubted that Ndende would return with Kanyoka and his elders before last light. The villagers might start their return journey today but darkness would catch them, making travel perilous. So, early on the morrow seemed most likely, he reflected. Two days and nights on his own, before the army moved in. As he thought out the permutations of the days ahead, his hands unconsciously caressed the automatic rifle resting across his knees. He could hear, distantly, the breaking of branches as elephants browsed.

The softly pitched call of the fish eagle, in the fast gathering dusk, caused them to stiffen. Here, miles from any water, the call was unusual. It was Ndende's prearranged location call. Kashili answered it. Once. Twice. They waited. The day's light had all but gone when the saw the small knot of figures picking their way through the twilight. Kashili whistled softly again and the figures changed direction towards them. Now Harry could make out the tall strong ranginess of Ndende. Behind him came Kanyoka and three other men. Harry and Kashili eased themselves upright to greet the villagers.

They sat in a close circle in the darkness. Around them the sounds of the night gathered strength. A zebra stallion barked shrilly. Lions grunted. Nearby a leopard sawed. They lit no fire and no one smoked. They chewed silently on sun dried meat, their conversation murmured. Harry digested the latest information they had given him, his anger and frustration tempered only slightly by the fact that he was now on the ground, and it appeared that the poachers were close. So, therefore, was retribution.

"How many are there on this hunt?"

"There are eight. Four of them have guns. The remainder have come to do the work. The cutting out of the ivory. They work fast, and seem to know this work."

In the darkness Harry could see the white of Kanyoka's teeth as he whispered. Well then, thought the warden. There we have it. The bastards are back. More organised than ever, bringing labour to do the hard work once they've shot the jumbo. Jesus Christ! It's open season! He spoke softly again.

"And you think they will still be where you saw them yesterday?"

He felt rather than saw the shrug.

"Perhaps. They had found more elephants, or rhino. We heard the shooting. So, they will need time to take out the teeth."

Harry grunted, saying nothing, his mind sifting through the information. When the silence was unbroken again it was Ndende who spoke. The man showed no tiredness from his mileage covered over the last days.

"There is that which we would discuss. Of which we spoke yesterday. My chief wishes to hear your words."

Harry nodded in the darkness, and when he spoke to the shadow close by him, he picked his words with care, striving to reassure the old chief.

"*Bava.* Father ... Ndende has told me of the concern that you and your people have ...,of the predictions of your witchdoctor. And, as I have spoken to him, so I say to you. We have known each other for many, many years. Since I was a young man who wandered this valley without direction. When the hair of Kashili held no white. We have always understood each other, you and I. I have eaten at your fire often. We have helped each other with many different things. I have killed the man-eating lions that attacked your village. You have been my eyes and ears in this part of the valley, helping me to protect the animals from outsiders. With all this that has gone before, bonding us, how can I allow harm to come to your people?"

The group of people, darker shadows amidst the blackness of the night-shrouded bushveld, waited as Kanyoka formulated his response. When it came there was a rueful irony in the ragged whisper.

"I hear what you say. And what you say is true. But times have changed. The trouble that is in the tribal lands is no small thing. It is bigger than you are, perhaps bigger than we. Although I know you speak with truth, I also know we can expect our lives to be disturbed ..."

The old man paused. Harry waited.

"This, I and my elders know, and we do not know how to prevent it. We must look to you for guidance. You know us. And you know how the world outside our home works. We have helped you protect the wild animals, because, like the sky and the rain, they are our animals also. And we will continue to help you. But you, in return, must help us when the time comes."

In the foliage around them a pair of Scops owls called in duet.

"You have my word," the warden replied. "These butchers from over the river will be stopped. I will do this, any way I can. With your help. Whatever troubles come out of this for your people, I will make my duty to undo. This I promise you."

There was a silence now for a time, broken only by the night sounds around them. Finally the chief sighed, a long low gusty exhalation.

"It is so. We shall see what we shall see. Let us look at the killings. What do you want to do?"

"I want to find them. Then they have a lesson to learn. Their heads for the elephant and rhino they've been slaughtering. But I need to have more information. So I need a prisoner."

Ndende cleared his throat, taking over as the elders' spokesman. "We would be wise to sleep here tonight. Let our minds and our bodies gather strength. Tomorrow, with the first light, I will lead you into the area where they have been shooting yesterday. I know the place well. Kanyoka and the others should return to the village."

"Thank you, Ndende. That makes sense. There is much to do before my time is up and the army become a part of this. And in my bones I feel that tomorrow will see good hunting ..."
As if in answer to his whispered prediction, the dark velvet of the night was cut by the screaming of elephants, distant, to the north, in the direction of the great river.

The faint whiff of woodsmoke came first. It was mid morning and the heat of the day was already hard on them. The tsetses were having a field day. The three men moved silently into thicker bush and waited, finely alert now. Harry hefted his .375, automatically checking the muzzle for any blocking dirt or vegetation that might have lodged there. He carried a dozen spare rounds for the weapon. Soft nose. So far today Kashili had carried his back-up weapon, the government issue FN, with four extra magazines slotted snugly in a canvas webbing pouch. Like Ndende, Kashili placed his faith in his hunting spear. He had not yet come to terms with the weapons of the twentieth century. The weapons of today, these guns that spat out many bullets, whilst one's enemy was a long distance away, were obscene. One needed little skill to fight these days, it seemed to Kashili. When one no longer looked one's opponent in the eye over the blade of a spear.

On the faint whisper of breeze then, came the smell of decay. Putrescence. It came and went, the death smell. Harry looked at the sky. Black specks, circling, dropping. A few hundred yards still, whatever was dead and bringing the birds down. What else? A honeyguide perched in a tree near them, twittering insistently. Hopping nearer to them, louder, when there was no response. Kashili glanced at the little bird speculatively, and then ignored it with a rueful grin. They had not treated themselves to a gorging of wild bush honey in a long while. The bush silent, except for the bird.

For half an hour they waited silently. Sweating. They did not smell the smoke or the decay again. Harry signalled his two companions over to him, waiting until the three men were crouched close together before whispering.

"Let us carry on. One at a time, keeping about ten paces between each man. I will lead. We are not achieving anything here ... Yes, Ndende?"

"Let me lead. I know that you are of the bush and the wild places. But I am also, and my longer years make me perhaps a little quieter, a little more wide-eyed, in such hunting."

The tribesman watched Harry's face. There was no challenge or belittlement in his words. He put across a fact which the warden knew made sense. Yet it was becoming a danger situation. They were moving into a new phase. He answered carefully.

"You are right. However, this is my trouble."

Ndende shrugged.

"This trouble is for all of us, not you alone ..."

A faint wry smile ghosted across his austere features.

"So let us go and meet it together."

The fire had been of the previous night. The poachers had moved on, leaving the fire to smoulder itself out. The fire had been made away from the carcasses. The vultures guided them past the fire to the dead elephants. The vultures and the smell. There were three. An old bull with his two younger companions. His apprentices. Harry inspected them and then the area around them. It had not been a clean killing. Each animal had several bullet holes in him, had milled and staggered around a lot before finally dropping. Kashili picked up a handful of cartridge cases and gave them to Harry. They were hot from the sun. Kalashnikov. Harry rolled them in a tight fist as he stood beside the old bull. He would have carried good ivory, if they hadn't been broken, he reflected. The other two would have carried smaller stuff, nothing like trophy size. These bastards move fast. In a hurry. Not prepared to wait until the tusks get loose in their sockets and it's easier to take them out. They slog away whilst the ivory is still tight in there.

Why the hurry, I wonder? He watched as Kashili and Ndende cast around the area for tracks, the .375 cradled readily. The fire, he thought. Sloppy. A fire can always give you away. One way or another. Keep it small, and the smoke down. And when you're finished with it, get rid of it properly. Yes, sure ... sloppy. Poor soldiering. Too fucking casual. Which is good news, he thought, watching the unhurried top heavy flight of a pair of hornbills. The more casual they are, the more sure of themselves, the more edge it gives us. Kashili materialised out of some scrub and joined Harry in the meagre shade of the young leadwood.

"There are eight of them, as the elders have said. They fear the night, sleeping close together like children. Their spoor is leading towards the river, with three of them carrying the ivory. Their spoor is heavier upon the ground."

The warden nodded, waiting for Ndende to join them before answering.

"All right. So they are not that far ahead of us ... about four hours. We may have luck on our side. The Zambezi is a hard day's walk from here. The ivory may slow them. Perhaps they are still hunting. Whatever, I feel in my gut that we will come on to them by tonight."

He watched more vultures slide out of the sky to join the squabbling, fluttering mass already feasting. A black-backed jackal stood watching them, tongue lolling. May as well radio the patrol, he reflected. They can move up to where I left the vehicle and follow our tracks to where we met Kanyoka last night. They may come in useful if they're closer when the deadline's up.

The sun was sliding to earth ahead of them, throwing long shadows and making him worry that they had crossed the river already, when they heard it. Murmured conversation. A suppressed laugh. The alien sound of metal knocked carelessly against metal. The three men could smell the river and see the dark evergreens that followed the course of the river, scarcely two hundred paces ahead. They sank into the obscurity of the darkening bush. They really are cock a hoop, mused Harry. Careless. I suppose they reckon the river is close and so is safety. I wonder why they haven't crossed yet? They had the light and the time. Perhaps they have to wait for transport to come over for them. Ah well, Harry old son, count your blessings. And make the most of it. No cock ups now. You've caught up with the murdering bastards, so let's extract a little payment for their mayhem. For the tusks and the horns. Not enough, not nearly enough. But a start. A little donation. A little blood for a lot of elephant teeth. What's the book say? An eye for an eye and a tooth for a tooth ... well okaaay, then. A few heads, for a lot of teeth.

He moved cautiously over to Kashili, motioning for Ndende to move in to join them. When their heads were touching he mouthed his orders.
"In an hour it will be dark. I want to move in and take them at last light. I would prefer to do it at first light tomorrow, but I do not have the time. One of them, one of those carrying guns, I want alive. Let us move in closer and see what we can learn. Ndende, please will you stay on my left side at all times. Kashili will be on my right. Any questions?"
His companions were silent.

Now, the radio and gear discarded, they moved in. From the river hippo grunted. Roosting francolin called. The muted conservation continued and the glow of a fire was bright now, in the dusk. Their guide in to the target. Harry grinned without mirth. They had covered over twenty paces. Movement then. Indistinct. Ahead. Pause ... More movement. Close to the first but left of it. The men waited, eyes searching the sepia of blurred bush in the fading light. Harry eased forward, bellying up behind a stunted patch of undergrowth. He had three people in sight now, with movement around them. Slowly the scene steadied and metamorphosed into clarity. The poachers were camped beneath the fallen spread branches of a great mahogany. In a far part of his mind the warden wondered why the big tree had fallen. Their quarry faced away from the three men, looking out in the direction of the river. The massive trunk of the evergreen angled away from the hunters, close by. Harry studied it, feeling Kashili slide up beside him. If they could make its sanctuary they would have a perfect launch pad for their attack. A person could run down along the trunk into the midst of the poachers, and be amongst them before they had time to react. Harry cradled the FN now. For close up face to face stuff he reckoned he'd need the full twenty rounds the magazine held. For any long distance accuracy work he'd have hung on to the .375. Once again his thumb checked the selector switch. He didn't want full automatic, too many bullets wasted that way. Too fast. Leaving you with an empty weapon, the working parts back, and a silly smile on your face. No, what was needed here was good quick single shot work.

Ahead, voices were raised. Harry listened. They were speaking Ndebele. Someone was arguing that it should have been him to go across the river ... He lost the rest of it in a babble of dissent. He looked at Kashili. The old man cocked his head in concentration. The hubbub died away. He put his mouth against Harry's ear.

"Two have gone across to collect more men. That is all I can make of it."

Harry nodded softly. That's two less to deal with now, he thought. That's good and bad. The more I can put out now the better. But it might be worth waiting. Who knows? Let's do it. From the movement and noise across the tree trunk he had an idea of where everyone was. He glanced back at Ndende and held a palm up at him to stay there. The tribesman nodded, his face wooden. In that position he would be at the poachers' backs when Harry attacked down the tree trunk. The warden was glad of his company. To Kashili he whispered.

"I will go down the tree into them. Come after me and stay behind me to watch my back, please."

The old tracker nodded. In the last minutes of light the white of his hair was still visible. Harry could feel his tension, in tune with his own, and his heart went out to him. He was getting too old for this kind of thing. Harry forgot his age sometimes. Kashili seemed ageless. He'd been around forever. The warden glanced around them once more and nodded.

The tree took him right on to them. Beside their fire he dropped, firing as he landed. His first shots he put into the legs of one of the gunnies, carrying on to the man and kicking away the weapon that lay beside him. Then he was whirling, crouched low, feet spread, moving, keeping himself as bad a target as he could, the FN tight against his side, hammering into the mêlèe of bodies scrambling around him. He felt Kashili behind him, at work with his spear. One of the poachers lurched on to him, already hit, but trying to get at their attacker with an axe. Harry guessed it was used for chopping out the tusks, levering the man away with his rifle, putting another bullet in him as the poacher grasped at the gun barrel. There was a garbled scream behind him and he turned to see a man go down with Kashili pulling his spear free. It had gone right through. Harry shot him through the head for insurance. Then it was over. Finished. Silence, except for groaning from the one he had hit in the legs. Harry checked the five bodies strewn around the fire, kicking spilt embers back into the low blaze. They were well down. The whole thing had taken less than a minute. Like a good cull, he thought. All down and kicking in no time. No break out. *Bastards.* He looked around for weapons. Two AK's lay on the ground in addition to the one belonging to the prisoner. Beside a rolled blanket, its wood gleaming dully in the firelight, an RPG 7 anti tank rocket launcher rested against a makeshift cloth bag holding four rockets. Bastards, he thought again.

Harry crouched beside the wounded poacher, searching him for any other hidden weapons. There were none. With his rifle barrel he lifted the man's head from staring at his shattered legs. He was dribbling freely and his eyes screwed up against the pain. The warden spoke quietly.

"Listen to me carefully, jackal. You are alive because I have let you live. I have medicine for your wounds that will stop your pain quickly. But this you will only be given once you tell me what I want to know. Do you hear me?"

The man's eyes opened, staring ahead. No reply, just a continuous whimpering incantation issuing forth. Harry moved the rifle, resting it across one leg, pressing softly. The man screamed. Harry took away the FN.

"Do you hear me, *hlati*?"

Kashili stirred the embers of the fire. Ndende was still in the darkness. Harry let him stay there. He felt better with someone out testing the night air. The blood soaked the ground under the poacher's legs. Harry moved the rifle.

"I hear you ..."

The answer, gasped in the Ndebele language, surprised him. He hadn't expected it so soon, had been at odds with himself on how to get it. Quickly. Quietly, and with the least damage to jeopardise the information he wanted. As he studied the wounded poacher, the man, reading his expression as doubt, gasped again.

"I hear you."

Okay then, thought the warden. Let's let him know that we know something.

"Where are the others? The rest of your group that hunted the elephants?"

Sweat poured, soaked the man's shirt.

"They have gone across to Zambia. For more men ... and boats."

"Why? Why more boats and men?"

Harry realised then that he had not seen any ivory. He spoke quietly to Kashili.

"There is no ivory here."

The poacher groaned, clutching at his thighs.

"The ivory is hidden. We have enough now to be collected and taken back over the river. They will ... aahhh ... The medicine. When will you give me the medicine for the pain?"

He slumped, blood loss hitting him. He babbled incoherently, head lolling. Well, thought Harry Kenyon. That's a start. Better than I thought. Let's get some morphine into him, and a drip, and let's see what we can do about stopping the blood. He's got a lot more talking to do, and I'm running out of time. Midday tomorrow is my deadline ... before the cavalry comes in. He turned to Kashili.

"Please collect the medic bag from where we left our gear. And ask Ndende to stay out there and keep watch for a short while longer. I think this vermin will talk. It is going to be a long night."

Kashili nodded, finishing cleaning the blade of his spear with cloth torn from one of the bodies.

"And Kashili ..."

The old tracker looked across at him.

"*Nikesile*. Thank you for once again looking after me."

"*Izona*. You performed well, little warrior. You moved fast and sure, as in the old days. You do not forget what you have been taught ..."

A wide grin creased the old man's features.

"I had forgotten the taste of such things. For a while it was like old, better, days, and I was young again. It is a pity there is no woman near to take advantage of this surge of youth."

From the trees above them a bird shrieked, tearing through the fabric of the night. Otherwise the night was quiet. The warden of Nemana chuckled.

CHAPTER TWENTY

In the night the hyenas came. Attracted by the smell of death they slouched and giggled at the edge of the firelight. As more arrived, called up by the first arrivals, they grew bolder. The bodies had been pulled back, lying in a sprawled line beside the vast trunk of the mahogany. The tree also protected the backs of the three men and their prisoner. They watched the hyenas across the fire, saw how the animals were starting to crowd them. Harry had no qualms about the scavengers having the bodies. It was the way of the bush. But he was not ready yet to give them up. They gave him a psychological lever whilst he methodically questioned his prisoner. The man was talking. With the morphine in his system and two saline drips into him, together with dressings on his wounds, it was apparent he could see a light of sorts at the end of his particular tunnel. The bodies beside him, and the mob of hyenas laying siege to the men, made a wonderful spur to his memory.

Through the pain and the treatment he talked.

And bloody how, mused Harry bitterly, had he talked. The revelations had left him aghast. His eyes felt grainy from lack of sleep. He checked his watch. Just after midnight. He thought it would be later. He stared out at the half circle of hyenas, counting at least fifteen in the flickering light. The noise was getting to him. The cacophony of witches' laughter, whoops and moans. A ghouls' chorus. And more would come, before first light. All in good time chaps, he remonstrated silently. You've had it too damn easy around here for a while now. Too many poor bloody jumbo and rhino carcasses for you to pick over, thanks to our friends here. You've had an absolute bloody banquet in this area for over a month now. Over fifty elephant and twelve rhino they've killed. Jesus Christ Almighty. The murdering bastards.

He watched a big female hyena, probably the pack matriarch he thought, edging out of the throng towards them, growling, head held high. Threat intimidating, impatient. Her teeth gleamed in the light of the fire. He let her push her luck to within five paces of them and then shot her. The force of the bullet slammed her back, scrabbling, into the pack and in seconds the rest of the hyenas were on her, tearing her apart. Chew on that for a while, Harry thought. It'll keep your mind off us for a spell. But he knew it would be short lived. She wouldn't take them long. More would come, giving the rest extra courage. There would be more forays. He looked at the faces of his companions. They were tight, fearful. These night animals were not their favourite animals, these scavengers who ate anything, even each other. Only Kashili returned his glance with an attempt at a dry-mouthed grin. The prisoner, whose *nom de guerre* was Bazooka Matiswa, watched in terror, unable to move.

It's about time for another round of twenty questions, thought Harry. Our friend is sufficiently overwhelmed at the moment to cast a few more pearls amongst us. He's told us how many they've killed so far, and the reason for this goddamned murder. The Ivory Section indeed, especially tasked to slaughter my elephants and rhinos, for their fucking war funds. What's happened to the largesse from Mother Russia, and the rest of the Eastern Bloc charity? My poor bloody game has got to die for these bastards to have a bit more money in the kitty. Well, boys, we will see about that. On my oath we will see about that. This joker says their latest cache, with over fifty tusks, is close by. Ready for pick up by the crew from over the river on the day after tomorrow. I wonder if the sound of the shoot-up reached them? Where's their base? How close to the river? It can't be too damn close with the SAS and the Scouts spending their time over the borders....

He reached out, and, taking the poacher's jaw firmly in his fingers, turned the man's head away from the hyenas to face him. He could smell his fear.

"Where is the base that you operate from? How close is it to the river?"

Bazooka Matiswa swallowed twice before the answer would come out.

"It is twelve miles from the big river, beside a smaller one, the Mushika, which runs into the Zambezi. Where the ground begins to climb."

"How long has it been there?"

"Over four months. I have been there that long and it was already there when I arrived."

The nationalist poacher's eyes slid back to the hyenas. The shot female had been consumed. Now they jostled at the edge of the firelight, their attention focused again on the humans. The noise level rose.

"When did your comrades leave here for the base camp?"

"There was two hours of light left in the day."

Eyes still fixed on the hyenas. Good, Harry mused. Food for thought.

"How long would it take to cross the river? What do you use?"

"They went in a dug-out, which would take almost an hour at this part of the river. We have rubber boats also, but they are still hidden on this side. More will come, for the ivory is heavy."

You fucking bet it's heavy, thought Harry. Some of the best ivory that's left in Africa is down here. He took a series of long deep breaths, calming himself. Okay then. All right. Just take it step by step. Cut out the hysterical crap, it's a luxury you can't afford right now. So ... maybe they heard the shots, maybe not. It depends how keen they were on getting across, and then hot-footing it to base. I doubt the noise would carry that far. The river is half a mile wide here. It's a fifty-fifty chance. If they come back on schedule, all well and good. We'll have them. If they don't, no matter. Because I'll make another plan ... do a bit of poaching myself. Over there. Give them a taste of being under the gun. My gun.

The hyenas were edging in again, the newcomers pushing at the front rankers. Harry eyed them watchfully, feeling his prisoner's terror grow.

"Where does this idea come from? This plan to poach ivory and rhino horn for your funds? You people have a lot of money from Russia, East Germany, China, and many other countries that support your cause. Why do you come here, into my game reserve?"

"Our leaders in Lusaka have said we should make ourselves more independent of our backers. They prefer to give us weapons only ... not so much money. And our leaders worry when the Russians or the others threaten to stop supplies. In Angola Jonas Savimbi has raised much money from ivory for his war against the Luanda government. The Ivory Section has been formed to do the same for our war. The Zambezi Valley is not the only target area. There have been patrols hunting in the Luangwa National Park for rhinos, but Kaunda has complained and that has stopped."

Bloody hell, cursed the warden silently. A regular extermination campaign.

"What happens to the tusks and horns once they have been taken back to your base?"

"I don't know. That has nothing to do with me. My job is to shoot the animals and get the stuff back over the river."

Two more hyenas had psyched themselves up for another attack. They came in, snarling loudly. Before Harry could shoot, Kashili and Ndende leaped forward, stabbing at them with their spears, not killing them, but hurting them and drawing blood as they worked the blades. The animals shrank back. The guts of one of them spilled, drawing the others on to it immediately. The hyena joined in the frenzy, snapping at its own wound, and went down under the pack. The snapping of jaws resounded loudly in the night. Harry shivered. Bazooka's eyes bulged.

"How many of you in this Ivory Section?"

"We are thirty, plus men for work as bearers."

"And you ... how many elephant and rhinos have you shot?"

The poacher shrugged, watching the mayhem at the edge of the firelight.

When he answered, Harry could hardly hear him.

"I have forgotten. About twenty. The Kalashnikovs are too light. Several of us shoot together. Sometimes we use bazookas. RPG 7's."

Harry nearly attacked him then, fought against it. It gets worse and worse, he thought. Anti tank weapons against the poor bloody animals. *Ahhh, the bastards.*

"You say you know nothing of the ivory once it arrives at the base. I do not believe this. This campaign is well organised, and you are a part of it. You are a part of the Ivory Section, therefore I am sure you know something."

Bazooka Matiswa shook his head.

"No. I speak the truth. Our commander handles this only. He deals with the man who comes to collect the ivory. No one else has anything to do with this part of the operation."

"This man who takes delivery of the ivory, is he of your army?"

"No. He is a civilian, and he is a white man. He brings his own transport."

"Who loads the ivory when he visits?"

"We do. Whoever is not out hunting."

"Then you have seen the man close up? You have heard him speak?"

The hyenas were backing off, whooping, looking back into the darkness. Reluctantly, but giving the men space. Harry heard a low rumble. Lion, he thought. Charming. A brand new ball game. He shifted his rifle to cover the area tighter. Then he saw the great dark shapes, shadows against darkness, and heard a shrill trumpet blast. Branches snapped close by as the elephants moved towards the river. Another shrill blast and a rush in the darkness. The hyenas still visible in the firelight broke into slope shouldered flight, dispersing before the agitated elephants. Must be a breeding herd with young calves, guessed Harry. Hyenas and lions tend to upset elephant mothers. There was welcome quiet now. The men could hear the elephants in the river. The hyenas would come back, but only when the herd had moved off. Kashili put more wood on the fire.

Harry stood and stretched, pushing the tiredness away. Then he turned and knelt beside the prisoner, resting the FN very lightly on one of his bandaged splayed legs. The hyenas were gone, but he still wanted the poacher to talk. And he wasn't fussy how the pressure would keep up.

"So, my hunting friend. Tell me about this *mukiwa*, this white man, who collects the ivory and rhino horn ..."

Muddy eyes stared back at him, blinking at the pain even the slight weight of the rifle caused.

"He is a big man. Strong. He has a beard ..."

Bazooka Matiswa licked his lips. They were very dry. He had been given no water for a long while now.

"I have heard that the man's name is Gant."

Harry Kenyon felt it start then. The control snapping. The poacher's face swam before him, blurring, steadying, then clear, sharp. *Gant.* He stood up, away from the temptation, feeling it surge through his system. He moved past the fire into the fringe of darkness, breathing deeply. Feeding the oxygen into the blood. *Gant.* Hands on hips he stared up at the canopy of stars above, searching out the formations he knew. *Gant.* There was Orion. And the Plough. The Cross. *Gant.* Like the hyenas, always there was Gant. But the hyenas lived off death. He caused it. A meteor burned earthwards. Harry waited for the knot in his gut to unwind.

Dawn had flushed across the sky an hour earlier. Pewter to mother-of-pearl. Ripe mango to citron. In the early freshness of the new day Harry stood staring at the pile of tusks and rhino horns. The cache was deep within a thicket of buffalo thorn. On top of the information given by their prisoner over the night, the sight of the cache had little extra impact. He felt drained. Washed out. He picked his way out of the thorn thicket to where the others waited. The poacher lay on a make-shift stretcher. He looked grey. The short journey had opened up his wounds. Kashili and Ndende squatted on their haunches away from him. Harry joined them and spoke to the tribesman.

"I am grateful to you for your help. It is yet another favour I owe you and Chief Kanyoka. There is not much else for you here. I have spoken with the army on the radio. They are making their way to this place. They should get here late today or early tomorrow. We will wait and see who comes for the ivory, and we will see what happens from then on. Let us move away from here and eat something. Then you are welcome to depart for your village. I know that from here it is an easy journey to make before nightfall."

Ndende nodded.

"I have thought this also. Kanyoka would wish to know how things have gone."

He gestured with a horny thumb at the poacher.

"What of him?"

Harry smiled.

"We shall see. He has not paid a full price yet for his actions."

Ndende grunted sourly.

"He does not look good this morning. It would be simplest to kill him now you have spoken with him."

Harry Kenyon shrugged gently, letting his gaze sweep the bush around them. Impalas, hides sleek and shining in the new sunlight, grazed serenely in the woodland fringing the floodplain. A waterbuck ram watched the men over the backs of his cow and calf. A troop of baboons grubbed and gambolled. Atop a fever tree a lone marabou stork balanced. Growing close up out of the thicket hiding the ivory a tamarind spread its delicate leafy canopy. Harry measured its branches. Good leopard baiting tree, he mused. Good for what I have in mind, too. He looked at Kashili.

"You remember that baobab we passed, a short way back? Once we have eaten please go and cut some bark for rope. It should be strong enough to hold a man. Several men."

He dreamed they were on a beach. The sand was very white and powdery, and it made soft squeaking noises when they walked on it. At the edge of the sea, where small waves washed gently in, the sand was firm and still white in the clearness of the water. The sea was shallow for a long way out, and as they walked there were small outcrops of rock, and then coral as the reef started. The water was very clear and the fish and underwater life showed sharp to the eye. Along the shoreline tiny sanderlings scurried, feeding behind the retreating waves. It was hot and clear, and the sea was beautiful, and there was no one else but them in the whole world.

They were eating oysters, out on the reef that they could walk to when the tide was low. The man and woman sat on coral chairs, slowly savouring the oysters. Somehow, out here, they were cold, just the right temperature. Somehow, too, there was exactly the right amount of lemon squeezed on to the oyster, and the dusting of coarse black pepper was perfectly judged. The brown bread was covered with fresh salty butter, sliced neatly. None of this was on plates, or anything else. It was just there. Only the wine worried the man. It was chilled perfectly. Absolutely. But it was red. A deep burgundy. Like heart blood, he thought. It was a pity the wine was wrong, on such a wonderful day. He looked at the woman. She looked beautiful, and he thought again how much he loved her. She wore a sarong that he had never seen before. It was made of raw silk and was a deep red colour. Like the wine, he thought. It's the same colour as the wine. It upset him. Why wear blood on such a beautiful day, he wondered. In such a beautiful place.

He looked around him, away from the wine and the sarong, and noticed that the sea had dirtied. It got darker as he looked, and he realised it was turning red. As red as the wine and her sarong. He stared at the sea in horror, feeling himself tremble violently. The tide was coming in fast. Faster than he had ever seen. The reef began to disappear. Water, heart blood, washed in over his feet. The man couldn't move, no matter how hard he tried. When he looked at the woman she was no longer there. He was alone. He could feel the trembling through his whole body, harder now.

Kashili's face then, above him. And, higher, green leaves and blue sky. Not red yet, he thought. There's still time ... The old tracker shook him gently again, concern in his eyes.

"Wake up, my friend, you are not happy in your sleep. I thought you were about to get up and run off, which would not be a good thing."

Harry stared at him, feeling the sweat trickle on his body, aware that his pulses were hammering. He swallowed and took a deep breath, the red still there behind his eyes if he shut them. Kashili spoke again.

"There is someone coming. It is late now. You have slept for almost an hour, although at the end it was not a good sleep. In the beginning you were smiling in your sleep. Come, let us see who we have."

Harry nodded. He wished he were somewhere away from here, with Peta Holt. Anywhere.

The bodies twisted gently on their braided bark ropes. The white of a piece of paper, torn from Harry Kenyon's note book, was cleanly stark against one of the bodies. A lively river breeze, slipping through the bush of the flood plain, made the note flutter. Harry and Kashili waited in the cool shade of a twisted wild fig as the army section made its way past the hanging things towards them. A soldier stumbled, looking back. It was late afternoon.

They've made good time, reflected the warden. Excellent. They can help keep the beasties away from the stuff on the tree tonight. While we wait for their friends to turn up. He saw that the grimace that had washed over the corporal's face as the soldiers had passed the bodies was still there. Harry remembered him from the base at Shingela. He was a youngster, not yet twenty, still reliving the glories of first team rugby at the evening mess. Harry smiled.

"Hello, David. You chaps made good time. Obviously no problems with your map reading."

"Harry." The young soldier's voice was carefully polite. His captain had told him all about Harry Kenyon. Nice enough bloke, he had said, but a bit fucking weird. Treated Nemana as his own private game reserve. And not interested in the bloody war effort. Doesn't give a stuff about all the mayhem around him. Even though he used to be in the SAS ... and got a gong. Doesn't realise that we're in charge here, and not him.

The corporal nodded back at the tamarind tree.

"What's that all about?"

Harry still smiled.

"Poachers," he replied. "There's some weapons for you guys to take back to the research people. And ..." He flicked a thumb at the dangling limp bodies.

"There's five bodies and accompanying hands for the Identification Team at Special Branch. Along with the already identified being of one Bazooka Matiswa."

Corporal Dave Morris stared at the bodies.

"How many were there?"

"Six. We took the lot last night. Two had already gone over the river."

"No prisoners? We could have done with some information."

The young voice wavering between remonstration and shock at the sight.

Harry kept his voice mild.

"There's plenty of information. Which I'll pass on."

The paper fluttered on a new breeze.

"What's that?"

Harry nodded at it.

"See for yourself."

He turned and looked at Kashili. The old tracker grinned dryly and shook his head.

The corporal walked over to the bodies, reaching up gingerly to steady the fluttering paper.

"Read it aloud," instructed the warden. "So everyone knows."

His voice was different now. He had finished with the politeness. The bullshit. The soldier heard the change, read it out.

" *'Caught, Charged, Convicted of poaching. Sentence, Death.*

Wanted for further questioning : Alex Gant and members of the Ivory Section.' "

The young soldier came back to the warden. He looked sick. Harry waited for him to speak.

"You don't play around, Harry."

Harry watched him without answering. Corporal Morris pushed on.

"I was given to understand by our CO that you were going to meet with the villagers downriver and see what up-to-date intelligence you could get for us to work on. After that it was army work."

Harry smiled without mirth, not really prepared to cross swords with a soldier pup, but full up with it. Sick of it.

"Well, old son, there is certainly enough to go round. You and your troopies won't be bored. I have spoken with Chief Kanyoka and his elders, and that business hanging from the tree is a direct result of my meeting. There was no time to bugger about ... and I had two days on my own. Compliments of your captain. Now ..."

He spoke more quietly now, slower. He moved closer to the soldier, fixing him with a hard stare.

" ... I have got information. Plenty. Which I have every intention of passing on to the army. When you've a minute to listen. Of immediate interest is the fact that some more of these bastards may be coming back over the river tomorrow, to pick up the ivory. We are here, on the ground, and we could, together, give them quite a welcome. So, what else have you got on your chest, corporal?"

The young man swallowed and, eventually, a weak grin drifted on to his face.

"I'm sorry Harry ... didn't mean to be snotty. It's just that the captain is standing by at Shingela ... wants an update asap. He's keen to get on the ground here. Let's make some plans."

Harry grunted sourly and then took a deep breath.

"All right. I suggest you place your men whilst we chat. Brief them that we expect some company. Kashili and I will be with the ivory in that thicket near the body."

The soldier nodded, and Harry turned away.

"Oh, Harry?"

He glanced back at the corporal, waiting.

"Who is Alex Gant?"

The game warden winced, as if a sharp sudden pain had twisted in his body.

"He is a person who will have to be put down. Soon. He's across the river, orchestrating the poaching we have here in Nemana."

He slapped a tsetse fly, his gaze following a flock of Lillian's lovebirds, a scattering of green jewels amongst the leadwood trees.

"And I don't care what I have to do to kill the murdering bastard."

CHAPTER TWENTY ONE

Black and white. Fluid motion. White and black. Balancing on the breeze. Feathered fingers splayed. Crimson. Talons and beak. Long sweeps across the hot blue sky.

Harry watched the bateleur patrolling. Kept his eyes on the eagle, away from the aeroplane that was banking away from the small airport of Kariba. Sunlight bounced off the Viscount's wings. Watching the bird, he saw that on the edge of his vision. He didn't want to watch the plane that was taking her away from him. Away from the valley. He didn't know when he would see Peta again. And it hurt. A deep aching hollowness. Leaning against the Landrover, feeling the heat from the metal burn through his shirt, he wished he smoked. It would give his mind and hands something to do. For a few seconds, at least. Then he could always light up another one. The airport was quiet again, slipping back into a still-life frieze. Some movement in the dark glassed tower, and across at the air force encampment. Three Alouette helicopters stood in line on the asphalt, stilled rotors drooping as if stricken by the heat. A

Dakota was being refuelled. Harry watched idly. He knew the general had flown up from the capital today, had seen him briefly, getting into the army Landrover, when he had arrived with Peta. *Peta.* Where would she be now? Further away. Closer to Salisbury, and the connecting international flight to London.

Okay, he thought now. Leave it alone, won't you. Cut it out. Grow up. That's just it, though. I am grown up. And I still miss her. *Already.* Why don't you go into town? Go and see what the brass want with you. You're already late. Get moving. That will keep your mind off her all right. Drummond and Garnet Clayton. All right then.

The bush tread tyres hummed loudly on the black tarmac. He drove steadily, deliberately, glance flicking occasionally away into the bush that fringed the road. Elephant browsing, off in the mopane. Warthogs paused in their rooting. His mind went over the past days. They had ambushed the ivory and rhino horn cache for two days. And nights. The poachers had come early on the third day, crossing the Zambezi in the darkness. It was hard to say how many because they came in carefully. Spread out and wary in the thickest bush. From the tracks, later, Harry and Kashili reckoned there were a good dozen of them. These ones weren't as careless as the ones Harry had annihilated. Maybe they could smell something ill on the breeze. For starters, where were their comrades? And why the vultures, crowding heavy perched in the trees in the fresh day's light, waiting for the first hot-breathed thermals? It all started too soon. One of the soldiers opened up too early, well before any of the poachers were into the killing zone. And that was it. A hail of scattered return fire from the enemy, a shout, and empty bush. Off like greyhounds. Harry had broken cover, Kashili on his heels, and gone after them, cursing. Caught a glimpse of a running form, snap fired, saw the figure stumble and the rustle of undergrowth. The warden slowed, moving in cautiously, Kashili bird dogging away to his right. His spear flashed briefly in the sun.

They found the Kalashnikov first, blood-smeared. Then its owner, in the long grass, right shoulder pulped by the soft-nosed slug from the .375. But alive. Kashili stayed with him whilst Harry moved on. The troopers were moving now, slowly. Warily. Searching their way through the bush towards the river. Harry waited for them on the Zambezi, hidden in the shade of a great fig. The dug-out canoes were all pulled up nearby. The poachers hadn't made for them. They would have been good targets out on the water. Instead, they had scattered, bomb-shelled. What a fuck up, thought Harry. What a bloody lemon. Now the bastards are all over the place. Biding their time. I'll have that trooper's guts ...

A soft whistle came from the scrub close by. He answered. The corporal emerged warily. The warden called softly.

"Here, corporal."

The young soldier joined him in the shade cover.

"That was bad luck, Harry. At least you got one ..."

"Bad luck, my backside," growled the warden. "Bad discipline. If he was under my orders I'd have him on a charge when we got back to base."

He paused, watching the river. Then he nodded at the dug-outs half obscured by the riverine growth.

"You've got yourself a fleet of canoes here. There's also two inflatables hidden further upriver. What's your next move, corporal?"

Harry had pushed the anger out of his voice now. He didn't want to rattle the youngster at the moment. Corporal Morris' answer was guarded.

"I'll contact base. I think they should send in more troops and we'll follow up. Should pick up some of these blighters."

He watched the warden. Harry kept his face impassive. You'll be lucky, he mused. In this bush, with them scattered to the four winds. Hope you've got good trackers because it's all yours now. You're the cavalry. It's time Kashili and I were getting back to Shingela. But first ...

They had, he and the old tracker, doctored the nationalist poacher as best as they could. Then they had taken him to the stiffened swinging corpse of Bazooka Matiswa. And his comrades. Harry had shoved him forward so he was crowded up against the body, and taken his note from its place. He turned the man around to face him, pulled him close, forcing his eyes to hold his own. The smell of ammonia told him the prisoner had wet himself.

"Look at me well, scum. Remember my face. For you will see it again ..."

He thrust the paper into a pocket, on the left, unbloodied side.

"Unlike Matiswa and your other comrades. For I will let you live. And I will allow you to return over the river, with my message. To the Ivory Section. And to Gant. Tell them that I am now hunting them, as they have hunted my animals. Before, I was not a part of this war. There are people enough on both sides for that business. But now, the Ivory Section and Gant have brought me into it ..."

Harry's voice dropped to a hoarse jagged whisper as he placed a hand at the man's throat, holding him there.

"Tell them what you have seen here, poacher. And tell them that if they come again into my game reserve and kill my animals, the same will happen to them. Have you understood me, jackal?"

The man nodded, hard. Harry took a deep breath, calming himself, and spoke softly to Kashili.

"Take him to the river and put him in a dug-out. It won't be a picnic but he should make it back, eventually."

He smiled now, without mirth, as he turned off the tarmac on to the track that led down to the regional wildlife headquarters on the shore of the lake. The corporal hadn't liked it, letting the poacher go. Nor had his officer back at base in Shingela. The soldier had moved to stop Kashili, and Harry had shaken his head wearily and stepped over, close to the young soldier. His

voice had been soft, even mild. But the corporal had flinched at
the expression in the older man's eyes.
"Leave it alone, son. If you push this you'll be needing a
chopper to casevac you out of here. That's not a threat ... it's a
fact of life."
Corporal David Morris had stepped back. Harry had nodded at
Kashili and he walked on. The warden watched the soldier, felt
the tension in the others as they waited. He waited also.
Finally the soldier swallowed, blurted.
"Captain Willis will not agree to this! He wants a prisoner.
You've pushed your luck too far. This is army business.
Letting that terrorist go is not your prerogative, Warden
Kenyon."
Harry stood unmoving, hearing the emphasis on the warden,
still concentrating on the tension around him. Keeping close to
the corporal in case they did something silly. He kept his voice
mild.
"I already have information that will keep everyone down here
busy for quite a while. Get on your radio to the captain and
give him a sitrep. Tell him I'm happy to wait for him here to
brief him, or I'll see him back at Shingela."
Harry moved away from the soldiers now, keeping them all in
view.
"And, corporal ..."
The soldier blinked, a vein throbbing visibly along his forehead.
Harry tapped a grimed finger against his own temple.
"In here are over twelve hours of interrogation. Any move to
stop that poacher making his way back over the Zambezi, or to
do anything else rash, and there's a case of amnesia on your
hands. Tell that to your captain as well, will you?"

Harry noted the vehicles parked in the scattered patches of
shade given sparsely by the mopane trees fringing the cultivated
hippo cropped lawns. He wondered what the army Landrover
was doing here at a departmental meeting. The same one the

General had used earlier, at the airport. A feeling of unease crept over him.

Out on the front cool shaded verandah, with the view of the lake and the air scented by frangipani, they were waiting for him. Quite a crowd, mused the warden, the unease forming into a tight ball in his gut. Looks like a first team fixture. He had left his beret in the car, which took care of the saluting. He greeted those present, watching carefully for reaction. Garnet Jackson grinned his welcome, but the grin was strained. Roy Thorson, sitting aside from the main scrum, grinned and winked before shaking his head slightly. The director's welcome was without enthusiasm.

"Harry..."

"Sir. Good afternoon."

Harry turned to the general and Scratch Peters, noting he was a major now. The army commander was smiling, held out his hand. Harry thought as he took it that the smile looked forced, a little sardonic.

"Hello, Harry. Long time no see."

"General. It is that. Good to see you again."

Harry shook hands briefly with Scratch Peters, watching his face carefully for any expression. There was none.

Okay, thought Harry, the first team it is. Is it a friendly, I wonder?

Alistair Drummond spoke.

"Take a seat, Harry. The general can't stay long, and we've a lot to discuss."

Harry sat, disliking the perfunctory tone of the director's voice. There was a brief silence as Drummond glanced at the general. Then he shifted in his chair and looked across at Harry.

"Since your run in with the insurgents a week back events have occurred that need discussing. Before that, however, there's a couple of things need clearing up ... which I hope will be done here and now."

He paused, glanced again at the army supremo, who watched Harry dispassionately. Not a friendly, decided Harry. This looks like heavy league stuff.

The director went on.

"The army representative at Shingela has charged that you've been obstructive, have far overreached your responsibilities, and have threatened one of his men. We'd like your comments on that."

Ahhh, thought Harry. Is that it? Have the general and Peters taken time out for that? Surely not. Not with their own fucking war to run. His glance swept briefly around the faces. Garnet and Roy Thorson looked worried. Harry replied carefully.

"This kind of issue is always better sorted out if all parties are present. It saves things getting lost in the translation. As far as I'm concerned the working relationship between Captain Willis and myself is fine. If I've overreached and been obstructive, someone will have to tell me how. As far as threatening one of his men goes … if you mean my handling of the corporal who did not wish the poacher to be sent back with my message … yes, I had to be a little firm with him. No more, no less."

Scratch Peters answered swiftly, sharply.

"You forget, Harry, that the army runs things. Not you, or the director of the Game Department, or Jesus Christ himself. The army. Operations in the Nemana National Park are our responsibility, which includes the hunting down of insurgents. Killing those six, and then letting one go free back over the river, is not your prerogative…"

He paused, his eyes hard. Then.

"You had your chance. Short of getting down on my knees I've tried to get you to rejoin on several occasions. To come back in the army and do something. But you're not interested. At this time of our history, you're not interested! When we need everyone we can get, especially with your background. All you want to do is play St Francis and count your bloody animals, and keep your nose clean. Well, all right … it's no good forcing you. But you forfeit the right to make your own laws. You will not play this by your own rules, Harry Kenyon. It's army responsibility. And from now on you don't lift a finger without our say so."

Harry felt it start, coming up fast. Fighting it because he knew he had to tiptoe this through, could not afford to lose control. He waited, fighting it, bemused by Scratch Peters' vitriolic attack. Trying to work it out. Wondering what the hell had happened that he had not picked up. Still fighting the anger that was spewing up inside him. Forcing himself to take this gently, step by step, probing his way. When he spoke, finally, his voice was quiet and restrained. Watching him, Garnet Clayton knew how hard it was for the warden.

"That was an army sanctioned operation. The army, in the form of Captain Jeremy Willis, gave me two days to recce the area, and act accordingly. On my own. Now hear me, Scratch. Watch my lips. Those poachers were in that area for weeks, with no one, including your army, knowing. If it were not for Kanyoka and his people we would not have known they were there. Those insurgents were poachers first, gooks second. They were totally involved in killing my elephants and my rhinos. Which they were doing bloody well, unknown, again I say it, to army or my limited patrols down there. My actions in those two days killed six poachers, or insurgents, and got you and intelligence a lot of information. What are you doing about it? Except for roasting me, that is."

"It's got f...."

The general lifted a hand, cutting off Peters' reply, going on to run it through sandy-coloured thinning hair.

"Harry, I have to leave. I have a press briefing in half an hour. Walk out to the car with us, will you?"

He picked up a canvas briefcase that leaned against a chair leg and stood up, excusing himself from the Game Department men.

"Sorry, gentlemen. Time isn't on my side these days. Please excuse Harry for a few minutes. Lead the way, Major Peters."

At the army Landrover they stopped, the general's gaze sweeping briefly across the clear blue afternoon sky before he turned to Harry. He grinned dryly.
"You're looking well, old chap. As fit as ever. I wish you'd accepted Scratch's invitations to come back in. The main jugular vein work in this shitty little war we've got is being done by a handful of blokes ... the pros in the small units. Special Air Service, the Scouts, a few other no-name brands. Guys like you.. from eighteen to sixty years old ..."
He let it hang between them. Harry was aware of Scratch Peters' oblique scrutiny. And sod you too, mate, thought the warden bitterly, thinking back to his tirade. He shook his head.
"I've had enough, Hugo. I've told this to your people already. Every time there's a shitty little war in Africa the game gets slaughtered whilst everyone's busy going at each other. The wildlife of the region takes a dive. Harry Kenyon isn't going to make a blind bit of difference to what happens here, in or out of the army. But he can help the poor bloody animals. To whit, sort out these murdering bastards from over the river who are taking out my jumbo and rhino. What's happening about the griff I passed on about that base in Zambia, whilst we're on the subject?"
The general sighed.
"Ahhh ... Yes."
He stared at Harry.
"That's why I wanted to have a chat with you out here. Privately. There is no way I should tell you this because it's red folder stuff. Top secret. Your director certainly does not know. Because I think I know you, and don't want you screwing things up, I'm going to tell you. If you blow it in any way you'll be responsible for the deaths of some very valuable people, as well as undoing a lot of dangerous work that's been done."
He smiled grimly, his eyes flat.
"I won't be boorish and threaten you with a quiet bullet and a one way trip down the Zambezi."

Pausing again, letting it all sink in. Harry didn't want to hear any more. Scratch Peters watched him from the other side of the vehicle, a sardonic expression on his face. The general went on, his voice lower.

"We know about the base on the Mushika. We have not neutralised it because we have an agent placed there who is very valuable to us. Some time in the future, we'll take it out. But not now. Any moves on that camp, at this time, are taboo."

The army commander held Harry's gaze as the warden stared at him. His thoughts cartwheeled through Harry's brain. Finally he spoke.

"The poaching? What about the poaching? As long as that base is there, with this so-called Ivory Section, they'll be coming over the Zambezi into Nemana, Chingusa, Katete and slaughtering the game. What happens about that?"

He was aware that his voice, pitched as low as the general's, had risen to a ragged shout-whisper. Almost cracked.

The soldier shook his head.

"There's not much to be done about that, I'm afraid. For the time being, anyway. I don't want to upset the flow of intelligence coming out of that area. You and your staff, without antagonising the army at Shingela, will have to do what you can to stop that."

"Staff? What bloody staff?"

Harry realised his voice was still rising, sounding shrill.

"I've got a skeleton staff at Shingela to basically keep a National Parks presence officially at Nemana. Myself and a ranger and six game scouts. And my personal tracker. Nemana is over nine hundred square miles. As is Chingusa and the Katete. The carcasses we have found to date are only some. I'm a game warden, not a bloody miracle worker!"

The two soldiers watched him silently, before the general shook his head again.

"I'm sorry, Harry. Really. For the moment that's the way it has to be. Perhaps I can arrange for the army contingent down there to be increased, to allow for more patrols. I don't know

... I'll have to review our troop strengths for the region. Whatever, you will not do anything without referring to the officer in charge down there."

He moved towards the passenger side of the Landrover, nodding to the major.

"What about your agent?" asked Harry, "Can't you signal him that the poaching is out of hand in the valley, and that the army is moving in more troops to counter the incursions of the poachers from Mushika base? Can't you arrange something, damn it? You seem to be able to do everything else."

The general stopped then, putting his briefcase into the vehicle. Then he turned slowly so his back was to the major, and spoke softly to the warden.

"Harry, old chap, I'm sorry I can't help you. Truly. Our agent is not permanently at the base. But he visits it often. He has to have reason to visit that camp, and other bases. The ivory is his reason. He organises the selling and distribution of it for the gook coffers. At this time, the information we get from him is worth a lot more to our survival than rhinos and elephants. Believe me..."

Harry stepped back a pace, feeling as if he had just taken a full kick in the gut. His head spun. He shook his head, kept shaking it to clear the buzzing there. When he tried to speak, his voice wouldn't come. It took long seconds to force his throat clear.

"Not Gant? He's not your ..."

General Hugo Winters reached a hand out, grabbed Harry's shirt, and pulled him back to him. When he spoke it was a harsh grating whisper.

"Never heard of the man. Remember today, Harry. Keep your nose out. You're not one of us, of your own choice. That's acceptable. But only just. Keep out of our hair, and never, but never, repeat what's been said!"

Harry stood in the dust of the departing army vehicle, long after it had disappeared. From away out over the lake he heard a fish eagle call, the sound floating sweetly on the still air. He stood, unmoving. He tasted bile in his mouth and spat, but nothing came. His mouth was dry. When he heard a footstep behind him, he didn't turn. Garnet Clayton walked around him, seeing the stillness.

"Christ, Harry. Are you all right? You're as white as a sheet!"

Harry felt as though he were outside himself, somewhere high up, maybe with the fish eagle, looking down at the shell that was him. He could see himself standing, tired, worn, unsure of himself, in the mid afternoon sun. He wanted to sit down, right where he was, in the dust, and go to sleep. Maybe he would wake up and it would all be a bad dream, maybe ..."

"Harry? For God's sake, man. What ..."

The chief warden stopped, sorely worried. Alarmed also at the flat dead look in Harry Kenyon's eyes. He watched as his friend took a deep breath, then another, turning his face to the sky. He saw that he was shaking, saw it steady on the third deep trembling inhalation. Harry smiled then, a sad, dry grimace. Pulling himself upright, straightening, blowing a long breath out now through pursed lips.

"I'm all right, Garnet ..."

He started back to the house and the others waiting.

"But life can certainly be a bitch on occasion."

Garnet Clayton cleared his throat uneasily.

"I don't know what went on out here that's upset you, Harry. But there's more of the same inside. Probably worse. I just wanted to give you some warning."

Harry paused, reached out and squeezed the older man's shoulder fondly, briefly.

"Nothing can be worse than what I've just heard, old friend. But thanks for the warning. Might as well fuck up the day well and good."

He grinned a rictus of a smile. Garnet Clayton shivered involuntarily.

They sat in the darkness, Harry and Roy Thorson, the only light coming from the crescent of a forming moon. In the trees above them bush babies leaped and chirruped, and, earlier, they had watched silently as a leopard ghosted across the lawn. Out in the inky darkness of the lake the lights of the sardine boats winked like so many fireflies. They were started on the second bottle of bourbon, with Harry setting the pace. He should have been drunk by now, but was not. The liquor that he hoped would dull the day's events hadn't done the trick.

Maybe this yank stuff isn't so potent, he thought, picking up the square black-labelled bottle that was empty. Wonder where Roy got this, in these days of naught? He hefted the bottle and threw it out into the night in a sudden savage movement. There was the sound of breaking glass.

"Thank Christ you picked that one ... not the full one."

Roy Thorson's voice was mild. He too, normally, would have felt the effect of the bourbon by now, but Harry's depression worried him, negating the effect of the booze. He kept talking.

"You'd walk a long way these days to find another bottle of that stuff. When I was up in Salisbury there was a bottle behind the bar at Meikles. They wanted five bucks a shot for it. It's as well my tastes are simple."

He watched Harry, saw him half smile, and pick up the other bottle.

Bloody hell, no, he thought. Don't go fucking rogue on me, Harry. He watched as Harry's hands played with the bottle, it hidden in the bigness of them.

"Good stuff. Not too strong though ..."

Harry's voice was mild.

"Where d'you get it?"

"A present. Two directors of AWF have been over the lake, at Sengwa Research. They donated a whole lot of telemetry equipment for old Roscoe's elephant study. They've been here a few times. I usually get the job of flying them around the country. They brought the bourbon across for me."

"AWF? What's that?"

"Foundation to save 'African Wildlife First'. Based in the States, a private funded outfit. They're impressed with our approach to conservation, and help us a lot with acquiring stuff for our research. Their main aim in life is to increase the chances of endangered species."
Harry grunted.
"Never heard of them. Wonder why?"
Roy Thorson answered carefully, noting the bottle was still balanced in one of Harry's hands.
"They've mainly been shown Wankie, Ghona-re-zhou, and the top end of the valley."
He didn't add that the director made himself solely responsible for all arrangements involving AWF visits. After today, Harry didn't need that.

Harry put the bottle back on the low verandah table and leaned back in his chair to stare up through the tree at the crescent moon. The horns of the buffalo, he mused. That's what the Shangaans call this moon phase. Kashili reckons it's the best time for night hunting. No shadows moving and no light shining off your spear. He chuckled, aware that Roy Thorson had shifted to watch him. Well, the old boy should be in his blankets now, back at Shingela, with some consenting *umfaazi* or other keeping his joints from locking. I'm glad he stayed out for a while longer down in that part of the Park, seeing what else crawled out of the woodwork. Shingela, he thought again. Nemana. Kanyoka ... What's happening to us all? Peta is well out of it. Tonight she's on the plane. London tomorrow. Here today, gone tomorrow. I wish she was here.
He sighed and hunched forward, reaching again for the bourbon. Pausing to swish the contents around.
"What else have you got, in the booze line?"
"A few beers, brandy, some Dumbarton. No gin, I'm afraid."
Dumbarton was a locally made whisky, unsmooth, distilled from the juice of sugar cane. Harry tossed the bourbon to Ron.

"You drink it, or save it for a better occasion. It's wasted on me tonight. Bring on the Dumbarton and let's drink with reality. Rough booze for rough times, a rough day."

He laughed aloud then, a harsh grating bellow.

After the revelations of the general he reckoned he could field anything else thrown at him with ease. But, on top of that, the news from Alastair Drummond was still another kick in the solar plexus. He thought back over the director's words now as Roy fetched the whisky.

"The authorities have decided to move Chief Kanyoka and his people. With terrorist incursions through his area, and in his area, he has been put firmly in the middle. Eventually, government repercussions as well as the terrorist threat make his position untenable. Who knows, for all their assistance to you, they may still have had contact with the enemy. If that's not so, then it won't be long before men armed with AK 47's will be knocking on their doors in the middle of the night. For their sakes the people have to be moved. And soon."

Harry had stared at the director. Speechless.

"Moved. Moved where, for Christ's sake? Those tribespeople have lived there forever, since Hector was a pup. They have always stayed out of any upheaval the country has had, and they've been my eyes and ears for a long time. I've known Kanyoka, and his father before him, for over twenty years. It's their land! They've done nothing to warrant having their lives turned upside down."

He'd stood up. Moved across the verandah to the director, slamming his words at him. Garnet Clayton had edged closer to the two men, praying that Harry didn't let it all go. It wasn't his way, but the chief warden could see he was on the edge, had never before seen him like that.

The director's reply had been brusque, hard, but Garnet had caught the unease. It had happened a long time ago, not far from where they now sat, and he knew that Dr Alistair Drummond remembered the thrashing given him by Harry Kenyon.

"Cut the hysteria, Harry. The decision's been made, and, I should add, it was a decision I did not agree with . I voted against it. But Police, Internal Affairs, and Army want it that way. Which, these days, makes it mandatory. Kanyoka and his people will be moved in the next month. Their new home will be near Kanyemba, downriver, seventy miles east."
Harry had shaken his head.
"My oath, whoever makes these decisions really should have their heads examined. Some policy making bastards back in some posh air-conditioned office in Salisbury turn an old friend into an enemy with the stroke of a pen. I ... Ahhh."
Harry spat disgustedly out into the bougainvillaea bordering the cool verandah, unable to go on.
Roy Thorson stared fixedly at the ceiling. Garnet Clayton watched warily, weighing up the charged atmosphere, knowing there was more.
Alistair Drummond spoke again, his voice determinedly sympathetic and even. It was an effort, and the best he could do. Harry Kenyon and his autocratic ways riled him sorely.
"I'm sorry, Harry."
The warden ignored him, remembering his words to the chief and his elders in the night before they moved on the poachers. He felt sick at heart.
"There's one other thing."
The director watched Harry. Garnet Clayton swallowed.
"You've been down in the valley for over five years now. As a warden, with the war restricting a warden's duties, there is a feeling at head office that the post should be re-evaluated, perhaps make it a senior ranger position. That would enable the department to transfer you to another area where you could get your teeth into a lot more of our problems ... use your considerable ability to best advantage. Perhaps the southeast. What are your feelings on that, Harry?"
Harry regarded the director with a flat steady gaze. Coming on top of all the other bad news today, it was like another boot in the ribs, the pain, dulled, flaring again. The silence on the

verandah settled oppressively about them. Finally Harry looked at each of them in turn, his expression dark and unfathomable. "You know my feelings on leaving the valley. There's no more for me to add."
Alastair Drummond cleared his throat.
"Well, give it some thought, won't you. It's early days yet, and it's only at general discussion stage. But it's a logical step."

Roy put the whisky down before him. It was a full bottle.
"Rather you than me, chum. That stuff is like sheep dip ..."
His eyebrows raised as Harry untwisted the cap and threw it into the night. He poured himself another generous measure of the bourbon, thinking, Oh well, thank Christ there's no flying scheduled for tomorrow.
"Harry," he spoke carefully. "You want to talk about anything? There was a lot piled on your plate today, a real bunch of shit ... We go back a long way, we understand each other. If there's any way I can help you, you know you've got it."
Harry Kenyon smiled crookedly, the smile not reaching his eyes, took a swig from the bottle, forsaking the glass now.
"Thanks, old son. I appreciate that. Maybe you could get on to your friends at AWF. They could put me on their endangered species list. Somewhere near the top, perhaps."

CHAPTER TWENTY-TWO

Peta Holt could not sleep, despite the two Rusty Nails she had drunk after the packaged aircraft dinner. Now, with the lights dimmed and the occasional patrols of the hostesses the only movement along the cabin, she stared out into the darkness from her window seat. The port wing light flashed hypnotically across the edge of her vision. Down there somewhere, she mused, was Africa. Not the Africa she had just left, not the Zambezi Valley, but still Africa.

It's weird, she thought. Today, she looked at her watch, yes, it was still today, just, at first light, I could smell the

Zambezi River. I could hear the fish eagles calling and the hippos grunting. Just after we left camp we had to wait for ten minutes whilst that herd of buffalo moved across the track; and later, Harry bluffed out the elephant, the young bull who was feeling his oats. *Ahhh, Harry.* I remember how petrified I was of those jumbo displays when I first went down to Nemana with him. I'm okay now, thanks to him nursing me through a few score more. And, tomorrow ... tomorrow I'll be in London. Could anything be more different?

She thought about the book then. *Her book.* Her first book. *'Valley Eden'.* My Christmas present to Harry, she thought happily. The publishers want it out for the Christmas buying spree. I still can't believe it! *'Valley Eden',* by Peta Holt. She smiled to herself through her reflection in the glass. It's a good book, she told herself. Even when I'm as objective and honest as I can be, it's still a good book. Photographs and text, all the knowledge there, all the moods. All Harry's teachings. God, I love that man. I wish he could have come with me. Whether he thinks so or not, he needs a break from the valley. No not the valley ... that's a place one could live forever in, just from its problems. That horrific poaching spree. Maybe the book can help the valley. I'm sure it will. Especially with the prince writing the Foreword. Oh my, I never thought the publishers could arrange that. Adrian is a wizard, and he's always put his heart and soul into good wildlife books. And it is a good book, Peta Holt thought again, hugging the proudness and the excitement to her, warming herself with it.

After a while she collected her thoughts, brought herself back to the present. And what next, she wondered. After the book's out? Back to the valley. Absolutely. Back to Harry and Nemana, and the river, and beautiful ugly old Kashili. But then? Are you going to be a one-book wonder, or do something else? It would be nice to do a study on one animal and its place in the rest of the wild society. Maybe concentrate on dear Harry's big love, elephants. That's a story in itself. Like

Harry. He'd make a good story. From poacher to saviour. And, oh, what a saviour. These last three years have been special. Apart from those horrible killings and this last poaching outbreak. Harry will stop it. For sure he will. And if the trouble in that country could be healed up, it would be total paradise. When I get back, she thought suddenly, and that's nearly three long months away, it will be Christmas. The rainy season. If Harry Kenyon doesn't get his act together and ask me first, I'll ask the bugger to marry me! Peta Holt smiled again, out at the darkness that cloaked Africa.

Harry waited whilst the big cow, the matriarch, held the track as the rest of the herd ambled across. Ears wide, flapping with loud wet-blanket sounds, tall standing, looking down her trunk, she faced the vehicle. Harry smiled fondly at the elephant. Get on with you, he said silently. I'm on your side. The last of the herd crossed, swallowed up swiftly by the mopane. With a final shake of her great head, the cow followed. He gave her a minute before driving on, bumping over the giant pockmarked corrugations of their tracks.

He'd left Kariba at first light, forcing himself to get on the move. Stopping at a garage and swilling back three ice cold Cokes to try and assuage the thick-headed biliousness that made him sweaty and liverish. On the escarpment, where he'd stopped with Peta so long ago, he pulled over and forced himself through ten minutes of push-ups. Which brought all the poison up. Once he'd cleaned up, using the water from the canvas jossaks that hung from the windscreen nuts, he felt a lot better.

Now it was a little after eight. He would make Shingela well before midday, taking it easy, keeping an eye out for any interesting spoor patterns, watching the bush. He cocked an eye up at the clear sky, automatically checking for vulture movement. The birds would be well away on the first thermals of the day now. And, thought Harry Kenyon, Peta will be landing at Gatwick about this time. I miss her already. And it's early days yet. With luck she'll be back for Christmas. He grinned suddenly, slowing as a warthog ran across his front, radio aerial tail erect, and wondered if she would consider marrying him. He thought of her here with him, always, in the valley. Maybe writing more books. Then he thought of yesterday's meetings and revelations. And his gut knotted. There's a lot that needs putting right before Christmas, and wild crazy thoughts of marrying Peta Holt, he mused bitterly.

And how are you going to play this one, old son? Warden Kenyon? Hey? Good question. A bloody good question. In truth, I do not really know. But, as sure as a frog's waterproof, I'll do something. Absolutely. And now I think one would be safe in saying that the gloves are off. The rules need a little bending. Oh, yes. He looked at the sky again, searching for the vultures.

Kashili squatted comfortably on his haunches in the deep-pooled shade of a Zambezi Ebony. In the branches above him he could hear the birds feeding off the sweet ripening berries. He had a hand cupped full of them himself, sucking on them absently. He had been unable to sleep last night, the first night back at Shingela for a week. So he had risen in the darkness, taken his spear and left camp, walking quietly out on the fringe of the flood plain, keeping the wind in his favour. Only once had there been danger. He'd come upon the lions suddenly, lying up on the edge of the plain. They had not moved off when he'd stopped, catching their strong scent on the faint night breeze, thirty or so shadowed paced away. A big lioness had got up and padded steadily at him. Kashili had climbed one of the evergreens, and the pride had moved on.

Afterwards he'd descended and continued walking. All the while thinking about the elephant. And Harry Kenyon. Now, with the sun well up, he crouched motionless under the ebony and watched the day's activities in the bush around him. Hau! thought the old tracker, these things that I have found mean new violence. It is a new war. It will hurt the little warrior very much to hear of this elephant. With his woman gone he will already be as edgy as an old buffalo living out of the herd. Kashili hawked and spat forcibly into the dust at his feet. These days are not good days. There is too much death in the bush. Too many people with guns. And now I have found more guns. I wonder if all will again be peaceful some time? I do not think so. I think this disease is here forever. I have heard that even in my ancestral lands, there on the other side of the country down on the Lundi, where life has always been gentle and kind, the animals are being killed. And people kill each other. Hau, he said silently again, perhaps it is as well that I am old, and have seen the good days. But this thing of the elephant ... The old tracker sighed.

It was the birds that led him to the elephant. Always the birds. The specks circling, dropping, as the vultures spiralled down. Volplaning into the carcass area. It was Katete, the first of the Big Four they had collared. Now a stinking faceless mass of flesh, tusks gone. The inevitable spoor patterns, tracks leading back to the river.
Kashili paused in his report to the warden, seeing the sad anger wash anew across his face. Then said finally.
"The plastic and the other thing were left hanging from a branch near the elephant. For you."
Harry fingered the heavy yellow plastic collar that had been hacked through and removed from Katete's neck. Thinking back to the day three years ago when he and Roscoe Daniels had drug-darted him and put the collar on. One of the first elephants in the whole country to be immobilised and studied at first hand. The collar to protect it, an insignia to the new wave of safari hunters, and the rest, that the elephant was protected. A living national monument. Not any more, thought Harry sadly, stroking the collar repeatedly then pushing it away from him across the desk. Opposite him Kashili sat uncomfortably in one of the visitor's chairs. The tracker would have preferred to sit on the floor, or stand, leaning on his spear.

However, out of politeness, and because they were back in headquarters, he did not. He watched silently now as the warden picked up the other thing that he had brought back, studying it anew. It was an effigy. A plaited grass figurine of a human, crudely sculpted, about eighteen inches high. It had been smeared with blood, no doubt Katete's, thought Harry, and a shaved sliver of wood, a spear, had been thrust into the figurine. Take that, sports lovers, thought Harry sardonically. This one's for you. Loud and clear. Abso-bloody-lutely. He looked up, caught the old tracker's eyes watching him. He did not look away.

"So, old friend. I have the message. What now?"

He put the effigy down. Pushed it away.

Kashili stood up, not able to stand the padded softness of the lounge chair any longer, moved to the wall and squatted on his haunches against it. He hawked and made ready to spit, eyed his surroundings, changed his mind.

"The moves are yours, little warrior. They have had your message ... now they have given you theirs."

The old man paused as he scratched at his groin meditatively.

"They are very sure of themselves, these hyenas. These dung eaters. Your next actions have to be powerful. At the same time you will have to move with care. For they know you hunt them now ... and they themselves are happy to add your head to the pile you started."

He cocked a shrewd rheumy eye at Harry, watched as the warden stood up and went over to the great curve of tusk on the wall. Oh yes, reflected Harry, his hand gently stroking the smoothness that was both soft and hard at the same time. The bastards are sure of themselves alright. Is it any wonder, with Alex Gant decreed Royal Game by the powers that be in this country? Hands off. Christ, what a sick, sick world this is. The poachers have got it sewn up, with Gant working for our intelligence. And with the army presence in this stretch of valley limited, and my own men too damn thin on the ground. Even now, with all this going on, no increase in troop strength. Harry lad, if you were a real cynic, you would be tempted to think it's all been planned that way. To give Gant the access he needs on that side. And now even poor old Kanyoka gets the shove. Move out, old chap, piss off, we have things to do here. So sorry.

Harry Kenyon sighed, a great gusty exhalation. He turned from the tusk and leaned his back against the wall, slid down so that now he squatted on his haunches as Kashili did, facing the tracker on the other side of his office. So, he thought, the moves are mine, are they? Along with the general's and the director's consent they are. Which means, old son, that you may consider yourself castrated. He smiled to himself then, a grimace that twisted his features.

"Old one, please may I have some of your snuff? I hope it is up to your normal standard, for I need to clear my head well and make plans."

Kashili unslung the horn from around his neck and tossed it lightly across the room to Harry. He watched as the warden tapped some out of the hollow cone of the horn, noting it was more than was necessary. Harry sniffed hard, taking the snuff deep into his sinuses, feeling the immediate effect and holding back as long as possible. Until his eyes watered and the sneeze was hurting and then the massive explosion. And his head cleared.

"Thank you ..."

He tossed the horn back. For long minutes he was silent. Kashili waited. Finally ...

"This that we have, this killing. It is very different from anything you and I have known before ..."

Harry spoke carefully, wanting his old friend to see it with him, to know the road he planned to take. To have no illusion.

"It has to stop. The poaching. It will be very hard to stop, and there will be few friends to help. I will fight it until it is stopped, or I am dead. It is my duty to do this ... not only because I work for the Game Department, but for myself also."

He paused, seeing Kashili's eyes on his face, his own impassive, unreadable.

"This that I will do is my decision. It is not for me to decide what you will do. You are not employed by the government. And the hunting that I foresee ahead will not be like old times, and I do not have the right to involve you."

Kashili watched him, his expression inscrutable. Eventually he shook his head, cleared his throat to spit and again managed to refrain, making do with a disdainful snort.

"This is old woman's prattle. You must be getting old, little warrior, to ramble thus. I would not like you to get lost during your hunting, in your seeming advancing years. I had better accompany you, to keep you on the right track ... As always."

Kashili laughed then, a great evil-sounding cackle of mirth.

"I am ready when you are. Let us go and teach these hyenas some lessons. Are we not sons of the bush, you and I? Is this valley not our home? Let us show these eaters of filth the true meaning of hunting."

The tracker laughed again, this time standing and striding to the door to hawk and spit savagely out on to the game-cropped lawn.

They had visited the remains of Katete. Harry wanted to take photographs of the bull's sad rotting carcass. He wasn't sure why, just that it made a start to the chronicling of the carnage. Now they crouched in the undergrowth, a day's walk from Kanyoka's village, and studied the arms cache Kashili had discovered. They had dug carefully with the two folding shovels they had brought, Harry concerned about booby traps. Previously, Kashili had just scraped away enough soil to establish what was buried at the end of the poachers' spoor he had followed. The old tracker had expected to uncover the dull gleam of ivory. Now it lay fully exposed, unprotected by any traps Harry could see. It was a small cache. Four Kalashnikovs, with several hundred rounds of ammunition, some canteens filled with water, and an RPG 7 anti-tank rocket launcher with four projectiles. A Dragunov sniper's rifle, wrapped in soft canvas, completed the hidden arsenal.

Well, well, thought the warden, brushing a hand through the miasma of mopane flies that surrounded his head, drawn by the sweat. What does it mean, I wonder? Extra weaponry for poaching sprees further afield? Something else unfolding in the area? Whatever, it's all bad news. His glance switched to a scrap of blue denim cloth hanging from the bush beside the excavated weapons. Unobtrusive, unless you were looking for it. Automatically his gaze went on to sweep the sky, inspecting it for vulture movement.

He had made his mind up about the cache. It would not be reported to the army. Nor would it remain here. Insurance, chum, he said silently. It's about time you started taking some out. This is a start. This stuff could do a lot more damage to the game. And you. So we'll say thank you and move on.

It had taken the rest of the day to move the weapons and erase their own spoor. Checked and cleaned, repacked in the wooden boxes with the Cyrillic writing, they were now buried half a mile away. In the last of the day's light the two men moved to the river.

They planned to wait out the night in hidden obscurity on the shore, monitoring any activity that might occur on the opposite side. The next day they would follow the river to Chief Kanyoka's village. For the first time ever, Harry Kenyon did not look forward to meeting the old chief.

They were not the only visitors. The late afternoon sun bounced off the windscreens of the two green government trucks. There was a stillness about the village. Kanyoka's people sat in scattered silence, watching as the chief and his elders met with the government representatives. Around the outskirts of the village a detachment of territorial soldiers were positioned in defence formation. Harry eyed them warily as he and Kashili entered the village from the river's edge. The soldiers, dozing and unalert had taken fright when the two men had emerged silently from the bush and been almost on them before they realised. Harry didn't want any scared over-reaction. They stopped at the knot of Kanyoka's elders and the four Internal Affairs officials. Kanyoka was speaking, his tone measured and patient, as if explaining something to someone who wasn't very bright. The interpreter passed it on to the visitors, without losing the restrained outrage of the chief. "… we were born here. Our fathers were born here, and their fathers before them were born here. Before there were white people and borders, before there were walls built across this river. Our ancestral spirits are here. Therefore how can you, or anyone, claim the right to move us?"

The patient expressions on the faces of the government men were forced, wearing thin. Kanyoka watched them, aware of Harry and Kashili outside the circle, not ready yet to greet them. Harry waited. He looked for Ndende, not seeing his face amongst those of the village elders. Not seeing him anywhere in the village. The government spokesman, a district officer with a south English accent who managed to look coolly elegant despite the heat, answered. It was obviously a repeat of earlier responses.

"Chief Kanyoka, I hear you, and I know you are right. I am sorry that this is the way things have to be. But these are troubled times. You have experienced that already. The government is doing this for your own safety. When the troubles are over, we will bring you back. For now, you must move. Twice, I have visited you, and we have run out of time. In five days I will return with many vehicles and people to help you move. If you are still stubborn in your refusal, we will have no option but to burn your village and force you to come with us."

The officer paused to ascertain the effect of his words on the chief and his men. In the way of Africa there was none. Their faces were wooden as they returned his stare. Somewhere in the village a chicken squalked. Eventually the district officer nodded and gave a faint sigh.

"In five days, Chief Kanyoka."

He motioned his companions away and they turned for their transport. It was then he noticed Harry and Kashili, stopping to study them critically. The warden returned his stare silently.

"Who are you, may I ask?"

Again Harry was struck by the incongruity of the accent out here in the wilds of the Zambezi Valley. He made his voice mild, kept his expression as wooden as Kanyoka's.

"You may ... Harry Kenyon."

The district officer waited for more explanation. Harry let his gaze leave the man and sweep over the rest of the contingent. Beside him, Kashili hawked and spat into the dust. Finally.

"What are you doing here? Do you realise this is a restricted area?"

Harry nodded, took his time replying.

"Sure. I'm warden of this neck of the woods. And Chief Kanyoka is an old friend of mine. Apart from that, it's got fuck all to do with you. Don't let me stop you leaving."

He kept his voice level, saw the flush colour the other's features, moved past him into the shade of the village conference tree. The district officer nodded, as if remembering something.

"Yes, of course," he said. "I should have remembered. They did tell me about you."

With a final disdainful sweeping glance around, he turned and walked away to the leading Bedford.

It was sundown. The pulse of the valley bush surrounding the village changed tangibly. The village itself was subdued, in shock. Harry and Kashili sat with the elders, absorbing their pain. Harry felt like a Judas. And the news about Ndende added to the whole goddamed witches' brew of events, his mind raged. The nationalists, the fucking Ivory Section, had killed him. Had come in the night and turned the village over. Beaten some, tortured others. Killed Ndende and another elder, using bayonets. Kanyoka had told them, his voice dispassionate and dead, a spark, though, in a dark eye when he had told how Ndende had spat at the leader of the gang, there at the end. When he lay in the dust, in the middle of the village, his intestines spilling out.

Harry took a deep, shuddering breath, knowing he couldn't put it off any longer. Kanyoka saw it in him, the question. Had seen it for a while, and let the warden suffer it out. Now he answered that which was unspoken.

"For helping you. Helping the government. But especially you. They said it was but the first lesson."

The chief looked out into the dusk, where the trucks had been.

"And now the government. They too will destroy our lives. Us. Who is worse?"

Harry shook his head. A small part of him heard the first calls of a fishing owl, out on the river.

"Truly, a question ... And, now, I have no answer for you. I am as you, old friend. As the buck choosing between the leopard and the hyena. My government has put things in my path. These times have caught up with me, snared me. I do not know what to say to you, Kanyoka. I gave my word, which now is nothing. Sand in the wind ..."

Kanyoka hawked and spat savagely.

"Our *nganga* told us of this. Long back. As I told you. This thing is bigger than you. Bigger than me and my people. I do not blame you. We have shared many fires, and I know you as a different kind of *mukiwa*, white man, to the others who have tarried here in this bush. But, certainly, your own people lack wisdom, lack vision. They are as misguided as the jackals that came in the night and killed Ndende. And they will destroy us. Whether it is slow or quick, the result will be the same. Do they expect me to sit and wait, do nothing?"

Harry watched the old chief, met his steady implacable gaze. Looked for something he could say that wouldn't be more lies, saw the man read it all in him.

Kanyoka shook his head and gave a harsh dry bark of a laugh.

"It would be best if you go away, my young crocodile hunter of past better days. We have many things to discuss amongst ourselves, plus tonight we speak to Ndende's spirits. I do not say you are not welcome, but things are changed. Go, you and Kashili. Go well and with care, and with my blessings. Beware of the vultures that gather."

Harry stood up reluctantly, Kashili moving in tandem at his right shoulder. He knew things had changed irrevocably. For him and the chief he had known for over twenty years. He felt very sad. Made a strong effort to stand proud in front of the watching elders.

"You and your people go well and in peace, Kanyoka. Whatever the bones have in store for us, I will always support you. Don't doubt that."

He shouldered his rifle, moved away a pace. Stopped and turned back to Kanyoka.

"When you speak to Ndende's spirits, tell them from me that the jackals who killed him will be joining him. Soon. That's a promise I can keep."

Harry Kenyon and Kashili moved slowly out of the village, tuning in to the night. Stars glinted out on the waters of the Zambezi. The night was unusually quiet.

So, thought Harry, there we are. Things do not get better. What now, Warden Kenyon?

The two men moved on through the night, two shadows merging with other shadows.

CHAPTER TWENTY-THREE

They found the boats on the second day, half way back to Shingela. Two banana boats and a dugout canoe. It was pure luck, finding them pulled up deep into the concealment of a mahogany that had fallen at the edge of the river, dense evergreen foliage trailing in the current. They had been resting at late morning, sitting quietly in the pooled shade, using the cover of a *capparis* that scrambled over an ancient termite mound. Monitoring the rhythm of the bush.

Two lionesses with a bustle of six cubs had appeared out of the long grass, a hundred paces or so away, walked relaxedly down for a drink. Near the fallen tree the lionesses had stopped, their demeanour suddenly wary. One of them had dropped into a crouch, tail whipping. An unheard command had brought the cubs to heel, silent, baby-lion games forgotten. They had remained thus, in frozen tableau, for a long minute. Then the mothers had turned back, led their youngsters back into the cover of the long grass without drinking.

The two men had waited a while, curious, watching. The binoculars showed Harry nothing. He thought maybe a male lion was lying up in the cool greenery of the fallen tree. A little later a group of kudu drank beside the tree, undisturbed. A quartet of egrets landed in the branches of the tree, perched unworried, a riffle of river breeze lifting their head plumes. More out of curiosity than anything else he nodded at Kashili. "Let's have a look. See what worried the ladies. We'll split, come in from different angles. Keep an eye on the long grass. They're probably still in there."

Kashili had grunted his reply, and they had moved in carefully. And found the boats. Harry felt his pulses quicken, looked at Kashili, saw his faint smile. They did the necessary, wordlessly. Checked the spoor, very carefully brushed away their own, moved well away into cover that overlooked the tree with the hidden craft.

Harry sipped from his water bottle and passed it to Kashili.

"How many?" he murmured, his gaze quartering their surroundings. "I reckon ten."

Kashili grunted another reply, swilling the water in his mouth. He too watched the bush around them. He swallowed, nodded his agreement.

"From yesterday. The gods are on our side."

They sat silently, both working it through their minds. Harry studied the bush intently, looking for ambush positions. There

was not much, strategically, to choose from. He wondered why
they had not left a guard. Maybe they had. Maybe he and
Kashili were compromised already. He did not think so. Didn't
feel so, more to the point. The game around was unworried,
unnervous of any foreign presence. Still, he whispered to
Kashili.
"Sentries?"
The tracker shrugged.
"I do not think so. But, we'll know soon enough. How do you
want to do this, little warrior? Do you want to follow up the
tracks?"
Harry thought about it some more, felt the embryo of an idea
kick in his brain. Pushed it away whilst he weighed up the
options. Shook his head finally.
"No. We'll wait, at least up to nightfall. Who knows how long
they will be inland. There isn't much cover for us, and when
they do come back, they're bound to send a scout in first to
check things out."
He grinned mirthlessly at Kashili, and the tracker saw the
flickering hard light dance in his eyes. Looking at the warden
the old man remembered long forgotten rituals, the muted
clicks of bones and cowrie shells tossed on shadowed sand by
the ancients, saw firelight bounce off sharp honed spear blades.
And he felt the blood stir anew in his old veins, felt the battle
fever.

Kashili watched from his hide, an antbear hole enlarged enough
to take his slim, wiry frame into its depths, as the scout held his
AK 47 aloft, signalling his comrades in. Minutes later the
poachers were all at the tree. From his distance Kashili could
only hear snatches of conversation, relied instead on watching
their body language for reactions. He saw the tusks, six pairs
carried across porters' shoulders, and the gunny sacks of rhino
horn. For half an hour there was discussion, the ebb and flow
of mild argument, various members of the group splitting away
to check for tracks. Their first nervousness began to dissipate,

Kashili could see. There was a brief snatch of laughter. He heard the thunk of a sack dropped on wood. Some of the poachers had disappeared into the depths of the mahogany, making ready the banana boats. Others remained atop the bank on watch. Within an hour the boats had pushed out into the river, the poachers watching their vulnerable rear now they were out on the open water.

Kashili took a long deep breath. It worked, he said silently, the little warrior's madness worked! So far, anyway. He stared unhappily across the river.

Warden Harry Kenyon looked around his lie-up position again, searching for any weak spot. It was hot, suffocatingly so, and the mopane flies were a miasma across his vision. He had been static for more than 24 hours now, had absorbed the rhythm of the bush and felt less threatened. His sixth sense was working overtime, and he felt confident that, for the moment, he was uncompromised. Had completed step one satisfactorily. His mind re-traced his progress. The idea to use the dugout to cross the river, ahead of the poachers on their return to Zambia, had passed quickly from germination to full bloom. It was a situation that had to be taken advantage of. What niggled at his decision was having to go in blind, with no planning, no back up, no fall back arrangements. However, it was a fact of life, he was giving himself the green light, ergo, Harry me lad, be positive. Into the breach, and all that. He was mildly surprised at how quickly his mind-set had tuned in to long unused military planning.

He was sure, by approaching the canoe through the shallows of the river's edge, leaving no tracks, it would not be unreasonable for the poachers to surmise that the dugout had drifted away on the current. He could cross the river at leisure in the night, sink it close to the Zambian shore, and establish himself in an observation position, after very careful anti-tracking, to wait for the poachers' return to Zambia. With luck he could shadow them back to their base on the Mushika.

For the rest of the day Harry had kicked the idea around in his mind, and finally told Kashili about it at sunset. His friend had not been happy, especially when he realised Harry intended to go across the river alone. Gently, but firmly, Harry had given his reasons, countered argument after argument, and in the last deep twilight they shook hands silently.

Harry had made easy passage, dodging hippo pods, pausing once to watch skimmers trimming the water in early quarter moonlight. When he closed on the Zambia shore, now in total blackness, his senses worked as far ahead as he could manage. Sweat running freely, wary, nerves strung taut, he had beached with mosquitoes in full cry. Putting his weapons, shoulder bag and binoculars above the water-lap mark, he had then gone back in the water to waist height and leaned heavily on one side of the dugout, capsizing it. Moving slowly, methodically, he had retrieved his equipment, removed his shoes and walked at a snail's pace inland from the river. When he found shadow and saw the mass of a copse of trees against the night sky he had sat down. Listening. Tasting the breeze. Feeling out the metabolism of his surroundings, here in enemy territory.

At first light he brushed out his tracks, keeping a constant watch on the bush around him. During the night there had only been natural wild valley sounds. No dogs, cockerels or other human indication. Now, as the day advanced, he moved, checking, always checking his own spoor eradication, watching for movement, wild animal or human, his eyes always alert to other human spoor. He guessed he had at least two days to wait, before his quarry came back. Which was fine. His objectives were many, he reminded himself. To find any ground sign that would tell him that humans regularly used a route or path to and from the Zambezi and, therefore, across it. To make sure he did not compromise himself whilst doing this. Ascertain from tracks or visual contact what game was in the vicinity. And, once he had found sign of human movement, to find a safe bolthole to lie up where he could monitor the river and some of the surrounding landscape. He wished, not for the first time, that Kashili was with him. And so here we are, mused the warden, all having a jolly good time. Sort of ... no, not really. If we are to be honest.

It took a long time, oh dear me yes, to find any tracks, and then to find, eventually, this place to keep an eye on things. Not the best hidey-hole one could have, but there we are. It's all there is. Henry Ford's choice. Kenyon, are you happy with this? Hmmm? I mean, you *have* broken rules before, but this is something else again. Absobloodylutely! There are people you know who would say you've flipped, gone over the top. Who would be getting the padded cell ready. This is not Malaya. You are not fighting for king and country. And you have given your particular establishment ... Scratch, the general ... a definite thanks, but no thank you. Yes. Sure. Okay. But what else can you do? At the end of the day, where does a person draw the line? When do you actually draw the sword out of its scabbard and make the mark in the dust? Who the hell cares enough anymore? About Nemana, the killings, the future of the elephants and rhinos. Who is prepared to walk the extra mile, and actually, positively do something? Apart from write reports, drag out working breakfasts, and have meetings about meetings.

Harry Kenyon took a long, ragged breath and let it out slowly. Out on the river he could see a goliath heron, standing so still it looked like some extraordinarily good art piece.

In the last hour of daylight of the third day, they came. Harry saw them by chance, alerted by the birds. A flock of white-faced whistling duck took off, alarming. A pair of hammerkops he had come to know well, suddenly left their favourite area of shallows, piping their own alarm calls. And the resident plovers, ever querulous, became noisier than ever. Harry's vision, restricted by shrubbery, had a small vector to scan. He moved position warily, looking for whatever had caused the birds to disperse. Maybe it had simply been small predators on the prowl, or a raptor patrolling overhead. He did not think so. Did not *feel* so.

The two banana boats were about a hundred yards from the bank, nowhere near, Harry noted thankfully, where he had beached and capsized the dugout. Well then, he thought, here we go. This is where we start earning our money. What money, old son? Alrighty then, let us re-phrase that. This is where we start playing things off the cuff. Where the balloon goes up. And I wish old Kashili was here, watching my back.

The poachers had guided the boats into a backwater, where high wind-sculpted sandbanks hid the craft. With business-like haste they had unloaded their booty and accessories and moved off. Inland. Long late afternoon shadows gave way to early twilight as the sun disappeared. Harry went after them, knowing he had little time left in which to formulate any kind of plan. Would they march in the dark? Were they confident enough of their surroundings, of their security, to make straight for the Ivory Section base on the Mushika? Or would they stop for the night, once they had put some distance between themselves and the Zambezi? Harry was glad of the deepening twilight. He would be harder to see, as he trailed them. Though in a matter of minutes visibility would be nil, putting an end to tracking or any chance of a sighting of his quarry ahead.

Harry Kenyon, warden of Nemana National Park, way out on a limb, ghosting his way quietly into the Zambian night.

An hour later, it felt much longer, he almost stumbled over them as they settled into their night bivouac. No fires, just muted conversation and the cocking of a weapon. He sank to the ground, mouth open, widening the ear canal. Then he withdrew, putting space between them. Harry was glad that their journey was paralleling the line of the Mushika river, some 200 paces away to the east. His earlier reconnaissance had showed him that the flood plain offered little cover for his follow-up. A wild open parkland, dotted with big Zambezi evergreen trees, similar to Nemana's riverine landscape. There was more vegetation, more dips and gullies, close to the course of the Mushika, giving him a little more concealment.

He spent the night again in solitary vigil. Listening to the crickets and night birds, his thoughts wandered, off on a journey of their own. For a long time he thought about Peta Holt, eventually, with difficulty, pushing the images away. Those kinds of thoughts were a luxury, not to be indulged here, now, with the job at hand. Such thoughts, unchecked, could weaken a man's resolve. He thought about his young carefree days, hunting crocodiles and elephants in a younger Africa that was less vandalised, a little more pure. Malaya came and went. Blood on the jungle track, the smell of cordite, a tiger in a forest stream, its stare holding his in silent communion. Close to sunrise, he heard the alarm snorts of impala, followed by the low moaning grunts of lions on the move. The deep canticle of ground hornbills tremored over the flood plain.

He waited, held back, when the new day arrived. He would track them. It was safer than trying to sit on their heels, bird-dogging them as they made for their base. He hoped fervently that the country would become harder, more rugged, inland. Giving him cover. He checked his equipment, hands patting over the items methodically. Knife, binoculars, water bottles – his and Kashili's, canvas shoulder satchel – in which were still some time tins of corned beef, a couple of onions, biltong, jelly powder, a last tin of peaches, luxury to be had after some minor celebration, plastic bottle of sulphur powder, sealed field dressings, bandages, disinfectant. The weapons, his FN and the sniper's rifle, chest webbing with spare magazines, crudely made belt pouch for the other ammunition.

All right then, he told himself. Let's go. With a hey nonny nonny, as the bard said. Let us see what this day has in store. Harry, old son, I have a feeling this is going to be one of the longest days of your life. In more than just miles covered.

The scorpion, one of the large black *parabuthus* types, Harry's mind noted absently, scuttled back under a rock. He had

almost put his hand on it, up there on the baking hot ridge
where he had eventually settled down in his observation point.
Far below, in a jumbled rock-strewn ravine that led off the
Mushika, with a line of tamarind trees giving shade, was the
headquarters of the Ivory Section. It was not, Harry's military
mind evaluated, the best sited base in terms of escape routes. It
would be easy to box the enemy in, if a large attack force was
sent against them. On the other side of the coin, anything short
of a major attack would be unthinkable, for he had already seen
trench systems and elaborately protected sentry positions. A
nightmare for anyone getting close in for a recon. His eyes
scanned the high ground surrounding the base, looking for
sentries. Could not locate any, which worried him. It made
elementary military sense for some to be positioned on the hard
high barren ground around their camp. And he wanted to
identify them as soon as possible. Once, he had seen a small
flash of sunlight, away to his left, on a high hill that overlooked
the dirt gravel road that led to the base. He continued to scan
the territory, taking care to shield the lens of his binoculars
from the sun. He did not want flashes of light giving away *his*
position, not after the blood, sweat and tears he had shed
getting here.

At the end of the day he had located two sentry posts on
the high ground, and had established a semblance of routine in
the comings and goings of the camp. He thought there were
about fifty men in Mushika Camp. Tents made up the
accommodation, and a conglomeration of aerials showed him
where the communications were set up. Weapons were in
evidence, thought not everyone carried them. He had seen light
machine guns, and, covering the approach of the road, a well
constructed guard position with a pair of heavy machine guns.
Goryunovs, Harry thought. But, overall, he found the
atmosphere of the camp relaxed, with the security aspect
wanting considerably. Which, mused Harry, with the SAS and
the Selous Scouts frequenting Zambia as much as they do, does
not make a lot of sense to me. Unless, the worm of an idea

wriggled anew, they were pretty damn confident here on the Mushika that no-one was going to gate-crash their particular party. Perhaps friend Gant's link up with the Ivory Section has put this camp on the Royal Game list. Harry's mind flashed back to Kariba, and Hugo Winters' warning. Harry swore. Long, silent, savagely. Sipped at a water bottle, wanting more but disciplining himself.

He wished he had seen the group he was following actually enter the camp. Where they took their plundered ivory. But Harry had been too busy staying in cover and working his clandestine way into a position where he could see what was going on. Without being seen himself. Without throwing the wrong numbered dice that would have him back-pedalling horribly in this particular game of snakes and ladders.

Tonight he would have to withdraw, make his way out and down into the Mushika river bed, to dig for water. I'm getting too old for this, he thought to himself, squinting up at the sun, judging its rate of descent, longing for the cooler darker hours. I wish I was back across the river, at Shingela. Or anybloodywhere, except here, come to think of it.

During the night Harry collected water and drifted off into an exhausted sleep. The throat rumble of elephants woke him, and he sat up, listening to the night. The elephants had passed below him, along the river bed. Had probably caught his scent as they passed, he thought. He was glad they had gone through, hoped their spoor had obliterated his own. He checked his watch. Two. After a minute of contemplation he used up two handfuls of water to splash his face. Felt better for it. Then he thought out his options. When he ran his tongue across his teeth they felt furry.

The good thing about this terrain, the rocks, this lower part of the escarpment, is that my tracks are almost non-existent. So, maybe, I should move around a little. Find another lookout point. A position closer to the road makes sense. That is where Gant is going to come from, one fine day.

Or night. Though it looks as if there may be a sentry point up on that western hill area, judging by that reflection I saw. He sat there, unmoving, weighing up his plan of action, knew he was vacillating, reluctant to get himself moving. God, but he felt tired. Okay, Kenyon, move your backside! Daylight is not far off, and you had better be in cover. Come on, move it!

A different hill. Rocky, with stunted pale-barked *commiphora* trees, scattered baobabs perched along uneven contours. Today there was some shade, for which Harry was grateful, compliments of a huge boulder, and, because of his new position, he looked over a different area. Harry evaluated his surroundings. Close to him a blue-headed agama bobbed its head in aggressive territorial display. The warden grinned. *Relax old chap, just passing through.* He had a good view of the road leading to the base, had already watched a clearance patrol shuffle past.

He wondered how much ivory and rhino horn there was now, stored at the camp. What constituted a full load, enough for Gant to move in and collect. I guess we take each day as it comes, reflected the warden. Until the food runs out, or until you are compromised. Or until Alex Gant pops in, and we have open season.

He heard it first. A vehicle. Or vehicles. Engines revving, gears changing, the roar of gravel, stones spinning off metal. Harry was galvanised into movement, shaking off the torpor the long hot day inevitably brought. It was mid afternoon. Distantly he heard baboons barking. Wiping the sweat from his binoculars, he cast a glance at his weapons, laid readily to hand. A truck came into view first, its make unknown to Harry, but a ten-tonner. In its wake, staying back out of the dust, came a white Landcruiser. Harry focused the binoculars, looking over the cab of the truck into the dust and windscreen dazzle of the cruiser.

Two men. One black, one white. The latter in the passenger seat, a brown arm leaning out the window. The muzzle of a rifle, in and out of focus. Harry kept his binoculars on the man, knew that in seconds he would disappear as the vehicle followed the curve of the road. Long dark hair, unkempt. Beard. A flash of teeth in a soundless laugh. Then he was gone. The two vehicles went past Harry's position, their dust hiding them as they followed the contour of the hill. Out of sight. To Mushika Camp, and the headquarters of the Ivory Section.

Harry leaned back against the rock, in shade, feeling the coolness of its hard surface seep through his shirt. Reviving. Refreshing. He was elated, grinned mirthlessly to himself. Yessss! *Jackpot!* Gant, Alex ... poacher of note, murderer of Harry Kenyon's elephants, was here! *In range, at last.* With no court rooms for miles. Harry took a series of long deep breaths, calming himself. Again his gaze moved to the rifles. Which to use? What were the circumstances going to be? How much light? Day or night? The Dragunov sniper's rifle, with its skeleton stock, short curved ten-round magazine, and the long sporting rifle-type barrel was ideal for a clear daylight shot. His trusted FN would be first choice if he was close to the target, needed extra firepower. Eastern Bloc or Nato Pact? Harry allowed himself the luxury of a long swallow of water. Wondered if it was the time to open the can of peaches. Decided any celebrating at this stage was premature. He checked the angle of the sun. When the balloon goes up, it will either be some time in the night, tonight, or daylight tomorrow, he judged. I can't see Gant hanging around here longer than necessary, even if he has got the nod from the powers that be. I'll wager he will get loaded, maybe grab some shut-eye, but sure as the Pope is a Catholic, he'll make a quick turnabout.
Proceed to GO, pass jail ... Harry picked up the FN.

CHAPTER TWENTY-FOUR

Through the powerful telescope mounted atop its tripod, the two vehicles now stopped at the machine gun post, dust swirling up, were easily clear to the eye. A minute later the truck and Landcruiser were waved through into the camp.

"Here he is again," murmured the man with the long beard and equally long hair. Out of the forest of hair a pair of penetrating blue eyes gleamed, as he glanced at his companion. "Our friend, Spider, has come to collect more tusks it would seem. And whatever else he obtains here, that makes him untouchable."

His partner, Corporal Josiah Obani, flicked a glance at the tall scruffy white man, though with the camouflage cream and accumulated dirt, it was hard to see that he was, in fact, white. Went back to watching their surroundings. It was basic operating procedure. Whilst one man used the spotting scope, the other half of the two-man observation team watched their backs.

Whispering Jim Lannigan put his face back to the eyepiece of the telescope, one hand fussing gently with the focusing ring. As he moved the scope slowly across Mushika Camp the new activity stirred by the vehicles' arrival floated in and out of his orb of vision. He watched Spider emerge from the cruiser, stretch mightily, a folding butt Kalashnikov slung over a powerful shoulder, saw the camp commander, who he knew as one Obert Hadebe, limp into his line of vision to meet the agent known only as Spider. The truck was being directed to its usual position, close beside a large pit, covered by tarpaulin and camouflage netting. The ivory and rhino horn storage area. Spider again, talking to the African driver of the truck. Beside him, the driver of the cruiser, nodding, looking at his wrist, giving a thumbs-up sign. Spider walking away with Hadebe, disappearing into the communications tent.

Whispering Jim moved the scope back on to the ivory storage area. Men were appearing, the loading detail. It would be several minutes before the tusks were uncovered. He lifted his head, rubbed his eyes, then, on a whim, turned the spotting scope away from the guerrilla base. Slowly traversed the rugged landscape of the terrain leading up to their OP. His Cyclopean vision passed over the road, noting a residue of dust still hanging in the air, drifted steadily on over scrub and rock, shadow and last day's sunlight, here a baobab, its swollen trunk a choleric purple in the dying light. Movement, just a flicker. Whispering Jim moved the lens back quickly, overshot, focused anew. There! Gone! He played the scope back and forth over the area. Leaned back, finally, scrubbing a grimy hand across his face, his expression thoughtful.
"We've got company," he murmured softly to Josiah.

Obert Hadebe watched Gant pour himself a generous measure of Camus, shook his head at the proffered black bottle. Gant had showered and put on a clean khaki bush shirt, his shoulder holster with the big Colt automatic lying within an arm's reach on the table. The AK 47 rested beside it. The ivory trader finger-combed his beard after a long appreciative sip of the cognac, then fixed an enquiring look on the base commander's face.
"So, Obert, what's the latest griff on our operations across the river?"
Hadebe gestured at a large map pinned to a board above the radio equipment.
"It is as I said in my radio message. The latest team came and went successfully, with no complications. Their ivory brings the total to 64 tusks. There are five sacks of rhino horn. There would have been more in this load, as you know, if the previous cache had not been discovered by Kenyon. Kanyoka's village has been visited, and the correct chastisement administered. Our information is that his village is to be moved. Relocated. Another idiotic decision by that government, but good for us."

Gant nodded dismissively. Which Hadebe noted, ignored as usual, but did not forget.

"And Kenyon? Any further news about him?"

The base commander noted the change of tone. Saw, just as much as he heard, the flow of bile in his visitor.

"Nothing new. He has not made any more moves against us. Not since we sent him *our* message, when we took the tusks of that big elephant. With the collar."

Alex Gant grunted sourly and took a long drink of the cognac.

"The sooner we cook that bastard, the better. He won't sit back and twiddle his thumbs, not after one of his precious bloody prize bulls has been chopped. I wish you guys would send people and scribble him."

Obert Hadebe let a faint smile slide across his face.

"Maybe we will. When the time is right. Which is not now. He has been warned, with that effigy. Lusaka command has told me to keep the situation at that. Don't ask me why. Dendera himself gave the order. Which is fine with me. We are small fish. There are bigger fish swimming above us."

Gant shook his head impatiently.

"You guys need more finance. Independent sources of money. Whether it's to eat more chicken-in-a-basket at the Ridgeway Hotel, or for more serious things. Like more weapons. And ivory and horn is the answer to that. Savimbi and the South Africans are a perfect example of that kind of business symbiosis. You bring the product to me across here, and I'll get rid of it. No problem. But if you lose any more caches, quite apart from your men being left swinging from ropes, the profits, yours and mine, will take a dive. And the way to ensure that does not happen is to get rid of Warden Harry Kenyon."

Obert Hadebe shrugged.

"Why don't you speak to Dendera then? When you are back in the bright lights of Lusaka? It is his decision, not mine. I am here to run the Ivory Section, along with gathering whatever intelligence is to be had coming out of that godforsaken piece of Rhodesia."

The guerrilla commander stood up and limped across to a water bottle hanging from a chair back. He methodically unscrewed the cap and took a long drink. Gant, and his attitude, annoyed him. Always had done.

"Rhodesia? I thought it was Zimbabwe, across the Zambezi." Gant's voice was mildly mocking. Hadebe kept his voice level. "Rhodesia. Disneyland. Atlantis. Who cares what it is called now. When we have won, taken our land back, then, oh yes, it will be Zimbabwe."

He could not stop the edge percolating into his voice. The dislike. Gant heard it and smiled inwardly. He enjoyed riling Hadebe. Anyone, for that matter. It was a good way of getting information. People tended to let things slip when they were irritated, and even little slips were valuable. Like, for instance, how come Denford Dendera had put protection on Kenyon? Dendera, the one the Rhodesian Intelligence wallahs called "The Black Russian". Public enemy number one. The man, who, as head of ZIPRA Intelligence, was in the Big Five of the most wanted on the Rhodesian's shit list. How come he, of all people, had put the word out to have Kenyon left alone? Shit! Alex Gant swore inwardly.

Obert Hadebe sat down again and lit a cigarette. He blew out a stream of smoke, watched Gant through the blueness, who seemed pensive now. Hadebe rubbed at his right leg absently, his thoughts detouring across the Zambezi. To another time, years ago, when things were clearer in his mind and the struggle seemingly poised on the brink of victory. ZIPRA Command had sent him across the river in December 1967. With a small task force of 27 men his mandate was to scout the Zambezi Valley east of Nemana National Park and establish a series of secure base areas for future infiltrations. Obert Hadebe had completed his task quickly and competently, and his report was in the hands of the guerrilla hierarchy by mid-January 1968. The season's rains had fallen well, and bush cover was correspondingly satisfactory.

Phase Two was soon up and running. Over the next three months, 175 nationalist guerrillas infiltrated the region and set up a line of Viet Cong pattern camps, six of them in a line across the Zambezi Valley floor. Commander Hadebe moved between camps, monitoring their progress, discussing strategy with the Chinese advisors, and making sure that camouflage and concealment was not found wanting. The armouries were underground, as was the main radio centre at Camp One, and the well equipped hospital at Camp Three. Camp Five, the most forward base, well entrenched in the escarpment, was the most heavily fortified, with heavy mortar and machine gun emplacements.

When Hadebe considered all was in order, he despatched a report and re-supply group of 44 men and women back to Zambia, and with his remaining 130 cadres set about expanding their patrols. He was very pleased at the way the offensive was progressing, was equally happy with the commendations coming from his leaders.

Then, in late March 1968, it all went haywire.

A game ranger on routine patrol found tracks. Many tracks. A veritable bloody highway through the valley wilderness. Within days enemy soldiers and aircraft were swarming all over them. Camp after camp was compromised, and a frenetic savage little war erupted in the once peaceful Zambezi Valley.

For the Rhodesian security forces it was a victory, eventually. A hard won victory. Hadebe's men dug in, fought back against the air strikes and attacks. Drew blood, much blood. But as days blended into weeks they also suffered losses. Men died, scattered, scrambled back for the Zambezi and the sanctuary of Zambia. In what the government military command dubbed Operation *Cauldron*, 55 insurgents were killed and 32 were captured, to later hang. The rest, a broken, battered, bloodied remnant, including Obert Hadebe with three bullets in a shattered leg, managed to get back across the river, or died of their wounds alone in the valley bush.

The camp commander took another pull at his cigarette, studied the tip, thought about his brother, who had been one of those captured. Their own intelligence links had sent back news that the boys had conducted themselves well. As prisoners of war. Had kept their heads high right to the end, singing their songs even as they were led out of the court room back to their cells after the death sentence had been passed. His brother, who had gained a degree in political science at a British university, in court referred to simply as Number 18, had smiled at the judge and the armed policemen when sentence was passed.

"I am so pleased," he had said, "that I am to die, as a soldier."

Obert Hadebe stubbed out his cigarette savagely, aware that his visitor had spoken, the pain in his leg stabbing anew, even after all these years.

"What?"

Alex Gant's expression tightened. There were times when he would like to do serious bodily harm to Hadebe, he thought grimly. The bastard is a little too smart for his own good. Nevertheless, Gant kept his voice even.

"I asked about the new road block. At Musengesa. They gave me a hard time coming through. Messed me around for an hour, hanging on to my papers. They were regulars, full of piss and vinegar."

Hadebe nodded, also keeping his feelings and mood in check with difficulty.

"It is a new base. To reinforce their guerrilla base across the Chakwenga River at Katema Nyaudi. The enemy special forces are becoming a problem. They are hitting us everywhere. We hear they will be attacking our base at Nyaudi so Command has sent down ZIPRA regulars with heavy weaponry and an anti-aircraft detachment."

The commander paused, looked at his watch.

"When are you starting back? I will radio them and tell them you are on your way, with the ivory. Ask them to be a little more easy on you."

"I'll grab three hours shut-eye. Jackson is watching the loading and checking the weight list. I want to be on my way by midnight ... he can catch up on some sleep whilst I drive the first leg. So, all being equal, I should be in their sector by sunrise."

Gant reached and pulled the big Colt automatic towards him, unlimbering it from his holster and removing the magazine. He inspected the weapon for dust, and then glanced at Hadebe.

"If the Rhodesians are playing cowboys and indians across here, it strikes me that some extra firepower wouldn't be a bad idea, when I go back. Can you spare me any men?" The guerrilla studied the map, rubbing reflectively at his jaw. Gant waited, watching geckos playing their own war games across the roof of the tent. Thought how the Irishman would be interested in the new ZIPRA base he had encountered. Wondered also how they knew that an attack was on the cards. Finally, Hadebe answered him.

"I need to meet with the commander at Musengesa. I have been waiting for transport, our scheduled re-supply. So, I will come with you, and have a six-man section prepare to escort us."

"Thanks, Obert. They can ride with the ivory on the Gaz. You can ride with Jackson and myself, in the cruiser. Just in case the Rhodesians are playing silly buggers with landmines in this neck of the woods tonight, we'll bring up the rear, even if we do have to chew a bit of dust. I'd rather the ivory went sky-high, than me have my undercarriage blown off."

Harry heard the motors start up, drowning out the distant orders and commands. He checked his watch. Almost eleven. All right then, he thought, I guess this is it. Time to score a few points for the elephants. Kenyon, old son, I hope you have still got the touch, haven't got too damn rusty. And I hope Gant hasn't collected a whole lot of gunnies, to ride shotgun with the ivory. That could make things complicated, a little messy.

He moved position, feeling his way downwards, closer to the road, aware that his breathing pattern had changed. Could feel new sweat breaking out. From somewhere behind him there was a small patter of loose stones.

In the windless night air the dust from the truck's passing swirled sluggishly, hung moodily over the road. Gant changed gear, slowed to allow more distance between the two vehicles. On the edge of his vision a nightjar fluttered. The lights from the dash reflected dully off his AK 47 that Hadebe cradled, sitting in the middle seat. His three-hour catnap had refreshed him, and the taste of the strong black coffee still lingered pleasantly on his tongue. The dust shifted reluctantly.
"What the ..."
Out of the dust, in the middle of the road, a figure had emerged, indistinct and disembodied. Gant's first thought was that one of the guerrilla escort had fallen off the big Russian Gaz truck ahead of them, but even as that thought flickered through his head he discarded it. The man wore no uniform, just ragged bush clothes. Khaki shorts, bare legs, sockless feet thrust into dirty plimsolls. Beneath the dirt and the grime, and despite the shroud of dust hanging about him, there was no doubting he was a white man. And the weapon he had swung up almost casually to point at them was a NATO Pact FN. Gant saw it all in slow motion, knew suddenly what was about to happen, and recognition suddenly hit him in icy cold shock.
"Jesus. It's Kenyon ..."
He saw the long spurts of fire from the weapon as he fumbled at his shoulder holster, felt the hammering, jarring shudder as the bullets slammed into the engine. The windscreen shattered, an explosion of bright silvered glass. A refracted part of Gant's mind saw red amidst the glass. He couldn't free his pistol. Slammed his door open.

As soon as the truck had passed, Harry sprinted from his cover on to the road, coughed at the dust that smeared the clean night air. The wash of light of the approaching cruiser metamorphosed into twin orbs of light, hazy in the dust. The vehicle was not going fast. Good, he thought, but I still can't see who's who in the cab. He lifted the automatic rifle, his thumb of its own accord checking the selector, could see figures now, in the cab. Three, but no details, only vague shapes above the lights. So, all right then, Gant's probably riding shotgun in the passenger seat, if he follows the same habit as when he arrived. Don't know who's piggy in the middle, but first we might as well stop the car. Ergo, hit the engine and then the driver. Get the party started. An errant part of his brain told him this was a bit like a cull. Being point man and selecting the first elephant of the herd to die. Except these were not elephants, and he had no flank men to help him.

The car was close now and he heard the motor decelerate, knew they had just seen him, picked out his form in the dust. Harry opened up, hardly hearing the shots, the recoil unfelt. Saw his shots strike, flashes of metal on metal. Heard them. One headlight exploded. After five shots he shifted his aim. Up to the windscreen. To the driver. Fired again.

Gant had the door open, could feel a small breeze. But he couldn't move. His brain was screaming at him to get going, get the hell out of the cruiser and run for cover. But his body wasn't listening, was not responding, was off on a mission of its own. The car had scrabbled to a grating, shuddering stop, putting up more dust. The smell of hot oil and burnt electrics was strong. Microseconds had passed. Gant, still trying to get out, looking down, seeing blood everywhere, realisation coming that it was his blood, had seen it amidst the shards of windscreen. Still did not know where the fuck he was hit, the shock still numbing him. His legs were not moving, not listening to his brain. And his left arm hung uselessly. Shit! He heard the FN again, felt more than saw Jackson taking hits. Heard him scream, felt blood spatter his face. Christ! Alex Gant rolled out of the car door, out of the car that had become a death trap, pulling himself out with the strength of one massive shoulder and arm, fear and adrenalin combining to give him extra power. He fell on to the road, horribly aware of the unresponding dead weight of his lower body. Struggled desperately to unscramble his limbs, feeling the first pain stabbing through his body. Cursing, cursing, cursing, a long savage litany.

Harry Kenyon saw a man trying to get out of the car, on the driver's side, could see by the uncoordinated movements that he was wounded, caught a glimpse of beard and pale skin. Then there was movement on the passenger's side. He fired. Four shots, double tapping twice. Could see the man had taken hits, counting his ammunition used as a reflex action. Like you did on the culls, his brain sang. Five. Three. Four. Twelve altogether, eight left. Car down, two men down, but hits inconclusive, so far. Middle target? Hit him now. No, wait. He's not moving, he's got hands up. Pink palms. So what? Clobber him now, while you can. While you're still calling the shots.

The driver was down on the road. Having trouble moving. Harry ran in, rifle held high at the shoulder. Now that he was out of the glare of the remaining headlight he could see better. Saw one man in the cruiser, on the far side, very dead. The man sitting in the middle seat looked remarkably composed amidst the bloody mayhem, hands held up more as a wave than as submission. Harry's gaze quartered the interior for weapons, saw Gant's folding butt Kalashnikov. He spoke levelly to the man.

"Don't touch it. Do not move a muscle. Or you're dead."

He switched his attention down to Gant, letting his peripheral vision monitor the cab. The poacher wore a shoulder holster, and one hand, his right, Harry abstractedly noted, had pulled a bloody smeared large automatic pistol from it. Gant was struggling to cock it, his left hand pulling feebly at the slide. Harry stepped forward and kicked, not bothering with the big Colt, aiming instead at the massive wound in Gant's thigh. Alex Gant screamed, a long hoarse roar of agony. Dropped the gun. Harry picked it up, stuck it in his belt.

He let the barrel of the FN drop. Watched the poacher over it, a quick glance into the cab flicking over the surviving member of the trio. The man still unmoving, watching the warden. Gant was swearing. Harry kicked him again. Another scream replaced the curses.

"Shut up, Gant. Your conversation was always limited."

Harry moved his rifle, prodded Gant's chest briefly, then stepped a pace backwards. The wounded poacher watched him, hate and pain fighting for supremacy across his face.

"Gant, I wish I could take you back. But, there again, you would probably talk your way out of court again. Or your friends in high places would get you off the hook. So, sport, the buck stops here, I'm afraid. I wish I had time to grill you. To have a nice long chat. But I haven't. It's problem animal control time, Gant. And you're top of the list …"

"Fuck you, Kenyon! And everyone who sails with you!"

Gant spat the words out. Harry grinned. Then he shot him. Using three careful unhurried shots.

"There's five left," he said to the man in the car. "Just in case you're counting."

He could hear the truck suddenly. Coming back. He was about to run out of time, once more thought over the pros and cons of shooting the man.

"What's your name? Your rank? How are you involved with Gant? Quickly!"

"Hadebe. Obert Hadebe. Base commander of Mushika. I command the Ivory Section, Warden Kenyon."

Harry swallowed. The truck noise was louder. Light bounced off rocks. The guerrilla leader watched Harry's face; saw the conflict of emotion, the indecision. Knew that, not since he had dragged himself, half dead, across the Zambezi, seven years ago, had his life hung by such a thread. He had an urge to talk, to say something, to plead his case. Instinctively knew it would be the wrong thing to do. He saw the attacker shake his head, finally.

"Gant was my reason for coming here. Him and his damn ivory racket. He's out of it now. At last! Hadebe, everything in me tells me to put you away as well. But I won't. But, you tell your people to leave my animals alone.   Leave my elephants and rhinos alone.   Stay the hell out of Nemana.   Or, I swear, I will come back and ..."
Gunfire. Splitting apart the night. Bullets singing past Harry, ricocheting off the cruiser. Hadebe wide-eyed. Harry ducked behind the vehicle, stumbling over Gant's body. He crouched, leaned inside, grabbed Hadebe's arm.
"Out! Come on, get out! Into cover, before your own bloody men do what I haven't done!"
    The guerrilla crawled, scrambled, lurched across the seat. A bullet shattered the top of the steering wheel, whining off into the roof. Harry gave one last tug. Hadebe dived out, falling on to Gant, scrabbled sideways towards the rear of the cruiser. The lights of the Gaz appeared around the corner, cutting through the dust. In seconds their full beam would be on the cruiser and the men beside it.
    Harry broke from the sheltering bulk of the cruiser, dragging Hadebe with him. Using the vehicle as long as possible, keeping it between them and the shooters out there in the dark. Off the road, into the hard rugged hill country beside it, Hadebe recovered and moving fast now. Harry·let go of him, moved faster. He heard new gunfire, as the men aboard the ivory laden truck fired at shadows, the cacophony of weapons on full automatic deafening.
    Who the hell was that, his mind shouted, who started firing first? All quick single shot stuff, no bloody automatic spraying the countryside. Who? A bullet cracked past him. He ran harder into the darkness, hoping he didn't fall base over apex over a rock. Wishing he could pull the darkness like a dark protective shawl over him. On the road the cruiser exploded, the flames turning night into day.

CHAPTER TWENTY-FIVE

S unrise over the Zambezi Valley.
The river flowing calm and deep and blue between white sand banks. It is hot already, with the sun not yet clear of the horizon. A kudu bull stands immobile alongside a thicket of buffalo-thorn. A pair of jackals sit alertly on the slope of a termite mound grooming, monitoring this new day. The challenge-bark of a dog baboon echoes across the flood plain, mingling with the hippo talk from the river. From a grass-filled depression comes the chirring alarm call of oxpeckers. The long grass whispers, shakes erratically, though there is no wind.

Harry Kenyon running, running for the river. Exhausted. On his chinstrap. Looking back for the hundredth time, standing close against the dark bole of an ebony and searching for movement. Not the warthogs or the impala, or the elephant having a giant scratch against a raintree. Human movement. He sees nothing, now. Did, earlier, though. A mile or so back. Shadow in shadow, dawns first light not easy on the eye. He lifted the binoculars to his face, swept the flood plain behind him. He had lost his shoulder bag and the water bottles. Had everything else. The fighting stuff. He listened to the oxpeckers, locating their position. Turned and pressed on to the river, keeping a wary eye on the long grass. Looking for landmarks, for where he had beached and left the dugout. So long ago now. Or for the high sand banks where the poachers had left their banana boats. He could smell the river, see the line of new sunlight upon the middle of the river, catching the big acacias on the far bank. Seeing the water made him more thirsty than ever, and he knew he had to drink soon. Take his chances out on the edge of the river. Across in the distance he could see the escarpment, blue hazed and beckoning, the sun already clean and bright upon its looming massifs.

For a while, back there, moving through the dark, he was not sure he would make it. He was bone tired, had caught his

mind wandering, on the edge of hallucination. He walked along
a beach with Peta, smiling at the ghost crabs around their feet
on the edge of the waterline. Kashili, sitting atop a monstrous
crocodile, smiling, pointing at its teeth. A tiger, swimming in a
jungle stream, also smiling. He had forced the images away,
shaking his head savagely and slapping at his own cheeks.
By God, he was tired.

He was not at all sure he was on any kind of safer ground.
Even with the river much closer. Water. To drink. Rhodesia
across on the other side. Nemana. The shots still worried him,
did not make sense. Neither did the niggling thing in his brain
that told him he was being followed.

He was sure the guerrillas back at the road would not
make any move until daylight. Would not move a muscle until
then, and even so would move warily. They did not know who
else was out and about, along with Harry Kenyon. The warden
did not think Mr Obert Hadebe would commit himself until a
lot of footwork had been done. Much checking for tracks.
Then, oh yes, he would be after him, a firecracker under his tail.
Which was fine, Harry reflected. I got a good head start. So
you just press on, old son. Keep going. *Pamberi* is the word in
fashion.

The oxpeckers alarmed again, and he thought he heard a
low growl, but he was past the *kasense* grass now, and the river
was right there. A crocodile slid off a sandbar. Dragonflies
dimpled the water. A flock of babblers caroused in a nearby
bush, competing with francolins screeching greetings to a new
day.

Harry Kenyon reached the water, dropped to his knees
and drank, fighting the overwhelming urge to bury his face in
the river and glug it down.

Harry opened his eyes, heard the sound again. A long soft hiss.
He was in the shade of a wild gardenia, close to where he had
watered. And he had, despite himself, drifted off. Fallen
asleep. He kept still, his eyes searched for the snake.

"Sssss …"

He turned his head then, quickly. Stared. At the figure crouched little more than a half dozen paces away. Stared at the weapon pointed at him. Knew there was no way on earth he could make use of his own weapon. Looked from the muzzle of the Kalashnikov at the person himself, seeing suddenly the tangled thicket of beard and the long ragged hair. Piercing blue eyes regarded him in return. A flutter of recognition stirred in Harry's exhausted brain.

"How you doing, Harry?"

The soft voice was conversational. Asking the time of the next bus.

Harry stared harder, the voice helping pull it together.

"Hey, come on … Just because I haven't had a wash or a haircut for a while, that's no reason not to say hello to an old mate."

The warden shook his head, a wide grin taking over his features. "I don't believe it! Whispering Jim! The last time I saw you was in some pub in Kariba. In your cups, challenging all-comers. As usual."

Harry rubbed a hand over his eyes, still not believing it. The man before him was a legend in certain little-known military circles, got his name from the soft ragged whisper to which his voice degenerated, the drunker he became. Before the fighting inevitably started. A founder member of the Tracker Combat Unit, he had transferred to the SAS. Had been twice decorated, to Harry's knowledge.

The soldier chuckled softly, letting his gaze sweep their surroundings. Harry noted that the AK 47 was still pointed at him.

"Hope you've got the safety on," he murmured, letting his smile dry out a little.

Whispering Jim Lannigan let out a long, long sigh. Lifted the barrel, a little.

"Harry, what are you doing over here? In Apache country? Hey? What the hell were you playing at, back there? Sneaking

around Mushika? Creating merry hell on the road last night? Jesus Christ, man, John Wayne's got nothing on you! And, mister, you have caused me a lot of trouble. So you had better have a fucking good story for me."
Harry watched Lannigan's face. Saw how anger had quickly blown in, like a valley rainstorm.
"Are you still with the Squadron?"
"Never mind who *I'm* with! Tell me what a bloody game ranger, a zoo keeper, is doing getting involved in covert ops? Which, as of last night, was no longer very bloody covert!"
Harry hesitated, weighing up his response, wondering how much he should, or could, say. His hesitation caused the soldier to point a dirty blood-smeared finger at him.
"Don't jerk me around, Harry. You screwed up an external operation, got my partner killed, and took out one of our main external operatives. So, you are between a stone and a hard place, my friend. I might add, so am I , thanks to you."
Harry took a deep breath and held up one hand. Took a quick searching glance around them.
"Okay, Jim. Okay. I came over to find Alex Gant. To kill him. Once and for all. No more, no less. No big clandestine operation. No-one knows I came over, except Kashili."
Lannigan was shaking his head disbelievingly. A twisted grin showed through his matted beard.
"My sainted aunt. You *do* get the bit between your teeth, even after all this time."
He paused, scratching vigorously at himself, keeping his gaze on Harry. Harry wished he would move the barrel of the AK a tad more away from him. Waited.
"I saw you, through our scope. Didn't recognise you, just caught a glimpse of someone new on the scene, mooching about below our position. Josiah and I were coming down to see what you were up to, once it got dark last night. We'd got close to where we reckoned you were holing up when Spider and his merrie men came along ..."
"Spider?"

"The guy you wasted, along with his major-domo. That's all I know him by. He's one of our deep cover types. He reports back to CIO in Salisbury. Or used to."

"That bastard is, was, Alex Gant. A murdering bloody poacher. I've chased him for years, had him in court. He walked out, laughing. He's killed hundreds of elephants, and the rest. And he has been the clever boy behind the killing of the elephants and rhinos in Nemana. Killing *my* wildlife!"

Jim Lannigan shook his head, gave a harsh bark of a laugh.

"Whatever he did to ruffle your feathers is not what's at issue here, Harry. Just hear me out, okay? Last night, when you did your number on Spider, you put me in a spot. I didn't know who the hell you were. As far as I was concerned you were some loose cannon going for one of our agents. That's why Josiah and I opened up on you. I had better get some more range work in. Don't know how the hell I missed you."

Harry listened silently, thinking back over the action. It already seemed long ago.

"When the truck came back, with everybody popping off in all directions, Josiah caught a stray round. It's always the stray fucking rounds. Straight through the head. Poor bastard. He was a good soldier. He had the Silver Cross. This was our seventh job together. So, Harry, I'm kind of pissed off at you, you know?"

Harry winced.

"I'm sorry. Really very sorry." He paused, hearing the oxpeckers alarm again. "So where does that leave us, Jim?"

It was Lannigan's turn to grimace, mutter a soft curse

"I had to make sure Josiah wasn't identifiable. Then I pulled out, with the radio and scope, plus our two packs. Not a nice load, in the dark, on the run. I was going to radio for extraction, but I realised those bastards back there weren't going anywhere. For a while, at least. The radio and other stuff is back a ways, a couple of hundred yards. I found you mostly by chance. Saw your tracks, found a water bottle, guessed you were the dude who put the cat among the pigeons last night.

Figured you were somewhere close to the river, whoever you were, so dumped the gear and tippy-toed in ..."

Whispering Jim Lannigan grinned then, but there was no mirth. "And found old Harry Kenyon, fast asleep. Getting his forty winks."

Harry smiled ruefully. Did not feel like smiling at all. Was aware that the other man had still not answered his questions. Wished the FN was in his hands. Asked again, making his voice conversational.

"And now?"

The soldier studied the game warden, allowing the silence to build. Fish eagles were dueting above the river. The oxpeckers called more insistently now. What, wondered a part of Harry's mind, are they sitting on? Whose cage are they rattling?

Jim Lannigan said, "Last night, at last light, I radioed Control. Told them I had an unidentified person close to our position, who looked to be doing exactly what we were doing. Monitoring Mushika. And Spider. I wanted to know if maybe some wires were crossed and we had two teams in one place. Which is never good news. They said no one else from our bunch, or any other unit, was anywhere near the area. That I was to do whatever the situation demanded, with the emphasis being to neutralise the party concerned if we were likely to be compromised in any way."

He cocked an eyebrow.

"So, Harry, you tell me, sport. We *were* compromised, lost a good man, lost an agent, and had the whole project blown sky high. Because of you. Because of your private little war with some bloke who you say has been killing *your* elephants. Elephants, for Christ's sake! You're worried about elephants when our fucking country is up the creek!"

Harry Kenyon knew the ice was thin, cracking already, great spiderwebs of cracks reaching out towards him. Looking into the eyes above the AK he knew he had seldom skated on such thin ice. And he knew that the next minutes were crucial.

316

"Listen to me, Jim Lannigan. I'll repeat to you what I've told Hugo Winters, Scratch Peters, anyone else who will listen. Every time there's some dirty scrappy bush war in Africa, anywhere, the animals take a beating. They are caught between a stone and a hard place. Now, you know my background, as well as anybody, so you know I'm not some bloody conscientious objector, some bible quoting dove who believes we should kiss and all pick flowers together. My contribution to this particular eye-blink of history in this part of Africa will not make one iota of difference to the outcome. But what I *can* do, is try and keep the game from being wiped out. As is happening, more and more. *Every week, every month, every year.* If I can give the wild animals on my patch of turf some more time on this planet, another decade or two, hell, any kind of stay of execution, then I reckon I've used my time on this earth well!"

Harry was aware his voice was ragged, that it had degenerated to the type of hoarse whisper for which Whispering Jim was well known. He shrugged then and spat in the sand.

"So, Jim, there we are. You there, me here. And devil take the hindmost."

The soldier stood up. Took a long careful look around them. The sun was well above the horizon now, the valley already sweltering. In the distance a line of elephants were crossing the river, towards Nemana. A waterbuck ram with two females stood near the water's edge, looking back over their rumps at the men.

Harry watched the Kalashnikov, then moved his stare to meet that of Lannigan, whose face was expressionless.

"You say no one knows you're across here? Except Kashili?"

Harry nodded.

"What about Hadebe? I saw you pull him out of the vehicle. Sticking your neck out to help the enemy, while we were pouring lead at you. Why did you do that? You killed Gant. Helped Hadebe."

Harry shrugged.

"It was one of those times when a person flips a coin. I suppose I should have hit him as well. He knew my name. I gave him a message, for his brass. To keep out of Nemana."

Jim Lannigan gave a snort, in which there was derision, disbelief, outrage, and, Harry thought, begrudging amusement.

"Harry, I do believe you belong in *Wind in the Willows*. Along with Toad. He's such a fuck-up. There again, you and Quixote would have made good travelling companions, giving the windmills a run for their money."

While Harry adjusted his thinking accordingly, wondering at Whispering Jim Lannigan's detour into literary realms, the soldier changed tangent again.

"You know you are in deep shit, Harry, don't you? Once the word is out back home, amongst the CIO, the special forces people, the big boys who call the shots, about your little escapade. You're finished. Well and truly. They will make sure you are discredited, lose your job, spend the rest of your life on your knees. There won't be many folks wanting to buy you a drink. I would probably be doing you a favour if I wasted you here and now. The warden on an anti poaching spree, protecting his animals. *His elephants*. Hey, Harry? Make you a hero, posthumous of course, killed in the line of duty."

The anger had gone, blown away as quickly as it swept in. What had replaced it, thought Harry, was possibly worse. Whispering Jim was restless suddenly. Was tired of this particular equation. Wanted to continue on his way. There were things to do.

"Well," Harry ventured, "you've got the gun. And you're the only person who knows it was me across here. And Kashili. And Hadebe."

Lannigan grinned.

"Yup. As far as Kashili is concerned, you end up as hyena food. And if you're not around, whatever Hadebe says will be hearsay. We'll probably take care of him anyway."

Harry watched as his captor, he realised now that he *was* his captor, stepped back a few paces. Cursed inwardly for being caught like this. For feeling so *useless*.

Lannigan let his gaze drift over Harry, his expression thoughtful. Shifted his grip on the AK.

"You see how easy it would be, don't you, Warden Kenyon? To get rid of you. Get rid of the problem. Feed you to the crocs. Make everyone's life simpler. Especially mine. What would *you* do, Harry?"

Harry was busy wondering how many seconds he needed to get his hands on the FN, bring it up and shoot. Too many. He needed micro-seconds. Remembered Gant's Colt 45 suddenly, in his belt. On his right side, unseen by Jim Lannigan. Mentally slumped. Too clumsy, and the pistol not even cocked. Lannigan's grin broadened, and he lifted the rifle up. Higher. Rested it across his shoulder.

"Ahhhh, Harry. What the hell. I have ..."

The buffalo exploded from nowhere, the oxpeckers fluttering above it. It had come out of the grass totally silently. Came now, already in head high full charge. Lannigan whirled, bringing the Kalashnikov to the aim. Harry scrambled up, on to one knee, grabbing the FN, seeing everything waft into slow motion. The buffalo, head thrust forward, an old bull, its pace . not right, an uneven lurching stride, but, my oath, still horribly fast. The dust line behind the buffalo, something glinting in the sun, wire trailing, a snare. The oxpeckers still fluttering, complaining, looking for a perch. Their one now a huge black mass on the move, coming like an express train at the human.

Whispering Jim Lannigan standing firm, feet solidly planted, firing fast, dust puffing off the scabby black hide, a chip of horn flying. But there was no way he was going to stop it. No earthly chance. Not with a Kalashnikov AK 47 and the adrenalin in the already injured, mad-angry buffalo flooding through its system.

Harry fired. Three times. The rapid single fire shots blending together. He was on the right flank of the animal, could see the tableau of man and beast, Lannigan and buffalo in sharp, clear focus, the slow motion still there. He saw the head lower, swing down into that terrible hooking smashing position, kept firing into the animal's face. Buffalo and man were almost a single entity. The buffalo head going down more, its muzzle scraping the ground. Legs buckling suddenly, and the massive killing machine falling, somersaulting with its own momentum. Dust. A thick explosion of form-obscuring dust. Harry Kenyon standing now, mentally re-counting his shots. Peering through the dust, rifle still at the shoulder. The oxpeckers gone now. To quieter haunts. A long, low bellow, becoming a shuddering dry rattle. The dust drifting away.

Whispering Jim Lannigan down, a motionless form on the other side of the buffalo. Harry stayed where he was. Watching man and beast carefully for a full counting-the-seconds minute. Walked slowly around the dead buffalo, looking at Whispering Jim, flat out on his back, noting the AK lying paces away. Stood looking down at the soldier, his gaze sweeping over his still form. Saw his eyes open, blink. Dazed expression clearing, eyes focusing on Harry. Then his head turning, his gaze finding the inert form of the buffalo.

He sat up gingerly, wincing, his hands checking over his dirty ragged form. Grinned up at Harry Kenyon, teeth yellow in the matted beard. He climbed groggily to his feet whilst the warden picked up the AK. Jim Lannigan let out a long gusty sigh.

"I *never* want to be that close to anything that will eat, beat or tread all over me again."

His voice was a croak.

"Well done, Harry. That was some shooting. The damn thing was so close at the end, before I jumped, I thought you would shoot me in the process!"

Harry watched him silently, the other man's weapon slung over one shoulder, his own held easily. Pointing in Lannigan's general direction. It was not lost on the soldier, who let his grin widen. A small smile came and went over Harry's features.

"Where were we, Jim, before we were so rudely interrupted? You were about to say something."

A pair of Egyptian geese flew over them, their asthmatic calls loud in the new quiet. Cicadas began shrilling anew. The elephants, Harry noticed, had reached the far bank, the sun shining on their dark wet forms.

He unslung the AK and tossed it to Whispering Jim, seeing the surprise in his face.

"Do you know how much I hate guns being pointed at me? Hmmm? Don't *ever* point a weapon at me again. Now, I reckon we're about quits, old son. We can discuss things further once we've found a boat and are getting ourselves back across the Zambezi."

CHAPTER TWENTY SIX

Sunday in London. Winter well and truly ensconced.

Peta Holt walked up Queen's Gate, passed between the black iron gates on to the grass and through the trees to the bridge over the Serpentine. There were no rowers today, and the ducks looked miserable on the cold water in the drizzle that was just starting. It was sharp biting cold and her breath misted out ahead of her. Her cold weather gear, packed away since Patagonia, so long ago now, had been dug out when she arrived in London as autumn winds scattered leaves across the city. When she reached the bench near the Peter Pan statue she sat down and unwrapped the loaf of bread. The ducks zoned in on her, trailing miniature wakes across the pond, quacking softly.

She sat there for half an hour, feeding the birds and ducks, enjoying the solitude that could be found here, even in London, when the weather was out of sorts and people stayed glued to the television. Sundays were her walk-about days. Never with any fixed destination in mind, but usually starting with a duck feeding session. As winter took a hold, the fewer people she encountered on her city rambles. Which suited her just fine, she reflected now, feeling the cold bite her ears and

SAND IN THE WIND

nose. I am about on overload. Have had enough of Old London Towne, despite what the man said about being tired of life if one was up to the neck with London. She tossed the last crumbs on to the water and set off at a brisk walk across the park, walking hard to get some warmth back.

London was fine, she mused, hands thrust deep into her pockets. It certainly has been kind to me, from the last nuts and bolts getting the book together, to the launch and the brief but hectic bout of celebrity wining and dining afterwards. But it crept up on you and got on top of you. Sure, you could see some shows, hit a lot of parties – oh my goodness yes, and have a wonderful time exploring. Then slowly it palled. The crowds and the dirt and the noise and the dog shit on the pavements began to ever so slightly irk.

She had covered a lot of ground, the focal points of her long busy days being her friend's flat in South Kensington and the publishers across town on Grafton Street. Had worked long hours during the final stages of the book coming together. But now it was out, in the shop windows. In Hatchards, Maggs Bros, Stanfords, Books Unlimited and all the rest. The publishers had wanted to change the title, and wore her defences down, so when they had the launch at Books Unlimited, on the cover was 'Vanishing Eden'. Afterwards, high on the occasion and the champagne, with the launch party spilled next door to the White Lion, she had finally felt happy with the title. Knew, in a small place in her heart, that the title was apt.

It had been a success, had taken off, her book with the exceptional colour photographs balanced with the sepia pictures of an era past, and the text that had been re-written a hundred and one times until it told *exactly* the story Peta wanted. Peta herself had been a success. Beautiful, articulate, still brown from the African sun, and unabashedly enthusiastic *and* knowledgeable about Africa, Nemana, its wild animals, she was pushed quickly on to the London celebrity merry-go-round. Interviews, expensive restaurants, book signing sessions, television appearances, weekends in the country, parties, it all blended into one long victory celebration. She wished Harry was with her, even if the whole show would have made him toe-scuffing- the-sand edgy.

The drizzle had turned to rain at Speakers' Corner, the soap box warriors running for shelter. She crossed the street at Marble Arch and caught a double-decker for the haul down Oxford Street. From the upper deck she watched the shop windows, looking for book shops, still hugging her excitement to her when she saw her book, *her* book, on display. The bus negotiated Piccadilly with Eros looking down on the tourists sprawled below, the pigeons drinking from the overflowing fountains, both seemingly oblivious to the weather. High above, the billboards were loudly dead, their colours and lights taking their habitual respite until lighting-up time came around again. She left the bus there, swinging down back into the rain and the bustle of the West End, crossed Haymarket towards Leicester Square. Tourists. Tourists everywhere here, even on a shitty day like this, she thought. The smell of roast chestnuts. Workmen busy with the Christmas lights.

Peta felt claustrophobic suddenly, stopped under an awning to think out the rest of her walk-about. The rain had changed back to drizzle and it was colder. And, she decided, she wasn't having fun anymore. Only another week, though. Then back. To Rhodesia, the valley, and Harry Kenyon. Ahhh yes. For now though, I think it's pub time, closer to home. A couple of warmer-uppers at the Denmark, and then full retreat back to the flat with the scandal rags. See if there are any new reviews on *Vanishing Eden.*

At the flat there was a note. Sarah had gone out to a lunch party. Another one! Peta smiled at the rest of the message exhorting her to follow on. Gad, that girl's feet seldom touched ground. A hard news reporter, blonde and beautiful, Sarah did not lack for social engagements. For a while Peta had joined in, and they had made a head-turning twosome. She had tagged along on the frenetic party programme, very different to the ones her publishers involved her in, with sherry and wine sipped by the literati. But both had one thing in common. Once the introductions were over and the congratulations bestowed on her book, things took a downward slide from there. Conversations re-plugged into the election/famine/wars circuit and it seemed to Peta that many Brownie points were given or taken according to concerts heard, books read, new wines discovered, names dropped, wives/husbands screwed, who was giving Aviemore a miss this winter in favour of Boulder. Would dear old Peter Finch get the nod for best actor in this year's Oscars and who said hairdressers were gay, did you see Warren Beatty in *Shampoo*?

She soon learned that, once away from her book and its contents, Africa was a little vague in people's minds. Yes, of course there was that man Smith in Rhodesia, where there was some complicated little war going on because he wouldn't let the blacks go to the same cinemas as the whites, or something like that. But not surprising really when you saw the television with that beastly man Amin who controlled that country called Kampala, and the way *he* behaves. Not to mention that fellow Kenyatta out in Zambia and that Emperor chap, Mobutu was it, in his palace in Zaire, down in the Congo. There were lions and tigers and bears in Africa, which started somewhere around Abyssinia and finished in the region of what was it again, Sharpeville? Peta had got used to the thousand-yard stare over her shoulder or the surreptitious squint down her dress, depending on the sex of the person she was talking to. It was a rare occasion, meeting anyone who had any knowledge of, or feeling for, the wild Africa she loved. Who understood her yearning for the smell of a mopane wood fire, the smell of the hot dry earth after the season's first rains, the roosting clamour of guinea fowl. Or watching elephants cross the Zambezi River, standing close beside a man called Harry Kenyon.

Peta sighed and turned on the television. A news programme ... the new civil war in Lebanon, Mozambique, five months into independence after 400 years of Portuguese rule,

Gerald Ford walking down the steps of Air Force One, Harold Wilson desk-thumping about the intransigence of the white settler government in Rhodesia ... She turned it off.

Walking up the Strand. Feeling buoyant because she had just collected her air ticket. Tomorrow she was out of here. Tomorrow she would walk across the bleak windswept apron to the waiting hunched-up VC 10 and sit through the night and half the next day. Nairobi. Johannesburg. Back up the continent to Salisbury. Peta paused on the edge of the pavement, opposite the dusty, curtained-off windows of Rhodesia House. She stood relishing the brief emergence of some watery sunlight. The lunchtime crowds were scrummaging along the city's streets. On the ledges of the empty sad-looking building the pigeons fluttered, making the most of the sun. She walked on up to Trafalgar Square and looked for a last time at the lions going coppery-green from the droppings and the fountains, cold and uninviting. Nelson was still atop his pinnacle, gazing blindly down Whitehall.

Tomorrow she was having an early dinner with her father, who was more Conservative than ever and much higher in the political ranks, though Peta still was not sure exactly what he did. He was based in London now, and after dinner he would take her to the airport. He had come to her book launch, had been good company, keeping adroitly back out of her limelight, and the next day had treated her to high tea in Palm Court at the Ritz. They got on better together now. He had never re-married, did not think he ever would, he said. And he worried about Peta being in Rhodesia. Did she know the score there? *Really?* Was she really that smitten with an older man, a game ranger for goodness sake! Peta smiled and told him about Harry Kenyon, about Kashili, about the wild animals in the Zambezi Valley. She left out the part about Kariba Lake one dark night, the soldier ants, her mother.

The late November air was misty and damp. A bitter wind bullied them as they left the restaurant, making inroads of chill in the short space between the door and the waiting car. Beneath a street light a policeman rubbed his hands together. Sir Courteney Hutton held the door open for his daughter and kissed her goodbye. Then, uncharacteristically, again he pulled her to him and hugged her soundly. Business had intruded and he had to go, had told his driver to take her out to the airport whilst he took a cab back into the city. At least, thought Peta, we managed to get through dinner before he was dragged off. Again, just like the old days. We even got as far as the port and Stilton. She settled herself in the back seat and waved through the window of the BMW. The mist had thickened in the minutes since they had left the restaurant, now swirled thickly in a Dickensian winter fog, swallowing up the figure of her father.

The car edged into the traffic in the Cromwell Road and headed out to Heathrow. And Africa.

CHAPTER TWENTY SEVEN

Harry Kenyon whistled silently through his teeth as he took the Landrover along the hard corrugated bush road. The song was 'Knees Up Mother Brown'. Behind the vehicle a plume of pink dust curled reluctantly away in the midday heat, bringing into view again the two trucks, one in army camouflage colours, one in Parks' green, that made up the three vehicle convoy. With the windscreen down, a cool valley-scented breeze blew over them. Up ahead, on the left, the escarpment reared, and he could see where the main road wound its way up from the valley floor. He checked his watch, calculating when they would reach the provincial warden's offices near Sinoia, and before that, the tarmacadam road at Entry Gate One.

Only a few minutes now, to the tar, he judged. Which is good news. With the landmine incidents increasing, further up the valley. I am certainly not in the mood to collect one today. Not when we are headed for the bright lights of Salisbury. And Peta Holt. I'm not sure about the rest of it though. The meeting scheduled for Monday with the director. No hint on the radio about the agenda. Ah well, my friend, we will just see, won't we? Coming into view was the boom, with the tar road after it.

"Wonderful," he said aloud now. "Good black tarmacadam. And I did not think I would *ever* be pleased to see such evidence of progress. But these days vehicles and dirt roads do not go together too well. Must say, I've always preferred walking."

Beside him Kashili turned from watching the passing bush over the half-door, Harry's FN cradled protectively against the lurching passage of the vehicle on the bad road.

"*Uti yini?* I cannot hear you above the noise. But perhaps you are talking to yourself, young warrior?"

Kashili grinned at Harry's sidelong glance.

"Young, hmmm. Does that mean I've graduated? Not 'little warrior'?"

The tracker watched a slender mongoose make its low-slung dash across in front of the car, the grin staying on his features.

"*Aizona*. No. With your last hunting you have set a new standard. Better than the elephant teeth and crocodile skins of the old days."

He paused. Then.

"Your friend of the long hair, who came back over the river with you. How is it with him? How much will he tell the army?"

Harry shrugged.

"I am not completely sure. Three weeks have passed since that time, with nothing coming to pass. If he had said anything, there would have been some action against me by now, I think."

The warden took a long breath, let the rest of his thoughts go unspoken. Whispering Jim would have been de-briefed, as standard operating procedure. He would have to have walked a

very fine line, to leave me out of it, if he stayed with his word to
me. By now CIO and anyone else in that particular game will
have come up with theories about Gant's passing on to greener
killing fields. Spider, I should say. Bastard. I have a feeling
that one or two people might join the dots. Scratch Peters.
The general. Maybe the meeting next week will be a little rocky.
Well, hopefully tonight you will pick up some recent scuttlebutt.
It will be nice to stay with Garnet and Jessica again, take them
out to dinner perhaps. A small thank you for watching my back
at headquarters. And Peta. Oh my goodness, yes. Back in mid
week, in time for Christmas. With her book, which sounds
bloody good. Doing well in the shops. He glanced at the sky.
No rain yet. Not a sign of it and we're into December.

They drove into town along the tree-lined avenue of Second
Street Extension. Looking past Kashili he could see the
Saturday afternoon golfers littered across the manicured green
fields of the Royal Salisbury Golf Club. Harry drove through
the town centre into the African and Asian quarter, to the long
distance bus terminus. He stopped the Landrover and turned
to Kashili.
"Okay, *bava*. Have a good time back in your village. It is so
long since your last visit, perhaps they have forgotten you! See
you a week on Monday, at the headquarters. Take care, now
you are back in civilisation. Try and keep out of trouble, as
befits an elder such as you. Give my regards to your people,
especially your eldest son. I hope Shadrek is well."
The African nodded, grinning.
"And you also. You take care, here in the town. For it is but a
big beerhall, and there are always strange people hanging
around beerhalls these days."
He hauled a worn green canvas holdall from the back, raised a
hand in farewell and started walking over to a line of buses that
framed the market square. Harry watched his retreating figure
fondly for a few moments before pulling away. It struck him, as
it always did in town, that Kashili always looked that much

smaller and vulnerable when in civilisation. There was no hint of his bush and hunting experience, of years spent out and about in some of the wildest places in Africa. Harry worried about him, in the towns.

It was Harry who got into trouble.
When he arrived at the Claytons' house, in the suburbs, where he usually stayed on his infrequent trips to Salisbury, only their teenage daughter was at home. Her parents, Julie Clayton told Harry, had had to go away for the weekend. Some annual presentation ceremony in one of the national parks, she said. But the guest cottage was open, there was a new bottle of gin, he was to make himself at home, and they would catch up with him on their return late Sunday. She linked her arm through his once he had parked his Landrover and was taking his gear inside.
"If you're feeling rejected, at a loose end in this town I know you're not that fond of, you could always come to a party with me tonight, Harry."
He grinned at her, seeing Garnet's features in tandem with the blonde ponytail, remembered when she had been a five-year-old riding horses on his swinging leg.
"Oh yes? Me? At one of your rave-ups? Thanks for worrying, young lady, but I think not. What would the current boyfriend say?"
"None at the moment. You could be my chaperone. Come on, Harry, shake the dust out of your system! Fluff the feathers a little. A party would do you good, truly it would."
Harry's grin became a laugh.
"You don't say. Julie Clayton, you go and party to your heart's content. Me, I'm quite happy to sit here out on the verandah with a drink or two, and watch the clock on your mum and dad's behalf."

But he had gone, despite himself. Had put on his top hat and tails, fixed on the party smile and walked into the mêleé alongside the pretty daughter of his friend. Had been assailed immediately by the music, and knew it was a mistake soon after. He had noted the expressions, the once-overs, from the townspeople. Did not think it was just because of the young girl on his arm. In his favourite grey flannels, sharply creased, and his pale blue button-down lounge shirt, his only one, even without the tie he had nearly worn, he was very much the interloper. The pterodactyl amongst the peacock-hued party animals. He felt his age suddenly, and was irritated by it. Braved it out for almost two hours, leaning against the poolside bar, nursing his drink protectively from the dancing merry crowd. Catching glimpses of Julie. Thinking, finally, okay Harry, maybe it's time to go, as the flashing coloured strobe lights from the mobile disco bounded across his face. He had eavesdropped on the conversations, all of them ending up shipwrecked on the same topics. War and politics. He noticed the clutch of journalists, looking very much at home here these days, supping at their duty-free whisky. Still hanging around, after covering the talks on the train at Victoria Falls in August, wasting their time, as much as Smith had been forced to waste his, humouring Vorster and Kaunda and the rest of the circus.

Just before midnight it all crept up on him. Smacked him firmly between the eyes. He couldn't wait to get away. Julie was with the journalists, laughing, when he stopped to make sure she would be all right on her own. She had gripped one of his ears and kissed him in a motherly fashion on the cheek and promised to be home within an hour. Harry ignored the sardonic looks from the hacks and made his way through the crowd and out across the lawn. Amongst the rose bushes someone was bent double, puking violently. Harry kept walking. Gradually the cacophony of the party receded and he stopped and took a series of deep breaths. Above him some cloud had scudded in and he felt a soft breeze on his cheek. He sighed and wished fervently that Peta was with him. That they were back down in the valley. From the party a snatch of a song reached him. He grimaced. *'I Want to Kiss You All Over'* really didn't suit his mood. Not at the moment.

The trouble came as he was driving back to the cottage. Waiting at traffic lights, he was slow to take off again. He had to admit, he was miles away, thinking about Kashili and his people down close to the Mozambique border. . Peta. Elephants. Journalists … So the impatient hooting behind him was deserved in a way, he supposed later. But a couple of gentle hoots would have been fine. And he and his old Landrover would have been away. The long strident hooting, and the torrent of abuse with the finger signs as the Alfa Romeo came alongside was not necessary, a little over the top. Harry watched them as they stayed level with him, young whites, hair shorn, the glint of overhead lights on beer bottles, faces distorted with drunken unreasonable anger. Four of them, he counted. An arm swinging. Crash of glass as the bottle hit the Landrover, splinters cutting his cheek. He felt it then, coming up out of the dark. Uncoiling. Slowed to let them get ahead, grimacing when they slowed also. The epithets increasing in volume. One of them half leaning out of a window now, another bottle poised.

Harry swerved. Toward the car. Heard the shriek of metal on metal as his bumper did damage to the skin of the Alfa. Saw the change of expression as he put out his right arm across the door, caught him by the throat and then swung away. The figure, gurgling and jerking frantically, arms scrabbling at the window. Harry widened the gap, holding hard. Judged it just right and then let him go, smiled mirthlessly as he watched him tumble out on to the road. Could still feel it flowing through him, stronger than ever. Crouching now. Ready to explode. He pulled over and stopped on the dirt. Got out. Waited, with the long steel jack handle held lightly in one hand.

The Alfa pulled up in a shower of dirt and gravel, the doors opening before it stopped. Harry watched as they piled out, noted the fit hard forms, heard the slang that confirmed they were soldiers, probably troopies from the infantry battalion. Everything was slipping into slow motion, just as it did on the culls, had done in Malaya and later tracking the insurgents in Wankie. As it had done when he stepped out on the road in Zambia, into the swirling dust, with Gant's vehicle coming at him through the night. He backed away a step, seeing their grins start, was conscious of passing traffic. No one stopping. The one he had pulled out of the window was moving, crab-like, off the road. Not interested in this any more. Three, then. Harry stepped forward. Hit one with the jack handle in the midriff, changed the position of his hands on the steel shaft and swept it up against the side of the head on number two. Seeing and hearing their reactions as he dodged a punch from his third attacker, dropping the handle and scrummaging tight up against him and hammering hard into the solar plexus. Smelling second-hand beer and cigarettes. Clubbing him with joined fists as he bent over groaning. Seeing him go down and turning fast, keeping his momentum on track, hearing tyres crunch on gravel in a distant part of his brain, hammering the one still clutching at his middle, twice against the ear, knowing he was out of it now and looking for the third one still on his feet.

Seeing the pistol, the muzzle not two feet away from him, identifying it almost distractedly as a Tokarev, with the knuckles white around the grip. Looking up over the black hole to the face, one side swollen from the jack handle, young seeming old, lips pinched tight in anger and pain. Harry straightening, looking for the gap.

"Don't be a prick."

The voice coming out of the dark. Familiar in a way, even with Harry's concentration on the weapon and the troopie. Coming again.

"Put the gun away. Not too bright, waving a captured weapon about under the street lights on a main road. Won't make you a hero back at barracks."

The pistol wavered, the expression above it also. Lips not so tight any more. The lump even bigger though. The voice again, conversational.

"There's a good chap. Put it down. Hear no evil, see no evil, speak no evil. Take it out of his face and you and your mates get the fuck out of here. Then there's no charges, no spell in Brady. I'm not saying it again, soldier. There's only half an hour left on your deodorant, anyway."

Harry felt his own anger boiling away now. The beast going back into its cave. Had the voice pegged as he watched the Tokarev drop, saw the tension leak out of the youngster. Hell, he's not long out of school, thought Harry. One minute playing first team rugby with his mates, the world his oyster: the next sitting in a chopper with a gun being flown into a whole new ball game. He smiled and nodded softly, then broke the eye contact. Turned, his smile becoming wry.

"We've got to stop meeting like this you know."

They sat on the verandah of the cottage. Julie had come home and made them coffee before going to bed. More clouds were blowing in, though still without moisture. Traffic noise muted, dogs barking down the street. Harry leaned back in his chair, watching his companion obliquely, thinking back over what he had been told.

"I guess I owe you one," he said finally.

Whispering Jim Lannigan grunted.

"Yes. I reckon you do. Quite apart from stopping that troopie plant you tonight."

Harry Kenyon's turn to grunt.

"The buffalo and you. The boy with the gun and me. We're even there. Tit for tat. But the other, you keeping your mouth shut about me going after Gant across the river, puts you in credit. Thanks again."

Whispering Jim scrubbed a hand across his face.

"Yeah, well, like I said. Watch your back. There are some people who are very unhappy about their man Spider being taken out. And I don't believe Scratch Peters is absolutely convinced that Warden Kenyon is not involved somewhere along the line."

The soldier stood up and stretched.

"Time to grab some sleep."

Pausing, before.

"I'm transferring out of the Scouts, by the way."

Harry looked up at him, the surprise on his face.

"Squadron. Selous Scouts. Medals earned in both units. What else is there for you?"

Lannigan grinned.

"In this business there's always the shadow units. The no name brands. Here today, gone tomorrow, two countries away the next day. The Irishman has always got something going. Contacts all over Africa, and beyond. On both sides of the fence. Plenty of money in the slush fund. I reckon he's more powerful than Smith or Walls. Of course, being on his payroll means things are usually more hairy, but good pay and good perks."

Harry stood up also.

"Well, good luck, whatever. We're all going to need it, I think."

They shook hands. Harry caught Whispering Jim's eye, seeing the hesitation there momentarily, seeing the shadow flit across his face.

"Watch your back," he said again.

CHAPTER TWENTY-EIGHT

"Hello, stranger! My goodness but it's been a long time since you paid us a visit!"

Mrs Pretty, eternally cheerful, secretary to the director, smiled at Harry, her Scots burr as strong as ever. Harry bowed theatrically, pleased that at least someone was happy to see him.

"Good morning, Isobel. You look younger every time I pass through these hallowed portals. Is it the clean life you lead, or have you kicked over the traces and found a younger man?"
She chuckled and wagged a finger in mock admonition.
"You're still a cheeky young devil, Harry Kenyon. And you're one to talk! I've heard these stories about the wee young lass you've had hidden down in Nemana, these past three years. She's about to return, I gather. When are you going to do the decent thing and marry her, the poor wee thing?"
Harry grinned, leaning against the doorframe.
"As soon as I can, if she will still have me."
The secretary smiled and looked at the clock on the wall.
"Go on in, Harry. The director is ready for you now. I've just taken in fresh tea. And ..." She winked, " ... mind you behave, young man."
Harry rolled his eyes and blew her a kiss. Crossed her office to the closed door, taking off his beret.

They had gone through the pleasantries, batted the conversational ball across the desk between them, service and delivery a little scrappy. Harry looked for the words between the lines, couldn't see them. Had not really thought he would. Finally Alistair Drummond pushed his chair back, crossed one elegantly tailored leg over the other and lit a cigarette.
"Peta Holt is due back soon, I hear," he said, past the stream of smoke he blew at the ceiling.
Harry nodded.
"That's right. Day after tomorrow."
"I gather her book has been well received. Doing well, put Nemana firmly on the map as a wildlife destination."
Harry nodded again.
"Seems so. She sent me some of the reviews in her last letter. I must say, I'm looking forward to seeing it."
The director's turn to nod.
"Likewise. A pity though, that people can't go down there these days. With the situation. Bit of a wasted effort, hmmm?"

Harry shrugged, kept his voice light.

"No effort is wasted. Any good public relations are a bonus, particularly these days. When the country as a whole is getting the bad overseas press that seems to be the order of the day."

Where is this going, he wondered. What convoluted bloody trail are we on here? Kept a poker face as he eyed Drummond. Saw the fingers tapping on the knee. Get on with it, man. Because I am not as good at this as you are. And I might be tempted to deck you again. Can't, can I?

As if reading his thoughts, the director stubbed out the half-smoked cigarette, concentrating on this task before eventually meeting Harry's stare.

"We're at the end of another year. 1976 is around the corner. Nemana National Park has had a rough time, with the poaching. So have you. I am fully aware of your efforts and your frustrations. The department generally has gone through some harrowing times. We've lost some good men, and not all the gaps are filled correctly."

He paused, eyeing the packet of cigarettes. Let his gaze move on across to the line of framed photographs along the wall. Harry waited.

"I've said this to you before. Nemana, with no tourist access and restricted Park administration, does not qualify now as a warden station. A senior ranger would be fine down there. Unfortunately, at this moment in time we are a bit thin on the ground with men in that position. Resignations and members killed by terrorist action being the reason. You have been at Nemana for a long time, way over the usual period for a field station. Not only that, although I know the spectre of promotion is not a happy thought for you, you are due for it. Which also means transfer. And if those reasons aren't enough, there is the situation with Miss Holt. Nemana, as you well know, is a bachelor station. The department has turned a blind eye to her presence there, living with you. With no tourists, and the place out of the public eye, the situation has not worried the department, me, overmuch. But there is a limit."

He paused to lift an eyebrow in Harry's direction.

"Paradoxically, with the book now out and available to the public, you will be subjected to some scrutiny. Not a good example to your juniors, Harry, living in sin. Nor will it reflect well on the department."

Now he met Harry's scrutiny, letting their stares clash. Smiled a man-to-man smile.

"So, Harry, what this is all leading up to is that I want you to get into mind-set for transfer. Not as soon as I would prefer, because of our shortage of relevant manpower, but in the new year."

He noted the warden's expression and shook his head.

"For Pete's sake, man! It's promotion! Up the ladder! Your career moving, not stagnating. Most people would be pleased!" Good news, wrapped up in bad. You do it so well.

"And the poaching? The elephant and the rhino, and whatever else is next on the list? Who looks after that?"

Harry's voice was level, despite his internal turmoil. He knew in his heart of hearts that this was what he had been expecting. Had been dreading this.

"Whoever takes your place. You're a damn good warden, Harry, but you are not a one-man band. No one is indispensable. You know that."

"Sure. Of course. But very few of our chaps, no one in fact, knows that valley like I do."

"Point taken. At the same time, that has not stopped the animals being killed, has it? Warden Harry Kenyon has not prevented the massacre that has been going on, has he? Despite his unorthodox approach, despite his autocratic ways, despite playing judge, jury and executioner. Am I right or not? You tell me, Harry."

Harry took a deep breath, letting it out slowly. Do I bring up Gant, he wondered. Maybe you know anyway. Maybe Winters told you as well. Maybe this is all a charade, part of my crucifixion. Shit!

The warden nodded softly.

"Fair comment. But let me say this. If I had not been down there, if I had not played things my way, there would have been even more carcasses And you may have noticed from my most recent reports, there have been no new poaching incidents for three weeks. You do read my reports, sir?"
Dr Alistair Drummond's eyes hooded, and he leaned forward to rest his elbows on his desk. Harry had seen the wash of pleased satisfaction, though. Because you've drawn blood. Because now you can see the jugular. Which is what this is all about.
"Pity about the last crack, Warden Kenyon. You've been doing so well, up to now, keeping your tongue under control. Yes, I do read your reports, carefully. And yes, I had noted there were no new killings of late. In fact it struck me as curious. Why? I asked myself. Why should they stop, just like that? Any ideas, Warden Kenyon?"
Harry shook his head, made a major effort to calm himself and ride this meeting through. Because if you get under my skin, here in Salisbury, on your own patch of turf, and I lose it, I'm finished.
"No. Maybe my extra patrols have paid off. It's early days ..."
"Early days? From when? To what? Explain that, will you."
Because you have decided it's time. Payback time. And perhaps because there is *something* on the wind. And now is the time to put the boot in.
"Since I hung that lot, earlier this year, and sent the message back." Which we discussed, in Kariba, with Hugo Winters. And which seems so long ago now.
Drummond was shaking his head, patiently back and forth. No, no, no.
"I don't think so. They killed one of the tuskers after that. One of the 'Big Four'. Katete wasn't it?
"Yes."
We won't bring up the message, the effigy. Not right now. There's enough blood in the water. No more sharks, please.
Harry watched Drummond watching him, in his mind seeing the man that long ago night on the lake, the woman staring, as

he thrashed the intruder. Peta's mother. Knew that somehow
Drummond had eavesdropped on his thoughts, because his
expression changed. But not that part, not Peta and her
mother. Because that was a secret. Between Peta and me.
"I hear whispers, Harry ..."
Harry again. Which means?
"One does in this country. It's so small, you know. At least,
I'm treating them as whispers. For now anyway, until anything
materialises out of these whispers. Watch your neck, Harry
Kenyon. Stick it out just a little, and it will be chopped off.
You do know that, don't you?"
Harry returned Drummond's stare, fighting it down again.
Kept the rock in front of the cave, just. To stop the beast from
coming out.
Grinned suddenly, letting his gaze leave the director to look
around the room. Bringing his eyes back, eventually, the rock
firmly in place now, to meet those of the director.
"Yes, Sir."
Dr Alistair Drummond nodded, made his own expression
neutral.
"Good."
He stood up, indicating that for him the meeting was over. Lit
another cigarette, before nodding at the door.
Harry stood up, kept the beret tight in one hand, and moved
towards the door. Had opened it when Drummond spoke
again.
"Oh dear, I'm so sorry, Harry ..."
Harry stopped and looked at him. The director pointed at the
tea tray.
"I forgot to offer you tea."

The day had not improved.
Early evening, sitting in The Blue Room at the Windsor Hotel,
the bar in the quiet time of flux between the after work
sundowners and the dinner trade. Harry sipped at his drink,
going over the meeting again, watching the mirror behind the

bar for Roscoe Daniels who was in town on research business. Looking forward to a friendly face, and also dinner later with Garnet and his wife. Feeling drained.

He didn't recognise him at first. Not in the blazer and tie, hair freshly wet-combed and considerably longer than when he had last seen him. It was the badge on the blazer first, the winged dagger, before his eyes met those of Scratch Peters, in the mirror. Saw the hard sardonic glint. He turned casually.

"Well, well! Harry Kenyon! Taking time off from your zoo keeping?"

Scratch was smiling broadly, hand out in greeting. But Harry had seen the first instinctive expression. He matched smiles.

"Hello, Scratch, how the hell are you? And you, giving the war a break? On a spot of R and R?"

The soldier slid on to the barstool next to him, calling the barman across with a nod of his head, pointing at himself and Harry. As he adjusted his blazer, Harry saw the gun under his arm.

"Yeah. Couple of days. Then back to the trenches."

The smile was still on show when he turned to Harry.

"So what's happening? What brings you up out of the valley to the bright lights?"

"Same thing. Departmental meetings and a few days off. Before the rains finally arrive and we get bogged in down there."

Scratch Peters nodded, letting his eyes inspect Harry. Waved a thank you for the drinks without stopping his inspection.

"And tonight? Hitting the town? While your girlfriend is away? Letting your hair down at Samantha's or Brett's, I'll bet. Old dark horse Harry."

The warden laughed, thinking about that choice of words. And the reference to Peta.

"You know me better than that, Scratch. A few gins around a quiet fire is my lot. No, I'm meeting some Parks people here, should be here any minute, and then it's a couple of drinks, and

after that, dinner. Where's a good place these days? The guinea
fowl with paté still good at *The Bird and Bottle?*"
Harry's voice as light as that of the soldier. As deliberately
banal. He poured the new drink and tilted the glass. Smiled.
Because we have both been around the block. Been there, done
that. And I have had plenty of practice today, playing games.
"Cheers. Keep to the high ground."
They both drank, watching each other over the rims of their
glasses.
"Ahhh. Nectar."
Scratch put his drink down, cast a glance around the bar.
"Hear you ran into a spot of bother. The other night, I mean.
Had a gun stuck in your face."
Harry chuckled. Drummond's right, he reflected. It is a small
place, this country.
"Uh huh."
Scratch raised an eyebrow.
"Slowing down, Harry. There was a time when you would have
flattened those troopies, with a drink in one hand."
Harry shrugged his answer, took a leisurely sip at his gin.
"Lucky that Jim was around," Scratch continued. "You might
have got hurt. Better be careful, Harry. Might not be so lucky,
next time."
The smile still there, playing at the edge of his mouth. Not in
the eyes though. Harry put his glass down. Shifted on the
barstool so that both feet were planted solidly on the floor.
"Next time I'll be ready."
Scratch Peters threw back his head and laughed, slapping Harry
on one shoulder. Harry waited, smiling also. The soldier shook
his head.
"Good old Harry. You haven't changed. Not much anyway.
Hell, but a lot of water has flowed under the bridge since
Malaya. Hey? Since we scribbled one Shorty Kuk and sent him
off to the great Chinese take-away in the sky. Since you got
yourself gut-shot. You know, there aren't too many blokes in

this country, even in these wild times, with your amount of bullet holes. Or your bunch of medals. What a bloody waste." He took a long determined pull at his drink. Something and Coke, Harry suddenly recalled. Scratch didn't order when he arrived, just nodded. Because they know you here. Because you know I usually drink here, when I do come to town. The soldier put his drink down and stared at it.
"I know it was you."
So quietly that Harry barely heard the words.
"What?"
"I know it was you. Who killed Gant."
"What the hell are you waffling about?"
Scratch Peters turned his head to look at Harry. Beaked nose. Blue eyes, very flat.
"I fucking know. No, Lannigan didn't say anything. He didn't say enough. I know you, Harry. And I know you went across the river and wasted him. It's the kind of thing you would do. You, here. Gant, there. Not too far apart, in our line of business. We've done it before, both of us, long before this crock of shit ever started. The others are still scratching their heads ... Flower, the Irishman. But not me."
Harry shook his head, returning the flat stare.
"You should change your drink, old son. Whatever sauce you're on makes you hallucinate. In a big way. If Gant is dead, and I hope the bastard is, it's news to me."
The soldier gave a derisive snort, answered in a quiet savage whisper.
"You screwed up a major scene, my friend. With that single-minded bloody stubborn outlook of yours. Cost people a lot of time and effort, maybe lives. It's not just Gant. You're right, he's scum. But he was *ours*. Wasted, because of *your* bloody elephants. Jesus..."
He shook his head and drained his drink in one long swallow. Waved away the barman coming down the bar to refill.

"So, Harry my boy. You had better watch your back very carefully, because the Gant business is not over. And that narrow line you have been walking is now almost invisible ..."
He stood up and stepped away from the bar, keeping his back to the other customers. Harry tensed. Scratch Peters winked and pointed an imaginary gun at his chest.
"... and you might just take a tumble."
With a last sardonic smile he left.
Harry took a deep breath. Well, he mused, there we are. The lines are drawn. Three warnings, threats, in as many days. Kashili was right about this place. I think I'll have another drink. Two perhaps.

CHAPTER TWENTY-NINE

The elephant lowered his head and charged.
It had taken a while for the bull to notice them, so busy was he harassing the other animals trying to drink at the last muddy water in the centre of the pan. Patrolling back and forth, head high and looking for trouble, throaty squeals and loud trumpeting challenges that echoed through the bush, the elephant had made an impressive sight. The liquid flowing from the temporal gland on the side of his head shone wetly in the sunlight, as did the viscous greenish emission from his exposed penis that swung and jerked spasmodically like some great serpent beneath him.

Before the charge came, they had watched him chase a pair of blacksmith plovers which had had the temerity to flash their wings at him. For more than two hundred yards, in full, jerky long-legged stride, he had chased the birds, screaming his pique all the way. On the way back to the pan from this little victory he had methodically trashed a wild gardenia bush that had dared to rustle slightly in the wind as he passed. With his testosterone level way up high, bubbling almost, the bull was in the peak of musth, and, for the time being, this was *his* patch of Africa.

Then he saw the Landrover parked unobtrusively in the shade of the tamarind. Had stared disbelievingly at this new intruder. Standing tall, head high, peering myopically down his trunk, moving forward a couple of paces to plant his front feet up on the fallen trunk of a mopane tree, so he stood taller still. Intimidating. Threatening. Sunlight flashing off his tusks.

"Here we go," said Harry with a smile. "Any second now, methinks."

Beside him Peta and Kashili were also smiling at the frustrated ill-tempered animal.

Harry started the motor, the new noise yet a new challenge to the bull, too much to bear. They could almost see the decision flame across his brain. And he was coming, incensed at this new interloper, who was now running away, escaping. He chased them across the valley floor for almost half a mile.

Inside the car the three of them laughing, Harry with an eye on the rear view mirror, seeing the elephant stop finally in a swirl of dust. Welcome back, Peta Holt.

Harry had been more than ready to take his leave of Salisbury. Peta had arrived back from London, eager for the valley, but they still had three days to wait for Kashili to return. They had booked into a hotel. Sealed off from unfolding history in the capital city, they had kept room service busy while they recaptured lost time, hearing what each had been doing in their months apart. On the first evening, with a purple twilight outside almost matching the colours of the jacaranda blossoms along Cecil Square, Peta had given Harry the book. He had looked at the gift wrapping, hefting it in his hands for a long time, before opening it. An early Christmas present, Peta had said, suddenly shy.

It was better than even he expected. She had caught that part of Africa perfectly. The peace and the violence. The wet and the dry. The hard and the soft. Big and small. The different light patterns. The sheer timelessness of the valley. When he read the inscription in front of the book, Harry Kenyon, for the first time in many years, had felt tears in his eyes.

"To Harry Kenyon ... friend, teacher

and midnight guru.

Always going a little further."

Later, laughing, she had said that she had more presents for Christmas Day, but some of them she didn't know how to wrap.

Now as she sat between Harry and Kashili in the Landrover, coming down out of the jesse thickets on to the flood plain, the pre-rain heat dissipated by the breeze blowing from the river, Peta Holt felt as if she was really coming home.

Christmas time in the Zambezi Valley. The rains now with them, falling hard every day, wiping away the dust that had smeared the air. The wild animals dispersed, making their own different ways to far wet-season haunts. The patrols still going out, but the pace of Shingela Base slowed, the seasonal isolation bringing a change to its metabolism.

The first flush of vegetation well established already, taking hold, fighting back against the erosion of the bare earth scarred by thousands of hooves. The dust devils gone now. The colour splash of wild flowers, with the invasive yellow of the devilthorn blooms hiding the cracks. Birds rivalling the flowers, in their new breeding plumage. Flashes of crimson, orange, blue and lilac amongst the reeds and bushes. Frog chorus competing with the insect cacophony, and every slowly filling pan with the splashes of white over it, where the tree frogs had made their foam nests. The spider communities had been quick to establish their different webs, raindrops asparkle in them when the sun reclaimed the sky. Around Shingela there were many new additions to the impala herds, the new crop of fawns already up and running on their spindly legs. And the resident bull elephants, too settled in their ways to move to firmer ground, waited out the rainy season alongside the Shingela staff.

Christmas brunch on Harry's verandah. Poached eggs atop smoked salmon, this luxury smuggled back from the food halls in Harrods. The blue-tinted bottle of Bombay Sapphire gin, one of Harry's presents, contrasting nicely with the white tablecloth and the green sweat-beaded bottle of champagne. No fir trees or Christmas lights. Outside, the decorations and baubles from London are sodden amongst the branches of the chinese lantern bush, its own purple and yellow flowers standing up to the rain well and making their own natural contribution to the occasion.

Peta Holt smiling, on her wrist a silver-stranded bracelet made to look like braided elephant-tail hair. On her left hand the new engagement ring, catching the light even on this rain-slashed December morning. Harry Kenyon's Christmas presents to her. Toasts. To the book, the future, old friends. And to the animals of the valley. And Harry Kenyon smiling, watching the woman who was now his fiancée, still not believing his luck.

Thoughts of Drummond, Scratch Peters, poachers and transfers pushed away for the time being.

The idyll continued on into the new year.

The rains, starting late, stayed on past their time. Only in May did the drying out period begin, delaying the annual repair of the roads and tracks. No sign of poaching. No new carcasses. Even though the rainy season was the time to worry even more, with the bush thick and inaccessible, hamstringing anti-poaching efforts. Harry located his three big tuskers, finding them all in good health. The collars had faded a little on the two bulls, Marula and Chiruwe, but nevertheless still looked bright and incongruous amidst the rain-green bush. Kabakwe, whom they had never managed to collar after the helicopter crash, still wandered further afield than the others, and the warden's pleasure at finding the big bull in one piece was tempered by his concern.

There were no messages about transfers or promotion on the daily radio schedules with headquarters.

He stood looking over the river, the vista sharp-etched after the rains. A pair of spoonbills fossicked nearby in the shallows, whilst a line of hadeda ibis flew past, upriver, their discordant cries still echoing after their passing. Behind him mopane squirrels chittered in high-pitched agitation. The army camp was quiet, as somnolent as the rest of Shingela. He glanced across at Peta, going through the mail that had come down from Karoi that day, sitting in her favourite spot on the riverbank. Scanned the river again. He felt restless, edgy, for no reason that he could identify. Maybe these months have been too good, he reflected. Things are going so smoothly that I'm starting to look over my shoulder to see what I've missed. We're halfway through the year, with not a peep out of Drummond, and no renewed poaching. There's even talk of reducing the army presence here, it's so peaceful. So, Harry, why don't you sit back and enjoy it? Thank your lucky stars that there are no more dead elephants or rhinos. And that the love of your life is with you, enjoying this peace and quiet because the ideas are forming for a new book.

"What? Sorry, I was wool-gathering."

He hadn't heard Peta speak, looked at her now. Faded blue denim shorts, old bush shirt of his, leather sandals, and not much else, he knew. He found it was still a novelty, looking at her, could not imagine it not being so. She waved a letter at him.

"I was saying that it never rains, but it pours, dreamer."

Harry walked over to her and planted a kiss on her lips.

"Right, you now have my undivided attention."

"You are becoming famous. We're becoming famous."
Peta tapped the letter.
"From the publishers. With me heading back for the wide, blue yonder in Rhodesia, I left them as a contact for any work that may crop up. This is from my editor. *National Geographic* want me to do an article on Nemana. They like the book, have heard how the poaching down here has stopped, and want a piece featuring both you and the Park. Something along the lines of one man and his wilderness, the calm in the middle of the storm. That being the peace and quiet here as opposed to the rest of the country, I suppose. There's talk of a BBC documentary link-up as well. And Conservation Africa want to do a big piece on all the national parks of Rhodesia, with Nemana being the anchor. Again the theme is how life goes on in the wildlife sanctuaries whilst the rest of the country faces off against the world.

"And if I, and you, honey child, are happy with the idea, they will go ahead and start making the relevant contact with government here, and get the show on the road. What do you think, lover?"
Harry whistled.
"Sure. Why not? I've always said that the more positive exposure the wildlife scenario gets, here or anywhere, the better. With their credentials, those outfits shouldn't have a problem getting the necessary clearance, even with our increasing xenophobia."
He hugged her, smelling the sun on her skin.
"That is damn good news, Miss Holt. Have we any champagne left?"

*****

The small boy watched the billy goat stop feeding and look around, once again, nostrils working. It snorted, turning one way and then the other. The rest of the animals picked up its unease and milled. Past them, gurgling amidst the riverine undergrowth, the Kukuku River made its way northwards to the Zambezi, still flowing vigorously from the late rains. The boy looked at the sky, judging how far away sundown was, and how long it would take him to drive the goats back to the village. He had left it a little late, losing track of time with the windfall of nyala berries he had found, which he now carried wrapped tightly in a cloth balanced on his head.

He caught the goats' unease. Was also worried about what his father would say if he allowed anything to happen to them. There were hyenas and leopards around, the elders had said, and especially there was the talk of the spotted devil further east, near Mushimbi Pools, who had killed four people this year. Killed them and eaten them! But Mushimbi Pools was a long way from here, he reassured himself, and I have yet to see leopard spoor in this new place we live.

Little Tendarayi Phiri, seven years old and into his second year of goat herding, got the animals moving along the path, chivvying them when they tried to stop and eat. Through big eyes he swept the bush around them. Gasped aloud.

The leopard was crouched on the far side of the goats. They had not seen it yet, but its scent was in their nostrils. They stopped and bunched, bleating. It came straight at them, a yellow blur shooting through the greenery. Oh my mother, my father, the boy wailed silently, standing petrified stock still, please do not let the leopard take Tongwe. He's my favourite goat. The leopard scattered the goats, not giving them a glance. Came straight through them at the boy. Tenderayi tried to scream, couldn't, and then the leopard was on him. The goats bleated in panic and ran, following the billy goat towards the village.

Harry took the handset from the scout, nodding his thanks.
"Kenyon on set. Go ahead, Garnet."
The chief warden's voice floated over the ether.
"Harry. We have a report of another killing by that leopard. The one the press has dubbed the Mushumbi Man-Eater.

Though this time the victim is a long way west of its normal stamping ground. This makes number five. Roger so far? Over."

Harry frowned.

"Copied. I didn't know there were any problems with a man-eater. I haven't read a paper for weeks, and I sure haven't heard anything about it from HQ. Where exactly? Over."

"So far it's been doing its thing in the tribal areas on the Hunyani River. This latest case is in the Dande, and the victim is from your old friend's newly established village. Chief Kanyoka. A little boy was taken late yesterday. As I say, the animal is far out of its normal range. I hope to Christ there aren't two of them. We've had someone from the Problem Animal Control Unit down there since the first attack last month.

Geyser Fletcher has been running himself ragged trying to cure it of its bad habits. To date he hasn't even laid eyes on the thing, and it's turning its nose up at baits, so poison or trap guns are out. Copied so far? Over."

"Copied."

"Kanyoka has asked for you. Says you sorted out those man-eating lions they had, way back, so he has faith in you. Can't blame him for not having the faith in Geyser, I suppose, but this cat is another story. It's writing its own rule book. How is your schedule, Harry? When do you think you could get across to the Dande? I would imagine the top road is fine now. Over."

Poor Kanyoka, thought Harry. He will take this as another sign that the spirits are not on their side. First the move, then this. And if this leopard has taken five people, not touching any bait, then you can be sure it is a smart cookie. Geyser is no slouch when it comes to this sort of work. Funny how every ten years or so the man-eating habit pops up. It will be good to see the chief. Kashili and I were only talking about him the other day, when we were down near his old village checking on Kabakwe. He lifted the handset.

"Roger that, Garnet. We're on full muster at the moment, so one of the rangers can hold the fort here. I'll head across with Kashili tomorrow. Should manage it in a day and a half. Over."

"Good, Harry. Once you've got yourself set up, get on the radio to me, will you. I think I'll fly down and see the situation at first hand. There's a choice of two or three strips in that area. Anything more from your side? Over."
"Negative. See you in a couple of days. Out to you."

Making love again, for the second time that night. Moving slowly, this time standing. In the doorway of the bungalow, half inside and half outside, the night sounds of the valley their background music. The geckos on the ceiling above them making the most of the insect invasion, with the door open. Harry stopping suddenly, freezing, still holding himself inside her. Peta biting him on the shoulder.
"Don't stop."
Voice ragged, nails digging into his back.
"Look," he whispered, his own voice hoarse. "Outside, just here."
Peta swivelled her head, her breath fanning his face, balancing against him. She gasped softly.
"God, isn't he beautiful!"
A big leopard stood immobile on the lawn, watching them. Harry recognised the animal as the resident male of the Shingela Camp territory. They had met many times. He showed no unease at being discovered, surprised Harry when he drew up his haunches and sat, still watching them. Peta giggled.
"Talk about a peeping Tom. This is crazy!"
Harry nodded wordlessly, his eyes on the animal. Started moving again, lifting one of Peta's legs up around him, bending his knees lower. Felt her responding anew. Both of them watching the leopard watching them. Peta bucking against him now, hair flying, breath coming in long gulping sobs, Harry's

hands low behind her, keeping her there, feeling the weakness
building in his knees. All the time his eyes locked on the
leopard.

Sitting, later, sprawled in the doorway where they had
collapsed. Leaning against the frames facing each other, legs
entangled. Breathing slowly returning to normal. Starlight
gleamed in the faint patina of perspiration on Peta's breasts,
made her eyes luminous. The leopard gone away. They could
hear him sawing his way around his territory. Heard the alarm
barks of bushbuck, the sneeze-warnings of impala. Harry still
had the leopard imprinted on his retina.

He shook his head, chuckling quietly.

"What?" she whispered.

"What's that saying? Something about 'a cat can look at a
king'."

She reached out and ran a finger over his lips. Giggled.

"*You're* a damn cool cat, Harry Kenyon. How did you know he
wouldn't do anything? We must have looked absolutely
helpless."

"I didn't. Fun, wasn't it?"

Hair swirling as she shook her head once, softly.

"Sometimes you're a little crazy. Off the wall. Do you know
that, Harry?"

He smiled, drinking her in with his eyes, this beautiful woman
who was almost twenty years younger than him. Wearing his
ring now. Wanting to be part of his life.

"An omen, maybe. Something to do with the other one, the
man-eater. I'm a great believer in omens."

He reached across and cupped one of her breasts in his hand,
stroked it with his thumb.

"I don't know how long I'll be on this man-eater thing. It's my
experience that if you don't make contact in the first days, you
can spend forever trying to get close to them. I'll keep you up
to date over the radio. In the meantime you keep working on
the *Geographic* piece."

She smiled, putting a hand over his.

"You take care, Warden Kenyon, and come back in good working order."

The smile became a giggle.

"Because there's also a man-eater back here, you know, waiting."

They heard the leopard again, followed by the screams and barks of the baboons.

CHAPTER THIRTY

Green. Tangled. Form obscuring. The undergrowth reaching up to interweave with the low canopy of trees, the yellowy-green bole of a fever tree providing the only solid form amidst the riotous confusion of vegetation. Mosquitoes whined in this dark, heavy bushed place, even though it was midday, though a person would not think so in here. The bubbling call of an oriole was the only other sound. Except for the noise we're making, thought Harry. Not much, with just the three of us going softly, softly, but still noise. Enough for the leopard to know exactly what we're up to. Edging forward, a step at a time, eyes searching amongst the gloom, ears straining for the slightest sound. Kashili in front, three paces away. Garnet behind him, three paces back. Any more and they wouldn't see each other. Harry felt the tickle of sweat running down from under his arm.

They were well into the big thicket now, Kashili still managing to hold on to the tracks. Which of course, thought Harry unhappily, are leading us straight into the middle of this stuff. I think I'm getting too old for this kind of business. He waited, shotgun poised, getting heavier, as Kashili checked the direction again. He did not dare even glance back at Garnet, not in this horrible, bloody tangle. Not when a second could be the difference between living or dying. Not when Kashili's only protection was Harry's shotgun, and his ability to use it. More ants were biting him, making steady passage up his bare legs. And the mopane flies had managed to follow them in here, were swarming happily after the sweat. Of which there was plenty, the warden reflected.

We were lucky, he thought again. The old thing of being in the right place at the right time, even if it was by chance. The leopard wasn't interested in that goat we tethered out, after we had dragged the carcass of the second goat around and about, sending out the invitation. But he had a look at it, all right. And he left his tracks for us to find, not an hour after first light. From his pug marks and his pace today, there's no sign of injury or deformation. He's a big boy, bloody huge in fact. Haven't found any of his droppings, so can't establish anything from that. Wonder what made him turn man-eater?

Leopards! They walk by themselves all right. They all write their own rule books, not just this one. Look at that fellow the other night, on your lawn, watching you and Peta. Like he was in front of the telly. I suppose he wondered what on earth we were doing. Although it was pretty obvious. Okay, Harry, let's stop that line of thought. Right now! It will just get you killed. Or Kashili. My oath but he's done well today, the old man. Six hours he's been on the tracks. And I moan that I'm getting too old for this rumble in jungle stuff. I wonder wh... Shit, just that bird hopping around.

Harry lowered the shotgun, just a little, feeling the increased adrenalin flow. Opened his mouth again to widen his ear canal. Taking some long slow breaths at the same time, feeling once more the dryness in his mouth. No spit at all. Kashili had stopped, his head cocking slightly. Harry could see new tension in the tracker's back, the way he held himself. The warden stepped back a pace, keeping some distance between them. Too close and they would be getting in each other's way, doing a Laurel and Hardy act, when things became critical. He willed his senses to strain harder, to lock in with Kashili's and find the leopard for them. Not for the first time in the last hour, he wished he had brought something to wrap around his neck. Like chain mail, a part of his mind whined. Shaddup. Just something, to keep the leopard's teeth out of his throat, if they had got it all wrong in here, in ambush alley.

Kashili still motionless, his left hand down by his side plucking unconsciously at the hem of his green bush shorts. His head moving slightly, to the right, taking his line of sight that way, but keeping his left periphery working as well. Harry could feel the concentration of the old tracker, as well as the sudden unease that had surfaced now, showing in his body language. He pulled the stock of the shotgun a fraction more firmly into his right shoulder. Looked straight ahead so that his own periphery vision could cover left and right. Behind him he heard Garnet swallow. Hoped the chief warden didn't shoot him in the arse by mistake, when it was bingo time. Or worse, do a Francis Macomber on him. Kashili, he noticed, was getting shorter. Was ever so slowly lowering himself to the ground, still with his attention focused to the right. But his left hand, still down by his side, was not plucking distractedly at the shorts any more. *It was a fist now, with the index finger angled in a point. To the ...*

The leopard was there, floating in the air already. At shoulder height. Not even any time for things to slide into slow motion. Thank Christ the shotgun was already pointing halfway in its direction. The leopard's front paws almost touching the barrel. Its teeth very white in the gloom, one canine broken. The brain still finding time, squeezing it from some recess, to record that. And also the big red hole appearing in the chest suddenly, skewing the mid air course of the leopard, the paws not reaching for him now, but the force of the leap still taking the animal over Harry's left shoulder. To fall in an uncoordinated black and yellow bundle between him and Garnet. Harry Kenyon not even being aware of pulling the trigger, not hearing the shotgun blast. Pulling out his handgun and shooting it again, very carefully, just so it didn't get up, as dead leopards have the habit of doing, and cause grievous

bodily harm to anybody. Harry Kenyon with an intense urge to
have a pee, now it was over.

Brassy cold, when a person stepped away from the fire, the
weather changing over the course of the afternoon. The heat at
midday, on the spoor of the man-eater, just a memory. No
stars tonight. Typical winter weather, in the valley.

The firelight skittered in the fresh breeze, making
harlequin masks of their faces as they nursed after dinner
coffee, Garnet also with a whiskey. The Landrover behind
them as a windbreak. The drums from Kanyoka's village
beating, coming to their ears softly. Others answering, across
this different part of the valley floor. No animal sounds. Not
here. Kashili back in the village, as guest of honour, having his
beer brought to him by Kanyoka's wives. *The spirits were happy
now*, they had said. The chief staring at Harry for a long time
that afternoon, while the leopard was being skinned, before
telling him of the news he had, from across the river. That the
nationalist poachers, *the boys from the bush*, would not be killing
any more elephants or rhinos. No reasons given. The camp on
the Mushika had been moved. No one knew where Obert
Hadebe was. They were still coming across, *the boys*, but they
were going on through the villages in the tribal area. Inland, up
the Kachuta Trail and into the white farming areas. Many
sections of them. And the spirits were on their side.
Chaminuka. Nehanda. See how the rains have fallen, a sure sign
that the spirits were on the side of the *Vakomana.* See how they
have let you kill this leopard that was troubling us.

Harry did not ask how the old chief knew, pretended not
to notice the new phrases that had crept into his vocabulary.
Neither of them mentioned Ndende, or their forced move out
of their ancestral home. It had happened. The *nganga* had said
it would.

Garnet pushed another piece of wood into the fire, and then looked across at Harry.

"You okay?"

Harry nodded, flashing a small smile.

"Sure. Just thinking."

The chief warden took a sip of his whiskey.

"Good news, about the poaching."

"Yes."

"I have some more good news. For the time being, anyway."

Harry looked at Garnet.

"It looks like you've had a stay of execution."

He grinned at Harry's nonplussed look.

"No move this year. Out of Nemana."

Harry stared at him, a grin breaking through for the first time that evening.

"Why not?"

"For sure, it's not the director going soft on you. It's circumstances. There is no suitable person of senior ranger status that we can put down in Nemana at the moment. And nowhere to put you. There have been a lot of changes this year. People leaving, mostly. Others, in senior positions, hanging in for the sake of their pensions, opting to stay on rather than take early payout. Nowhere to go, or don't want to go, yet."

Garnet Clayton studied Harry over his whiskey.

"Are you sure you're all right?"

Harry took a deep breath and manufactured a soft laugh.

"Yeah. Absolutely. Tired, I suppose."

"Have a drink, for Christ's sake. You've got reason to have one! The man-eater sorted out within two days of getting here. The news about the poaching. And any moves to Siberia have been shelved for the time being."

Harry laughed genuinely this time.

"Okay, Garnet. Okay. One of your whiskeys would be good. Must say I'm not a cold weather person. Been down here too long probably, and this change of weather has caught me flat-footed."

He paused, watching his friend pour a generous tot.

"I've been thinking about Kanyoka. What he said. What he didn't say. In a way his situation is an encapsulation of the whole scenario in this country. He is an example of how not to do things. I've known him for twenty-five years. In the old crocodile and elephant poaching days I used to re-supply at his village, used to hunt with him, shoot the occasional crop raider that hassled his people, and sorted out those lions, the two man-eaters. I would help with any medicine I had when anyone caught malaria, and there were times when I was under the weather, with no medicine, or not knowing what exactly was wrong with me. Then, he or the *nganga* would fix me up. Herbs, potions, mumbo-jumbo, whatever it took.

"When I stopped poaching, spent some time just rambling and looking, wondering what I was going to do with my life, and then when I joined the Game Department, I still saw a lot of him and his people. As you well know, he was my eyes and ears down in that part of the valley. It was him who put us on to the poaching last year. And so, indirectly, he helped us stop it."

We won't go into any detail here, thought Harry. No four-letter words, like Gant, mentioned. Not at this time.

He was aware that Garnet had not taken his eyes off him. Went on.

"He was, in the parlance, *on sides*. Then we moved him. Not far, and still in the valley, sure. But, out of his ancestral home, where he had been for years. Like we did with the Shangaans ten years ago, down in the lowveld, when Gona re Zhou was made a game reserve. And, with the stroke of a pen, in some dingy government office in Salisbury, the villagers were no longer *on sides*. We ... government, nudged them across into the other camp."

Harry took a sip of his drink, feeling the weight of the chief warden's stare.

"So, Garnet, the way I see it, is this. No matter how good our security forces are, no matter how many medals are won, no matter how many terrorists are killed, it's no go. No matter how inventive we are in business, no matter how good we are at sanctions busting, no matter how long old Smithy tries to make the Kissingers and Vorsters and the various British prime ministers see things our way, we're scuppered. Christ, Malaya taught me that, the hearts and minds business. I would have thought a few others would have read the same book. If the tribespeople are not on our side, we are in the smelly stuff. Savoury was right about that bit. So, Garnet, someone is not doing his homework. Internal Affairs, Police, none of us, are doing this right. Because the villagers, the *povo*, are throwing in with the *boys in the bush*."

Garnet Clayton stood up and turned his back to the fire, warming that side now. Stood thus for a long time staring up at the darkened sky. Not looking at Harry for the moment. Finally he turned and sat down beside the warden again.

"So what's new, Harry? Tell me something I don't know."

Harry grunted. The drums were still thrumming on the night air. The chief warden looked at him.

"And you? Where do you fit into the equation? Where will you be, when this particular bit of history is finally resolved, whichever way it happens to go? And, I'll ask the question that someone asked me recently. Whose side is Harry Kenyon on, these days?"

Harry met Garnet's enquiring stare, before giving a soft, rueful laugh.

"Me? I'll be here. In the bush. Looking after the animals. That's when I stand up to be counted, Garnet. I won't be going anywhere. Whether it's Rhodesia, Zimbabwe or Noddyland, it's the country that I love. The valley. And whatever happens, the wildlife will need to be protected. Properly. And I will do that, Garnet. Absolutely."

Harry stood up and walked to the other side of the fire. Met the chief warden's eyes across the flames.

"Africa is fucked, Garnet, for anyone who wants to be a *pukkah* white man. No doubt about it. We're all here on borrowed time. I accepted that a while back. So, I will dig in, I'm here for

as long as the spirits decide. I don't want to go anywhere else.
As for anyone asking whose side I am on, hell ..."
Harry grinned widely at the chief warden.
"... I would have thought that was obvious."

~ PART FOUR ~

Summer - 1976-1979

*"I loved you, so I drew these tides of men
into my hands and wrote my will across the
sky in stars."*

SEVEN PILLARS OF WISDOM by T E Lawrence

CHAPTER THIRTY-ONE

They moved back silently, the two men, retracing their steps on the meandering game trail they had been following. In the heat of late morning the bush here on the edge of the flood plain shimmered. There was little other movement. Harry scuffed a foot softly in the sand, noting the direction of the barely discernible breeze as the dust drifted slowly away.

Only just on our side, he reflected, returning Kashili's dry grin. Good thing there are no oxpeckers. We can back off and make a detour around our sleeping friend. Hate to disturb his siesta. And it's too darned hot to start climbing trees. The low mournful cadence of an emerald spotted wood dove floated over the bush. A bateleur eagle sliced across the blueness of the sky, in the direction of the still sleeping rhino. They had come upon the animal suddenly. Rounding an old termite mound, he was there in front of them, hull down beside a large-leafed *cassine* with its mantling shroud of spider web adding to the pooled shade. They were so close they could see the puffs of dust near the rhino's nostrils as he snored softly in midday repose.

Their strategic withdrawal completed, Harry and Kashili continued quietly on their way, with not a word necessary between them. Another night under the stars, and then they would be back at Shingela. The seven day patrol downriver had been uneventful, with little to raise the adrenalin level other than circumventing the increasing amount of elephant family groups that were to be encountered at this time of year down near the Zambezi. It was mid November, and as with the last wet season, the indications this year were that the rains would again be good. Harry had wanted to check the vicinity around Mtawatawa Pan, before it became inaccessible, and, as a matter of routine, pay a visit to the safari group currently in temporary residence at G Hunting Camp. He knew that Orville Cunningham, a roving warden with their department, was at the camp, playing host and professional guide to VIP guests of the government. Headquarters had already briefed him on the visit to the Safari Area, and although mildly curious that he himself had not been delegated to the chaperone duty, Harry was pleased to be out of it. These types of safaris were more frequent nowadays, as the beleaguered government courted new friends and cosseted old ones, and the favours increased.

One night at G Camp had been sufficient. Orville Cunningham had everything running smoothly and had picked up little of local import for Harry. The size of the group had surprised Harry, though. The main guests were two middle-aged, though well preserved Frenchmen, they in turn having a retinue of a dozen people that included personal bodyguards, a pair of exceedingly young and beautiful women, and a gaggle of personal aides. Seconded to the group was a Rhodesian Army section, and, the most interesting aspect of all for Harry, a member of the police Special Branch.

Jack Breen had grinned his usual shark's smile when he saw the warden. They knew each other reasonably well, had met several times in the past, usually in out of the way places. Breen had been the Special Branch representative attached to Harry's tracking team during the nationalist incursions in the late sixties, had visited him in hospital when he had been shot up. Harry liked tough, laconic Jack Breen, was aware that he moved in the rarefied air of top intelligence circles, knew also that his penchant was definitely not the safari life. Which was why his presence down here in the wilds alongside the French VIPs came as some surprise.

Jack the Knife, as he was known in certain circles, could not tell an impala from a giraffe, thought elephants belonged behind bars, and had no interest in lions unless they were on a certain local beer label. It was well known that, on his very rare spells of leave, he would take a rowboat out into the middle of a small dam outside Salisbury, and stay isolated there until his accompanying case of Lion was empty, whereupon he would radio for a new one. That, for Jack Breen, was a safari.

There had not been the opportunity for a quiet chat with the SB man. In fact, Harry had mused, it was almost as if Breen had ensured that no such opportunity presented itself. Seldom did he stray more than a few paces from the Frenchmen, and so the limited conversation between the policeman and the warden had been banal.

The next day saw Harry and Kashili begin their return to Shingela. For some time they had stayed close to the river. The carmine bee-eaters had returned and flew in iridescent parabolas above them. River music played, this morning dominated by the liquid bubbling notes of coucals. Then they had angled inland, cross-graining the country, watching for alien spoor patterns, or for vultures spiralling down. They sniffed at the slight breeze constantly, checking for any hint of putrescence in the air. But there had been nothing, not one single sign of anything being out of kilter. So uneventful had been the patrol, that the few seconds of tenseness with the rhino brought welcome excitement.

Apart from that, Harry ruminated now, this patrol has been as quiet as the rest of the preceding year, in fact as far back as the man-eating scenario near Kanyoka's new village. And here we are almost at the end of 1977. It's enough to make a person nervous. He thought about this as he automatically noted the spoor of a small group of nyala crossing ahead of him. A male with four females, his mind registered.

Paradoxically, though the country of Rhodesia itself was in turmoil, Nemana and its neighbouring wildlife areas were now enjoying a state of grace. Peace and quiet reigned. There had been no sign of poaching for over two years. Not since he had taken his own private war across into Zambia and terminated Alex Gant. Almost equally important to Harry was that he was still here, in Nemana. He was still chief guardian of the region's wildlife, with very little interference from headquarters. From Dr Alistair Drummond. Scratch Peters seemed to have dropped off the face of the earth. And , just for good measure, Peta Holt continued to be a permanent fixture at Shingela.

Her article for *National Geographic* had been published in February. A film documentary, incorporating Nemana amongst other foremost wildlife sanctuaries of Africa, had been made just before the last season's rains and was scheduled for imminent release. This exposure of Nemana, and, in tandem, of Harry, was a contributing factor, the warden was sure, to his continuing unharassed sojourn in the valley. In influential external wildlife circles he had become synonymous with Nemana National Park, and in a period of history when there was little enough good publicity appearing in the world media about Rhodesia, his niche in conservation, and in particular his successful efforts to stop poaching, had been too positive a piece of public relations to sour with a move out of the limelight. That no one knew just how he had put a stop to the poaching, Harry thanked the spirits, often. He did not know how long he could count on the situation remaining so, and grabbed each and every day with both hands, here in this patch of paradise on the great river he loved so much.

He listened to the staccato trilling of a woodland kingfisher, not too long ago returned from its seasonal migration to West Africa. Pausing, he studied the cheetah tracks, fresh, going in the same direction as the nyala spoor. He moved the weight of his FN across to his other shoulder, unaware of the shadow that passed across his features, as his thoughts marched on. We might be in a state of grace down here, but overall we sure as hell are not in good shape. Sure, we're still punching, and the gloves are still up, but we are taking a pounding. The Geneva peace talks were, to quote Ian Smith, "a dead duck". That's after Kissinger and Vorster read us the message, loud and clear ... move along, folks, because we've got bigger fish to fry ... because we are pulling the plug on you. The communiqués take longer and longer to read, and the death toll goes up by the day ... the farmers, the tribespeople, the missionaries, as from this year, playing their

little games both ways, and our security forces ... no matter
how many of the enemy are being killed, inside or outside the
country, their gaps in the ranks are quickly filled. We had the
Mapai raid, and everything was jolly hockeysticks, and then the
Woolworth's bomb, right in the middle of Salisbury. It's a
spiral. Tourism is shot to hell ... we've even just had tourists
ambushed in Wankie National Park, for Christ's sake. Our
flagship Park! And now we have Field Marshall Lord Carver
and friend Chand on the gin and tonic circuit in Salisbury,
trying to make us see the error of our ways. I wonder what
Jack Breen is doing down here with the French types? Old Jack
the Knife. Hmmm? Harry grunted softly, watching a pair of
parrots screech their way overhead.

All doom and gloom, he thought sadly. Not much good
news out there, even between the lines. Speaking of which, I
wonder what's happening across the country in Gona re Zhou?
Kashili looked very glum, after his most recent trip home.
Shadrek gone, no one knows where. Or why. The stories of
poaching filtering out. Elephants, some of the biggest bulls in
Africa, found dead. Deep inside the Park. Do we have another
Ivory Section scenario? Are the laddiebucks focusing their
attention on that region now? And if they are, who is playing
piggy-in-the-middle now that Gant is dead? Ahead of them a
matriarch led another family unit of eight elephants down on to
the flood plain. Perhaps you should stop wool-gathering, Harry
Kenyon thought to himself. Maybe you should concentrate a
little more on the job at hand. So you don't get yourself
trodden on, nor have something bite you. Not now, not when
everything is going so swimmingly.

CHAPTER THIRTY-TWO

May in Rhodesia, the weather perfect in this part of Africa at this time of year. Champagne month, people call it. And it is no less so this year, in 1978, down in the Zambezi Valley, with the air crisp and the view across the river to the northern escarpment in Zambia clean and clear. No smoke from the almost permanent bushfires at this time of year, over there. Explosions though, and much gunfire, as the soldiers of the Rhodesian Light Infantry and the Special Air Service harry the nationalist ZIPRA enemy across the northern valley floor of their host country. The sounds of battle echoing louder as Cuban instructors are deployed there to reinforce the Zambian based wing of the Patriotic Front alliance. The elephants do not swim across the river these days, not with the sound of guns there.

At Shingela base Harry Kenyon and the lovely Peta Holt discuss marriage plans. Long engagements went out with *Gone with the Wind*, she tells him. And it has been so peaceful down in Nemana for so long now that they think the time is right. Even the permanent army presence that has been here since that first landmine explosion in late 1972 has been reduced. A platoon of the Rhodesian Defence Regiment mans the bulldozed ramparts of the fort these days. Fish eagles call from their respective territories along the river. The tugboat chorus of hippos echoes reassuringly from the middle of the Zambezi. Impala rams, in tune with the arrival of the May full moon, are in full rut, their hoarse barking challenges floating everywhere across the flood plain. It's that time, Peta says, bestowing one of her widest smiles on Harry. *Carpe diem, quam minimum credula postero*. You know what that means, lover?

Harry Kenyon cocks an ear often at the gunfire over the river. Squints against the sun at the swift, low flying helicopters that occasionally sweep over Shingela on their way across the river. Sometimes at night he wakes to the faint drone of high flying aircraft, dropping more men into Zambia. A part of him is with them, and he thinks frequently about Malaya these days. Malaya and the early heady days with the Tracker Combat Unit. He wonders at his own restlessness, puts it down to almost three years of peace and quiet. Perhaps he's overdosed on tranquillity.

It is not like that in the rest of the country. Rhodesia is still on her feet in the ring. Taking hard hits and low blows. Needing more clinch time, needing more damage control, but still managing to land some punches of her own. The external operations are an everyday occurrence now, with designated names like *Manyatela, Miracle, Snoopy* and *Vodka*. On other playing fields, Rhodesia has managed to hold Transvaal to a draw, in the Datsun Shield cricket semi-final at the Salisbury Police Ground. Which helps keep people's minds off the communiqués from Combined Operations Headquarters. There is some euphoria to be found, amidst the mixed emotions ebbing and flowing across the country in early March, when Ian Smith joins with Muzorewa, Sithole and Chirau to form a transitional government. The end to white rule is written clearly on the wall. In black chalk.

Carver and Prem Chand are still tap-dancing their way around Africa. If it's Tuesday, it must be Cairo. David Owen, Cyrus Vance and Andrew Young blackbottom their way into the cabaret, just as one hundred political detainees are released to sing and dance their way to freedom from Wha Wha detention centre near Gwelo. In Dar es Salaam the bogeymen, the leaders of the Patriotic Front, watch the whole score from the wings, unimpressed.

Full moon is on the wane. The early winter days of June slide in. Cold, crisp nights give way reluctantly to the dry flat heat of the winter sun. Long dappled grasses rustle. Leaves fall. The valley bush is fast losing its colour, the greenness is going, giving way to the parched drab brown uniformity of the season. And the smoke from this year's first bushfires begins to haze the horizon, again.

In Salisbury there is ecstasy as the Rhodesian rugby team holds Transvaal to yet another draw. Out at Andre Rabie Barracks, Selous Scout Captain Chris Schulenburg becomes the first soldier to be awarded Rhodesia's highest medal for bravery, the Grand Cross of Valour. And down in Nemana National Park, Warden Harry Kenyon thumbs more bullets into another twenty-round magazine, his eyes flicking over the recently cleaned FN, and the pack that waits beside the doorway. His gaze drifts outside to rest briefly upon Kashili, squatting on his haunches on the lawn, his spear stuck in the ground beside him, as he talks quietly with their visitor. One of Kanyoka's men. *Again.* Bless him, thought Harry. It's one hell of a hike from their new home to Shingela, even as the crow flies. And things are very different now, since Kanyoka sent Ndende to me, so long ago. Oh yes, the times they have a-changed all right. But, the story is the same. So it's back to the trenches. It's bully beef and raw onion time again.

Harry finished filling his magazine and pushed it beside the others he had charged. Then he stood up and moved across to the big wall map, finding the spot with his eyes and then placing a finger on the name. Rushamba. An abandoned mission station. Right against the eastern border of the Chingusa Safari Area. Another finger on Mushumbi Pools. He frowned at the map. Two camps, they say. Recently established. With about a hundred white soldiers split between the two. And four dead elephants, with the tusks removed.

Harry sighed, following the red line of the road along the foot of the escarpment on the map. Roads. Ergo, landmines. Not to mention the chance of being ambushed, he thought unhappily. But I'll have to do it. There's no time to walk it. So, okay then. If that is what you have to do, so be it. No good whining. We will drive slowly, with our eyes peeled and our fingers crossed. At least that road is seldom used, and will still be damn rough from the rains, so it does not make for a prime mining target. We'll spend tonight on the road, hopefully well past the halfway mark. With two vehicles we should carry

enough fuel for the return trip. Kashili and me in front, with
three game scouts in the second back-up Landrover. I'm glad
Sergeant Fumbi is back from his leave. He's a bloody good
man. Peta should be fine back here, with the rest of the
manpower. So much for wedding plans at the moment. He
paused, listening to more distant shooting from across the river.
Plenty of automatic fire, punctuated with explosions. He
grimaced. Wonder who's doing what to whom, he mused. He
swept a long look around his office, drumming fingers softly
against his holstered revolver, making time to tick things off his
mental list. It seemed to take longer these days. Nodded to
himself, eventually. Well, let's head 'em up and move 'em out,
as the cowboys say. He did not have a good feeling about this
business.

The road had been worse than he anticipated.
Washaways and caution had eaten up a lot of time, and nightfall
at the end of the second day was almost upon them by the time
they had bisected the large gravel road that snaked across the
valley floor from Centenary to Kanyemba. Harry weighed up
their night-stop options. It was one thing to ease quietly off the
road into the security of pristine bush along the escarpment,
but down here in what had long been a hotly contested war
zone, with villages to be seen and the area a well established
insurgent infiltration route, it was another thing entirely. He
stopped the Landrover at the junction of the two roads and
climbed out to stretch, not moving far from his FN. Their
route to the left would take them another five hours, landmines
and ambushes notwithstanding. In a straight line Rushamba
would not be far, but the road followed the easiest contours.
Five hours of Apache country, in a very small, lightly defended
convoy of two vehicles. Where the security forces travelled
with heavy machine guns and never less than four armoured
trucks. To the right, he knew, but a few miles away, was the big
concrete bridge over the Angwa River, where a permanent
reinforced security force presence was well entrenched to make
sure the bridge did not get destroyed. He wondered who had

the duty these days, decided it did not really matter, with the lengthening shadows blending quickly into early twilight. Guinea fowl were already winging into night roosting positions.

Two sections of Police Support Unit defended the bridge, commanded by a young quietly spoken section officer. Harry and his men were made welcome and given cramped but adequate sleeping areas. Dark was full over the land by the time Harry had washed and shaved and joined the young policeman for a cup of coffee. Hawk moths were on the wing, battering themselves against the hissing gas lamps in the mess area. The smell of cooking blended with gun oil and musty canvas. They sat away from the light, beside a sand-bagged bunker, their weapons close to them. Now and again the cupped glow of his host's cigarette revealed the camouflage face veil now draped as a scarf around his neck. Their voices were soft as they chatted.

"You say you're headed for Rushamba?"

"Uhuh."

"That's a sealed area these days. Has been for a couple of months. The same with Mushumbi Pools. You know that, do you?"

Harry shook his head, then realised the movement could not be seen in the darkness.

"No, I didn't. Any idea why?"

"Sure. Frogs."

"What?"

For a second Harry's mind went off and played a game of its own. He imagined a large stretch of Zambezi Valley a-crawl beneath an invasion of yellow and green bullfrogs. The policeman chuckled.

"Frogs. A bunch of Frenchmen."

Harry grunted.

"What have you got in that coffee? I thought you said you ran a dry base?"

"It sure is, sad to say. There's a company strength unit of French soldiers at the two bases. Seven Independent Company they are down as, on our radio network. Mostly ex Foreign Legion, so the story goes. They've been given their own patch of turf to look after. It's all very hush-hush, under the counter stuff. Don't know who wangled it, getting them into the country."

Harry was silent for a while. Crickets shrilled. He had heard a Scops owl chirruping as the other man talked.

"How the hell do they fit in with the rest of the security network?" he wondered aloud. "Radio messages, communications generally ... Do they all speak English?"

"I hear that a handful do. That's all."

Harry drew in a deep breath, gave a soft laugh of incredulity.

"Well, well. We sure are casting our net wide. How come you know so much about them?"

"I don't actually. It's just that they were trucked in through here. So I saw them when they first came down. Plus this position is in the middle of their designated operational area, so I still see them on occasion. And, now and again, we pick up their transmissions on our radio net. All in French."

"You've seen them? Have you talked to them?"

"No. They keep their mouths shut. But there are always a couple of our guys with them, acting as liaison. Special Branch and SAS, and other special force types."

Harry stared through the darkness at the other man, something beginning to stir at the back of his mind. Leaves rustling, in a new-born breeze.

"Have they had any success down here? Foreign Legion or not, this messy little war we're locked into will not be a fun situation for anyone who hasn't had good on-the-ground experience."

He felt rather than saw the shrug.

"They've had a few contacts. It's difficult not to, in this neck of the woods. Both bases have been clobbered ... heavy mortars and rockets. There have been some casualties. The word out is that they are not enjoying themselves. There's already been a couple of them shot in the foot."

Bloody hell, thought Harry. This is like *Alice in Wonderland*. Things get curiouser and curiouser. I'm glad we ended up making this little detour. I suppose another hundred fighting men is that many more fingers in the dyke, with our own emigration figures increasing monthly. It can't be easy, keeping them in step with our modus operandi. SB and SAS hmmm ... I suppose it would be too far fetched to think those French types I met hunting out of G Camp last year had anything to do with this. The ones that Jack the Knife was sticking to, like mud on a buffalo's hide. Hey, Harry? Why the hell not. Even if there are some people who would say that you're reaching, being a wee bit paranoid. But if ... The sound of an explosion, muffled by distance, interrupted his ruminations. Others followed, not all of the same timbre. His companion stood up. Harry could sense him listening, heard him grunt, finally.

"Rushamba. They're getting another rev. Eighty-two millimetre mortars. RPG 7's. Some other heavier stuff, maybe 75 Recoilless. The terrs are giving them a real stonk. Glad I'm not down there."

He paused, taking a final drag of his cigarette, not bothering to cup it this time. Harry saw his young face in the glow. Looking old. Resigned.

"We'll Stand-To, for the rest of the night. There might be plans to let us have it as well. It has happened. Advise your chaps, will you."

He chuckled without mirth.

"If you are going down there tomorrow, I'd be awfully careful if I were you. Never know who's likely to take a shot at you. Quite apart from the mines. They're bound to have put one down. Or two."

Harry leaned against the front of his Landrover, hoping he looked more relaxed than he felt. Some red-billed wood hoopoes scrambled garrulously amongst the branches of a tall mopane nearby, where he could see bark chipped by bullet strikes. A crested barbet's incessant monotone echoed in the midday heat. He caught a whiff of explosive as the wind changed direction, and glanced again past the soldier at the base. The faded white-washed walls of what had been Rushamba Mission looked incongruous amidst the flurry of military activity. Amidst the smoke that still swirled across the landscape. Vehicles and soldiers moved amongst the scattered buildings and tented positions, their tops peeking above deeply dug shell scrapes. Several buildings looked the worse for wear, and there was blackened rubble blocking pathways. Even from where he was standing, Harry could see many bullet scars.

The perimeter of the base was a maze of deep bunkers, topped by thick recently hewn mopane poles and layers of sand bags. He could see the snouts of machine guns, poking out of the narrow dim slits of the bunkers. His gaze drifted back to the sentry, who leaned against the shady side of the fortified guard post, watching him. Pale blue eyes in a hard lined face. His haircut was convict-type stubble. Although he wore the camouflage of the Rhodesian military, he was most certainly not a Rhodesian. His challenge and questions had been in rapid fire French, as had his orders to his colleague, who had trotted smartly away into the confines of the base. Now he and Harry traded stares, as they waited for whoever had been summoned.

Harry felt tired, knew it was from the tension of the drive from the Angwa to Rushamba. They had driven slowly, off-road wherever possible. My oath, but I hate roads, especially roads with landmines, Harry had said to himself, often. Several times helicopters had flown over them, and he had caught a glimpse of a stretcher sticking out the fuselage of one. Another had circled them twice, in radically banked turns, the technician crouched over his cannons in the doorway, peering down. Harry had waved. Then the chopper had levelled out, tilted briefly and disappeared away over the mopane wilderness that dominated this stretch of valley. They had met two teams of sappers, together with well armed escort sections. On both occasions their two vehicle convoy had earned disbelieving stares and terse comments. You fuckers crazy? This is the Badlands. Don't you zoo keepers know about landmines? A base got badly zapped last night ... five killed, thirteen wounded. Harry was glad when they finally reached Rushamba. Even if his work had not started yet.

Now he watched as the French soldier returned with two men. Even from a distance he recognised them, and he knew the day was unlikely to improve. He remained leaning against the Landrover, arms folded, as he waited for them. They halted behind the rolls of concertina wire that barricaded the road into the mission that was now a French mercenary base and stared with deadpan expressions at Harry.

Scratch Peters spoke first, his voice surprisingly mellow.

"Jesus, Harry, you are one bad penny. What the hell are your doing here?"

Harry made his own voice light, letting his glance inspect them casually, noting the heavy calibre handguns at their waists. No signs of rank. He was comforted by the weight of his own revolver on his hip.

"If I said I'd dropped in for tea and cucumber sandwiches, would you believe me?"

Whispering Jim Lannigan laughed softly and shook his shaggy head.

"You're like a bloody jack-in-a-box, Harry. Don't you know there's a war on? Especially down here. What are you doing out and about around here, in two Landrovers, just five of you? In country that is most definitely not National Parks territory, I might add."

Harry made a grin appear.

"Are you chaps going to keep us out in the noonday sun, chatting? Or are you going to be sociable, and invite me and my men in?"

Scratch Peters' right hand disappeared distractedly behind his back as he stared at the warden. Harry could see the faint scratching motion that he knew so well. Knew by this small sign that the soldier was not at all as relaxed as he appeared to be.   Remembered firefights and bar room brawls that had followed the idiosyncrasy in the past.   His voice was tighter now.

"No way do you come into this base, Harry Kenyon.   No bloody way.   I am extremely pissed off that you have got to where you are standing right now.   This is a no go area.   You should not be here.   And unless you have got a damn good reason for being here, I'm thinking of changing my mind and bringing you inside.   Under arrest!"

Ahhh … Here we go, thought Harry.   Once more into the breach.   The gloves, I think, are now off.   He let his own grin fade.

"Okay, gents.   Then let us get down to business.   There are four dead elephants lying out in the bush near here, with their tusks gone.   Four that I know of, that is.   This has happened since Rushamba became a military base.   Since you moved in with your foreign friends.   Now, is that a coincidence, I ask myself?   Especially as there has been no poaching for three years in Nemana or its neighbouring Safari Areas …"

Harry stepped forward, away from the Landrover, to his edge of the concertina wire, so that a couple of paces separated him from the soldiers.   He directed his next words at Scratch Peters.   "Not since I stopped it."

He let his own stare clash with the icy rage now coming at him from Peters.   Did not really know where this was leading, but could not stop now.   He saw the soldier's gaze move past him, to sweep over the vehicles and his men.   Was aware of the knot of soldiers that had gathered further back within the base confines, watching the proceedings curiously.

Scratch Peters took a long breath and brought his attention back to Harry.

"I told you once before that you walked a very fine line.   That one day you would take a tumble."

Harry returned his stare silently.

"You see, Harry, I reckon you're doing this in your usual balls to the wall fashion.   I would put money down that you have come across here on your own initiative. You have climbed up on your white charger and galloped off on another bunny-hugging mission. Except this time you've bitten off more than you can chew."

He paused, allowing a grimace of a smile to slip and slide across his face.

"This is top secret, Harry, this participation in our war by our frog-eating friends. This is a sealed area. Which means that no one comes in, or goes out, without the necessary permission. Which, on the ground, down here, is given only by me, or my SB counterpart. Now, it's my turn to ask myself ... is Harry Kenyon a threat to national security? Does he have the interests of the country at heart? Or is he still a loose cannon? Is he still only interested in his goddam elephants?"

Scratch Peters cocked his head and let his expression become bland.

"You don't actually have to answer that, Harry Because we all know it, don't we?"

Harry kept his own expression neutral, made his voice conversational.

"You've got it wrong, Scratch. Again. In front of you, you have one Warden Kenyon, investigating a poaching incident, with his National Parks team. This poaching incident has taken place near a Rhodesian military base, with the dead elephants themselves located in the Chingusa Safari Area. Which commences less than rifle shot distance from where we stand talking. The incident has been logged, and the information passed on to National Parks headquarters."

Harry paused, squeezed an easy going smile across his face.

"Copied so far, Scratch? Now, it's one thing for Jack Breen to chaperone a bunch of Frenchmen on a government sponsored safari in the Chingusa ..."

Harry saw he had hit the mark. Peters' eyes blinked once.

"How is Jack the Knife, incidentally? Give him a shout, why don't you. We didn't have much of a chance to chat the last time we met. As I was saying, a government jolly is one thing, but it is a whole different kettle of fish for elephants to be shot illegally, without permission, off the cuff, so to speak, by a bunch of cowboys."

Harry let the edge come into his voice. "Don't give me the national security bullshit, Scratch. Not me. You do your work, and I'll do mine. Keep elephants out of the equation, and we are on the same side. But if you or your comrades-in-arms want to start using elephants for target practice, or earn some extra pocket money from the ivory, then you have a brand new war on your hands."

Scratch Peters' eyes had narrowed to hard glinting slits. His right hand moved to rest on his hip, brushing the grips of the revolver holstered there. Harry was aware that the barbet was still calling, the only sound in the midday heat. He let his own hand drop to rest near his own handgun. The pair of French soldiers, not understanding anything but feeling the increase in tension, fidgeted, their FNs gripped in both hands now. Whispering Jim Lannigan put a restraining hand on his companion's arm. Kept it there. Behind him, Harry heard movement, turned slightly to flick a glance back. Sergeant Fumbi and the two scouts had moved up to stand behind him, their FNs held ready. Kashili stood alongside them, his spear resting lightly on his shoulder. Harry brought his eyes back to the soldiers, studying both of them very closely. The crested barbet had stopped its alarm clock trilling, his mind noted of its own accord. He felt sweat running down his back. Things were beginning to slide into slow motion.

Whispering Jim spoke levelly, his hand still on Peters' arm. "We've all got better things to do than replay *The Gunfight at the OK Corral*. Harry, you've made your point. It's taken. Five elephants were in fact shot. It was a breach of discipline by our new-found friends. Let's just say they took the words 'Safari Area' too literally. It's happened. It won't happen again."

He paused before directing his next words at Scratch Peters. "Boss, he's doing his job. We've given him the time of day. There's no sense in complicating matters. Let's have him turn

around and get the fuck out of our hair, so we can get on with running a war. We've only got the time for one war."
Scratch Peters still stood tensed, his stare unblinkingly locked with Harry's. The sentries stood immobile now, no longer fidgeting. The group in the background had been joined by others, all watching intently, weapons held loosely pointed in the direction of the confrontation.

Harry Kenyon waited, outgunned, way, way out on a limb. Not only out there, but dancing on it, doing the old soft shoe shuffle. With the limb close to breaking. He could not read Peters, did not know which way he was going to jump. Another rivulet of sweat ran ticklingly down his back. The soldier nodded, finally, a slight inclination of the head. Said nothing.

Lannigan spoke again to Harry, his voice as level as before. I'm glad he hasn't slipped into whisper mode, thought Harry. Because then this would get messy.

"Harry, I suggest you call this a day. Use what is left of today to put some space between you and Rushamba. And, trust me on this, let the situation end here. Don't make any more waves."

Harry took his hand away from his revolver, held it palm up. He nodded softly at Whispering Jim Lannigan and then at Scratch Peters, watching them watching him. He stepped backwards slowly, until he felt the vehicle at his back. Looked across at his men, seeing his tension mirrored on their faces. Winked and gave them a half grin.

"Okay, Sergeant, well done. Back off and take your vehicle away first. I will follow on."

He brought his attention back to the soldiers, glanced past them at the grouped men in the background. Saw a familiar figure now alongside the ex-legionnaires, watching the hair-trigger scene at the edge of the base. Even with the distance he could see the wide shark's grin on Jack Breen's face. Saw him shaking his head. The sound of the vehicle engine loud, suddenly, as Sergeant Fumbi prepared to withdraw. The noise fading with his departure. Things still in slow motion. The barbet began calling again.

Harry and Kashili climbed warily into the Landrover. Lannigan had taken his hand off Peters' arm. A faint ironic grin had crept on to his face. Harry started his vehicle, its noise drowning the call of that damn bird. He felt cold, despite the valley heat.

CHAPTER THIRTY-THREE

Vultures. Everywhere. Every large tree in the area settled with the big birds, gorged and sluggish. More, new arrivals, coming down out of the circular patrol patterns on the thermals. Others, disturbed by the intruders, flapping heavily into the air, squabbling their way on to already overcrowded perches. Not happy at being disturbed on their booty. Feathers drifting slowly past, flitting like bad spirits. Lion and hyena spoor abundant, in this place of great feasting. The air thick with decay. Apart from the vultures only the noon hush in a sepia-coloured landscape, time slowed to the ooze of treacle. The October sun white-hot in a colourless sky.

Harry Kenyon, staring at the hulks in the bush, mantled white by the bird droppings. Aware of Gordon Holmes' oblique scrutiny, of the others watching him. Harry Kenyon feeling old, one toe testing the tepid waters of middle age. Not at all keen to put the whole foot in. They had walked inland from the Lundi River, all of them feeling the weight of the lowveld summer heat. The eastern perimeter of the pink buttresses of Chilojo Cliffs reared up to their right, blurred and trembling in the heat waves. Not his patch of turf, this, not his parish. Not for a couple more days, when Gordon Holmes, warden of Gona re Zhou National Park goes on annual leave. With Harry delegated to fill the gap as acting warden-in-charge. It does not matter whose parish this is. The elephant carcasses

are a kick in the solar plexus for all of them. The two-finger
sign thrust in their faces.

Harry walked slowly around the killing ground. Nine of
them. With, according to Gordon Holmes, another three, a
little further on. A week old. All with their faces hacked off
and the tusks gone. All bulls, of differing ages. Bulls, so why
so many so close together, he asked himself, looking around at
the vegetation. No trees fruiting, wrong time of year anyway.
He wondered what Kashili would have made of it. But he was
at his village, downriver near Murumbi, where the Lundi joined
the Sabi and flowed on together into Mozambique. This stand-
in assignment had suited him well. It gave the old man some
extra time to be with his people, to see how the fortunes of
unfolding history were treating them. And to find out if there
was nay more news on his missing son. Harry stopped in the
spangled shade of a *tamboti*, resisting the impulse to reach for
his water bottle. He had already used it too freely, on their walk
in to the murder site. I'd forgotten how hot it could be down
here on the other side of the country, he reflected. Give me the
Zambezi Valley heat anytime.

Gordon Holmes joined him, the other members of the
reinforced Parks escort section seeking their own boltholes
from the sun. He lit a cigarette, blowing the smoke upward in a
thin blue stream. It remained, motionless, in front of him.
Harry wouldn't have minded a smoke himself right now, to
help dilute the smell of the putrefaction. To keep the flies at
bay. He glanced at the other warden, who he had not seen for
some years. Short and lithe, brimful of nervous energy, he was
a little younger than Harry. Had been notorious crocodile
poacher himself once, before he turned a new leaf and joined
the Department of National Parks and Wildlife Management.
Another poacher turned gamekeeper. Ebullient and with an
eye for pretty girls, the devil danced in Gordon Holmes' dark
eyes. His name had come up in more than one divorce case.
Harry had been amused, only a little, at his reaction to Peta,
when they had arrived at Chipinda Pools headquarters two days

ago. Peta herself had smiled, accepting homage, before laying the cards on the table gently. No problems, after that.

Now they stood in companionable silence in this patch of stinking African bush, watching the vultures return. Harry matter-of-factly checked the setting of the gas regulator on his FN. Two and a half. Fine. A little more recoil, but no jams. Funny how we seldom use the sporting rifles any more, he mused. Haven't even fired my .275 or the .458, for ages. Because it's all thin-skinned stuff now. Thin-skinned animals killing each other. His thoughts switched to the carnage in front of them, recalling what Gordon had told him.

They had been on a routine vehicle patrol. Not too many routine patrols these days, vehicle or foot. Not with Gona re Zhou a war zone, and every man and his dog running around shooting from the hip. The firepower in this neck of the woods nowadays was awesome. The birds had led them in. Ahh yes, Harry had thought, always the birds. Or, *makhoti*, as Kashili would say. Any spoor had been wiped away by the vultures and other scavengers. Some cartridge cases though, glinting on the sand. Communist Kalashnikov and NATO FN. Which was not awfully helpful. Pin the tail on the donkey stuff, if truth be told. Because, these days, every man and his dog carried one or the other. Both, on occasion.

Harry turned away from the elephants.
"How many did you say you'd found, this year?"
Gordon lit another cigarette from the tip of the previous one.
"This makes sixty-two, in this part of Gona re Zhou. Down in the southern region, Mabalauta, Mopani Wilson has found twenty-four carcasses. All bulls."
Harry shook his head, succumbing now to his thirst and unlimbering one of this canteens. Squinted away into the distance, through the brittle heat towards Mozambique, just over the blue of the horizon. Mozambique ... another war zone. Much mayhem and destruction next door. Lots of people dying. Lots of animals also. Plenty of smoke in the sky.

The law of the gun, over there, for a long time now. Harry took a long swallow of water, closed his eyes against the glare. I'm getting too old for this, he thought.

A small mopane wood fire, with glowing embers raked to one side, over which is a metal grill. Meat sizzling, smelling wonderful, tended by Gordon Holmes. They have not eaten all day. Harry and Peta sitting in frayed green canvas chairs pushed back into the dark from the heat of the fire. No lights out here, back within the security fenced confines of Chipinda Pools. Bunkers constructed of teak railway sleepers and sandbags loom nearby and there is the occasional murmur of conversation on the hot still night air from elsewhere in the base. Calls of night birds. A hyena duet, once, coming from the river. Distant hippo chorus, lonely sounding. Harry, not as tired now, after a cool shower, enjoying the strong gin drink in one hand, Peta's soft grip in the other. He wondered how Kashili was faring, hoped he was all right. This might be his home territory, but it was a different country now. The rules were different these days, oh my goodness, yes, to when we last took part in that *sayela*, that fish drive. Centuries ago now, it seems.

They had got back to headquarters at last light. There had been little conversation en route. Each man had been in the company of his own thoughts as they watched the road and surrounding bush warily. For a while they had driven between the Lundi River and the cliffs, and Harry had let his gaze sweep along them often, thinking back to less troubled times. They were clearer now, with the sun well over its zenith and its rays picking out the thrusts and crenellations of the eighteen-mile long massif. Soft pink turning to crimson. From the colour of lung-shot blood to heart blood, a part of Harry's mind had whispered of its own accord. He had shaken his head brusquely, wondering where that had come from.

Supper on their laps, some more wood on the fire giving them light, flickering liquidly across their faces. Shadows dancing, Gothic creature figures, in the branches above them. The soft yelps of side striped jackals now, outside the security fence. Gordon Holmes talking quietly.

"So, as you've no doubt gathered, it's been a messy year down here. With not much to be optimistic about. Worse, across in Mabalauta. Young Mopani Wilson has turned out to be a damn good senior ranger. Filling dead men's shoes can't be too encouraging, and the two guys before him were killed within four months of each other. He's been ambushed twice, in the time he's been here. Plus there have been some sniping incidents. He sleeps in a different bunker every night. But the lad is still chirpy, full of bounce. Gets the thousand-yard stare though, now and again. He's actually started leaving messages, notes on trees, for the gooks, poachers, whoever ... telling them he's going to get them. Down here he's being called the Mabalauta Kid."

Harry smiled.

"Good for him. Good to hear there's some young blood out there, standing up to be counted. Let's hope he makes it through to the finish. Whenever the hell that may be. Does he have any lead on the poaching?"

The other warden shook his head.

"The carcasses he's found have been all over the area. On both sides of the railway line. Gorwhe Pans, Manjinji Pan, along the border within spitting distance of Mozambique. He followed tracks once, leading south towards South Africa. Lost them,, outside the boundary of the Park. The last time someone took a shot at him was when he had just found the three bulls near Gorwhe Pans. Shot through the top of the head, all three. That's the time he heard the helicopter taking off, west of the pans. Though, as I said, he never actually saw it."

He lit a new cigarette and poured himself another brandy. A strong one, Harry noted. Neat. He lifted the glass to Harry, aware of his scrutiny.

SAND IN THE WIND

"Cheers. Can't tell you how much I'm looking forward to this leave. I hope you're in one piece when I get back. I know you've managed to sort out the poaching in Nemana, even heard about your showdown with Scratch Peters and his French outfit, a little while back. This is a different story down here, Harry. There are a lot more players in this game."

Harry watched him, nodding.

"Sure. I can see that. Peters?"

Holmes grinned.

"Bush telegraph. Actually, he was in this neck of the woods, a couple of weeks back. Running some operation out of Chiredzi. I ran into him on the road, along with a few other tight-eyed types. All in civvies."

"You know Scratch well?"

"Not really. He's been in and out of this area for three or four years, doing one thing or another. Our paths have crossed at briefings, we've chatted in passing, had an occasional beer together, that sort of thing. Never know what he's up to. Don't even know who he's with, these days. He's another character with a nickname. 'Superscratch', they call him."

He paused to cock an ear at distant elephant trumpeting. Went on with a wry grin.

"I get the feeling you are not his favourite person, Harry."

"Yeah?"

"When I bumped into him the other day I mentioned in passing that you were filling in her whilst I was on leave. He didn't actually say anything, just grunted."

"The French? How do you know about that?"

"Another friend of yours, who's down here. Jack Breen."

Harry grunted, his gaze quartering Gordon Holme's face, more than a little surprised at the other man's knowledge.

"Breen told you? That surprises me. He's a pretty tight-mouthed chap, and I'm sure the French connection is something all concerned parties keep close to their chests."

"Don't worry. Jack the Knife and I go back a long way. He said to tell you he would call in some time."

Harry grunted again, switching his attention from the warden to the fire, staring into the flames. Not really seeing them. So I'm not Peters' favourite person, hmm. The feeling's mutual, pal, he said silently. Absolutely. We sure do keep crossing paths, don't we? Here and there. 'Superscratch' hey? Well, I wonder what friend 'Superscratch' is doing down here, at this time? Harry took a long deep breath, held it before sighing it out. My oath, but the poaching is way out of control down here. We're looking at, what, eighty-six carcasses. All big bulls carrying good ivory. That is what has been located. Christ knows how many others are out there. Can't really blame Gordon, I suppose, the whole situation being the wild card that it is. Like he says, there are a lot of guns on the loose.

He took a long pull at his gin, letting his mind wander over the spectrum of who could be responsible. A grimace twisted his features at the eclectic line-up. The nationalist ZANLA forces were all over the place. So was RENAMO, the rebel movement in Mozambique fighting against that country's Marxist government, who used this part of the country at will, supported as they were by Rhodesian Intelligence. The regular army of Mozambique, FPLM, crossed into eastern Rhodesia often, reinforcing the insurgent campaign of their ZANLA blood brothers. That's just to start with, Harry reflected sombrely. Let's dig a little deeper. Let us throw some dice here, shall we? Because there are a lot of other people with guns who have not been mentioned as yet. Like the French, for example. If Peters and Jack Breen are down in this stretch of country, where are the French? And, if we are going to be picky, let us look a little closer to home. At our own players, in this big game where the bloody goal posts are being moved with monotonous regularity. We have got a lot of units running on long leashes. With the wheels beginning to fall off, and some people already looking over their shoulders, there is bound to be some bending of the rules.

Let's throw the dice again. Gordon mentioned the helicopters that young Mopani Wilson has been seeing. The

South African Defence Force choppers based at Pafuri, right there on our southern-most tip of Rhodesia, flying in support of our air force. They are back and forth across this stretch of country all the time. That makes for a lot of very mobile air transport, which, when I look at what is happening in Angola, with Savimbi shipping out tons of ivory through his South African conduit, makes me bloody nervous. Oh yes, to be sure, there are an awful lot of FNs and AK 47s out there all right.

Harry leaned back in his chair, taking another deep breath. Aware of Peta sitting silently beside him, also staring into the fire. He looked across the fire, meeting Gordon's stare. Shook his head ruefully.

"It's scary, the amount of military weapons floating about. Leaving a whole bunch of military cartridge cases to account for. Wish I had an answer to that particular problem."

Gordon Holmes had a new cigarette and a new drink to hand. "Not to mention .375. There's been a fair share of those cartridges around as well. Close to where the biggest bulls have been killed. I didn't mention those. Didn't mention Shadrek, either."

Harry stared at the resident warden of Gona re Zhou, feeling his pulse trip.

"Shadrek?"

"Yeah, Shadrek. He's a Shangaan, from Chief Murumbini's area. But he's out in the bush now, on the move. A real travelling man. You know how the Shangaans have always had a reputation for being the best hunters, the best trackers, the best poachers? Well, this guy is in a league of his own. We have always kept an eye on him, because of his reputation amongst the local folk. And, sure, he would do some judicious illegal hunting. For meat. Okay, fine. Then came the first elephant, with rhino quickly added to the list. And he was in business. Off and running in a big way. That was about three years ago. And, as the war has escalated down here, and our control has slipped, he's gone for the jackpot. I'm damn sure it was he who nailed Kambanji, our biggest bull recorded, complete with bright plastic collar, earlier this year."

Harry continued to watch Holmes, silent, his gaze hooded now. The man gave a short bark of a laugh and shook his head.

"We've never got anywhere near him, the bastard. I don't even know what he looks like, apart from local descriptions. Even his records with Internal Affairs have gone missing."

Harry's voice was level, as he let his glance switch to Peta. She too watched the resident warden steadily.

"How do you know which are his kills? Especially these days, with open season declared. Do you base it on him using a .375?"

Holmes shook his head, flicking his used cigarette into the fire.

"In the beginning, yes. Because we had our fingers quite firmly on the pulse, and because we knew who he had pinched the .375 from. But he's got access to the military stuff as well now, and uses other weapons. So we can't be absolutely sure any more which are his kills. But we know he is still in business. Our undercover unit had gradually put together a dossier on him. We know all his family, and informants have helped us put together a pretty good picture of him and how he ticks. He is a bloody unbelievable bushman, a fantastic shot, and absolutely fearless. And I wish he would get the hell out of my area."

Harry returned his attention to the fire.

"The ivory? No idea where he sells it? How he sells it? It might be useful for him to have a whole bunch of other folks wandering around doing their own poaching thing, but it means he also has to tread damn carefully. So he doesn't get fingered."

"Nothing. The bastard runs a tight ship."

Harry put some effort into making his next question casual-sounding.

"You say you know his family. All of them? All the brothers, uncles and cousins? Not just mum and dad and the kids?"

"Sure, the lot. There is no father, though. Seems he went missing ages ago. We've never found any references to him. We've never quite established the where, how or why of that. But he certainly makes for a gap in the family tree. By all accounts, Shadrek must be fifty years old. So his father is probably long dead."

Harry nodded. Grunted softly. Not quite, he said silently. Not by a long chalk. My, my, this little country of ours gets smaller and smaller. Oh hell, yes. I do hope Kashili is all right.

CHAPTER THIRTY-FOUR

The elephants stopped, eventually, pulling up in a cloud of orange dust. Still trumpeting their rage, the small family unit of five females stood in the road, trunks aloft. Reluctant to leave off the chase. Harry slowed the Bedford truck to a gradual stop and clambered up out of the cab on to the roof. The ten-man patrol section perched atop the rows of sandbags shook their heads, nervous laughter coming from some of them. It had been a close run race. The Bedford, made heavier by the steel layers of landmine protection, the sandbags and the men, together with a service that was three months overdue, had made heavy weather of the going. Harry, driving, could tell from the intensity of the encouragement from his passengers that the angry elephants were catching up. Could not do much about it. Then had come a long downhill stretch, and the old sick truck had responded to his whispered urgings. He stood now, hands on hips, and watched the distant animals, listening to their angst. The Gona re Zhou population of elephants were living up to their reputation. They were as aggressive as ever, only too ready, willing and able to attack. Poor bastards, thought Harry. Can't say I blame them. With the tsetse control slaughter over the years along with the poaching, they've had a tough time.

He lifted his head, listening hard. Turned as he tried to pinpoint the direction of the tremor, hearing it increase quickly. Tremor to low growl, to high-tide washing roar. The ventriloquil throbbing coming fast at them, preceding the four helicopters that swept into sight above the tree line seconds later. Four great prehistoric dragonflies, in line abreast, hugging the contours. Coming straight at them. Harry glanced back towards the elephants. They were running. Heads down and tails curled high, they stampeded away through the scrub and bush. Even with the noise of the helicopters, Harry could hear their terrified shrill screams. Them, in a buffet of ear-hurting noise, the helicopters swept over them, over the track they had just used, over the spot where the elephants had given up the chase. The jet whine decreasing as they dwindled into specks that were swallowed up by the landscape. Eastwards, towards Mozambique. Eastwards across Gona re Zhou. Harry listened for a long while. Did not hear any change in engine pitch. Could still hear the elephants though, in the distance. Screaming.

Harry, in front of the maps, again. Pondering. Looking for answers, finding, instead, new questions. Seeing the scores of red-topped pins stuck all over the map. Tombstones. Each pin denoting a dead elephant. It is already hot, and it is not yet seven. Peta outside with a camera, stalking birds. Her heart not really in it. She would like to be back home in the Zambezi Valley. Back in Nemana. Last night, for the first time since they have met, they have argued, cast the first stones. Stared across the cottage at each other, the realisation of this swirling with the tension on their faces. *Where does all this end, Harry?* Don't know. *I don't know anymore.* The map mocking. Not giving any answers.

Kashili in the doorway suddenly, a small figure in a shard of sunlight. Spectral, almost. The sun anointing the point of his spear, and the white marching through his hair. Harry standing very still, feeling the great gladness sluice through him, feeling this morning's depression lift. Before striding across the office to seize the old man by his shoulders, to stand grinning before crushing him in a bear hug. Smelling the smoke intermingled with sweat and snuff, smelling the bush. Breathing it in.

Later, with weapons slung, they had walked slowly beside the river.

"Tell me," said Harry, "about Shadrek."

Kashili had told him. It took some time. None of it surprised Harry too much. With the end of the telling they stopped walking, stood looking across the water. Watched weaver birds busy with their nests. They're not building them high, Harry noted. Maybe the rain spirits are not too happy this year.

"Shadrek has asked if you would meet with him," said Kashili. "He wants to tell you some of these things himself. There are also other things that he would talk with you about. Things which he has not seen fit to tell me."

Harry nodded, his gaze still on the weavers.

"I would be pleased to meet with him, of course. Because he is your son. Because I will do anything to stop this killing of elephants. Because there is a need for communication here. This business with the elephants, with him, does not make life simple for me. You know that."

Kashili nodded also.

"Yes. But if you are prepared to match his trust, in meeting together alone, I believe all will benefit."

"When?"

"In four days."

"Where? Not too far away, I hope. I am feeling old, these days."

Kashili chuckled.

"He will meet us at his office."

Harry stopped looking at the weavers. Looked in some surprise at the old tracker.

"Office? We'll be driving, then. Or will he send a car?"

Kashili chose not to hear the dryness in his voice.

"No. We will walk. It will take three days."

They watched the herd of eland feeding slowly past their position, sitting silently within the confines of a caper bush. Even in here there was the irritating blur of mopane flies in front of their faces, constant companions since they had left Chipinda headquarters. It had not been a particularly hard journey. For most of the way the Lundi had been on their right flank, sometimes close, at other times only evidenced by the swathe of riverine evergreens that followed its course. So water had not been a problem. The heat was a fact of life, needed to be treated as such. On several occasions they had had to manoeuvre past herds of elephant, and last night lions had padded around their sleeping position for a while. They had not made fires. There had been no sign at all of other humans. But they had come across their work, finding eight elephant carcasses, old, with the skin dried and stiff over the bones. Once they had heard helicopters in the distance.

Now they waited, where Kashili had stopped, eventually, and nodded wordlessly at Harry, their minds blanked off to the heat and mopane flies. Watching the eland. *Namutla*, Kashili had said. He will come today. Then he will take us to his office. Fine, said Harry. I look forward to that.

Mid afternoon. The shadows lengthening. Baboon talk, somewhere away behind them. Bird song. Kashili cocked his head, listening. Sat that way for several minutes, before grunting softly.

"Let us go out. He is here."

They emerged into the sunshine, the rays still hot. Harry let his eyes sweep over their surroundings, saw the figure standing in some scrub, a hundred paces away. Kashili led the way over to his son. He watched them come, his body language relaxed, a Kalashnikov lightly balanced on one shoulder. Harry studied Shadrek as they approached. There was nothing to show he was the most successful, and wanted, poacher in the region, perhaps in the country. He was not big, no taller than Kashili had been, in his prime. The clothes covering his slight frame were ragged and much patched. His bare legs had several bush sores, and a filthy piece of cloth served as a bandage around one ankle. The Kalashnikov, Harry saw, was clean. Shadrek's gaze met his openly, man to man. The three men greeted each other quietly, conversing in Shangaan. Then the poacher looked Harry in the eye again.

"*Nikesili.* Thank you. For agreeing to this."

Harry nodded, letting the irony of the situation show in his smile.

"*Izona.* You're welcome. I hope something comes from it."

"*Eh.* Yes, myself also. Come, let us go. I will lead the way. It is not very far."

"To your office?"

"Yes, my office."

The baobab was not that prepossessing, by baobab standards. There were others in sight with wider girths, more dramatic shapes, more choleric purple in their trunks. This one stood in the middle ground of a long sparsely covered slope. Red-billed buffalo weavers had built several of their untidy community nests in the upper branches, and white streaks showed where some raptor's favourite perch was situated. There were some recessed hollows and slits in the trunk that suggested other nest sites or boltholes for small creatures. The inhospitable spiny denseness of a *cardiogyne* bush hugged one side of the baobab, its small tightly packed orange fruit bright amongst the foliage. Shadrek stopped, fingering one of its leaves, grinned at Harry.

"Good for snake bite. Plenty of them around this place."

Then he disappeared. Harry blinked. A hand beckoned from within the greenery.

It was cool inside. There was far more space than was indicated by the outside proportions of the tree. As his eyes adjusted to the gloom Harry could see that Shadrek was well established. A sleeping mat and blankets were rolled against one rounded wall. Close to them was the folded soft grey hide

of a kudu. A zebra skin, well cured, covered half of the floor
area. Shelves, carefully adzed mopane, arranged between tiers
of stones, occupied another space. Three wooden stools sat on
the zebra skin, along with a massive buffalo boss. Harry caught
the faint smell of gun oil. Saw the shapes of three rifles
wrapped carefully in clean linen cloth. Knobkerries. Spears.
Bows. Quivers, with arrowheads protruding. A panga. From a
wooden peg hammered into the pithy wall of the baobab, a pair
of small crude figurines hung, twisting slowly. A miscellany of
shoulder bags and satchels hung from other pegs, together with
several water bottles. A double row of pegs stretched up the
trunk, to a hollow where light splashed through. From high up
in the dark recesses came the squeak of bats. No tusks here,
Harry noted. Shadrek grinned again at him.
"My office," he said. "I'm afraid it is not as smart as some I
know in Chiredzi, or across the border in South Africa. I do
not have as many elephant teeth as they do."

They had talked long into the night, candlelight flickering across
the hollow of the baobab. Outside, the territorial roars of lions
rolled through the dark. From the branches of the tree came
the resonant grunts of a Giant Eagle Owl. Harry lay awake,
listening to the owl, sleep eluding him. Shadrek's face, earnest,
not grinning any more, in the glow of the candle, came back to
him, time and time again. Kashili's also, there between the
poacher and the warden, inscrutable, listening to the litany of
horror stories which heralded the end of the elephants in Gona
re Zhou. Yes, I have killed many elephants, Shadrek had said.
But few only, compared with other people, in this place. For
which I am blamed, more and more. The bottom line of all
this, all we've heard tonight, thought Harry, is that the sooner
the war ends, the sooner the war on the elephants ends.
Because every son-of-a-bitch is having a go. Everyone is taking
a turn at the coconut shy. Roll up, roll up! Take a shot at the
jumbo! Get the prizes while they last.

Okay, Shadrek has certainly got plenty to answer for. He's got tusks buried all over the place. With buyers lined up. Like the South African Defence Force at Pafuri, who are doing a fine trade in ivory. What they don't buy from him, they go out and shoot themselves. Wham, bam, thank you Sam! Anyone for a helicopter safari? And the maintenance crews along the Caborra Basa power line are having a field day. Plenty of field days, thank you. As are various assorted citizenry down here in Chiredzi and environs, including some people who should know better. Not to mention our own security forces, for Christ's sake! Our revered headline-making warriors. In their air chariots. Not all of them, okay, but enough. Spending more time hunting elephants than hunting terrorists. The carcasses that have been found down here are just the tip of the iceberg. I've got names for Holmes that will blow his mind.

And Shadrek, what do I do with him? Very good question, Harry. All right, so a lot of the stuff he's been blamed for has not been his handiwork. I believe that. The facts and figures, names and dates, make a lot of sense. And he need not have set this meeting up. He could have simply continued along the merry path he's chosen. He says this is his own personal vendetta against the government, for moving his people out of their ancestral homes, when Gona re Zhou was made a game reserve. Okay, I buy that as well. There's not a Shangaan I've ever met who does not harbour a grudge about that. But they haven't all gone out and declared war on the wildlife. Not all of them have gone for the elephant a day keeps the DC at bay routine. Just Shadrek, who has killed enough for all of them put together. He should go the same route as the bastards who came into Nemana, the same route as Alex Gant. But then what about the rest of them? Hey Kenyon? That's a long list you've got this long night, mister. With some star performers amongst the names. It would keep you busy for years. Chasing after the clever boys putting down the salt blocks, to attract the elephants into the guns. And the heroes in the helicopters, herding the elephants into a nice suitable spot and then plugging them. Which is why those nine they showed me were all close together. Shadrek has certainly been a revelation. He is Kashili's son all right. He sure as hell makes his own trail. At least he hunts them on his two flat feet, on his own. Meets them face to face. Which brings us back to the question, doesn't it? What are you going to do about him?

CHAPTER THIRTY-FIVE

The tyres hummed on the tarmac. Peta Holt also humming a tune, enjoying the breeze flowing through the doorless Landrover that the increased speed, now that they are on good road, brings on this otherwise hot November day. The outskirts of Chiredzi town ahead, the list of things to do there is in her shirt pocket. Pleased, paradoxically, to be back in civilisation, with the domesticity of the chores to be done making for a pleasant interlude. Happy to be out of Chipinda headquarters, even happier that the sojourn there is almost over. Gordon Holmes is due back within the week, which means she and Harry can get back to the peace and quiet of Nemana National Park. Strange, she mused now, how I have not managed to like Chipinda. There never seems to have been the right spirits there, for me, anyhow. Part of it has been the security aspect, not being able to get into the bush whenever I liked. And not having the river, the Zambezi, to look at, any time of the day or night. God, but I miss that river. There is just so much horrible news coming out of Gona re Zhou. Which has made Harry very tense. He has been like a bear with a sore head, down here. I think there is a permanent state of angst in Chipinda. I could feel it in the air. It sure as hell made Mr Kenyon morose, as well as me. He's been even worse since he came back from that secret outing with Kashili.

Ahh, Harry, tilter at windmills, always trying to right the wrongs done against the animals. Which is so infra-dig, at the moment, it seems. Even if you are a game warden just trying to do your job. She smiled, lifting her face into the breeze. He turns fifty soon. The big five-oh, just around the corner. He doesn't look it. Still carries himself and his age jolly well. Even when he's bleak and disillusioned with life. He needs to get drunk more often. Needs to live a little. He used to. She looked at him now as they slowed for the police roadblock on the edge of town.

"How about it, lover? Want to get drunk and fool around?"

He looked askance at her, one eyebrow arched, his foot slipping a little on the accelerator.

"Hey, I don't mean right now. Later. How about you and me having a party? Booking into a seedy motel and talking dirty. Sound like fun?"

The mock innocence on her face at odds with the words. Harry grinned slowly, which turned at last into a laugh. She laughed also. Harry swept his eyes over her face, his expression lighter.

"I don't think there are any seedy motels around here."

She gave a mock pout.

"There must be. There has to be!"

He realised there was some seriousness behind the levity. Was suddenly glad that he had managed to see that.

"The best we could do is the Ebony Lodge. Shall we do that? When I've finished at the briefing later, and you've done what you want to do? Shall we declare today null and void, and play truant? Have too much to drink, and, as you so delicately put it just now, fool around."

Peta reached over and run a finger down the side of his face.

"Why the hell not? Screw the consequences, give the cat another goldfish!"

The weekly briefing was held in the combined operations centre on the Buffalo Range airfield. Here, the various representatives of the region's security forces met together to correlate their efforts in the spiralling war situation, as well as update themselves on the overall situation evolving in and around Rhodesia. When necessary, other government representatives or people having a current relevance to a situation were invited to attend. The National Parks representative was a regular visitor, with Gona re Zhou occupying a big chunk of strategic territory on the border with Mozambique. Harry had a nodding acquaintance with most of the men involved. He had little to say at most of the briefings, spent more time listening and following the progress of this part of the war on the large scale map. He intended to be as low key today, but, after the revelations of Shadrek, would pay much closer attention to the deployments of certain units. His digging had started; the homework had already begun, learning about the people who were playing their own war games, against the elephants.

The overall picture was, as usual, depressing. Rhodesia was still there in the ring, bobbing and weaving, feinting with the left, punching hard with the right. But some brutal punches were also getting through the defences. There were cuts and bruises now, bad ones. Blood showing. The country was still reeling from the shooting down of the Air Rhodesia commercial aircraft, *Hunyani*, by ZIPRA in early September, and the subsequent massacre of the few survivors. The downing of the Viscount, and the following outrage, had brought to an end the secret negotiations between Ian Smith and the ZIPRA leader, Nkomo. The death toll and emigration figures made for sad reading. Terrorist attacks within the country were increasing weekly, even with the external raids hammering away at their bases in the neighbouring countries. Operation *Gatling*, mounted against ZIPRA bases in Zambia, causing many hundreds of enemy casualties, brought some solace to the Rhodesian man-in-the-street, if not to the outside world. Green Leader, in his Canberra bomber orbiting high over Lusaka, reading out his succinct, no-nonsense message to the Zambian Air Force, had been the toast of the country. But, even with dramatically successful operations like *Gatling*, the country's military supremo, General Peter Walls, still had to admit that ZANLA and ZIPRA were by no means neutralised. That there were in fact so many of their cadres operating within Rhodesia that the government security forces were not containing them. A ZANLA group had driven into Salisbury and rocketed the main fuel storage deport, destroying a quarter of the country's fuel reserves. High on the day's agenda was the sudden postponement of the imminent elections that the multi-racial transitional government had planned, which would herald black majority rule, and, hopefully, a return to normal. The delay of four months, until April 1979, did not bode well for a quiet Christmas.

The cloud of depression that the briefings usually induced in Harry was no different this time. Afterwards he stood outside in the sunshine, hoping that, like the winter morning mist in the valley, the depression would burn off with the sun. He looked forward to the evening. Needed to do precisely what Peta had suggested. Drink too much, yes. Fool around, absolutely. But most of all he needed to let his guard down and forget about dead elephants, and the people and machinations that were making them dead. He walked slowly over to the Landrover, his eyes automatically quartering the hot sky for vulture movement, the old tracker's words still there, floating in his mind. *Tiko lingahava zvihari itiko lingafa.* His parting words to Shadrek. *Stop it, Harry. Just today, okay? Okay then, but Kashili is damn right.* A land without wild animals is a dead land.

"Yo, Harry!"

He turned. Jack Breen leaned nonchalantly against an army Unimog, the habitual predatory grin in place.

"Well, well. Jack the Knife himself. Whose balls are you twisting today, Jack?"

The Special Branch officer chuckled.

"Not me, sunshine. I leave that to lesser mortals. I concentrate on the hearts and minds."

"Sure. Of course."

Harry leaned against the Landrover and eyed Breen sardonically as he walked across.

"No Frenchmen around, Jack?"

Breen shook his head, wry amusement on his face.

"Nah. A waste of time, that."

"Who's nursemaiding them now?"

"No one. They've gone. Only stayed five months. It didn't work. Not their cup of tea, you know."

Harry smiled dryly.

"You sure as hell kept a low profile, when I paid them a visit down at Rushamba. How come you didn't do the Gary Cooper bit alongside Lannigan and Peters?"

"That was essentially Scratch Peters' show. So I didn't think I needed to be a part of the showdown."

Harry grunted, his answer laconic.

"Typical SB assessment. Sit in the wings and pull the levers. If Jim hadn't been there, I think Scratch would have pulled his gun."

Breen shrugged.

"You would have handled it, Harry. Him, anyway. I don't know about the rest of the shebang. That was why I stayed back, so I could keep an eye on the Frogs if they started getting trigger happy."

Harry grunted again, noncommittally.

"Where is Scratch these days? I heard he was in the neighbourhood."

Jack Breen nodded, the shark's smile coming back.

"Yeah. He's around. He's not with SAS or Scouts these days. He's Group Nine now, one of the various no-name brands that have surfaced as the war gets hotter."

"You see much of him, Jack?"

"Nah. Very occasionally. Group Nine has its own SB attachment. He has always walked by himself, if you know what I mean. He's a bit like you, Harry, in that respect."

He winked broadly.

"Funny, he was asking me about you, the last time I did see him. Wondered if I'd seen you around. Your time is about up here, isn't it? Gordon Holmes should be back soon."
Harry nodded, curious about Jack Breen. Affable, easy-going, chameleon-like Jack the Knife.
"What are you up to these days, Jack? I know it's not the right thing to ask a Special Branch type."
The policeman shook his head, shrugging.
"The usual SB field stuff. Working with Fire Force and whoever is on the ground. Everybody's down here these days... RLI, RAR, Scouts. All out on OPs, with 2 RAR on Fire Force duty. There's so many bloody gooks around."
"So I hear," said Harry. "You reckon we're on top of this, Jack old son?"
Breen shook his head again, back and forth.
"No, sunshine, we are not on top of this. We are snookered, well and truly. You mustn't believe what you read in the papers."
Harry grinned.
"Never read them myself. It's *Playboy* and *Men Only* for me. For the pictures, you understand."
He turned and climbed into the vehicle. Jack Breen, grinning, threw him a half salute. Harry, watching him carefully, spoke again.
"Is Gordon Holmes a friend of yours?"
Mild surprise registered on Jack the Knife's face.
"You could say he's a mate, yes. We've worked together over the years. I liaise sometimes with your undercover unit, and so I've done some work with Gordon. Why do you ask?"
Harry shrugged.
"Just curious. He said you had mentioned the French incident to him, which surprised me."
Jack Breen looked at him.
"Not me, chum. I haven't said a word."

The second gin and tonic tastes better than the first, as they sit out on the lodge verandah under the cathedral-cool canopy of riverbank trees. Peta has visited the hairdresser. Harry, is not sure what she has had done because she is almost always there on his retina. Tawny, beautiful, immutable. He compliments her anyway. It is early afternoon, and very pleasant sitting doing nothing, with nowhere to go. Contemplating what they will be doing later. Harry has contacted the office at Chipinda, advising that he will only be back tomorrow, feeling guilty about it, knowing he shouldn't. Not with the ground he has covered, with the information he has turned up.

He would be glad to leave, and get back to Nemana, he reflected. Give Gordon all the information and say cheerio. Leaving Shadrek out of the equation, for now. He stopped his train of thought, halted it now, before it ran away with him. He owed Peta a break. Another drink, then, he thought, and ...

"Harry Kenyon? Warden Kenyon ...?"

The voice interrupted his reverie. He looked around. A tall young man in the uniform of National Parks stood on the verandah. Harry nodded, standing up.

"Hi. How do you do? I'm Mopani Wilson, from Mabalauta."

Harry took the outstretched hand.

"How do you do? Damn pleased to meet you at last. Gordon sang your praises before he left, and I've read some of your reports. Pull up a chair and join us for a drink, or a spot of late lunch."

Open schoolboyish smile.

"Thanks, but I can't. I was actually driving out to Chipinda, when someone mentioned you were here. And now my Landrover has gone lame, so I had better get it sorted out."

"What's wrong with it?"

"Just dirty fuel, I think. Causing the usual stop-start hassle. Won't take me long to fix."

"Why are you headed out to Chipinda?"

"Couple of reasons, actually. There's a month's mail for my station been collected and taken there by mistake, which is not too good for morale. Plus I need to draw some equipment, an extra rifle, and ammunition, which are all issued through Chipinda office. I've already been on the radio to the sergeant-in-charge there."

Harry looked at his watch.

"It's no problem making the trip out now. But if you were delayed there, you would be pushing your luck coming back. A little close to the witching hour. Come out with us tomorrow morning."

"Can't unfortunately. I've got to send patrols out. I was hoping to get the mail to the guys before they left."

Harry pursed his lips, nodded, feeling in his pockets. Took out the keys.

"Okay. Here, take my Landrover. It will save you some time messing around with yours. Mine is fuelled up and goes like a bomb. Pick yours up on your way back through, when the lateness of the hour won't be so critical. I'm not going anywhere today. If you don't see me around, just leave the car out front near Reception, with the keys in the dash."

Mopani Wilson paused for a moment. Harry could see him thinking it through. Not too long ago, the warden imagined, the youngster would have had the same expression on his face as he placed the rugby ball just right for the kick at the posts.

"Okay. Much obliged. I'll head off right now. My sergeant is with me, riding shotgun. Thanks ... er .."

"Harry. Harry's fine."

"Thanks, Harry. Maybe I can grab a quick beer with you later."

Harry watched the young ranger walk out, then sat down again.

"Nice young bloke. He'll go far, from what I've heard and just seen."

Peta nodded, grinning across the table. Her glass was empty. One fingernail tapped gently against it. Harry returned her grin.

"Another drink here, young lady? Or shall we order a bottle of gin and a bucket of ice and head for the room? Perhaps they've got some bubbly. A couple of bottles of that wouldn't be amiss. I'm sure we could think of something to celebrate, don't you think?"

The grin widening. Damn, Harry thought, certainly not for the first time ever, she has a wonderful grin. As opposed to a smile. She stood up.

"You talk too much, lover. Get a bottle of anything. See you at the room. You'll recognise me, I think, from what I won't be wearing."

"When are you going to make a decent woman of me, and marry me, Kenyon?"

"Tomorrow, if I could."

"It had better be soon. I'm beginning to think you're giving me the run-around. Just keeping me because I'm good in bed."

"You're lousy in bed. It's your cooking I cherish."

She laughed softly, a finger moving in lazy circles in the sweat on his chest, fingernail jabbing into him now.

"Liar. It doesn't have to be a grand affair. Though a church would be nice. A handful of people. Who would be your best man? Garnet?"

Harry stared up at the thatch of the room.

"Maybe. Or Kashili. I would say he's my best friend. He could keep the ring on the point of his spear so it didn't get lost."

Peta giggled, letting her fingers trail over his skin as her hand moved down his body.

"Idiot. Talking of spears, is it too soon, lover? Oh, no, obviously not. Don't move, Harry Kenyon, it's my turn on top."

The telephone woke them, the noise loud in the dim secret confines of the room. A ribbon of late day sunlight shone through a gap in the curtains, splashing across their bodies on the bed. Harry leaned over her and picked up the heavy black receiver, tasting her still, seeing her again in his mind's eye.

"Hello ... Yes ... Hello, Jack ... Out front? Sure, I'll be with you in two minutes."

He looked down at Peta, who lay silently watching him, as he put the receiver back on its cradle. He kissed her gently on the tip of her nose.

"Jack Breen is here, in Reception. I won't be long. Don't go away."

Harry found the policeman in the late afternoon shade of the car park, leaning against a Landrover. Young Mopani Wilson's vehicle, Harry noted, so he's not back yet.

"Hello, Jack, what made you track me down?"

Jack Breen rubbed a hand along a bristled jaw. Harry could hear the rasp.

"Saw the Parks vehicle here by chance. Hoped it was you. Bad news, I'm afraid. Two of your department's people were killed this afternoon. An ambush. Out on the road to Chipinda headquarters. Young chap ... Wilson, and a sergeant. Both shot."

Harry felt the chill come in, despite the summer heat that still lay thick on the land at this time of the day. He squeezed his eyes shut for a moment. Opened them to get rid of the image, the schoolboy placing a rugby ball carefully for the kick at posts.

"What else? How badly were they shot up?"

Breen shook his head, grimacing.

"There's not a lot to tell. Someone on Police Air Wing duty flying over saw the Landrover off the road in the bush. Circled and saw the bodies in the cab. Radioed JOC and got the ball rolling. We choppered in and found what I've just told you. Two guys shot, with the car stalled away off in the bush. We found the ambush position and trackers got on to spoor. Lost it in half an hour when it led on to the main gravel road."

The SB man looked at Harry, pausing to scratch at an insect bite.

"The trackers reckon the ambushers were picked up by a vehicle. They wouldn't swear to it, but are pretty sure. There were only two ambushers. And there were only three bullets hitting home. One each killed Wilson and his sergeant, the third ricocheted off a roll-bar. That, in case you didn't realise, is some shooting. Taking out two people in a moving car, even a half open slowly travelling Landrover – it was stalled in third gear – is no mean feat."

Harry stared at Jack the Knife, the chill in him turning to ice.

"Any idea on the weapon? Or weapons?"

Breen shook his head.

"There were no cartridge cases at the shooting position. Which means they had to have been picked up. The autopsy will be able to tell us something, later. Looking at the force of the strike on the roll-bar, I would guess at an FN."

Harry took a long deep breath and looked up at the sky. Too late in the day for the birds, he thought. He looked at Breen.

"What do you think, Jack? Between you and me? Three shots? Just three bloody shots! Not the usual style, would you say? With a bunch of the bad guys all having a bash ... AKs, RPDs, and the odd rocket. Not the usual Fourth of July stuff."

The policeman met Harry's bright, hard stare, took his time replying.

"It's different all right."

The eyes of each man holding the other's.

"Did you know he had been shot at before? Not just ambushed, but sniped at as well?"

Breen nodded.

"Yes. Yes, I did."

He pushed himself away from his leaning position against the Landrover, walked a few paces out into the car park, turned and walked back again. Repeated the exercise. Harry watched him silently. Jack Breen stopped the pacing, stood frowning at the back of the vehicle.

"This your Landrover? It doesn't have the same registration number as the one you were driving earlier today."

Harry shook his head.

"No. It's Mopani Wilson's car. There's some problem with the fuel. He was driving mine, out to Chipinda."

Jack the Knife nodding, looking at Harry now, his eyes quartering the warden's face. The sun easing behind the horizon, thorn trees in stark silhouette against the crimson. A silence, a singing desert silence, over the two men and their surroundings. Harry could almost hear the shift in the Special Branch man's thinking.

"So ... he was driving your vehicle, when he was shot. Killed very efficiently out on a stretch of road used by you quite regularly."

Not a question, a statement. Jack cocked his head, still scrutinising Harry.

"When I first heard the news at JOC ... two Parks guys taken out in an ambush, on the Chipinda road ... I thought, damn, old Harry Kenyon's finally caught it. But, here you are. And somebody driving your vehicle has bought it instead, compliments of a most efficient ambush. Something smells. Something makes me nervous, here. Doesn't it make you nervous, Harry?"

Harry shrugged. He was not going to say that the same thoughts had trickled through his mind. Had begun to meander their convoluted way at about the same time as the lump of ice had settled in his gut.

"Mopani also had shots sent at him, remember?"

"Sure. But that was in his own area, Mabalauta, which is a long way from here. And, from what I remember, both sniping incidents occurred when he had just found poached elephants, a long way off any beaten track. Today he was minding his own business, driving out to your patch of turf. In your Landrover."

Jack the Knife bestowed the rictus of a smile on the game warden, his voice laconic now.

"Somebody out there doesn't like you, Harry."

CHAPTER THIRTY-SIX

F irst light. The bird sounds already constant, punctuated by the rough wake-up calls of baboons. Bees loud amongst the bright yellow sprays of the long-tail cassia above the Landrover. Beyond the red of the fire creepers, starting to fade now, with November well established, the hills around Chipinda headquarters emerge out of the fading dark like mediaeval fortresses. The cloying heat already causing sweat to run. No sign of rain, not a cloud to be seen. The rain spirits are out to lunch. Harry Kenyon and Kashili making a last check, before they take their leave of Chipinda. Weapons, with magazines full. The remaining glass in the two bullet-shattered windscreens has been removed. The metal scar up on the roll-bar is already rusty. Weapons cocked. The steering wheel, that had been coated with the young game ranger's blood, has been cleaned many times. Weapons ready, including Harry's revolver, now close to hand in a shoulder holster. Gear and equipment neatly stowed away behind the cab, under green canvas. Peta Holt not with them. She is in Salisbury already. Harry put her on a plane out of Chiredzi, two days after the ambush. He will meet her in the capital, on their way back to Nemana.

Gordon Holmes stands on the stone-paved verandah, nursing a mug of tea, silently watching the two men make ready. The revelations of the twenty-four hours closeted in his office with Harry still swirl in his mind. The extent of the killing that has been going on in Gona re Zhou, in his back yard, is almost not to be believed. But it is all there. Names, map references, dates, weapons, descriptions, vehicle registration numbers. Now under lock and key. Shadrek's endowment. But not the man himself. Harry will not give him up, not the only person alive who is able to identify all the worms in the can. Who trusted him. How the hell did he do it, Holmes asks himself again. How did he catch up with Shadrek? The son of a bitch!

The gravel road stretched out ahead of them, Harry and Kashili. The two men silent, watching the bush on either side carefully, the safety catches on their weapons off. Harry's swerving pattern not entirely due to the corrugations and pot holes. The weight of the FN balanced across his lap is comforting. Movement on the left drawing the eye quickly. Kashili already covering it with his rifle. Impala, copper pennies in the sun. *Combined Operations Headquarters reports the death by terrorist ambush of Warden Harry ... Shaddup!* Stop snivelling. Just pay attention to the road and the bush. Not terrorists, anyway. Not the bastards who killed Senior Ranger Wilson and Sergeant Mpofu. Instead of me. It was someone on that list. Someone who knows that we are starting to pin the tail in the right place. That long list, now in Holmes' safe. The other one, the original, with me, with Peta actually, in case something happens to me. Which it won't, with a bit of luck. Who, on that list? *Who?*

Gordon Holmes looked a little tight-eyed this morning. Not surprising, I suppose. He's come back to one hell of a pile of dirty laundry. Hope he's got the sand to put things right. Why didn't you bring up Jack Breen and the French connection, Harry? Why indeed? Can't answer that, not right now. Ask me one on sport, instead. Because... Harry tensed. A flicker of movement on the edge of a large termite mound ahead snagged his attention, and he swore softly. Good ambush spot killing ground leading the target, *them,* straight in difficult no, *impossible* to break out of the killing zone *off the road,* because there are too many trees right here so *hit the brakes hard* make some dust and let's get the hell out of the car and ... A kudu bull leaped gracefully down off the mound, the sunlight catching the tips of his horns. A pale grey ghost amongst the grey mopane trees. Harry took his foot off the brake pedal, let out a long whooshing sigh. It is going to be, he said to himself, an awfully long day. I think I'm too old for this shit.

CHAPTER THIRTY-SEVEN

The buzzing of an insect, almost lost amongst the rest of the insect noise, the shrill monotony of the cicadas. A bird party, bulbuls and starlings, with a sextet of white helmetshrikes, in full clamour amidst the lower canopy of a leadwood. The scolding chitter of squirrels. Otherwise there is little else to add to the rhythm of life on this hot morning on the flood plain. Around a small glistening-wet hole in the bend of a sand riverbed there are butterflies colourfully aswirl. They dance, too, around the pillared front legs of an elephant that has dug the hole, and who now stands sucking up cool earthwater. The elephant is the bull, Chiruwe, whose Africa-map ears flap indolently here in this silent, peaceful place, where many piles of droppings across the sand attest to many other visits made. The soft companionable murmur of elephant flatulence echoes in the quiet river bed, mingling with the slushing of water being squirted far back into his throat. A bright yellow butterfly perches on the sandy, wet tip of one of his magnificent tusks, almost as brightly coloured as the thick plastic collar. The insect noise is louder.

Harry watched the pattern made by the wind on the water, a slowly advancing shimmer across the sheltered bay near his bungalow. Out in the middle of the river, small fretful whitecaps heliographed in the sunlight. The wind had become more bullying in the last few days, a portent of things to come in the next traditionally windy month of August. Small plovers fluttered, seeking escape from the wind. He turned and walked back to his office.

Nemana National Park in July 1979, a serene Constable-like scene far removed from the Daliesque cut and thrust paroxysm that is the rest of the country. On his return from Gona re Zhou, half a year ago, Harry had slipped very easily back into the rhythm of Nemana life. There were still the sounds of war echoing from across the river, and aircraft of the

Rhodesian Air Force passed over the Park regularly. After the slaughter in Gona re Zhou, Harry had been anxious when he returned to his own parish, had mobilised his staff and led them out into the Nemana hinterland to look for signs of poaching. There had been none. Peta had planned another book in her mind, the new one centring on the life of elephants. A chronicling of their fortunes, from hairy-baby stumbling-over-trunk days, to the decline of old age, with the last set of molars worn down and starvation looming. Peta. Peta Kenyon now, since that Friday afternoon in December, in the small stone country church in Karoi, with the wet-earth smell from the passing rain shower following them inside to the altar. Counting the rain as a blessing from the spirits, as so little had fallen, the country suffering. The game was still concentrated, on the flood plain of Nemana, with no new water beckoning, away up in the hard hot escarpment. Harry Kenyon, turned fifty and married in the same week, shook his head softly now, thanking the gods responsible for the peace that reigned in Nemana, in his middle age and newly married status.

Chiruwe dozing the middle day hot hours away in the cool, spangled silence of a tamarind. Dreaming elephant dreams. He has leaned his great bulk against the tree, and his trunk hangs loosely, the end of it curled limply in the dust. The insect noise suddenly louder, a buckling of the air, with the trees stirring and then whipping frenziedly in the wash of the helicopter over them. Flaring, nose high, until it has almost stopped in the air. Hovering. Elephant dreams shattered. Chiruwe wide awake, startled, afraid, a bubbling blast of confusion blaring from his upraised trunk. The bull running, out of the shade, away, anywhere, to escape from the cacophony of noise that has invaded his siesta. The broad plastic collar, his protection, a bright yellow splash of colour against his hide. Head turning from side to side, looking for the cause of this sudden mayhem. Long tusks catching the sun. The insect above him, following his terrified bustling stride away from his peaceful haven alongside the Chitembe River. Chiruwe feeling the pain in his head, hearing the sharp loud reports distantly, unable to keep his legs moving, knowing that there is something very wrong with him. Not feeling his own impact as the earth comes up to meet him. Chiruwe not seeing or smelling the thick cloud of dust that has billowed up around his massive fallen body.

In his office, Harry Kenyon lifts his head from the paperwork on his desk, wincing at the brief savage spasm of pain that has forked through his brain. Sits staring out through the open doorway at the river sparkling in the sun. Wondering.

Rhodesia on the ropes. Stumbling. Gloves fending off the hits feebly, trying to protect the vulnerable areas. Return punches hitting wildly. Referee hovering, smiling. The whole crowd baying, scenting blood; East, West, the OAU, the frontline states, the Patriotic Front. For a while, in April and May, there had been a comparative lull, with the election and its results allowing recovery time. The UANC, under the cherubic-faced Muzorewa, had attained a major victory, in a high poll that showed the defiance of the tribespeople to succumb to ZIPRA and ZANLA intimidation. The results gave pause for thought to the Western string-pullers, sent all manner of representatives scurrying to and fro across the globe. The diplomatic safari set. Thatcher and Carrington, the new British front rank, played pass the parcel with Carter and Vance. To Vasily Solodovnikov, the Russian KGB master planner of military and diplomatic offensives against white rule in southern Africa, working out of Lusaka, it was just another day at the office. Both internally and externally, ZIPRA and ZANLA were taking numbing uppercuts, were back-pedalling. The external raids reached new heights, hit harder than ever before. In Operation *Grovel*, Canberras bombed two ZIPRA bases near Lusaka. Operation *Vanity* saw Canberras fly a thousand kilometres to bomb a ZIPRA training base near Luso in Angola. *Neutron* involved bombers, fighters and helicopters laying waste one of

ZANLA's training bases at Chimoio, in Mozambique. Chokwe. Munhava. Solwezi. Mulungushi. Tete. Names on maps in neighbouring countries where Rhodesian Intelligence sent its troops to nullify the nationalist war machine. Intelligence that became suspect, as the flames scorched higher. Because there were leaks, bloody great holes, resulting in the loss of soldiers' lives. Operation *Bastille*, mounted by the SAS against Nkomo in Lusaka, was compromised before the Rhodesian troops had a chance to get anywhere near their target. Leading cadres of ZIPRA based in the Roma suburb of Lusaka were warned of another top secret attack. Operation *Carpet* killed many enemy, but the ones at the top of the list were long gone. Perhaps there were also leaks in the nationalists' intelligence networks. Because tit for tat, they too would have their misses. Notably the two assassination attempts made on the life of Rhodesia's military supremo, General Peter Walls. In the first, on 7 February 1979, ZIPRA shot a second Viscount out of the sky, missing the general who flew out of Kariba on a similar Viscount. On 4 July they tried again, this time attacking his house in Salisbury, except that they raided the wrong house.

The end of May saw ZIPRA and ZANLA with a second wind, bouncing back from their corner. The war intensified. Intelligence predicted that it would intensify even more, with the Commonwealth heads of state conference scheduled to be held in Lusaka, *Lusaka*, in the first week of August, and points to be scored. There were, Intelligence said, 13 000 terrorists inside Rhodesia, with another 30 000 waiting at camps in the neighbouring frontline states. The new prime minister of the new majority rule government found he had an increasingly difficult product to sell. It was not what the people wanted, the string-pullers. More and more doors were being slammed in his face. Carter, at Camp David, on 10 July, smiled his presidency-winning smile, patted the African leader's shoulder soothingly. Muzorewa got little more than that from Thatcher at Downing Street, three days later, on his way home to beleaguered Rhodesia.

Momberera Pan sweltered in the noonday sun, the dew from the cold of the winter night long evaporated. The water in the pan had dried up months ago, with the rains poor and the heat intense. But this large, grey, saucer-like depression in the bush, fringed with ebonies, tamarinds and acacias, still attracted animals. The holes, shallow and smoothly-round, were many, where the salt occurred. The four elephants had been digging up the salt for over an hour. All bulls, they made an impressive sight. The senior bull, with thick, medium length tusks, stood well above the three younger bulls, the *askari*, who had travelled in his company for several months now. The pan was a good two-day's journey from the river, in country that was wild, even by Zambezi Valley standards. A dust devil, a shifting miasma of grey dust and dead leaves, whirled across the dry surface of the pan. One of the *askari* paused in his digging and peered myopically at the disturbance. Heard also the tremble of noise on the air. Stood with ears outstretched, turning away from the small whirlwind to face in the direction of the new sound. The other elephants picked it up now, and stood listening. The younger bulls moved instinctively to bunch protectively with the big elephant, the four animals making a real-life sculpture in the middle of the dry pan.

Kashili took the hook out of the mouth of the bream and placed the fish on the wet sack at the bottom of the canoe. It was his third catch in two hours of fishing. Two more, he thought, then I will go back to the camp. It is not so good now, the fishing, but it is good to be sitting in the sun. These winter nights are making my joints ache, and I need the sunlight more often. He tossed the newly baited hook back into the water, letting his glance sweep routinely over his surroundings. Nothing much had changed in the last ten minutes. Except the crocodile had left its sunning spot on the sandbank. He looked at the river, saw the knobs of its nostrils and upper head, motionless, between the canoe and the bank. I see you, *ngwenya*. You are wasting your time with me. I am thin and old, and I'm sure I would not taste very good, not much food for you, even in the cold period. He let his attention drift to the northern bank, noting again the blue haze that almost obscured the escarpment. The fires started early over there, this year, he reflected. Hau, I think every Zambian that is born has a box of matches in one hand when he comes from the womb. The nylon line tightened momentarily across one finger. Yes, come, he said silently. Do not be shy. His thoughts moved on. I wonder how is Shadrek? Has he listened to my words about the killing of the elephants? I hope so. For there are enough people killing them. And I believe our destiny is linked with that of *ndlovu*. What affects them will in time affect us. I wonder if that warden has caught anybody? With the names the little warrior gave him? I am not sure about that man. He is not of the same substance as my adopted son. Hah! The little warrior, married! I am glad he has taken this step whilst I am still alive. Although I think it is too late for me to teach his children, as ... The fishing line went tight, pulling strongly. Kashili struck. Felt the slack. You should pay attention, he told himself. You are sitting dreaming like an old man in the sun.

The helicopter came over the trees. Straight at the four elephants. The animals stood defensively, held their ground with ears outstretched and growling screams thrown at the sky. One of the *askari* charged forward a dozen paces in the direction of the increasing tumult. Stopped, bewildered. The helicopter turned and banked, slowing, keeping the elephants on its left, below the open door. The machine flared, hovered. The first shot came. The *askari* that had charged, dropped. Legs buckling, great head flung back with trunk swung aloft in a parody of a salute. The firing continued. The big bull lurched, went down, tusks ploughing into the earth. Struggling, struggling. Battling to regain his feet. Amidst the cacophony of the gunfire the two surviving *askari* placed themselves on either side of the patriarch, manoeuvred tight against him, bending, pushing with the sides of their heads, lifting, heaving. Trying to get the bull back on his feet, to get him up and away from the madness that enveloped them. Seconds. Microseconds. A lifetime. The bull fighting to get up, levering against one of his companions, straining. More shots. Explosions of dust on wrinkled grey hides. The bull not struggling any more. Motionless, except for one back leg kicking spasmodically. The *askari* slumping beside him, going down. A trunk moving slowly, twisting, reaching across to rest finally on the dead bull's face.

Peta closed the thick note pad and sat quiescent on the verandah of the bungalow. She had the new book mapped out now, had at last established the route she would take. It had occupied her time for three months, working her way through the tangle of ideas and notions, plucking at one thought then another. Testing it like a fruit, holding it up for inspection, looking for the wormholes, turning it around, tasting it finally. Liking it perhaps, taking another cautious nibble, perhaps discarding it, dropping the germ of one idea for another. The bowl of ideas slowly filling.

Now as she sat quietly, she experienced the special feeling writing people enjoyed when things had eventually taken shape. When the butterfly shrugged free of the chrysalis. Like birth, she mused, watching African skimmers flying past, glued to their reflections on the water. A finished book, published or not, is like a baby. You look at it and you can't believe it's yours. That you made it. Peta smiled. Oh yes, Peta Kenyon? Mrs Harry Kenyon. Where did that train of thought come from? Well, why not? Life marches on. *Tempus fugit*, and all that. Harry is not getting any younger. Neither am I, for that matter. He would make a good father, whatever the age gap. Ahh, Harry, my tilter at windmills. My warrior saint. Peta's smile widening, her eyes hazy and far away.

Below the helicopter the elephant was in full jerky-legged stride. Tail curled high in terror, head moving frantically to the left and to the right as the bull tried to see his tormentor. Long squirts of excrement marked his passage, as, loose-bowelled with fear, he tried to escape from the clammering noise that ripped the valley quiet apart. From this thing that dipped and swayed in the air just behind him. Across the sand the elephant ran, the cool water of the river forgotten, the middle age elephant musings shredded. Aiming for the trees, feet kicking shallow water high into spray as he stampeded through the remnants of a backwater. Not hearing the first shot, above the tumult of the clattering blades, above his own screams. But feeling it, and the next, disoriented suddenly, his body not listening to his brain, the trees which had been so close, now far away. The bull fell in the backwater, amidst an explosion of spray. For an instant, minute rainbows shone amongst the droplets. The elephant shivered and lay still, a thin stream of blood trickling from his trunk. Discolouring the water.

The helicopter landed in a swirling maelstrom of sand. Sand, whipping across the dead elephant, blowing away in the wind. The sun bounced off the metal blade of the chainsaw in the hands of the soldier who jumped lightly from the belly of the great steel insect.

Harry Kenyon lifts his head from the vehicle engine he is working on, frowning at the peppering of the sand that blasts him. Although the wind has died now, for the moment.

CHAPTER THIRTY-EIGHT

‘‘The radio stopped working, so it was not possible to contact base. I did not worry too much at first. The shooting was very far away, and these days there is much shooting, especially from across the river. But we heard more, over the next few days, all far, but each time there were only three or four shots, maybe six at the most. Single shots, never any automatic fire, which began to make me nervous. That is why I cut the patrol short and returned to Shingela."

Sergeant Fumbi, round face sweating and anxious, hoping he had done the right thing. Webbing showing signs of wear, green issue shirt patched neatly. Portuguese-made G3 clean, the plastic furniture matching the green of the shirt.

Harry nodded, turning away from the map, giving the sergeant a brief grin.

"Exactly right, sarge. I'm glad you came back. Even if the shooting was so far east of your position that it was faint, it still puts it within the safari area. You say you heard four lots of firing. Any particular time of day?"

"It varied, sir."

Harry sighed. Damn, he said silently. What is this, I wonder? Fumbi cleared his throat.

"There were two occasions when I thought I heard a helicopter, sir."

Harry felt his scalp tighten then. Felt the sudden chill in the pit of his gut. Stood for long moments. Nodded eventually.

"Okay, Sergeant Fumbi, have your men re-provision. Also have them draw an extra forty rounds of ammunition each. Please will you find Kashili and tell him that we will be leaving for patrol in two hours. I cannot advise the duration, but everyone should carry food for at least a week. To save time we will go by vehicle as far as the Katete River, on foot from there. We will use the two Landrovers, sarge, so please make sure that they are both fuelled and checked. We should make the Katete by last light. Tomorrow we start sniffing the air."

He returned the sergeant's salute, a thin grim smile creasing his features.

It was the birds, as always, that guided them in. That showed the way to the carcasses. Two elephants, faces missing, covered in vulture excrement. Large-bodied bulls, even shrivelled as they had become, a week dead. Their tusks gone, and no tracks at all to be found. Bullet holes in the tops of their heads. Harry looked up at the sky, stood staring. As if the answer could be found there, written across the blue of it. How, though, do you track a helicopter across the hot unused space of the African sky? Looked down at the map, finally, at the marks he had made. The reference where they had found the murdered elephants. 685490. Apart from that, he reflected, it's *November Tango Romeo*, I'm afraid. Nothing to report. Not at this time, anyway. He turned to Sergeant Fumbi.

"Sarge, we'll cover more ground if we split up. You and your three men work due north from here, as far as the Zambezi. Then follow the river east for three kilometres, before cutting back in and patrolling south, inland. Kashili and I will work our way due east from here. We will RV with you at, say ..." Harry followed their respective patrol patterns on the map, and gave a grid reference.

"I hope your map reading is up to scratch, because I want any carcasses you may find marked on your map. We will make radio contact at specific times, and maintain listening watch for an hour at the beginning and end of each day, from five to six. Let's arrange to meet up on day four, unless something out of the ordinary develops."

Like what, Harry? What, exactly, is out of the ordinary? Do we count more elephant carcasses as the norm, or do we classify that as extraordinary? Hey, Warden Kenyon? Let's just see, shall we. Let us take this one step at a time, and make plans accordingly. What did we say, way back in Malaya, ah yes ... *perlahan lahan* ... slowly, slowly. Because, to be honest, I'm not sure where we're headed on this new killing. And we may as well start with a body count. Just to see how far along is the disease, and what remedy is needed. Will a couple of sticky plasters be sufficient, or will major surgery be the order of the day? Will we have to get radical on this, and take off a hand or two, chop off a few heads? Ahhh ... I hate this, this ... This what? This goddamn murder, that's what.

Harry and Kashili found the remains of Chiruwe the next day. His yellow collar clashed grotesquely with the hacked, stinking, maggot-infested place where his face had been. Again there was no sign of spoor, and again there were bullet holes in the top of the head. Harry stood looking at the carcass, oblivious to the flies and the smell. That's two down out of the 'Big Four', he thought. We have only Marula and Kabakwe left. Maybe they have been killed too. What the hell started this? Why now, after so long? This is Gona re Zhou all over again. If helicopters are being used, how high does this go? I mean, a person does not just go out and whistle up the services of a helicopter, to go and blast a bunch of elephants. Especially these days with choppers more than ever the backbone of the counter-insurgency war. You would have to have some damn good connections. To organise it and keep the whole bloody operation secure. This, old son, is heavy stuff. Almost Mafia. Harry looked away from the elephant, squinted up yet again at the sky. Grunted sourly. Aerial spoor, all right, no doubt about it. You've got your work cut out for you on this bit of tracking, Harry boy. This is anti-tracking like you have never seen before. So, what to do? Jolly good question. We can only keep moving. And hope they make a mistake whoever the hell 'they' are.

Full moon, with the valley cast in silver. The shadows of trees running in long, black stripes across the silvered landscape. Night sounds taken over from those of the day. The six men sat silently together, each engrossed in his own thoughts. They had met in the late afternoon of the fourth day, Sergeant Fumbi's patrol and Harry and Kashili. Compared notes for an hour. They had found fourteen bull elephants between them, all carrying the same trademark. Shot through the top of the head, faces slashed off, tusks missing. With no tracks to follow. Harry chewed steadily on a stick of biltong, staring unseeingly out into the night. He had folded his map and put it away.

Could still see it, in his mind's eye, see the crosses that denoted the sites of the carcasses. X marks the spot all right, he ruminated. Dig here for the treasure. Except the treasure had already gone. The chickens had flown their coop. Flown being the operative word. His brain moving in circles, casting for its own sign, searching for the line that would connect the dots. Not finding any signs. Okay, what do you know? You are not hearing any shots or aircraft noise at Shingela, except for what's going on over the river. Nor have you heard anything in this neck of the woods over the last four days. The kill sites are all over the place, on the river and way inland. That's just what two short patrols have located. So, wherever the chopper is coming from has to be east, or south. Or north, for that matter. And it has to be working out of a base, because it has to have fuel, be serviced. One chopper? Several? More than one means more crews, more pilots and technicians, more people in the know, so more chances of a leak. Are they even worried about leaks? Christ, flying around the Zambezi Valley clobbering elephants is not exactly clandestine. Which means that they are pretty damn sure of themselves. They sure as hell must have some very potent top cover. Maybe you should have some top cover, Harry. It's about time for you to share this can of worms around. This is headquarters emergency session stuff. Garnet. Drummond. I'm not sure what else I can do, down here on the ground. For once I'm having a bloody hard time following any tracks.

Garnet Clayton sat out on the patio of Harry's cottage, sipping a cool beer, his attention diverted from the map on the table by the last of the sun disappearing behind the escarpment across the river. Harry and Peta watched him silently. He looks terrible, thought the warden. As if he's got one foot in the grave and the other already lifted, shaking the slipper off. These last seven years have not been kind to him. He's not much older than me, but he looks an old, beaten man. Thanks to head office and unfolding history. Above them, a flight of white-faced duck whistled past, arrowing downriver. Harry had a pretty good idea which sandbank they were heading for. The inane wheezing laughter of hadeda ibis reached their ears. Harry and Peta Kenyon, watching Garnet Clayton, watching the sun go down over the Zambezi Valley.

Harry, on his return from the patrol, had made radio contact with headquarters, requesting a priority meeting in Salisbury. Dr Drummond, he had been informed, was away on department business, and would be for some time yet. The chief warden had come on set, listening to the tension in Harry's voice that had been obvious, even floating through the ether. Although the warden had not given any reasons for wanting the meeting, not on an open network, Garnet knew it had to be bad, had promised to fly down to Nemana himself the next day. For the whole of the day they had discussed the latest elephant killings, the ramifications as shocking now as when Harry had first found the carcasses. And they had not, to their own satisfaction, come up with any kind of a decent answer.

"I'll make it known to Joint Operations Command that this has come to our attention, of course. The report will go across as soon as I get back. That will be the first step. Though, to be honest, I'm not sure how concerned they are going to be, at this stage of our history. The whole bloody country is in upheaval, each new day worse than the last. The security forces are horribly stretched, between trying to contain the terrorists inside the country, and hammering the bastards outside. In a couple of days the Commonwealth heads of government conference begins in Lusaka, and the Patriotic Front are escalating this war as much as they can. So, I'm not sure some elephants shot through the tops of their heads, probably, possibly from helicopters, is going at the top of any agenda right now."

Garnet Clayton had absently stroked the great tusk on the wall of Harry's office as he spoke. The warden snorted.

"Hell, Garnet. This might be something new down here in the valley, but it sure as hell is not a new phenomenon across the country in Gona re Zhou. Either our own military, or the South African Defence Forces operating alongside our people, have been enjoying open season there for an awfully long time. Elements of both, I would bet. What's happened about all the information I passed on to Gordon Holmes, copied to headquarters? I hear bugger all on the grapevine."

The chief warden shook his head, his expression bleak. "Not a heck of a lot, I'm afraid to say. Gordon Holmes did make some progress. In fact he started off well. There were arrests made, a couple of pillars of local society. A policeman and an army officer, ours, were had up on their respective carpets, but were allowed to walk. In the interests of security, naturally. They were amongst the names on your list. Then of course Gordon had that damn terrible accident."

Harry looked at Garnet.

"Accident? What accident, for Christ's sake?"

"His body was found at the bottom of Chilojo Cliffs. His vehicle was at the top. It seems that he slipped."

Garnet paused, took his hand from the tusk to run it through his thinning grey hair.

"There are some who reckon it could have been suicide. Gordon was very much a ladies' man, and apparently he was pursuing his old habits. He was caught with someone's wife, and there was a potentially very messy divorce case coming up. This, added to previous indiscretions, meant it was on the cards that he was about to be dishonourably discharged from the department. You didn't know?"

Harry shook his head.

"No."

He tilted his chair back against the wall.

"I wouldn't have said Gordon Holmes was suicidal. He was always pretty quick on his feet, and, as you say, he liked the girls. He's been caught with his hand up someone's skirt before, so this was something to be considered as being standard behaviour. Why would he take a swallow dive off Chilojo Cliffs just because he had been caught, again, and cited in divorce proceedings, again?"

The chief warden shrugged.

"True. So he slipped. The end result is the same. The man's dead."

Harry grunted, gazed speculatively out through the open door, not seeing the distant sparkle of the sun on the river. *So he is, whether he slipped or jumped. But I do not see Gordon Holmes opting out, of his own accord. He wasn't that kind of person. Besides, there were still so many pretty girls out there. He used to half joke about it himself. So many women, so little time. So, no, huh-uh, I do not think so. Besides, to be out alone in that part of Gona re Zhou would be downright stupid. And Gordon was not stupid. Why don't you come out and say it then, Harry? Stop beating around the bush.* He switched his attention back to Garnet.

"No evidence of foul play?"

I mean to say was he pushed? Did someone give him a wink and a nudge, perhaps? Did he get clobbered and get slung off into the wide blue yonder? An irate husband, or someone on the list? Or are you reaching on this? Being a little paranoid? Have you been reading too much Raymond Chandler?

Garnet shook his head, an ironic smile slipping on to his face. *Yes, it said, you are stretching.*

"There's been no suggestion of foul play. There was an autopsy. He was rather badly bumped about. He fell a long way."

One. Two. Three. Four. Who's that knocking on my door? All right, then. *Gordon Holmes, it has been decreed, slipped, and in so doing, went for the long goodbye. I, personally, do not buy that, excuse the pun. But if everyone else is happy, hey, who am I to rain on someone's parade. Mopani Wilson took a ride, looking for Harry Kenyon. Found instead a piece of lead, and Gordon flattened at attention.* The words came unbidden, jangled in Harry's mind. Roller-balled around the inside of his head. It

423

took some time to shake the verse out, the words sticking doggedly, filings on a magnet. He gentled his thoughts, brought them slowly back under control. *Whoa there. Steady.*
"Who has the helm at Chipinda, these days?"
"Roger van Horn. He's part of the newer order. Just been made up to senior ranger. Good chap that he is, the promotion has been too fast. That's the way it is though, with men leaving, and getting killed. It's a fact that we have too many square pegs in round holes."
The chief warden smiled wearily and shook his head. Harry watched him fondly, feeling sorry for him. Old Garnet. Boss, good friend, always in his corner with the oranges and the vinegar. He stood up and stretched.
"This bingo session in Lusaka. You reckon there's any good news in it? Will Zimbabwe-Rhodesia be recognised? Will Muzorewa get the nod?"
The two men drifted out on to the verandah of the office block. Stood staring across the river at Zambia. Garnet took his time answering. Shook his head, in the end.
"No. A thousand times, no, I'm afraid. We have damn few friends at court. Carrington has never been a supporter of our internal agreement, and now he's brought Thatcher around to his way of thinking. Waldheim and the UN circus are certainly not backing it. The West was kicked into touch the day Jimmy Carter left his peanut farm to take over America, so no light at the end of that tunnel. The OAU has still got the so-called free world bowing and scraping. The Queen has been tripping the light fantastic in Tanzania, Malawi and Botswana, and now she's in Lusaka for the kick-off. Malcolm Fraser is the nigger-in-the-woodpile. No-one knows what's on his agenda. He's organised a 'working group' consisting of himself, Thatcher, Kaunda, Nyerere, Manley of Jamaica, some Nigerian general, and they've got themselves a bloody great soap box and are handing out leaflets with gay abandon. All screaming the same message about us. Unclean. Don't touch. Not with a barge pole."

The chief warden gave Harry a twisted grin.

"So, my friend, enjoy your bit of paradise down here. Because out in the real world, things are a little messy."

Harry nodded sombrely.

"I hear what you say. I have a feeling, though, that things are about to change down here. It's been creeping up on me, this feeling, taking its time. But it's there now. Like a piece of lead in my gut."

Harry lifted his gaze from the river, let his eyes search the sky.

"Garnet, I would appreciate knowing the response you get from JOC as soon as possible. I will wait to hear from you on that. Then ..."

Harry turned to look at the chief warden, swept his eyes across his face before halting to hold his eyes with his own. Made his voice matter-of-fact, a hard tight grin curving his lips.

"... I am going out on a long patrol. I'll take Kashili and do some deep penetration work. Head back into that area and stay there, until something breaks. Like we used to do in Malaya. Wally Conway is back off long leave, so he is in position to run the station. I have something like three months leave in hand, so, if necessary, I would be happy to use that. Sort of a private safari, if anyone objects to me going off for too long on company time. Even if it is business."

He paused, seeing the wry smile slowly taking hold on Garnet's face.

"Harry Kenyon, off to the wars again? You and Sancho Panza, with visors down and lances up?"

The chief warden shook his head softly, the smile still in place.

"Why don't you leave this one alone, Harry? At least until we know more. These are crazy times we are living in right now. Priorities, and loyalties, shift almost daily."

Harry returned the smile. Said nothing. Waited. Garnet Clayton grunted.

"Methinks you're getting too old for this rubbish. Not to mention that you are a married man now. But, sure, what the

hell, get out there and see what you can find. It's one of the things you do well. Or used to."
Harry chuckled.
"Thanks, pal. For those few kind words. One other thing. If I should ask, one day, if Peta could stay with you and Jessica up in Salisbury, is that a problem?"
"Not at all. We would love to have her, anytime."

A swift African twilight, sifting across the valley. Becoming the darkness of the shroud. Harry, Peta and Garnet, each of them in their own pocket of silence, sitting beside the river. Distant gunfire, a whisper on the breeze.

CHAPTER THIRTY-NINE

Dust rose above the massed black hides of the buffalo, obscuring for some moments the snowstorm of egrets accompanying the animals. They stood, heads high and necks outstretched, watching the two humans walking across the flood plain, curiosity again fusing them, holding the buffalo shoulder to shoulder. A few senior-ranking cows took tentative steps forward, breaking rank. Then they were off again, charging away.

Harry and Kashili carried on walking. They were six days from base, well over the Katete River, the boundary of Chingusa Safari Area another two days' hard walk. There, Harry planned to cache their extra food and main packs. They would be able to move faster after that, cover more ground. They had discovered two more groups of dead elephants; a trio of bulls, and, for the first time, some cows. A family unit of five lay in a jumbled rotting bunch. Only three of the animals had had tusks. Harry had looked at them, silently. Shaken his head once, and moved on. There had been nothing else out of the ordinary. It had, in fact, been particularly quiet, as one season gave way to the next.

Harry cuffed his floppy bush hat back, and peered once again at the sky, gave a thought to the irony of it. How, on the one hand, the birds coming down out of the blue were his pointers to new killings. How, also, the helicopter used its space, coming and going at will, leaving no sign of its passing. His thoughts moved on, to the radio message from Garnet. The chief warden had, at last, received an acerbic answer from Joint Operations Command. Elephants, dead! Really! Shot from the air, probably from a helicopter? No! What had this to do with the military? Was the Department aware that there was a war going on? That at this time history was proving to be most unkind, and, ergo, there were far more pressing items on the agenda than a few dead elephants. Besides, afterthought heavily tinged with sarcasm, even with the extra South African helicopters and crews on attachment, there were not enough choppers to go round, so even one gap in the ranks would be sorely felt. Elephants, indeed! Helicopters! Tush, tush. It had been couched in official terms, of course, but that had been the message, sure enough.

Harry had stood for a long while in his radio room, reading over the message. Had been surprised at his own equanimity regarding the response. Realised he had not expected much else. He had gone, then, to the wall-size map in his office, once again marked with his eyes the spots he had chosen. Followed the contour lines of the lower escarpment and again checked over the last parts of the plan that had taken hold in his mind. He would put his total field strength out, in two-man observation sections, three to four kilometres apart, along the southern perimeter of Nemana National Park and into Katete Safari Area. Their sole task would be to watch for helicopter intrusion, maintaining radio contact with each other and also with Harry, working the valley floor generally eastward of their positions. They would stay in position for two weeks, before returning to Shingela, whilst the warden stayed out in

the field. The enlarged patrol would leave Shingela made up of
nine sections, led by Harry and Kashili. At the appropriate
places each section would peel off, and head due south inland
to their given map references. Their presence behind him,
watching and listening, would allow Harry a free rein of
movement in the rest of the Katete and Chingusa Safari Areas.
His first port of call would be Kanyoka's village, to see if they
chief or any of his people had, or would give him, any
information they might have learned.

Now, with the sixth day drawing to a close, Harry felt
fitter than he had felt in a while. He did not feel fifty years old.
The hard walking, the meagre field rations, the decision taken
to get out and do something, all had honed him down over the
last days. The hard light of battle gleamed once more in
Warden Harry Kenyon's eyes.

They sat in the dark on the visitor's chairs near Kanyoka's hut.
The barking of the village dogs had at last subsided. The main
nose now was that of mosquitoes attacking them. Harry could
feel the sweat on his body slowly drying. The drawn out
greeting ceremony was behind them, and now they took pause,
listening to the night. Harry sensed a feeling of withdrawal on
the chief's part, behind the polite courtesies whispered in the
dark. Was not surprised, not these days, with fortunes difficult
to interpret by the straightforward throwing of the bones. He
spoke.
"There have been more elephants killed. This time I believe it
is being done by members of the government. By soldiers of
Rhodesia. This is why I have come thus in the night to see you.
I am hoping that you may have heard something of this, which
might help me in my search for the people concerned."
Silence, broken by the whine of mosquitoes. A dog scratching
nearby. Thump, thump, thump.
"I believe the soldiers come to the killing places by helicopter,
shooting down from the sky. I think this because the wounds
in the elephants we have found are in the tops of their heads,

and there are never any tracks. Have you see any helicopters moving over the Park whilst you and your people have been going about your business?"

More silence, swirling about them, almost as tangible as the night mist on the river. Kashili speaking now.

"The times are many that my thoughts return to your village, when there was much happiness. When you brought me so much beer. After we killed the leopard that had killed one of your children. We were fortunate to kill it so soon, when other people had been tracking the animal for such a long time. The little warrior and I were very happy that we managed to stop the killing habits of that leopard, especially with it moving its territory to include your village."

The fading-away call of dikkops. That is all, in the night. Eventually, there came a grunt, punctuating the latest silence. And, Harry thought, once again, there were words, whole sentences, uttered in that soft, sharp exhalation. Chief Kanyoka cleared his throat.

"In these times there are many helicopters in the sky. We see them almost every day passing above us. Visiting Zambia, visiting Mozambique, travelling in and out of Kanyemba. On occasion they are almost like flies. So, with such movement, it is not possible to say which of these machines are involved with the killing of the elephants. My people do not travel far from our village these days, because it is not safe to do so. There are too many people with too many guns. I am sorry I cannot help you in this business of the helicopters."

Harry nodded in the dark, pausing, allowing time to let the disappointment filter out of his reply.

"It is so. These were but thoughts on my part, that you may have seen something. I will look elsewhere. Thank you for your time."

He stood up, shrugging his shoulders to adjust his webbing back into place. Saw Kashili's shadow standing also, caught a glimpse of moonlight reflecting off the head of his spear. Kanyoka and his elders remained sitting.

"It is only the helicopters that interest you?"
Harry stopped adjusting his kit. Looked down through the darkness at the chief. Picked his answering words carefully.
"Helicopters, yes. As with anything that affects the fortunes of the animals."
"There have been other *ndeges*, birds, that have visited this place. Twice, they have come down and landed. I do not know what you would call these machines. Unlike the helicopters, they need space when they leave and enter the sky, and they have solid wings. Their colours are the same as those of the uniforms of the government soldiers. They have two motors, one on each side of their body, and in their body, on the side, is a doorway. Through this doorway we have seen men entering and leaving."
Harry stood motionless. Not quite sure where this was heading. Mentally ticking the seconds off in his mind. Forty-five, forty-six, forty ...
"Once, we saw elephants' teeth being loaded into the *ndege*, through the doorway into its belly. It was during the middle of the day. We were returning from fishing. The soldiers shouted at us, when they saw us watching."
Harry felt it then. Uncurling. Stretching. Claws unsheathed, pricking at his stomach lining. Forced himself to remain calm. Knew that, despite his control, the chief had caught the whiff, had tasted his tension on the night air. He made his voice matter-of-fact.
"Where, Kanyoka? Where did you see this? When did you see it?"
The old man shifted his position on the stool. Harry could hear fingers scratching. The rasp of knotted woolly hair.
"At the same place that your friend came, with his small *ndege*, when you came to rid us of the spotted devil. There are also other places for these machines to land, but it was at that place. When? Hah, it is hard to remember the last time that the big *ndege* came. I think it was sometime close to the last full moon, when the night shadows ran straight. The helicopters, also,

came to that place, on occasion. For a short while the soldiers had a small camp there."

Harry Kenyon's turn to grunt. A grunt for all seasons. So, there it is. In plain sight. The airstrip where Garnet landed, when he flew down to give me a hand with the man-eater. They've been flying ivory out of there. We're looking at a Dakota, from Kanyoka's description. Someone's using a gooney bird to fly out the ivory from the valley. Helicopters. Dakotas. Oh deary me. He grunted again, and the chief knew, in his turn, what thoughts were passing through the white man's mind.

"Thank you, old friend."

There came the soft, dry hack of a chuckle, like the wind rattling the drying pods of a snake-apple bush.

"You had better go now. And you should not come here again, for we have visitors often. It is not safe for you. Even tonight we are expecting people. Travel well, and with care, you who worry about the elephants."

Heat waves shimmered over the airstrip, in the quiet of late morning. The only sign of life was a lone impala ram wading through the mirage of water at the end of the gravel. Bird calls sounded desultorily from the vegetation surrounding the strip. Harry and Kashili stood in the grudging shade of a large mopane, surveying their surroundings. The warden's murmur finally broke the silence.

"Let's take a look round. Can't say I expect to find anything. But it's a start. Once we have checked the strip out we'll start back. We'll probably find water in the Chingusa River, if we dig. Tomorrow, once we have re-supplied from our packs, we'll travel once we're there. Not a peep out of our guys on the OPs, so it looks like the choppers are busy elsewhere. Don't know whether I'm pleased about that or not. Any ideas, Kashili?"

The old man squinted at him. Shook his head silently.

There had been little of import. A few empty rusted tins, some assorted cartridge cases, a couple of patches of discoloured earth caused by spilled aviation fuel. Harry swept a last glance across the airstrip and led off. They had the lowering sun in their faces, and were still getting into stride when Kashili whistled softly. Harry stopped, senses ratcheting up a level, looked back at his companion. The tracker jutted his chin towards a bush near them. A ribbon of camouflage cloth swung from the end of a branch, neatly tied. Harry remained still, his eyes quartering the immediate area around them. Kashili did the same. There was nothing else to be seen. The old man moved cautiously across to the area from this new perspective. Nodded, using his spear to point at another strip of cloth, low on a branch, some thirty paces distant. The two men made their way warily across. Again Kashili studied the ground, grunting his discovery eventually.

"There is something buried here," he murmured.

Sunset. The bush cooling, though the flies were still with them. The hole in the ground already shadowed, the freshly exposed earth smelling pleasantly. Beside it lay the weapons, gleaming dully on the well-worn canvas inside a dark brown wooden box. An RPG 7 portable rocket launcher, two AK 47s, two FNs. Ammunition in sealed metal cases for the rifles. A second wooden box, painted pale green, with yellow Cyrillic lettering, containing six projectiles and six cardboard propellant cylinders. Also inside the second box a Makarov 9 mm pistol, with full eight-round capacity magazine slotted. Cocked, with the safety catch down, ready to fire. All were cocked, with safety catches in the off positions.

Harry and Kashili squatted near them, looking at the cache wordlessly. Whose, I wonder, the warden asked himself. They haven't been there very long, I would guess. And they are all ready to go. Ready to rock 'n roll. What a useful little arsenal. Perfect for a five-man patrol. Stuck out here in the middle of nowhere. I was bloody worried about booby traps.

Who put them there? What plans have been made involving
them? Well, they have new owners now. They're going to be a
bitch for the two of us to haul, but that's okay. And we've got
some work to do, filling the hole back in, and getting rid of our
tracks. But that's okay too. Because we've got all night. We'll
re-bury the ammo. I have a feeling this is the break we've been
looking for. So, all right then Warden Kenyon, let's get this
show on the road.

The extra weaponry had slowed them down.
Momberera Pan had taken an extra twenty-four hours to reach,
and they had got there at last light. The bodies of the four bulls
killed six weeks earlier were dark shapes in a forming half
moon, the smell of putrescence still there when the wind
changed. Harry and Kashili selected a termite mound, where a
thicket of *capparis* tumbled down one side, on the inland
leeward side of the pan. The mound stood in close company to
a huge ebony that reared up out of its abutments, dark and
solid, its leafy canopy virtually a roof over the termite castle.
Before they settled own to share a can of corned beef, they
manhandled the boxes under the shrubbery. Then, even
though darkness had settled around them, they worked back
over their own tracks for a hundred paces, eliminating the sign
of their passing. The sweat ran down their bodies freely by the
time they returned to the mound, climbed it and sat down to
rest. Both men feeling the tiredness that had crept up on them.
Harry would have liked a very strong gin and a hot, hot shower.
With Peta in attendance. The twelve days they had been out
had slipped by, one day blending into the next in typical bush
fashion. Only his notebook, with each day's events, or non-
events, had marked the passage of time. Harry envied the rest
of the men their soon return to Shingela. The eastern-most
team, consisting of Sergeant Fumbi and a game scout, was but a
few hundred metres from where they now rested. They had
spoken briefly on the radio, during the end of this day's

listening watch. They, like the rest of the call signs, had nothing to report.

Harry grimaced now. November Tango Romeo. Still, after all this time. Not a bloody dicky bird. He had, despite himself, begun to hope that the killings had been a passing squall. That whoever had been in the helicopters, flying them, shooting from them, had moved on. A part of him felt guilty that he should wish this, that he should secretly hope the poachers had departed. Unidentified. Untried. Untouchable. To other wild places, killing other elephants. Around them the night was coming alive. Out near the salt licks, kudu and impala moved silently. A zebra stallion shrilled his dog-like challenge. Roosting baboons squabbled and screamed briefly somewhere nearby, and in the distance hyena chorus had just began. Some small creature rustled the undergrowth near the two men. Harry leaned his head back against the trunk of the ebony. Took a long, slow, luxurious swallow of water from his canteen. God, but he was tired.

With first light the radio crackled into life.
"Three nine, three eight."
Harry used his face veil to dry off the bit of water he had used to wash his eyes and face. Reached across for the hand set.
"Three nine, go ahead."
"Three eight. Good morning. We can see one of the 'Big Four' bulls approaching your position. It looks like Marula. He is not in a hurry, coming from the direction of the big river. He should arrive at yours in a few minutes. Over."
"Three nine. Roger that. It will be nice to see him again. Anything further?"
"Negative. Out."

The bull elephant ambled into view as the sun cleared the trees. The men watched him fondly, Harry's thoughts going back to when they had darted him and fastened the collar in place. God, that was almost exactly seven years ago, he mused. Seven years gone by, and the collar still looks good. A little battle-scarred perhaps, but still in place. Hooray for science. Seven years ago also, since Peta and I finally succumbed and consummated our relationship, when we couldn't stand it any longer. Just looking at each other. As from that first day at Bumi, when I was giving the talk and she was in the audience. That night before we went out and darted old Marula here. My, my, a lot of water has certainly flowed down the Zambezi.

The elephant ignored the salt depressions, strode solidly, slowly past, to the carcasses beyond them. Stopped, stood unmoving beside them. Remained thus, immobile, for ten, fifteen, twenty long minutes. At last there was movement, as his trunk reached out to play gently to and fro over the wasted putrid remains. He shuffled closer, feeling over more of the area of the bodies, and now he was throat-rumbling, a long, sad elephant murmuring as he held his own communion. Harry and Kashili watched silently, the warden feeling the lump swell in his throat. Marula edged his way slowly around the quartet of fallen bulls. Touching, caressing, elephant-murmuring last rites. Prodding now and again with his great tusks. He picked up a scrap of dried, warped hide, holding it delicately in his trunk, passing the piece of elephant back and forth across the front of his whiskered mouth. Then he replaced the piece of hide, stood unmoving again. The radio hissed asthmatically into life. They had, reported Sergeant Fumbi, picked up a helicopter, a long way out. A speck. Just on its own, hugging the landscape.

CHAPTER FORTY

The helicopter swept into view, just above the tree line. Coming fast, it jinked and changed direction as they saw it, banking to come over the pan. Marula trumpeted and wheeled to face the machine. Harry was amazed at how quickly the invasion had happened, at how little warning there had

435

been. He wondered if Marula's low ground swell of noise had masked the sound of the incoming helicopter, as he scrambled into the prone position, dragging the radio behind the flared bulk of the tree. Saw the red glow flashing on the face of the set, knowing that meant someone was talking, couldn't hear a damn thing above the engine noise that buckled the air around them. Lifted his rifle, thumbing the safety off, aware of Kashili low beside him, saw that Marula was turning away, preparing to flee. The jet whine and rotor slap boiling over the pan, surging across the two men, the trees buffeted by the blade wash. The chopper came straight at their position atop the termite mound and for a moment Harry was in a panic. *Christ, they've seen us! Somehow they've picked us up!* The plexiglass bubble of the helicopter was only a dozen paces away, in front of them, swinging from left to right. The warden could see the pilot clearly, helmet, sunglasses, lips compressed in concentration, green flight suit with leg zips catching the sun, gloved hands on the yoke, grey suede boots working the pedals. Beside him, the back of the flight technician hunched over his machine guns, peering down. Watching Marula.

The helicopter banking now, showing the two men on the ground its underside momentarily as it wheeled away in a tight left-hand turn above the elephant. Harry Kenyon aware that the situation had slid into slow motion, seeing the left side of the machine come into view. Door back. Man crouching in the open doorway with an FN. The automatic weapon being raised. Shadowy figures of others behind him. A hand gripped his shoulder, holding the shooter, steadying him. The helicopter slowing, the pitch of the rotor blades changing as they clawed at the air. The giant insect hovering now. The FN coming up, the butt socketing into the shoulder, one leg bracing against the mounting of the machine guns, the other, the left leg, planted firmly on the step.

His FN firing. Not hearing the shots. Not feeling the recoil. Double taps, just as they had been taught, so long ago in their SAS training. *One two. One two.* Over-compensating, with

the swaying movement of the chopper. Readjusting. *One two.*
One two. Out of the corner of his eye seeing the elephant
turning back, trunk raised. Not running after all. Confused by
the terrifying alien chaos above him. Head and tail up. Massive
tusks gleaming white. Above his sights, also confusion. Plain
as day. Good. Bloody marvellous. *One two.* The bullets
hammering into them, coming fast and furious. From where?
How? *What's fuckin' happening here?* One of the figures inside
the chopper jerking, flopping spasmodically. The shooter still
there, no hand on his shoulder now, his rifle not pointing at
Marula any more, lifting uncertainly instead to cover the
landscape, face white above it, eyes staring. Glaring angrily.
Blue, Harry could see, recognition coursing like ice through his
system, his gut feeling as if someone had kicked him there.
Scratch Peters searching the landscape below for their attacker.
Scratch Peters. The helicopter caught between a rock and a hard
place, caught by surprise in that area of translational flight, that
time between hover and forward passage when the lift from the
rotors is decaying and the lift from the forward flight has not
yet built up. *One two.* The FN spinning out from the chopper
in a slow arc. The shooter, Scratch Peters, punched back into
its shadowed confines, one leg kicking wildly. The helicopter
straining, beginning to swing ever so slowly away. The chopper
tech tensed over the twin Brownings, also searching for the
unseen unheard assailants. Twin steel baffled fingers pointing.
In counter-insurgency warfare most choppers were destroyed in
the thirty feet between landing and taking off. The guns
opening up. Their hammering perfectly clear above the engine
noise. No target for them, but nevertheless, heavy suppressive
fire sweeping over the pan, fountains of dust exploding.
Parallel lines of explosions marching across the pan, slamming
into the termite mound and over it, forty rounds a second.

Harry pumped the rest of the magazine at the helicopter,
released it when it was empty, slammed a new one in place. In
the second this had taken, the chopper had swung away from
the pan, finally gaining height, scrabbling its way into the sky.

Marula was running now, back the way he had come, screaming, his baggy-trousered stride carrying him away from the madness that had descended upon him. Harry tracked the helicopter over the sights of his weapon, slammed more shots at it, cursed savagely when the trees hid it. Cocked an ear, listening to the aircraft, hearing the scream of the turbines fading. *Damn.* The sudden quiet loud in his ears. The bulb on the radio snagged his attention before the voice registered. Sergeant Fumbi, his voice hoarse with anxiety.

" ... three nine, three nine, three nine. Come in, three nine."

"Three nine, roger. Got your fives. Couldn't hear you above all the noise here."

"Roger. Are you all right?"

"We're fine. Maintain your position there. Keep your head down and your eyes open for that chopper. We'll stay put for now. Over."

"Roger. We have the helicopter visual again. We lost sight of it for some minutes. It was moving away, but now it is turning. I think it is coming back."

Harry grimaced. So be it, he thought. Let's ...

"Call sign three nine, identify yourself. I say again, identify yourself."

The voice from the radio contained barely controlled anger. The chopper, Harry realised. We're using the same channel. He looked at the set speculatively, then lifted the hand set.

"Last caller, this is three nine. Give your call sign. Over."

Silence. The bush sounds around them returning to normal. Somewhere, a woodpecker busy at work.

"Last caller, I say again, give your call sign. Over."

The response came immediately this time.

"Call sign three nine. Never mind my fucking call sign. Who the fuck are you? We have taken heavy ground fire from unknown source, and we have sustained casualties. Now, who the hell are you?"

Not Wee Willy Winky, that's for sure. The noise of the helicopter increasing. From its pitch, flying higher. Harry looked at Kashili, then patted the bulk of the ebony.

"I have a feeling we had better get ourselves behind this, pronto. The chopper is going to be swarming over us any moment now, with those horrible bloody machine guns. Let's see if I can put across one last message."

"Cyclone, three nine. Request your call sign. We are friendly forces on routine duties in this area. You have fired on us. Request you clarify your position with regard also to attempted shooting of elephant. Over."

There, thought Harry, now it's out in the open. They know, and they know we know. So, boys, what next?

The helicopter swept over them, much higher this time. Swung into left-hand orbit over the pan. They caught glimpses of it through the foliage, saw the sunlight wink steadily off the blur of its rotors. The guns spoke, flat explosions of sound preceded by the smack of bullets hitting the ground. Geysers of earth bursting skywards. Harry winced at the sound, eyes fastened on the exploding earth, watching its progress over the pan, around it, now advancing towards them. The termite mound shuddering beneath them, leaves and twigs whipping across their bodies, the tree trunk suddenly pocked with white scars, dirt and muck and dust swirling over the inert cringing forms. The noise, God, the noise. The firestorm passing on, moving over them. Kashili's face alongside Harry's, eyes squeezed shut, a litany of fear pouring from his lips, unheard amidst the turmoil.

Harry was aware that the helicopter was some distance from them. Moved his jaw to try and improve his hearing, his senses overwhelmed by the noise. Frowned as new sound registered in his mind. Shots, barely discernible above the helicopter's jets. Leaped up and scanned the sky, saw the helicopter sweeping away behind him. Saw it buck as the machine guns fired again. Swore suddenly, as realisation sluiced over him. The shots had been from Fumbi, firing long distance at the helicopter as it had hovered above Harry and Kashili, its guns seeking them out. Fumbi had initiated supporting fire, to help the warden and to draw the helicopter away from its

murderous task. He had succeeded. For a second Harry stood
immobile. Frozen. Feeling utterly helpless. Then his mined
clicked back into gear.

"Kashili, help me with the boxes. I need the RPG 7, and damn
quickly. I hope to Christ I can remember how the bloody thing
works. It's been a long time since I did any training on one of
those things."

Hands fumbling. Seconds drifting by as lazily deceptive
as tracer rounds. Harry had the propellant screwed into the
rocket and the projectile slotted into the muzzle of the
launcher. Fiddling, all thumbs, as he aligned the cap with the
percussion hammer. Years, tumbleweeding past. Up off his
knees, in a crouch, racking his memory, knowing there wasn't
any more time. The firing had stopped, both from the chopper
and Sergeant Fumbi. The helicopter continued to orbit, its
circle wider now. Lower, also. Harry finished his mental check
and stood up beside the ebony. Apart from the noise of the
aircraft the scene was again peaceful, with no hint of the earlier
mayhem. The warden remained motionless, watching the
helicopter. If it had ceased its attack, he had no great plans to
re-open the engagement. Go on, he muttered silently, bugger
off. Get out of here. Let me see how Fumbi has weathered
this storm. As the thoughts filed through his brain, movement
caught his eye. It took seconds for realisation to sink in that it
was the sergeant and the game scout, bent low, running towards
them. Sprinting through clearings of sunlight when shaded
areas were not to be had. Nervous glances directed upwards
towards the orbiting helicopter. Silly buggers, screamed Harry's
thoughts. Why don't they stay put? Why draw attention to
themselves? Damn! He scrambled down the termite mound,
balancing the rocket launcher. Heard the change in the pitch of
the motor. Saw the sergeant's eyes find him, relief giving way
to uncertainty, *come on*, the sergeant staring, *come on*, the
helicopter sweeping over them, Jesus Christ, *come on*, realising
that Fumbi had seen the RPG 7 on his shoulder, his brain
tripping with an enemy weapon in the warden's hands.

"Fumbi! Move it! Get over here!"

The hesitation costing him dear. The terrible slap of earth and the staccato hammering of the guns. Dust flying around the sergeant and the game scout. Harry Kenyon hefting the rocket launcher, noticing only now the tip of the rocket. Cursing. The nose cap, the damn nose cap and the safety pin! I haven't taken them off the fuse! Ahhh ... The shadow of the Alouette sweeping over them like some apocalyptic angel. Harry seeing the machine itself turning, out on the edge of his vision, its left side swinging around into view, showing the machine gunner fused to his weapons. Kashili at the warden's side suddenly, using Harry's FN, brass cartridge cases flying in a steady parabola, sparkling in the sun. The helicopter impervious, seemingly, to the bullets. Nose cone off, pin out, discarded. The tube on his right shoulder, nestled alongside his cheek, sights flicked up, left hand on the rear grip, right hand up on the front one, finger feeling its way over the trigger. The helicopter above his sights, there, now wavering in the rectangle. Its machine gun speaking again. Harry Kenyon's finger taking up the pressure on the trigger. Squeezing. The sergeant down in the dust. Harry wincing at the machine gun's savage assault. The helicopter turning towards him. Rocket sliding behind it. *Because I cringed at the last moment. Because I yanked at the bloody trigger.* An explosion. Fire and smoke and metal debris scything through the sky. The tail section gone, taken by the rocket. More by luck than by design.

The helicopter already slewing to the left. With the tail rotor destroyed everything headed for hell in a hand basket. For the tail rotor is what makes a helicopter travel forwards. The vital anti-torque coming via the drive shaft from the main engine prevents the machine spinning on its own axis. Now instead of going forward the fuselage was turning on itself. Like some huge damaged insect the helicopter gathered momentum, totally out of control. Spinning across the sky, main rotor blades whopping louder, spinning like a giant top. Faster and faster, all the way down into the ground. Then it was gone, in its place a great ball of flame. Harry stood, stunned, feeling the heat of the explosion roil over him. Watched what was left of the helicopter come hurtling headless out of the inferno, a great twisted piece of steel bucking violently across the flood plain.

Harry paused beside a mangosteen, watching the file of men picking their way silently past him, across the valley floor. The silence was not just bush discipline, he knew. They were still in shock. The rough stretcher they took turns carrying between them was a horrid reminder of the recent events. The mangled bloodied remains of Sergeant Nathaniel Fumbi were already a little high, and Harry was glad the vehicles would be waiting for them at the Katete River. The observation teams, responding to the warden's radio message, had quickly converged on the scene of the battle with the helicopter. Had seen the signs of the conflict, had been told the story by the three surviving Parks' men. The game scout was still ashen, could hardly take his eyes off the covered body of the dead sergeant. Harry was amazed that he too had not been killed by the helicopter's machine guns. The radio had been shot off his back, and his weapon smashed from his grasp, a buckled mess. Kashili was unnaturally silent, and the warden thought he looked, all of a sudden, old. That was enough to age anybody, he thought. He looked back. The twisted, charred remains of the helicopter lay near Momberere Pan, a few equally mangled pieces strewn over the surrounding area. There had been no way of separating twisted flesh from twisted steel. The explosion and the inferno had incinerated everything. Everyone. He could still see Scratch Peters in his mind's eye, glaring angrily over his FN. Searching for whoever had disturbed them in their shooting of the elephant. Automatically his gaze lifted to check the sky. Looked for vulture movement.

Rhodesia down on the canvas, being counted out. Almost universally there is the collective thumbs-down. On 2

September the green and white flag had come down for the last time. In its place went the flag with those colours so favoured by the newly independent African states; black, red, green and a splash of white, with, in this instance, a gold Zimbabwe bird in one corner. The externals still going one. Operation *Uric* sweeping across southern Mozambique, destroying bridges and roads, laying waste communications. *Dice* doing the same thing in Zambia. Messages to Kaunda and Machel, the fairy godfathers of the Patriotic Front, that there is still life in the body down on the canvas. The all-party conference at Lancaster House well under way. Dragging on. The last nails in the coffin of Rhodesia being hammered in. Lord Carrington, master of the side-step, tangos his way amongst the factions gathered in London. Smiling, smiling. Doing it so well.

CHAPTER FORTY-ONE

Through the telephoto lens the clean white symmetry of Marula's tusks contrasted perfectly with the green sedge that covered Mbera Pool. The purple of the hyacinth flowers added to the composition, and Peta clicked away happily. A pair of jacanas entered her frame occasionally as they darted around the bull, which looked serenely content, deep in the remaining slush of the pool. It was a typical Nemana scene, enhanced even more by the presence of the great elephant whiling away the hot hours of the day. The December pre-rain heat lay stolidly over the valley, and Peta was sweating freely. Nearby, Kashili rested in the poolside shade of some evergreens, watching her work with her cameras, his gaze drifting off now and again to the elephant and the surrounding landscape. The old man was sweating also, and he wondered again when the rains would come. The first thunderheads piling up looked promising. There had even been lightning, on the last few evenings.

The rifle barrel moved slowly. Swung across from the elephant, over the pool to the two figures opposite. The eye behind the sights rested first on the woman and then the old man, studied each person dispassionately. Moved back to settle on Peta Kenyon. An easy shot. All of them easy, really. Compared to some he had made.

In his office at Shingela base Warden Harry Kenyon finished the report. It seemed to him that he had done little else since his return after the chopper incident. Hoped this was the last one. There had been a lot of radio traffic between Nemana and Salisbury, once he had made his initial report, and the director and Garnet had flown down, accompanied by Hugo Winters and various airforce hierarchy. The debrief had been acrimonious, the subsequent visit to the crash site very tense. There had been no middle ground. That a Rhodesian Air Force helicopter had been involved in shooting elephants, firing on members of National Parks and killing a person, had absolutely no bearing on the fact that said aircraft had been shot down and destroyed along with its crew and members of a crack special forces team. This, whilst on normal counter-insurgency operations in the Zambezi Valley, which were continuing, even with the big-top performance at Lancaster House. Harry had stood his ground. Garnet and, Harry was pleasantly surprised to note, the director, backed him solidly. But it had not been a good day. At the end, before they climbed back into their waiting helicopters, Hugo Winters had taken Harry aside.
"Have a good look around you, Harry. Enjoy the place whilst you can. Because your days are numbered. I used some top contacts to make sure you were not taken out. Because you were, *once*, one of us. I will make it my duty to make you pay for this latest nonsense, no matter what happens in this country over the next few months."
His voice had been calm and measured, at odds with the cold rage in his eyes. Harry had responded in kind.

"You, General Winters, have lost touch with reality. The rarefied air in Salisbury has finally got to you. Yes, there's a war going on, yes we are headed for even tougher times, yes I may be pissing in the wind. This 'nonsense' is the tip of an iceberg. I cannot believe that what has been going on here, reported to JOC less than a month ago, and what has been going on down in Gona re Zhou, has managed to go unchecked for so long. Unless it has the highest sanction. And I am very happy to meet you, anyone, with pistols at dawn. Anytime."

Hugo Winters had glared at him and then turned away. Harry spoke again.

"By the way. Shame about Scratch Peters."

The hard irony in his voice matched the expression on the warden's face. The general paused for a second, looked as if he were going to speak, then strode across to the waiting Bell. Harry had been aware of the intense unfathomable stare of Winters, peering down, as the chopper swung away.

The shot echoed flatly across the pool. A flock of parrots erupted out of a nearby tree, and the jacanas flew off. Marula went down. Legs collapsing, great tusks ploughing beneath the sedge and hyacinth. One tremor shivering through his great frame, and then he was motionless. A grey weathered rock jutting up out of the greenery. The man switched targets, a predatory smile forming. The two over there, standing frozen, staring around them, the man with the spear now poised. Settled his cheek a little more comfortably against the stock, steadied his sights on the tracker.

Harry read his report over, satisfied at last with its content. Had had enough of paperwork, needed some fresh air. A stroll across to Mbera Pool where Peta and Kashili were busy taking elephant pictures made a therapeutic alternative to the office. He stood up, paused, hearing the not-too-distant shot. Not sure, in the confines of his office, of the direction. Pushed his chair back and went out on to the verandah. The heat lay on Shingela like a heavy suffocating blanket.

The bullet, travelling at 2455 feet per second, hit Kashili in the chest. He did not hear the shot that killed him, that catapulted him backwards against the bole of the fig tree. To lie sprawled like a discarded doll, his spear still locked in one clenched fist. The smear of blood on the tree from the exit wound innocuously bright. Peta screamed, knocking the camera tripod flying as she scrambled to Kashili. Burst into tears when she saw the damage wreaked on his frail form. Picked him up and held him against her, her tears splashing down on to his face.

With the second shot echoing across the flood plain, a surge of unease pulsed through Harry. It had come from the direction of Mbera Pool. Neither Peta or Kashili had weapons with them, the old man, as always, confident of his bush knowledge and his spear. As was Harry. He snatched his FN from its rack by the door and began running for the Landrover. Wally Conway emerged from the radio room.
"Grab a weapon, Wally, pronto, and come with me."
The ranger nodded wordlessly.

Peta Kenyon now firmly in his sights, crouched by the old tracker. Not a clear shot, with her holding the old chap like that, but passable. The grin wider now, shark-like. He cocked his head as the sound of a vehicle, coming fast, reached his ears. Nuzzled a cheek against the stock. Payback time, Harry Kenyon.

The Landrover bounced over the flood plain, careening wildly when it hit patches of long dried mud, with old elephant footprints deep sunken, playing havoc with the car's suspension. Wally hung on to the steering wheel grimly, saw Harry's knuckles also gripped white on the open metal dash, his FN clasped tightly in his left hand. They both heard the shot as they bounced high over the lip that sloped away down into the long depression that was Mbera Pool, more sand than water at this time of the year. The last remaining muddy water surviving at the far end of the depression. Wally glimpsed the yawning cavity of the ant bear hole at the last second, yanked desperately at the wheel. The Landrover slewed sideways in an explosion of dust, tilting on to two wheels. Harry thought they had lost it, were going to turn over. As the thoughts kaleidoscoped through his brain the windscreen starred and he heard a bullet whine off steel beside him. The Landrover was sliding sideways, Wally's arms locked at ten to two on the steering wheel, the momentum of its sideways passage not slowing as the slope increased. Dust swirled thickly over the two men. Harry heard another round bounce off the vehicle. Jumped free of its confines. Landed flat and hard, nearly lost the FN. Scrambled up, his free hand automatically checking the muzzle for dirt obstruction. Was aware of the Landrover still in full slide, in the eye of a miniature dust storm. Heard the weapon once more, got some direction at last. Also identified it as an FN. *Who, though, using it?* Ran for the shelter of nearby trees, wishing, praying, that he would see Peta and Kashili. Trying to ignore the foreboding that had gripped him.

He could not see the vehicle at all amidst the pall of dust. Waited relaxedly, his weapon in the general direction of the dust storm. He was surprised the Landrover had stayed on its wheels, the speed and angle it had achieved, sliding down the slope. He levered himself up on to one knee and lifted the rifle. The car had stopped and the dust was beginning to thin. He could see a figure, Kenyon, squirming across the seats, away from him, as he attempted to exit the vehicle on the side away from the shooter. He was pushing his FN ahead of him. Was almost out. One hand, his right, lifted, gripped the edge of the cab. The shooter grinned, squeezed the trigger.

Harry heard the shot and the scream, superimposed. Searched for the source, again, of the shot. Found it! There was the figure, a man, kneeling behind the line of a fallen tree on the far side of the pool. Harry fired, saw the man flinch and duck. Fired again, double-tapping now. Counted off ten rounds. Saw splinters of wood chipped from the tree trunk. An old, grey, fissured mopane, he absently noted. Wally Conway was out of the vehicle, screaming.

"My hand! He shot off my fucking hand!"

He was only a dozen paces away, further down the slope. Harry spoke sharply.

"Wally, listen to me. Stay behind the vehicle. Whatever you do, stay there. Don't show yourself. Do you hear me?"

Wally nodded, gripping the stump of his arm with his surviving hand, staring disbelievingly at it. Harry went on.

"Get something around that hand, Wally. Now, before the shock gets you. Tight. Then, Wally, you've got to help me. You've got to keep that bastard's head down while I get across to him. You've got to pump lead at his position. Can you do that, Wally?"

Harry kept his voice level and distinct, hoping it would help calm the ranger. Wally lifted his gaze from his missing hand, met Harry's eyes. Nodded.

"Let's do it now." His voice was shaky. "We'd better do it now, because I think I'm about to fall over. Where is the bastard? Who is it?"

"I don't know who it is. When you look over the bonnet, he's behind a long, fallen, dead tree. The only one across that side of the pool. I'll pump a couple more shots at him in a moment. Will you be able to handle your rifle?"

Wally Conway's face was white. He nodded wordlessly. Harry could see the man's teeth chewing into his bottom lip. The ranger levered himself upright, his FN gripped one-handed.

So, there were two of them. You slipped up there! Okay. No sweat. No problem at all, to get Kenyon on the wrong foot. Time to finish the job. He moved his rifle and raised his head slightly. Muttered a curse when a bullet clipped the top of the log, sending splinters into his face. Heard the shout from across the pool. *Go.* More shots. The tree trunk shuddering. Couldn't get his head up to see what the fuck was happening. Damn it. Felt blood trickling down his face. Vision in his right eye blurred. The whine of a ricochet. *Go.*

Harry was in full stride. Hit the bottom of the dry pool, went up the other side. Wally doing bloody well. The firing quick and controlled, just like the old days on the culls. Harry could see the log clearly. See the splinters flying from it. *Who?* Ten more paces, with his legs getting rubbery suddenly. The firing had stopped. No more chips of wood off the tree. Pounding, lifting his knees. Waiting for the gun to come up over the log. His breath ragged, shot to hell in fact. *Come on!*

Nothing. Not a damn thing, except for some empty brass cases winking in the sun. The bastard had chosen his position well. There was a huge area of dead ground behind the fallen tree, leading off into the hollows and gullies that criss-crossed the plain. Harry could see the shooter's tracks leading away. Toe areas indented deeply. Because he was running, the son-of-a-bitch! Harry swept his gaze once more over the firing position, noticed a splash of blood on the tree. Good. . Nothing else, though. He scanned the plain again, saw movement where the jesse thicket bordered the open parkland. Saw him then. Saw him slip up out of the dead ground and into the jesse. Far away. Too bloody far, for now. Harry marked the spot in his memory, carefully. Turned and gave his attention to Mbera Pool and its surrounds. Saw Wally Conway where he had fainted beside the Landrover. Saw the figures across the pan, in the solid shade of a massive fig tree. Motionless. Began to run, feeling horribly sick.

The shooter trotted along the game trail that twisted through the jesse. He was mildly irritated with himself. It had taken a long time to get into a position near Harry Kenyon, where he would have control of the situation. And now he had blown it. The whole thing was a bit of a lemon, with Kenyon still in the game. Still walking on his hindlegs. Instead of down, with a bullet in him. Still, there would be another time, it didn't matter when. He wasn't going anywhere, not now, the way things were going in this country. And he had given Harry enough to keep him occupied, to grieve over. Don't know why I pulled that last shot, though. Getting soft. Nah. Maybe I should slow down and take this trail a little more carefully, especially with my bloody eye the worse for wear. Bastards. I would hate to bump into a rhino or elephant at such close quarters. Not right now. Later maybe.

Harry cradled his wife in his arms, held her close as he stared over her head at Kashili. He felt numb and there was a roaring in his ears, the pounding of heavy surf. He could feel, rather than hear, her sobbing beginning to subside. Continued stroking her hair. Above Kashili was the white scar mark of a bullet. The old tracker, as small as he had been in life, looked more shrunken in death. Like lion and rhino, Harry mused. They always look smaller when they're dead. So you're in good company in that respect, my old friend. *Bava.* Father. What a sorry way to end your days, when you, *we*, have walked the length and breadth of this valley and taken everything it threw at us in our stride. Our home, the Zambezi Valley. Vandalised by these people playing their war games. I felt bad, after that business with Scratch Peters and the chopper. I had no right to involve you in something like that. That was beyond the call of duty, friendship. You were too old for that kind of violence. Me too, I reckon. Africa has been kind to you and me, apart from that. We have gone our ways quietly over her spaces, and she accepted our presence, our respect. Not any more, it seems. What am I going to do without you? I'm sorry I never had children for you to teach, as you taught me. It would seem I've been remiss in that department. Ahhh. *Africa, bloody Africa.* Harry Kenyon could not see Kashili any more, through his tears. Could not see the vultures sliding down out of the hot sky.

CHAPTER FORTY-TWO

They lay silently, listening to the growl of distant thunder. In the aftermath of their lovemaking, Harry could hear the night noises clearly. Even the territorial rataplan of the geckos seemed louder. The beating of his heart was taking longer to return to normal, because tonight they had made love with an almost savage intensity. It had gone on for a long time, the sweat running off them in the thick fabric of pre-rain humidity. There had been a catharsis in their coupling, for both of them, a purging of so many fears and emotions that had cross-grained through them in the last days. Now, staring up through the dark, feeling Peta's eyelashes like butterflies against his skin when she blinked, Harry thought again about Kashili.

He had buried the old man this morning. To a quiet, cool place on the edge of the flood plain he had gone on his own and dug a grave. Working methodically, he had gone deep, unheeding of the sweat pouring from him, unfeeling of the blisters that formed and then broke, rubbing raw as the hole went deeper. A few paces away a major game trail slanted past. So you'll never be lonely. *So there will always be someone for you to talk to.* He had placed Kashili at the bottom of the hole, together with his spear, knobkerrie, kaross, and a gourd of beer. The grysbuck horn that held the old man's snuff he had arranged just so, on his chest. Then he had refilled the hole, unmindful of the tears streaking through the veneered sweat on his face. Towards the end he had placed a solid bed of rocks across the freshly-turned earth, and then, when there were only a few inches to go, he had poured petrol over the area as further deterrent against hyenas. He had covered the grave fully then. He used the Landrover to tow a large chunk of long dead leadwood, worn and sculpted by the elements, over the grave. Your headstone, he said to Kashili. It should make a good scratching post for elephants and the smaller stuff. So you can keep an eye on them for me. I'm sorry I've put you in a grave. I know you wanted your body left out on the plain for the hyenas and other scavengers, when the time came. As I do. But I couldn't, I'm afraid. Getting silly in my advancing years, probably.

Harry had sat near the grave for the rest of the day. In the late afternoon Peta had brought a small basket she had made, containing white baobab flowers, and hung it on the driftwood. In the gloaming they had driven slowly back to Shingela, their own silence a smaller part of the great African silence that comes briefly with twilight. Harry had not felt like a drink, which surprised him. That would come later, he supposed.

Now, in the dark, Harry felt becalmed. The things that needed to be said had been spoken of. Tomorrow Garnet Clayton was flying down to Nemana to collect Peta and take her back to Salisbury. Harry did not know who had shot Kashili and Marula. Could not even guess. That the person knew him, he was in no doubt. The message had been very clear. Peta had been allowed to live, for reasons only known to the assassin. He wanted her to keep on living, and so had asked Garnet to take her out of here. While he finished this business. Or was himself killed. She had not tried to dissuade him. Peta Kenyon had spared them both that. Wally Conway was in hospital so Garnet would be bringing with him someone from headquarters to hold the fort during Harry's absence. He was aware that this was but a small ripple caused by a small stone, creating only a minor disturbance amongst those larger ripples flowing across the country. Agreements were still being hammered out at Lancaster House. The advance guard of the cease-fire monitoring force, of Operation *Agila*, had already arrived in Salisbury, along with all manner of strangers. There was a veritable beehive of activity, not to mention the much attended cocktail circuits. The rumour factories. It was all exciting stuff, this bringing to heel of the intransigent Rhodesians, and, by Jove, the beer was jolly good out here. So, the isolated death of an elephant and an old Shangaan tracker was not high on anyone's agenda. Just mine, Harry thought now, hearing Peta's breathing change as sleep claimed her. Tomorrow we start tracking. Correction, I start tracking. From where I saw him go into the jesse. Until I catch up with him, wherever the hell that may be. I wish Kashili was coming with me. It's so much easier when there are two of you working on tracks.

He travelled light. Rifle, ammunition, handgun, knife, binoculars, three water bottles; the essentials. A small pack, containing salt, sugar, cans of corned beef, onions, and, a single ultimate luxury, a can of peaches. When that ran out he would live off the land. He took a small medic pack and a light blanket, around which was wrapped his old army waterproof, on a rope slung over one shoulder. And the clothes he stood in. No toothpaste, soap or comb. No plates or cooking utensils. No radio. This was a private safari. No one else was invited.

He had got on to the tracks at first light. Given that they were now almost forty-eight hours old, they were not exactly as plain as day. The killer had used animal paths a lot, so there was a fair amount of disturbance caused by the animals. It did not bother Harry too much. Whenever he lost them he backtracked, circled, searched anew. Moved forward again. Always forward. The tracks led up on to the first hard contours of the escarpment. Here in the hill country there was none of the luxuriant greenery of the flood plains, no soft blue haze to gentle a person's eye, no great sense of timelessness. The escarpment was a no-man's land of little compromise, where all life forms lived on the edge. It was a place that did not suffer fools.

Harry kept moving all day. The tracks left by game were fewer now, with water at this time of year almost non-existent. He still saw tracks of kudu, rhino and, once, lion. Baboon sign was still to be found, which was encouraging, for they needed water almost as much as their human cousins did. Harry kept an eye on bee movement and birds' flight, also positive water indicators. He knew this part of the country well, had passed through it before over the years. In his mind were places he remembered where water had once been found. A certain hollow baobab, a cleft of rock in a sandy seasonal riverbed, a hidden seep at the foot of a lone fig in a rocky cul-de-sac. But there was no guarantee that there would be water there now. And the direction of the tracks might take him into unknown country. In mid afternoon he paused, studying the earth intently. The tracks of a lone elephant entered the game trail he was following; travelled in the direction he was moving. He gave a soft grunt of surprise. Partly because he was surprised at an elephant being in such a dry hostile place at this time of year, and also because he recognised the huge creped lily-pad tracks as those of Kabakwe, the sole remaining bull of Nemana's 'Big Four'. He travelled on, the spoor of both the killer and the elephant preceding him up into the hard country. He hoped the elephant did not cross the path of Marula's executioner.

Before last light he found where Kashili's killer had made camp two nights before. There was little obvious sign, some scuff marks where he had lain, a place where the butt of his weapon had stood, under a flat rock a small pile of excrement. Harry kept moving, halting only when the fading light made it impossible to see the faint sign his quarry had left. The elephant tracks had meandered here and there, occasionally off Harry's line of march, but then returning again to the trail. The warden was intrigued that the bull should be up here, away from the easy life of the flood plain and the Zambezi. It made him hopeful also, for the elephant would have to have water, and if he was up here he must know where there existed some secret source. He made a dry camp, with no fire. Sat on his bedroll, listening to the night. In the late afternoon, distant thunder had echoed over the hills. Now it was louder and he could see sheet lightning in the east, flickering like far-off artillery exchanges. It was very hot, and the sweat did not dry on his body. Tomorrow I'll have to find water, he thought. Better to find water whilst I still have some. What were the ground rules they taught us in Malaya? The five horsemen, those five enemies of survival ... fear, fatigue, thirst, pain and haste. I wonder what he is doing about water? The assassin? Because if he is not used to this place he will come unstuck. Which would be a good thing, of course. And the elephant? Kabakwe? What is his secret, about water? Where is he now? What food has he found tonight? Harry watched the lightning ripple along the horizon. Rain, he thought, would be nice. But, please, no rain. Not yet. Not on the tracks.

Leaden heat. Very little animal spoor now. Mainly insects and snakes. And Kabakwe's trail, no longer meandering, but journeying purposefully. In mid morning the tracks of the shooter and those of Kabakwe parted ways. The human sign continued along the contour, travelling east, while Kabakwe had pushed in towards the main escarpment. Harry stood in the sun, feeling dessicated, hesitating with his decision. The elephant, he was sure, would lead him to water, eventually. He would lose valuable tracking time, but if he ran out of water he would slow down and probably die before he could find another source. The heat today was more intense. It lay cloyingly on him, mingled with dust and grime. He could feel the dust in the air. Today, for the first time, the thunderheads on the horizon had not disappeared with the coming of the sun. They lay, bank upon bank, dark-hued and sullen. The sun had appeared later, climbing above them with seeming difficulty. Harry shook his remaining canteen. It was a little over half full. He set off again, across the landscape the colour of old bones.

Under a magenta sky. Following the tracks of the killer. He was starting to hallucinate about the can of peaches in his pack.

Four hours later bees led him to a tiny seep of brackish water. He made himself study the surroundings for a long time, staying in cover. The tracks of the killer had led here also, and Harry judged that he had caught up in time on his quarry. Now he could see the deeper indented marks where the killer had crouched beside the seep, taking water. And he was sure those tracks looked more fresh, could not say for sure until he could get closer to them and make an appreciation. Perhaps it was simply that the earth around the seep was firmer than the ground they had travelled so far. Harry would have loved to clear the scum off the water and methodically refill his canteens, compounded this simple pleasure by washing his face, pour water over his head. He could feel it, taste it. He scanned the landscape again, not seeing anything, not a damn thing to indicate the presence of another being. *But he felt it, by God.* The hairs on the back of his neck were telling him something all right. Harry eased back deeper into cover, looking for a rock or scrubby bush that would give him a modicum of shade. Once again he checked the sky, noted the strange colour that still washed the heavens. No vultures. And another three hours until darkness. When he could get to the water, taking it nice and slow and easy. *Perlahan lahan.*

He sat high up among boulders and struggling thorn bushes, watching back over the way he had come, and the approach to the seep, which was itself below the foot of the knoll, out of sight. The eye did not make the watching a simple task. There was now a deep throbbing behind the socket, and it was weeping continuously. His vision, at best, out of his right eye, was like opening his eye underwater, and it irritated him mightily. Once he had gained the high ground, with the going subsequently harder, his passage had slowed, because of his limited vision. He had seen no sign of pursuers. Which surprised him. He would have laid bets that Harry Kenyon would have been hot foot after him. Well, he thought, maybe he is and you just don't know it. Which is why it's a good idea to sit the day out and watch the lay of the land. It gives you a chance to saturate your gut with water, which in turn allows you to top up on dried meat, which would otherwise make you thirsty. Then when it's dark you can re-fill your water bottles, have a last long gulp at the seep, and be on your way. Places to go, sights to see. It's reassuring to think of the pocket money you've got stashed, thanks to your moonlighting. And the Irishman has guaranteed you a contract elsewhere, now that Rhodesia is down the tubes. Christ, but it's hot. Can't say I enjoy running around the *bundu*. Never know what the hell is going to eat, beat or tread on you. Never could understand why Harry loves it so much. Weird bastard. I hope he comes. He's one bit of unfinished business that needs finishing. And I did give my word.

CHAPTER FORTY-THREE

Full dark, with a sluggish heat coagulated over the landscape.

Tonight the thunder was louder and the sheet lightning was punctuated by jagged forked discharges. Even though the display was still on the horizon Harry could feel the electricity in the air around him. He stood up, patting a hand exploratively over his items of equipment in the dark, making sure he had everything. Then he made his way, a few paces at a time, stopping, sifting the night air, towards the seep. His thumb felt for the safety catch once again. Yes, fine, off. A wind had come up, not much, but he could almost see the ripples and eddies it created in the thick, hot air.

When he reached the seep he stood, listening. Lowered himself into a crouch, put out a hand and felt for the tiny patch of water. Found it, smeared away the surface scum, keeping his head up, all his senses probing the night. Brought his hand up, running the dampness over the back of his neck and around his face. Repeated the process, relishing the cool of it. Untied his face veil, bunching it in one hand, put it into the water, squeezing, releasing, soaking up the cool reviving wetness of it. Brought it out, pushed it into a pocket. He would re-tie it later, when his attention could be safely diverted. Stopped any movement now, for a minute. Two. Three. Crouched with his mouth wide open, helping the ear canal to do its work. Continued, one-handed still, unscrewing the top off one water bottle, holding it back with a finger while he immersed the bottle in the water. Adjusted the angle as best he could to keep the noise of the inflow down. Glob, glob, glob, it still sounded like bloody Victoria Falls. Went on and on. The weight of the ever-so-slowly filling bottle settling gradually in his hand. Come on. The damp on his face and neck already dried. The bunched face veil in the pocket deliciously cool and wet, seeping through his shorts, against the skin. Bottle full. Okay, cap it and move back. Away from the seep a ways. Let's just sit quietly and listen before we refill the other two. See what goes bump in the night.

He took his time coming down off the high ground, stopping to listen often. He thought that somehow the worsening condition of his eye was beginning to affect his hearing. Hoped to Christ that he was imagining this. Because he still had a good long day's travel to where he had cached the pack and the radio. Before he had gone down to settle the account with Harry. Thank Christ for the radio. It won't take long for the chopper to come in and haul my arse out of here, once they get my message. Eventually he reached the level ground which surrounded the seep, moving his head left and right, searching out the pulse of the night. He reached the seep and dropped to a crouch, fumbling one-handed with his first water bottle. Got the cap unscrewed and balanced it on one knee whilst he moved the free hand to clear the surface slime aside. Was mildly surprised that there was none, that it had not reclaimed the surface during the day, after he had filled up at first light. Found himself wondering about that. Shifted position slightly, and felt something under his foot. Brought his hand from the water to feel it.

Harry heard the movement. Strained his senses. He reckoned he was about a dozen full paces from the seep, and the sound had come from that direction. He moved the barrel of the FN so that it pointed that way. Felt the sweat griming his body. More sound. Muted. Stealthy. But sound, to be sure. He thought it could be some animal drinking under cover of the night, pushed that speculation aside. It did not sound like an animal, didn't feel like an animal, something wild. The sweat trickled down from his hairline, over his face, stinging his eyes. He put his left hand down to his shorts, to retrieve the face veil, and wipe the humidity off his face. No face veil. Just the dampness where it had been. *Damn.* Heard the scuffle at the seep. Snatched his hand back to the FN.

His hand felt cloth, explored it. It felt like a bloody face veil! And sure as hell, not his! Which meant ... Shit! He crouched lower and swung his weapon up. Silently cursed his eye, as his finger sought the trigger. Almost dropped the rifle when the first shots split the darkness, saw the flash of the weapon firing at him, almost up his bloody nostril! Heard the whip crack of the bullets close alongside his head. Jerked his FN across and returned fire, hammering off six rounds in the direction of the muzzle flashes, dived away from the seep, rolled, kept moving. Cursing silently. *Shit shit shit!* How did he get in so close? Bloody Kenyon, it must be him! *Shit!*

After his first double-tap, Harry dropped, squirmed sideways. Heard and felt the darkness ripped apart where he had been, saw the flashes of the killer's rifle, caught the brief spectral silhouette of a figure behind the flame. Fired again, double-tapping twice. Heard a loud grunt, followed by a scraping noise. Caught the metallic clink of metal on rock. Fired twice again at the sound. Waited. Tried to separate the slight noises coming from the seep from the strident ringing in his ears caused by the gunfire. Focused his senses on the night. Heard thunder, much closer now. Lightning flickered across the higher ground of the escarpment, briefly illuminating rocks and trees. Go away, he thought. Come back later. Warden Kenyon busy with problem animal control, lying silently in the night in the no-man's land of the Zambezi escarpment, looking for a target.

****

Rain. A dense swirling grey curtain pulled across the land. Pounding down, the sound of it drowning out all other noise. The day well advanced, but no colour, no sun. Just the low dark cloud and the rain coming down. Harry sat cross-legged, his waterproof draped across his shoulders, forming a tent across most of his body. The brim of his floppy hat kept some of the rain out of his eyes. The barrel of his FN angled down, keeping the water out. The heat and humidity were a thing of the past, a memory. Now he was cold and wet. The rain had swept in two hours before dawn, preceded by an increasing crescendo of thunder accompanied by white hissing lightning bolts that speared into the earth.

Harry heard and felt the water cascading off his hunched Buddha-like form as his gaze swept over his surroundings one more time. The seep area was now a pond. Small streams gushed past his position, gathering momentum as they mill-raced between the rocks. No tracks now, he reflected ruefully. They're out the window. So now we just search. I think I hit him last night, but, impossible to say now. The rain has washed away any blood spoor, as well as the tracks. One could say that rain has stopped play. Almost, not quite. Because as soon as this lets up, we move on. The rain is not going to stop me catching that bastard. No wonder the heat and humidity was so bad. It was leading up to this. I wonder where Kabakwe is? Bet he's enjoying the rain. Maybe he knew this was on the way and that's why he was quitting the flood plain.

He had forced himself on through the darkness. The wound had not felt too bad at first. But then, as the adrenalin cooled, he had begun to feel it, moved more slowly. Cursed, often. Dammit to hell, he swore again. A lucky shot got him. *Unlucky.* Two, actually. One had shot off the bottom tip of his right ear, which was nothing except it tended to bleed like a stuck pig. It was the other wound that was a bitch. Straight through his upper thigh, just below the crown jewels. It had, thank Christ, missed bone and major blood vessels, but it sure as hell had slowed him down to a gallop. And now, with daylight, it hurt, Jesus did it hurt. Wish I had morphine. Haven't, because it's in the pack. Stupid move, that. He stopped, leaning against a rock, and inspected the damage. Did not dare sit down, in case he couldn't stand up again. The rain had kept it clean, had at the same time made the flesh soft. He could see the jagged exit hole, blood oozing again from it. He re-tied his face veil, using it as a tourniquet, made it tighter still by twisting the knot with his knife blade. The situation with his eye was but a minor problem now, with the new damage. One-legged and one-eyed. Shit. I've got to get to the radio. Get the chopper in. He was cold, heard his teeth chattering. Knew he was also beginning to feel light-headed. Dammit. *Bloody Kenyon.* How had he caught him like that, in the pitch dark? And now the rain, freezing his balls off.

He grunted, shoved himself away from the rock. At least it was wiping out all sign of his tracks. Which was how Harry found him in the first place, of course, plodding along the spoor he had left. He had not thought the bastard could still do it, especially with the way he had used the hard ground, and lost his footprints amongst those of the animals on the game trails. And his major-domo, what was his name, Kashili, pushing up daisies now, had sure as hell not been of much use this time. But, he had always been an incredible tracker, Harry Kenyon. Could follow fish through water. Christ, I should know that, if anyone should. He squinted up through the rain at the sky. If anything, it was raining harder. The FN was getting heavy again, so he changed hands, gritting his teeth when his wounded leg took his weight. Out on the fringe of his vision there was movement, wraith-like in the rain. He did not see it, with his eyes half closed.

By mid-morning the rain had slowed to a steady drizzle. The three water bottles he had put out were long ago full, though he was not thirsty now. Harry cast an eye over the sky and then the landscape, and shrugged to himself. Okay then, so we get wet. Wetter, I should say. He stood up, readjusting his waterproof. It was not so efficient, now that it had become waterlogged, but at least it helped to keep the body warmth close. He slushed through the pond and surveyed the terrain close above where the seep had been. Saw two of his bullet strikes, and then the black metal of the FN magazine. Picked it up. It was fully loaded. That must have been the metallic noise I heard. So I wasn't shooting at shadows. Good show. And if you did hit him, and he could still move, which way would he have gone, out of this place? Harry stood, peering through the drizzle, around him. Sighed, eventually. Moved off slowly, squinting past the miniature waterfall draining off the brim of his hat.

He had been on the move an hour when the rain petered out. Harry had let his intuition guide him from the seep, feeling, more than anything else, that he was still on the trail of his quarry, easing his way steadily and warily through the rain-drenched country. Now, with it stopped, he could hear the dripping of water off foliage and rock ledges. Heard a lark break hesitantly into song, under the gunmetal sky. He crouched beside a stunted *albizia* and let his eyes quarter his surroundings, getting the feel of the new rain-free situation.

Took his time having a swig of water, his hands doing all the work, whilst his eyes kept on with their inspection. Continued looking, over the top of the water bottle, whilst he savoured the taste of the rainwater. Ahead there were only the tops of trees visible, indicating where land must drop away suddenly. A ravine, Harry calculated, or maybe one of the steep-sided valleys that lead north down on to the flood plain. He screwed the cap back on the bottle, listening. Squirrels were scolding from the trees ahead, and a loerie complained querulously. Harry stood up. He could also hear the rush of water.

Goddam it to hell. He stood staring at the torrent of brown water sweeping past. Coming down off the high escarpment, the first flood of the season. And impossible to cross. Equally galling was the knowledge that to deviate up or down the river would be a waste of time. It was too new and too wild. He leaned the FN against a tree and gripped his leg with both hands, feeling the new heat in his flesh. Grimaced with the pain. Against his better judgement he collapsed to sit beside the water, and was immediately glad he had. The pain in his leg lessened. So maybe you should rest up here, while you wait for the river to go down. It will probably do you good, and anyway, these flash floods don't last for long. Find yourself a place where you can cover your trail, and wait. Above him squirrels and birds were making a noise, loud, seemingly, in the new hush of the rain-sodden bush. He forced himself back up on to his feet, thinking for a second that he was going to black out. No, he remonstrated himself. You can't do that. There's a way to go still, to the morphine and the radio. So pick up your gun, sorry, rifle, and find yourself a good position. What was it that old Cockney bloke sung? Harry used to do it so well. *Pick up thy musket, lad.* Yeh, that's it.

Harry could still hear the squirrels and the bird as he studied the tracks, no more than ten paces from where he had stopped. Well, well, he thought. Lookey here. Where has he come from,

I wonder? He must be very close, because these have just been put there. Fresh out of the oven. He smiled. Well, all right then!

He must have closed his eyes, he realised. Because he had company, suddenly. Because now there was a fucking great elephant standing looking at him. *Christ.* He sat, frozen, staring up at the elephant, that was regarding him from a distance of a dozen paces. *The tusks.* They were like bloody tree trunks! Bigger than anything he had ever seen. A few quid there, a part of his brain calculated, while the main part directed his hands to lift up his musket. *No, rifle.* The movement irritated the elephant. He shook his great head and his ears clopped like tentflaps in a gale. *Shoo! Go away! Fuck off!* I would love to shoot you, you son-of-a-bitch. Can't though. Not with the chance of Warden Harry bloody Kenyon being in the neighbourhood. And he is first prize. You can be second, if you like.

Harry heard the slap of the ears, continued on along the tracks. Saw, suddenly, the other tracks. Those of his quarry, coming on to the trail that led down into the ravine. Kabakwe's footprints were over his. His thumb slipped off the safety catch, and he eased forward, adding his tracks to those already there.

The elephant lowered his head and came at him, making absolutely no sound. *Damn.* He fired, saw white splinters explode off the edge of a tusk, was aware of the mass of wrinkles at the top of the trunk, which snaked out towards him. Felt the blow, and things breaking inside. Was aware of tumbling through the air. *Goddam the bloody elephant.*

Harry saw the beginning of Kabakwe's charge, saw the head go down, heard the shot. Kept going, rifle up at his shoulder. No reaction from the elephant to the shot. A body hurled into the air, dropping out of sight again. He stopped near Kabakwe who stood poised, growling now, head high as he looked for his quarry. Harry slapped the magazine of his rifle and called sharply.

"Hey! Kabakwe!"

The bull wheeled to face him. Peered across his massive tusks at the warden. Harry could almost read disbelief on his face. What, another one? Spoke again, his voice level, now that he had the elephant's attention.

"Go on with you. Move off. I reckon you've done him some serious damage, which is fine with me. Nothing at all wrong with that. But leave it at that, don't take things out on me. I'm on your side, remember?"

The elephant stood tall. One massive front foot lifted, swung back and forth in indecision. A long, low growl reverberated from deep in his throat.

"Sure. I know. But just bugger off. *Please.* The rains have come and there will be lots of good things to eat. You're pretty smart, aren't you? You knew the rains were close. Which is why you moved up here."

Harry kept his voice conversational, watching the bull across his FN. Wished Kashili was here, to see Kabakwe at such close quarters. The animal moved his head to the left, swung it back to the right, his gaze staying riveted upon the man standing in front of him. The warden could see his long eyelashes, and the fresh chip out of his left tusk. No blood anywhere. Good.

"Go on, there's a good chap. Just mosey along out of here and let me finish this business. You've done your bit. We've known each other an awfully long time, you and I. I would hate this to end in tragedy. Okay?"

Kabakwe wheeled slowly, swung his immense bulk away, still watching Harry. Began to move, reluctantly, still making a show of it, letting the warden know he was not sure he was doing the right thing. Well done, Kabakwe! Thank you, sir. You're the only one left, so it would have been terrible if I'd had to shoot you. He stood motionless, watching the elephant

465

out of sight, seeing the bush tremble with the great bull's passing. Checked his FN briefly, then, and moved in.

He found him close to the stream. Stood for a long while watching him, absorbing the shock that had percolated through him. The way he was lying had to mean that his back, at least, was broken. It was hard to say what else, there was so much blood. Harry knelt beside him and moved the FN away, saw where he had shot him. Good. Checked for other weapons, removing a knife and a revolver. Felt then for the pulse in his neck. Found it, fluttering. Moved back to sit on a rock, keeping his FN pointed loosely in his direction. Unsnapped a water bottle to have a drink, squinting up at the sky as he did so. It was hard to tell the time, with the clouds, but he guessed it was sometime after midday. When he looked back, his eyes, one anyway, was open. Watching him.

Harry raised the water bottle.

"Cheers. I thought I'd killed you."

Scratch Peters blinked. One blue eye glared out of the blood at him. His mouth worked. It took a while for the words to come, and they were a strained whisper when they did.

"Flak jacket. You just knocked me over. When the pilot decided he was coming back, I made him drop me first."

A faint ironic smile wrinkled his lips.

"Reckon you've got me now, though."

Harry looked woodenly at him.

"Wish I had killed you then, you bastard. Before you killed Kashili. Before you had your second crack at Marula."

"Marula?"

"The elephant you almost shot from the chopper. Which you killed along with Kashili."

Scratch Peters winced at some sudden spasm. Squeezed his eye shut. Harry waited for it to open. When it did, asked.

"Why, Scratch?"

The eye met his.

"Because you're a fucking nuisance. Because you got in our way. Because you made other people get in our way. We should have taken you out long ago. When you killed Gant. Long before you got to Gona re Zhou and stirred up things there. You were lucky, I thought I'd topped you on the road to Chipinda. But it was some other bloody zoo keeper."

Harry grimaced, felt like using the FN on him then.

"And Gordon Holmes? Did you kill him as well?"

A faint nod.

"Sure. He was starting to get delusions of grandeur ... needed to be taught a lesson. So I took him for a ride. He ... ahhh ..."

Peters lapsed into agonised silence. Harry waited a few seconds, feeling his questions build up. Then.

"How long have you been killing elephants, Scratch?"

Peters' eye had closed again, whilst he licked dry lips. Stayed closed. Harry reached over with his weapon and prodded the man's face with the muzzle.

"Scratch."

His eye opened.

"Forever. Years. Long story."

The whisper more ragged now, his eye flinching with the pain. Harry felt nothing, shook his head.

"You were one of the blue-eyed boys of the military. An officer in the Selous Scouts, the SAS, and whatever outfit you were in after that. Malaya, the Tracker Combat Unit, and everything in between. Medals. With a future anywhere in the world. What made you get into the ivory racket, for God's sake?"

"Because I knew we were fucked, long ago. The white man is finished in Africa. We're on borrowed time, so I figured to cash in on my pension sooner than later. Join in the rape. Everyone's in on it, Harry, the ivory racket. The South Africans are the whizz kids at moving it, the military especially. With our liaison over the years there are channels all over

Africa. All heading south. It was so easy, especially with the frozen areas."

Harry was shaking his head again, could feel the depression mixing with the anger.

"Everyone? The whole military system?"

Peters smiled, his gaze moving from Harry to stare at something only he could see.

"Huh-uh. Don't be daft. The more people involved, the more the leaks and less the return. There's twelve of us, 'The Dirty Dozen'. We run the scene in Rhodesia, with the support of the South Africans. All roads lead to Johannesburg, Harry."

Harry eyed him dispassionately. Saw again the groups of dead elephants in Gona re Zhou and here in Nemana. Malaya filtered through his mind. He could see the rise and fall of the wounded man's chest, saw that the breathing was erratic. The eye had closed again, and his face was screwed up against the pain.

"Scratch."

Nothing but the breathing and the face screwed up in pain.

"Scratch."

The eye fastened back on his again.

"What?"

Harry ran his eyes the length of the battered body and then met the one-eyed stare.

"You know it's the end of the line, don't you? You're going to die here."

Scratch Peters managed to grin.

"So?"

"You want to tell me some more about it?"

"No."

"I'll make you a deal. Tell me some names, give me some details, and I'll be happy to do the honours. Put you down quickly. Which is more than you deserve. You're going to hurt a lot before you die from the wounds. What do you say?"

"Fuck you."

The voice a whisper that Harry could hardly hear. He grinned, making his expression non-committal, looking into the man's staring eye. Knew it hadn't worked, because he saw his own hatred mirrored in that hard blue eye. Shrugged.

"Remember the barracks at Johore, Scratch? There was that sign on Hugo Winters' desk that used to give us all a giggle. Funny how it's only just come back to me. 'Death is nature's way of telling you you fucked up.' Well, I reckon that's you all right."

The blue eye blazed. Harry stood up, collected Peters' weapons together. Gave him a long sardonic grin.

"I hope it hurts like hell, Scratch. I hope you die screaming. I'm always pleased to hear about pseudo-hunters being killed by elephants. It restores my faith in Africa."

In Salisbury, on this twelfth day of December 1979, as Harry Kenyon took his leave of Scratch Peters, history was being made. At fourteen minutes after two that afternoon the concourse of Salisbury Airport echoed with the announcement that *The Royal Air Force wish to announce the arrival of Ascot 1175 from London Heathrow'* and up on the main terminal balcony a small group of sombre-faced citizenry watched the Royal Air Force VC 10 trundle in from the runway to stop with precision before a gathering of journalists, politicians, an honour guard and a brass band. The Air Rhodesia steps that were wheeled into place alongside the RAF jet looked incongruous somehow. The newly appointed governor of the country, in a blue lounge suite, took only a short time to go through the welcome proceedings and depart the area in his imported Daimler. On the balcony Sir Humphrey Gibbs, the last governor of Rhodesia, wiped a tear from his eye, as, up in the green-glassed control tower, the special sniper team relaxed. No one had tried to kill Lord Soames or any of his entourage. Peta Kenyon thought with some disappointment what an anti-climax it had all been, and hurried for the car as the rain, which had only just held off for the historic occasion, started falling gently. As she

469

drove back into the city she looked forward to seeing her father again. He had, somehow, managed to locate her in Salisbury, leaving a message at the Claytons, saying he was in town for a short while and would be delighted to take Mr and Mrs Kenyon to dinner. She wondered how he was, in fact, her husband. Gave a small prayer, stopped in the rain at the traffic lights, for him to be all right.

Warden Harry Kenyon paused, then shook his head. Retraced his steps back to where Scratch Peters lay. Unlimbered the man's revolver and cocked it. At the sound the soldier opened his eye. Stared up. Harry gave him a brief mirthless smile.
"I made that mistake before, thinking you were dead. Don't want to make the same mistake again. Say hello to Gant when you see him in hell."
He lowered the handgun and fired one shot. Then he tossed the gun into the stream, turned and made his way up out of the ravine, seeing again Kabakwe's tracks. The cloud was still lowslung over the escarpment, and there was a cool gusting breeze. No thermals today, for the vultures, *makhoti*, to get up into the sky, he thought. Pity really, with that nice piece of carrion back there by the stream. He thought he would stop a little later, and have his can of peaches. In celebration, sort of.

CHAPTER FORTY-FOUR

Jack Dent's Trio swung into *In The Mood* and they left the dance floor, both ignoring the scrutiny and the not quite *sotto voce* comments of the journalists who held court at a table near them. Peta flashed a smile at her father as he held her chair out for her, moving adroitly ahead of their attendant waiter. She watched him as he seated himself. He really hasn't aged, she thought. He looks jolly good for someone who's just topped sixty. That's something he and Harry have in common, holding their age well. And that's not all they have in common, if one cares to roll back the years a little. Which we won't dwell on right at the moment. He caught her look, raised an eyebrow.

"Yes?"

She smiled again.

"I was thinking how well you're looking, Dad."

"Thank you, daughter dear. It's the clean life I lead. Along with the thirty cigarettes a day, decent whisky, and never eating anything but fruit before midday."

Peta Kenyon met his eyes with hers.

"How come you've never married again? Mum has been gone such a long time."

He raised his eyebrows and shook his head slowly back and forth.

"I never thought that I had given of my best, with Monica. Always away, playing games here and there for Queen and country. And for myself, of course. My lifestyle hasn't changed at all, so I would be subjecting someone to the same thing all over again. And Monica would be a hard act for anyone to follow. Besides, with the liberalisation of attitudes these days, I'm not sure one has to be married."

The maitre d' had been hovering unobtrusively, moved now to Sir Courteney Hutton's elbow.

"A refill, Sir Courteney? Perhaps some port at this stage? We do have some of your favourite."

Her father grinned amiably.

"Thank you, Albert, a last whisky, please. Peta?"

"I'll stay with gin and tonic. I've caught the gin habit from Harry."

The man inclined his head politely and moved away.

"They seem to know you well," Peta observed.

"They would do, I suppose. I've been staying at Meikles off and on for donkey's years. It's so civilised. Makes any visit to Salisbury an absolute pleasure. Let's hope the same applies when the city becomes Harare."

Peta put an elbow on the table and rested her chin on her hand. "Do you know, I don't have a clue as to what you really do, to earn the Queen's shilling. All these years, with you all over the place, popping up here and there. What did you do to earn the 'Sir'? I'm sure it wasn't for writing any pop songs. What do you do, in fact?"

Sir Courteney Hutton leaned back in his chair, smiled around the cigarette he had just lit.

"Don't you know you should never ask a politician a direct question. It's liable to give the old pacemaker a vapour lock. However, as a businessman I will give you an answer. I am on quite a few boards, around the globe. Advisory stuff, mostly. The most time consuming is Hutrhon Limited, of which I am chairman and principal shareholder. It dabbles in a bit of everything, agriculture, mining, import, export, major construction work, earth-moving equipment, you name it. Even hotels. We've tried to buy Meikles. Hutrhon is principally involved in the Third World and the Pacific rim. As far as politics goes, I'm rather a rare animal, in that I do it more as a hobby. To complement my business, to be frank. I have no aspirations to Ten Downing Street, or anything like that, and, anyway, I'm probably a little too difficult to label to get the nod for very high office. I'm probably best described as a left leaning Conservative, which makes me welcome in both camps. It's a bonus, because it means I'm not too easy to manipulate, which is the bedrock of politics. I have the ear of very powerful people, and my forte is behind-the-scenes lobbying. Very shadow secretary type of stuff."

He paused to take a measured sip of whisky.

"That's it in a nutshell. It gets oh-so-boring if I go into any details."

Peta eyed him speculatively.

"And Rhodesia? Which hat are you wearing here at the moment?"

Her father chuckled.

"Both actually. I know Christopher Soames personally, and will be going fishing with him up on Lake Kariba, where we will have some time for a quiet chat. I've also got rather a lot on my plate with regard to Hutrhon. These are delicate times in this part of the world, and it isn't easy keeping one's finger on the current pulse."

Hutton leaned forward and looked his daughter in the eye.

"Let's talk about you, Peta. *Mrs Kenyon.* When do I get to meet the famous game warden? It's long overdue, I feel."

Peta grinned.

"Soon, I hope. Garnet Clayton said he spoke with Harry on the radio today, and that he intends coming up in the next couple of days. I can't tell you what a relief it was to hear that he was all right."

"Why? Is something wrong?"

Peta sighed and gave a rueful smile, running a hand through her hair.

"No. Not now, anyway. There have been some horrid things happening down in Nemana, and he had some business to attend to that was very dangerous." *How do you tell your father that your husband has been out in the bush hunting down a man in order to kill him?* "I've been worried sick about him. But, it would seem all is well."

Her smile changed, became whimsical.

"I hope you do get to meet him. He's very special, and I love him very much. He's a bit of a dinosaur in some ways, so progressive in others. I don't know if there's a patron saint of wildlife, but if there is, it should be Saint Harry. I call him my warrior saint. He's forever lowering the drawbridge and charging out to do battle with anyone who wants to harm his animals. Especially his elephants."

She paused and shook her head once, softly, fondly. Looked at her father.

"He ruffles a few feathers, Dad. No doubt about that. He's a paradox, really. Africa's wildlife needs a person like him to stand up for it. On the other hand, I sometimes wonder, *worry,* if Africa has grown out of people like him. Moved on, so to speak, without him."

Sir Courteney Hutton drew in a long breath, nodding, keeping eye contact with her. His voice was quietly earnest, when he spoke next.

"Peta, are you sure you want to be here, in this country, at the moment? I ask this because things are a little obscure right now, and my sources tell me that it could get bloody here soon. Lancaster House is still dragging on, but the end result is certain. There will be elections, and they might not give the result that people are hoping for. Why don't you take a break and stay out of the country until things are more cut and dried? This isn't the politician or the businessman talking, it's your father. I know we haven't seen much of each other over the years, but I very much hope that will change. I need to make up some lost time with you."

"And Harry?"

Hutton looked at her steadily, thinking how much like her mother she looked now. Smiled at the thought.

"Ah, Harry. I don't know anything about this man who has captured my only daughter's heart, who I suspect has been the inspiration behind the wonderful stuff she has written and photographed about Africa. And I would never presume to meddle in your affairs. But I would like to say this, and I would have liked to say it to both of you. If your situation here in this country should ever become untenable, I would be happy to unconditionally pull any strings required to help you. And I would find a place for Harry that is worthy of him, somewhere in my business ranks. I'm sure there would be room for a decorated ex SAS soldier and game warden of the most beautiful game park in Africa."

Peta reached across the table and took hold of his hand, squeezed it as she looked away, down out of the window of the restaurant. It was a soft, blanket-like night outside, with a gentle rain causing the lights of the city to reflect off the wet tarmac, as did headlights of cars going silently down Stanley

Avenue, past the dark shrouded gardens of Cecil Square. The relentless heat of the valley was hard to recall, and she wondered if it had rained there yet. Could almost taste the wet-earth smell of the first valley rains. Thought about Kashili. And Harry, hoping he was on his way. Looked back at her father, eventually, pausing, so that she got the words right.

"Thank you. I'll say that for both Harry and myself. I don't know what the future holds for us here. Neither does he, anymore, I suspect. For him the valley, Nemana, is everything, and he has fought so hard to protect it. But there is no doubt that his, our, time is limited now. We've been lucky to have remained there so long. He's been dodging promotion, because that means leaving Nemana. But it has to catch up, sometime. Then, of course, we have unfolding history, whichever way things go. And I don't know where Warden Harry Kenyon fits into the brave, new world. You know, Dad, he has this idea of parallel civilisations. It has to do with the quality and respect of living things ... all things ... termite mounds and baobabs and elephants and snakes and humans. Learning to love the scorpion as much as the butterfly. All pretty much down to earth. But life, Africa, is not that simple any more. Churchill said something that has always stuck in my mind. 'This is not the end. It is not even the beginning of the end. But it is perhaps the end of the beginning.' What do you think, Dad?"

Sir Courteney Hutton smiled wanly.

"If I knew the answer to that, Peta dear, I wouldn't count so many bloody sheep at night. And I'll quote you something, not as profound, but very well suited to Africa. 'In the land of the blind, the one-eyed man is king.'"

The Jack Dent Trio was easing its way through a particularly melancholic version of *Moon River*. Peta's thoughts were up there on another river, where it swelled to be a huge new lake, twenty years ago. On a night when soldier ants had invaded the tent she and her mother were sharing, biting them horribly. And a young game ranger scraping them from her naked young girl's body in the starlight with his knife. Watching the girl and

her mother unfathomably afterwards. Ahh yes, Harry Kenyon,
you left your mark. No doubt about it.

~ PART FIVE ~

Summer 1980

"The past is another country,
They do things differently there."

THE GO-BETWEEN by L P Hartley

CHAPTER FORTY-FIVE

Provincial Warden Harry Kenyon gazed at the tusk on his office wall. Had been doing so for many minutes. Another office this. Not the one he was used to, with the view of the river through the open doorway and the escarpment blue-hazed and ethereal in the distance. His new office, paradoxically, was smaller, as his position was now higher, with the red polished verandah outside and the rectangle of lawn, in the centre of which stood a bird bath. In this country with a new name and government, Harry Kenyon with a new base and new duties to match his promotion. At least it's not Salisbury, he thought, his eyes still on the tusk. You were spared that, being buried in the warren of headquarters, with the palliative drinks in the .470 at the end of each day, before wombling your way out into suburbia. Thank you, God. Sinoia is a pleasant little town, and you are still out of the mainstream. You were lucky that the post of Provincial Warden for this region was free, with the resignations. Nemana is still under your jurisdiction, so you still get to visit the place. If you can keep the increased paperwork at bay, that is. And Peta has somewhere peaceful to work on her book. So count your blessings, Kenyon. Someone up there still likes you. From outside he heard a cock crow stridently, winced at the sound, the incongruity of it.

Rhodesia dead and buried. Zimbabwe the latest name on the maps, with official independence less than a year away. The result of the elections had left no doubt as to who was now in the driver's seat. Operation *Quartz* had been stillborn, getting no further than the nudge and wink stage, and the cease-fire monitoring force had dispersed. The bobbies were already back on their beats in England, as was Lord Soames, who had eventually, with a little help from new-found friends, managed to shoot his buffalo. The tone of the prime minister elect, in his radio and television broadcast on 4 March 1980, had been one of moderation. It was surely time, he intoned, to beat swords into ploughshares. The optimism generated by his conciliatory outlook made for balmy days and starry nights ahead, in place of the civil war that had ravaged the country. Harry Kenyon, now a rung up the ladder in the ranks of the Department of National Parks and Wildlife Management, wondered if it was time to uncross fingers, to let out the breath that had been so long held. Because it looked as if, contrary to some pessimistic opinion, things were going to actually work. That he could get on with the normal duties of a game warden, and not freeze at the sound of distant gunfire and low-flying helicopters. There was even talk of Nemana National Park being re-opened to the public, once a final check of the landmine situation had been made.

The white pages of the memorandum of agreement made a stark contrast against the polished teak of the boardroom table. The six men gathered around it looked expectantly at each other, the temporary silence almost as thick as the cigarette smoke that clouded the room after four hours of final discussion. Outside the tinted glass windows of the skyscraper the city of Salisbury went about its business under a clear, blue sky. The distant wailing of sirens just reached the ears of those in the room, for a few moments competing with the crows outside on the high window ledges. Sir Courteney Hutton bestowed a smile on the two visitors from Zambia.
"Would you care to sign first, gentlemen? I'm sure your Zimbabwean colleagues would be happy to accord you that honour. I will sign on behalf of Hutrhon last. Then, I think, a small celebration would be the order of the day."
As the executives of the Zambezi River Authority went about their signatures, the Englishman gazed over their heads out of the window. One of the crows was pecking at its reflection in the glass, feathers raised in anger. Another held station near it, waiting its turn at the reflection. Is that symbolic, Hutton contemplated, the gathering of the crows? No, I think not.

Not yet, at least. I must say today has gone remarkably well. So it should, after all this time. All the months of meetings here and in Lusaka, all the junkets. But we've got it now. We have the go-ahead to bring in the surveyors and the geologists. They have had it soft, long ago contracted and sitting on the sidelines twiddling their thumbs, while I hammered the agreement out. Now they can go in and earn their wages, get the show on the road. The sooner the core samples are analysed, the sooner we know if we are in business.

The forms had been pushed across to him and he signed his way through them quickly. Capped his pen with a small flourish afterwards, beaming around at the small group. "A red-letter day, gentlemen. Now, allow me to take you to lunch, and to sample some rather good champagne I brought in for the occasion. It's from a small vineyard near Reims, in which I happen to have a few shares. Perfect for a toast to the Mupata Dam Project in the Zambezi Valley."

CHAPTER FORTY-SIX

Holiday euphoria once again echoed through Shingela tourist camp. Nemana had been opened in time for the last three months of the season, and already there were visitors out and about in the Park. Facilities were still Spartan, and there was much to do, shaking the mothballs out of a place that had been closed to the public for over seven years. Harry paused in his conversation with the senior ranger now in charge of the station to watch a trio of children clasping fishing poles trudge across the sand from the river. It was nice to see people enjoying the place again, he thought, not for the first time on their visit down to Nemana.

He and Peta had visited the place where Kashili was buried, noting with pleasure where elephants had used the driftwood atop his otherwise unmarked grave as a rubbing post.

They had stood silently, both remembering the day almost a year ago when the old tracker had been shot. Had strolled slowly back across the flood plain to Shingela. The bungalow that had been Harry's for so many years, to be shared with Peta, was now the domain of the resident senior ranger. They had pitched tent between the headquarters and the camp site, and walked along the riverbank to where they used to feed Methuselah. Harry had whistled and scanned the surface of the backwater, but there had been no sign of the giant vundu. Some tourists had noticed them and walked across, asked eventually what they were doing. He had smiled and explained that they were calling a fish, and received strange looks.

In the night, as if to welcome them back, there had been fine lion music echoing over the river, and under an almost full moon they had watched a rhino trundle past their tent, down on to the sand bank. Elephants had browsed around them all night, shaking the acacia trees, and Harry had had to get up once and dissuade a honey badger from its purloining of their safari trunk. He had risen long before dawn and sat in his camp chair on the high river bank, listening to the night sounds slowly give way to the day chorus. The sun had come up out of the river in its customary splendour and African skimmers had drawn lines across its calm surface. He did not hear any shots from across the river, just the hippos and the rest of the early day river music. Which was, he thought, so therapeutic to hear, after the roosters at Sinoia headquarters. When they drove back, weathering once again the hard corrugated dirt road to the main tar highway, it seemed strange not to be looking for the disturbed earth that could mean a landmine. Not to be watching the bush for signs of an ambush. And it was not the same, not having Kashili with them.

Bad news does not always come with the jangle of the telephone in the dead of night, just as hell is not necessarily as it is described by Dante. For Harry, both came without fanfare, secreted in one of the department's buff-coloured envelopes, typed routinely upon the coarse dirty-white governmental paper. When he had read it, he stared unseeingly at the firefinches and mannikins that sported in the bird bath, feeling that his breathing had changed and that a pain had lodged itself solidly just under his heart. He thought that if he were to stand up and walk to the door, he would not make it. So, he said to himself, it never ends. You think you have stopped it, but you haven't. You think you have scotched the evil, but it appears somewhere else. Like Medusa's heads. Ahh … He picked up the letter and re-read the bulk of it.

"This office has been advised by the Zambezi River Authority that preliminary geological exploration has commenced in the Mupata Gorge. This is in keeping with original plans to construct three new hydro-electric schemes on the Zambezi River, and is a continuation of the survey process first initiated in 1953 by the relevant bodies in then Northern and Southern Rhodesia. It is considered that the Mupata Gorge site will prove to be the most economical of the dam sites to develop, providing the required 500 MW that are needed to boost the national grid, and thus meet the increased power requirements of Zimbabwe. Core samples have been extracted and processed in London and we are advised that the information attained from these samples meets with required parameters, setting in place the next phase of the geological work to be initiated.

This Department has been advised to give consideration to the possible effects of the flooding of the dam on the wild animal populations. It is thought that if hunting may be permitted within Nemana National Park, to the same degree as the adjacent Safari Areas, the effect would be to push the larger animals back to the escarpment foothills. This, in conjunction with a major capture and translocation exercise, would go some considerable way to lessening the impact of the planned inundation on the wildlife of the region.

The Provincial Warden of Mashonaland North is required to report to Salisbury Headquarters on the date given to put forward his views on this subject. Needless to say that this development is viewed with considerable alarm by the Department, the ramifications of which, for the Middle Zambezi Valley region, are radical and far reaching."

How, he asked himself. How did they get in there and set up shop so easily and so quietly? Without the department hearing about it? *Who?* How is it that things are so far along, yet the first I hear about it is when questions are being asked on how to sort out the wildlife? So sorry, elephants, so sorry lions, pardon me waterbuck, but move along now. Get the hell out of this nice, fertile, unique, vitally important flood plain, because we want to drown another, *another*, part of the Zambezi Valley.

Oh dear, thought Harry Kenyon, I'm not sure I can take this.

Tea cups and cigarette butts, standard debris for the average meeting, and both well represented in the director's office this summer's day. Harry sat back and swept his eyes over the room again. It had changed little since he had last been in here, years ago. Not long after he had left his mark on the Ivory Section, and terminated Alex Gant's ivory dealings permanently. But a long while before Scratch Peters and his onslaught on the elephant populations of the country. Both of them gone, now, oh yes, helped on their way by yours truly. But how does one fight City Hall? He tuned back into the director's summary of the situation, caught the tail-end of it. Chief Warden Garnet Clayton nodding his agreement, his expression sombre.

"Harry?"

Dr Alistair Drummond was looking at him expectantly.

"Do you want to add anything more at this stage? As the department's senior field staff representative in the area where this development has arisen."

He shook his head.

"No." "Sir," he added.

Because we've said it all, been saying it all morning. With not much to show for it. Plenty of questions and precious few answers. Some facts as well. If the dam at Mupata Gorge goes up, there will be 130,000 hectares of water over the Zambezi Valley. No more Nemana, no more wilderness, no more animals. Add that to Kariba and Cabora Bassa and that's a horrible amount of valley drowned. Down the tubes. Down on that Nemana flood plain, in September and October, *right now*, before the rains break, there are some of the biggest concentrations of game animals to be seen anywhere in Africa. And they want us to can it. *Shoot it, move it or drown it.* Thank you and goodbye. We don't even know who is doing the exploratory work down at Mupata, for goodness sake! Drummond says all his contacts with government and the Zambezi Water Authority have gone silent. *No calls returned, no one home, who did you say you wanted?* Not today, thank you. So, all right then, if the shutters are down here, what say you that we start at the other end? Start knocking on a few tent poles. Let Garnet and Drummond continue with their efforts in civilisation, and you head for the valley. Because that is your home ground. That's where you belong. I wish Kashili was riding shotgun with me on this one.

CHAPTER FORTY-SEVEN

The geologists' camp on the edge of the Mwanje River, where it joined the Zambezi at the beginning of the Mupata Gorge, was well established and a hive of activity, even in the October heat. A kitchen and mess area had been sited where the view of the Zambezi was stunning. Half-a-dozen large safari-style tents formed a line along the river bank, with thatched ablution areas strategically placed in a shorter row behind them. Behind the camp stood workshops and a vehicle park close alongside a security fenced stores area, in the centre of which four metal quonset huts sent heat waves out. Harry could see that extensive use of mopane poles had been made.

The invasive thudding of a large generator echoed across the camp, and diesel fumes overloaded the valley air.

He let his Landrover idle slowly through the organised chaos that had become entrenched on the edge of the river he had loved all his life. He was in his own vehicle, as opposed to a Parks Landrover, and he wore ragged nondescript bush clothing. He looked relaxed, his expression only mildly curious as his eyes scanned his surroundings, guiding the vehicle slowly towards the mess area in separate splendour atop the river bank. He remembered the last time he and Kashili had camped here. They had had to make strategic withdrawals twice in the night because of the persistent attentions of various rhinos coming down to water. He wondered what the rhinos thought of this hubbub in their territory. Behind the kitchen area he noted a buffalo skull. Saw kudu horns also, and then a zebra skin pegged out to dry. Heigh ho, he thought, remember that you are not Provincial Warden Harry Kenyon today. You are Henry Stumblebum or Abner Thistleprick or whoever, sometime prospector and occasional elephant hunter, looking for a bit of company. He looked at the sun lowering towards the far side of the river. You've judged it just right, he reflected. The day's work should be almost done, it's tea or sundowner time, and it would be jolly rude to turn a passing stranger away at this time of day. Not bush etiquette at all. Just remember you've got to smile your way through this, Harry. Smile away and do the old soft shoe shuffle.

He parked behind the mess building and walked around to the front, meeting the curious stares of four men having tea. "Afternoon, gents. Hope I'm not intruding. I was passing through and thought I'd drop in and say hello. Don't see too many folks down in this neck of the woods."
Nods. Half smiles. Given cordially enough, if a little guarded. Appraising stares drifting over him. The man pouring the tea stood up, gestured with the brown enamel teapot.
"Come in out of the sun and have some tea. Can't say that we see many folks either. You're the first, in fact."

Harry entered the mess, nodded around at its occupants.

"Thanks. The name's Willie James."

The main speaker put the teapot down and held out a hand.

"Greetings. Jeff Swain. This is Vic, Ken and, the guy with the scruffy hat is Ian. Take a seat. Sugar in your tea?"

"Sure, thanks, three or nine."

"Sorry?"

Harry grinned.

"An old bush joke. Three if it's a mug, nine if it's an old jam tin."

Jeff Swain laughed.

"You say you're passing through? From where, going where, exactly? We are pretty much the end of the line here. There aren't many places a person can go, a fact we established a while ago. To the disappointment of some, I might add."

His voice was English and confident. Harry made his own casual.

"Anywhere. I'm prospecting down in the valley. Been doing it, off and on, for years."

"Prospecting for what?"

Harry shrugged noncommittally, the ever-wary prospector. Let his eyes slide away from the other's questioning stare.

"You name it. Gold, tantalite, garnets."

"And you make a living from it, Willie?"

Harry grinned.

"Sure. Enough to keep me in whisky and Paludrine, anyhow. I live off the land, shoot for the pot when necessary. Catch a few fish."

Jeff Swain nodded, looking at Harry, who thought it was time to throw out a few questions of his own. He didn't want the question and answer routine with Swain to get too well established.

"What about you chaps? This is some set-up you have here. You prospecting as well? Looking for oil or uranium maybe?"

He grinned engagingly.

Swain glanced at his companions before continuing with his role as spokesman.

"No, we're not mining. At least not here. We're doing the groundwork for a dam. Across the Mupata Gorge over there."

Harry whistled appreciatively.

"That's some project! How long have you been down here?"

"Since early this year, after the last rains."

Harry grunted his amazement.

"I don't envy you blokes being down here for any length of time. It's always hot as Hades and it's damn tough country to boot. How long will it take you to build the dam?"

"Once the final survey is done, which we hope to wrap up before the coming rainy season, and if the last geological samples sent back are up to scratch, the main work will start next year."

Harry let his face show he was impressed. Thought privately that he deserved an Oscar, the way his gut was churning. The way he was managing to keep himself under control.

"Sent back where?"

His voice only mildly curious, sliding the question in. Hoping to get the ball past the slips. Jeff Swain grinned, giving him a wink. No run.

"There."

Harry held up a hand, grinning also.

"Sorry, don't mean to pry."

He looked out at the river vista. *Bastards.*

"That's a hell of a lot of valley you're going to put underwater, I reckon. Including national park areas. Are they happy with that?"

He hoped it didn't show in his voice, the anger.

Swain shrugged dismissively.

"It's not our problem. We're just here to do a job. To get this particular show on the road. The company will have sorted that side out, I'm sure. And the dam has the backing of the government. So I can't see a few elephants and monkeys getting in the way of progress."

Harry finished his tea, nodding his agreement. Made his voice bright and tried again.

"Maybe they'll need someone to shoot fresh rations, once you're properly dug in here. It's one of the things I do. Did it for Impresit when Kariba was going up. I see you've shot yourself some already. Wouldn't leave the trophies around where some zoo keeper from Parks could see them, by the way."

Swain's laughter, joined by the others guffawing.

"Can't say we're too worried about that. We've got a lot of big guns on our side, in more ways than one."

Damn you and your big guns. His cup still empty. No attempt being made to refill it. Such were the small signs starting to show. Thought it was time to push a little, in case the old heave-ho was coming.

"Any idea who I would speak to in your outfit, to see if I could get some work supplying rations. It's one of the things I'm good at, the shooting business."

Yes indeed. Trust me on that one.

Swain shook his head.

"Not really, Willie. It's early days yet, and at this stage we shoot our own. Sorry."

Harry shrugged his acceptance of the rebuff.

"No sweat. Maybe you'd be good enough to give me the name of the company, so I can make contact with them later, when the time is more suitable. Or," he added as an obvious afterthought, "I can leave you my contact address."

Jeff Swain shook his head again, and made a point of looking at the early sunset.

"I'm afraid that's confidential information, which we are not at liberty to disclose at this stage. The company is very security conscious. In fact we are not supposed to allow any person to set foot in here. Not that that is a problem. This part of the Zambezi Valley is as remote as Mars." He paused. Then. "I know it sounds rude, but there's enough time left for you to find yourself a camp for the night."

Harry made a moue of disappointment, which was genuine enough.

"Okay. Sorry we can't chat some more. A chap gets sick of talking to himself over the fire at night. I was going to say that I had some of the best biltong you'll ever taste in Africa, and a bottle of Jameson, as my contribution to a bush party. But, not to worry, I'll move on."

He stood up, nodding amiably at the four of them.

"Hope you guys are taking your malaria *muti* regularly. It's pretty damn bad down here."

He eased his way outside, his eyes flicking over the mess area as he moved through it. Stood for a moment when he had made his exit, staring out over the river. Whistled softly.

"It's a hell of a view," he said.

Which you intend to spoil. You bastards want to build a bloody wall across the gorge and drown all this. Can't let a few elephants and monkeys get in the way of progress. He threw a half salute.

"Take care now."

They did not accompany him to his vehicle. He used up a minute to kick his way around the four tyres, checking their pressure, looking over the camp. Smoke drifted from the cooking fires of the labour force, the smell of it pleasant in his nostrils. Mopane, he said silently. They sure have made themselves at home with the mopane trees. Not to mention the shooting. So, what now, Harry? He grunted sourly and climbed up into the Landrover.

"Willie ..."

Jeff Swain stood by the thatched half-wall of the mess, his grin sitting awry.

"The guys tell me I've been a little churlish in my behaviour. For which, I apologise. It's only because our necks are on the block if we allow any kind of media people in here. I'm a little cautious, because I'm the head honcho on this part of the project. Grab your gear and I'll show you to our guest tent. There'll be hot water laid on for you in a few minutes. Don't worry about the biltong, we have some pretty good venison ourselves. The Irish wouldn't be amiss, for a couple of after-dinner drinks."

Hippo talk echoed back and forth across the darkened river. From the north bank a hyena called regularly, giving them a good part of its repertoire. They sat outside after the meal, the whisky bottle passing companionably between them. Harry had not asked any more questions, was happy to pick up any information in the general conversation, for the time being. Which had been varied and flowing. The men were good company, and, Harry realised, were all good at their particular jobs, were proud of it, and had been picked for the Mupata project because of that fact. They had all worked on large construction projects in different parts of the world, though this was their first dam. He supposed that, under different circumstances, he would have enjoyed their company more. Could not, here. Not with the dam hanging like the sword of Damocles over the valley. He raised his head, listening intently. Jeff Swain noticed.

"Something wrong, Willie?"

Harry shook his head, pointing a finger downriver.

"Hear that? That long, low moan? Pels fishing owl. I'm surprised there's any still around, with all the brouhaha here. They're shy birds and usually move on at the least disturbance. Haven't heard one for quite a long while."

The one he knew as Ken grunted.

"We've been wondering what the sound was. You sure as hell know the bush, Willie. How did you get to be so knowledgeable?"

Harry grinned. Careful, he thought. Let's not be too smartass about this.

"I've been in it all my life, doing one thing and another. Prospecting, hunting, shooting crocodiles, poaching the occasional elephant, taking out the occasional safari. You name it, I've done it. Jack of all trades, that's me."

"You've been an elephant poacher?" Jeff looking at him across the glare of the gas light. "Where? Down here?"
"Here and there. Different parts of Africa."
Harry, the sometime poacher, suitably vague.
"We've been told we can shoot for rations, and maybe sneak the occasional trophy, but we were told that under no circumstances were we to shoot an elephant. They are taboo. Seems there's some prickly colonial type who is the warden of this bit of real estate, based further up-river, who goes bananas if anyone with a gun goes anywhere near his elephants."
"Yes?"
Harry kept his voice mildly interested. The man called Vic chuckled.
"Yeah. We were told in no uncertain terms by our boss not to incur the displeasure of this bloke. Seems he has spies all over the place, and descends like the wrath of God on anyone who has a bash at his elephants."
Harry managed a soft laugh.
"Who is this guy?"
"Can't remember. Got his name written down on file somewhere."
"It's probably old Harry Kenyon," said Harry Kenyon. "He's been around forever. He can be a really awkward bastard. Thinks he owns the valley."
"Yeah, that's his name," said Vic.
Jeff nodded his agreement, pouring himself a whiskey.
"Your boss told you not to shoot any jumbo because of Kenyon? When you've got the big guns of this," he waved a hand in the direction of the gorge, "behind you. Strange that."
Harry's surprise was genuine.
"Sure. But ours not to reason why."
Swain shook his head dismissively and stared out through the night at the river.
"So Mr Kenyon thinks he owns the valley, does he?" he said, his voice quietly sardonic. "Well, he doesn't any more."
He raised his glass in the direction of the gorge.

"Because my boss does. Hutrhon Limited. That's privileged information Willie, like I said earlier."

The picnic, on a high rock beside the river, was, Harry considered, a five-star affair. By any standards. The white linen tablecloths fluttered fitfully in the breeze, kept in place by the impressive array of food on them. How did they manage with the hot buttered asparagus, he wondered. Out here? It was a pity about the guest list, though. That left a lot to be desired, my sainted aunt, but it did. He wondered what had prompted Peta to invite them, kept trying to get her attention. Could not, because she was taking pictures. He kept seeing her eye, smoky-blue, peering disembodied out from the lens of her Nikon, it taking the place of the lens itself. Saw, at the same time, the person she was photographing, the subject frozen, as if already in a photograph, laughing. Always laughing. The camera clicks sounded like explosions, and Harry flinched every time another picture was taken. Like gunfire, he suddenly realised. He wondered if perhaps he was drunk, because everything was floating along in slow motion, just as it did when he was on a cull or when the adrenalin of sudden action was coursing through his veins. Realised that he could not be drunk, not sipping tea out of these nice silver goblets. What the hell are they doing here? Where is Peta? Why did she have to invite these bastards? Alex Gant laughing. *Click!* Scratch Peters laughing. *Click!* The passing parade of waiters, who were all Frenchmen, laughing. *Click! Click! Click!* He didn't know how he knew they were Frenchmen, it wasn't as if they were singing the Marseillaise or waving the Tricolour. But they were, all right. Bazooka Matiswa, laughing. *Click.* No! He'd had enough of this! If Peta wasn't going to do something about this, he would call Kashili. Where was Kashili? Harry tried to push his chair back. Could not. It was too, too heavy. And it hurt him to try, a pain spearing up through his gut into his heart, making him gasp. *Kashili, where are you, dammit?* Bring your spear and we'll sort these murderers out. Harry looked desperately around. Over the heads of the others he could see the river, except that it was not a river. Not the one he knew that curved towards them from the west in a long graceful sweep. Now it was swollen, grotesque, and very still. The uppermost branches of a baobab were thrust up out of the water, as if in supplication. A last wave before the dam claimed it. Harry tried to move again, still could not, burst out crying. *Click!* Harry waking, fighting with his sheets. Lying supine, panting, staring up through the darkness, feeling the sweat run. Listening to the fishing owl.

CHAPTER FORTY-EIGHT

He couldn't remember the last time he had had a bath. A full and proper hot bath. Months, years ago, most likely. In Salisbury, when he had met Peta off the plane from London, he calculated, when we stayed in the hotel waiting for Kashili. It has always been showers or bucket baths otherwise, all the years on the Parks bases, or in the army. Taking a bath actually took some getting used to, but if one was going to get into that habit, even this late in life, this was certainly a fine one to start with. It was like a swimming pool on magnificent old brass claw legs. These thoughts trickled through Harry's mind as he felt himself begin to at last unwind under Peta's ministrations. Felt the knots untangling under her fingers, felt the soft insistent nudge of her breasts against his back as she worked on his shoulders.

It had been a long hot slog back up out of the valley, from Mupata Gorge. Made even harder with his Landrover being contrary, his hands collecting more and more oil and grease, his knuckles taking punishment amidst the vehicle's innards. The two days on the road had given him plenty of time to think, to weigh up the situation that now existed at the gorge. Nevertheless, he had not come up with any kind of solution, had got increasingly depressed the more he ruminated. Had never felt so helpless. He had reached Sinoia headquarters at last light today with the depression settled heavily upon him. Now he took another long pull of the gin and tonic that rested to hand on the edge of the bath. Felt it beginning to work, along with Peta's fingers. He watched the tiny grey tree frog, in its usual place hugging the edge of the bathroom cabinet above them. What to do, Fred the frog? he asked silently. Got any ideas? I'll listen to anyone. The frog as still as putty, a pulse tremoring faintly in its throat. Harry took another drink.

"When I went up against The Ivory Section, Gant, and then Scratch Peters, it was face to face business. It was personal in that I came to know who they were, whilst they certainly knew who I was. The lines were clearly drawn. This situation with the dam is something else again. Because it is government and high finance, the power game. And it's faceless. Unless a person decides to personalise it and consider the people at the very top as the figureheads, to be the ones who will atone for the dam's coming to pass. Which means, if I am going to try and stop this the best way I know how, that I target the president of the country and the head of this company, Hutrhon, whoever he is. It would seem that he sure as hell knows me, and where I stand, from the comments I heard at Mupata. Which would seem to give him an edge, so far."

Harry Kenyon was laying his cards out on the table. Looking for options. Not many, not at the moment. Nothing new coming up out of the mist of ideas and permutations that had swirled about in his mind the whole of the two-day drive from Mupata.

"So, if I continue with the process, the process of elimination, you could say, that I started with Gant and Peters, I have to add new heads to the pile. Illustrious VIP heads this time. But where the hell does it stop? Remove them, and then do I clobber the next ones in line, when they fill the gap? Because if one is going to wage war, do it properly. Don't mess around.

This country had some of the best soldiers in the world, but they fought with their hands tied. They were never allowed to chop off the head of the snake, and keep chopping until there was no more snake. Not until the end, when it was too late, when the whole system was riddled to hell, penetrated, and the operations were being blown sky high.

"The trouble is, I think I've lost the touch. I'm getting too old for chopping heads off snakes."

He was on his fourth cup of black coffee, as they sat on the verandah with the lights off. Fireflies made moving pinpricks of light across the garden in front of them. Peta had sat silently, listening to him. Harry thought that she had been unusually quiet and ... distracted, almost, the whole evening. He reached out and ran a hand through her hair.

"You okay?"

She nodded.

"Yes. A little tired maybe. And as worried as you are about this dam."

He sighed.

"On a less radical note, it's obviously important to get some media interest in this. To expose it, call for impact assessment studies, get various wildlife bodies mobilised. To have the public ask questions, like why Mupata, ahead of other potential hydroelectric sites? Perhaps, with what you have already produced ... the articles on Nemana, the book, you could write something on the threat of the dam. They are all steps in the right direction. But I have a feeling it will take a lot more than that to stop this Hutrhon outfit, and government. It's time I found out about Hutrhon, seeing as they know so much about me. Time to do some research, treat it as an advance recce."

"And then what, Harry?"

Peta gave him a searching look.

"Do you go back into battle again? Do you lower the drawbridge and charge out with your lance raised and colours flying? Against the whole new government of this country?

Against some massive organisation that has offices all over the world? Is that on the cards, Harry Kenyon?"

He slumped in his chair.

"Have you any better suggestions? Because I'll listen to anything even vaguely worthwhile. I don't want to fight any more, Peta my love. I've had enough. But someone has to. To stop this, and stop it soon, before the whole damn thing has gathered too much momentum to stop. So, yes, if there is no other way, I'll go against the whole bloody world."

Peta was shaking her head slowly, a fond yet sad smile on her face as her eyes sought his through the darkness.

"Ahhh, Harry. My warrior knight. What am I going to do with you? Because I won't let you march out, not this time. Because it's too big, this battle. You're outnumbered. They will stop you. Or worse. This is City Hall, Harry. And you cannot fight it."

He shifted in his chair, restless with his frustration. Knew she was right. Knew also that he would not be able to sit by and watch the dam happen, could not, whatever the consequences. Harry Kenyon, caught between the devil and the deep blue sea. He took in a deep breath and then let it out slowly. Listened to the night, wishing he could hear something. Hyenas, hippos, lion music, anything. A barn owl screeched.

"There's something else ..." Her voice subdued now, making him study her face. "The chairman and the main shareholder of Hutrhon is Sir Courteney Hutton. My father, Harry."

He stared at her. A firefly passed between them, its pure green light illuminating their faces for a moment, showing the tense expressions on each of them.

"Your father is Hutrhon?"

She nodded.

"I thought he was in politics?"

"He is. It seems he mixes politics and business very nicely. He's on various boards other than Hutrhon, all over the world. I only learned about it in December, when he took me to

dinner. Would you believe it, thirty-something years old and only then finding out what your father does for a living." Harry gave a soft rueful laugh.
"So he knew about me, from you ... his daughter, my wife. I'm sorry I missed meeting him. Imagine having dinner with the man who's about to drown the Zambezi Valley."
"It's not as cut and dried as that, Harry, and you know it. It is a government decision, so if it wasn't Hutrhon it would be some other organisation."
He nodded, reluctantly.
"Sure. You're right, of course. If Hutrhon were to become excluded from the equation, there would be other companies lining up to fill the gap. As long as government and high finance are calling the shots, the dam will go ahead. And I really am not sure what I can do about anything."
Peta's turn to reach over and run her fingers through his hair.
"Come to bed, Harry. Let me see if I can take both our minds off this business."

She lay staring up through the dark, sleep evading her. Poor Harry, she thought. He takes all this so personally. Which makes a bad situation worse. Can you imagine the wall completed and that Godawful dam filling up, drowning Nemana and the rest of the valley? That whole fragile eco-system gone, all the animals gone, dear old Kashili buried under a brand, spanking new dam. Where would the elephants go? A bull like Kabakwe, carrying that size ivory, where would he go that is safe? Just so there will be extra power for so long, until the population catches up, which it surely will, look at Kenya, and then another solution has to be found. Another dam, another power station. Harry's right about publicity. That has to happen very soon. He's also right in saying it won't be enough. I wonder where father is now? The Honourable Sir Courteney Hutton? Honourable? I wonder if his offices in Salisbury would know where he is? Why do you ask, Peta Kenyon? Why the questions? Don't know, to be honest. Wish

I did. I'm pretty darn sure about the other thing, though. Which I haven't told Harry about, not yet. Will do, oh yes, when the time is right. When he hasn't got so much on his mind.

Mr Aubrey Buxton was urbane, pleasant and most efficient. Peta knew that within minutes of meeting him, realised at the same time that her father was unlikely to have anyone less working for him. The lemon tea had taken two minutes to appear, and she sipped at it now, as he addressed her.

"Mrs Kenyon, Sir Courteney left instructions with me some years ago that if ever I should become aware that you had any problems, I was to contact him immediately. That instruction was reiterated last December. So, yes, certainly I can ascertain from his London office where he is at the moment. I might add that we expect to see him here next week, should you feel that your business with him can wait that long."

Peta gave him one of her best door-opening smiles.

"Thank you, Mr Buxton, but I really would like to make contact with him sooner than next week. Of course, should you establish that he is in Outer Mongolia or somewhere up the Yangtze River, then please don't rock any boats."

A smile came and went, passing across his eyes rather than his lips.

"Of course. It may take a little time. Can I show you to the boardroom? And I'll organise some magazines, though they may not be very exciting ones."

Peta shook her head.

"I'll be across the road at Meikles. Shall I call back in, say, an hour, two hours?"

"If you tell me where you'll be, I will have someone call for you as soon as something is sorted out."

It had taken, in fact, less than an hour. Buxton had called for her personally, whisked her smoothly back up to the Hutrhon office suite. Sir Courteney, he said, was almost next door, as luck would have it. He was in Nairobi, and was standing by at The Norfolk for her call. Some more lemon tea? Perhaps with a pinch of cinnamon this time? You can use his office, right over here.

Her father's voice was anxious. So strange, she mused, after all this time. She assured him that she was fine.

"But, Dad, you've really managed to send a bolt from the blue. I don't know how you could let yourself be a part of something like that."

"What are you talking about, Peta?"

Caution in his voice, and something else.

"The dam, Dad. Mupata Gorge."

Silence on the line, except for a long distance whistle coming and going.

"What do you know about Mupata, Peta?"

"Just that Hutrhon have people working there. That they have been there for months. That between Hutrhon and the new government of Zimbabwe they plan to drown the Zambezi Valley, one of the last great wildlife regions in Africa. You may once have read about it in a book. A book called *Vanishing Eden*. It turned out to be a damn, excuse the pun, Dad, prophetic title, didn't it?"

She spoke the words slowly and deliberately, punching them down the line. Could hear his silence. Longer this time.

"How did you find out about Hutrhon?"

"It's a small country. It's Harry's job to know what happens in the valley. It's his parish, his own back yard. He's spent most of his life in the Zambezi Valley, Dad. Did you think he would not find out? Even without the Game Department telling him that they had been advised that geological survey work was already under way and that preliminary plans should be made to get rid of the wildlife in the region. Good God Almighty, Dad, how could you sit and give me the blarney you did when we last met, knowing all the time what you had planned for the valley, knowing what havoc you were going to wreak on Nemana?"

His response was swifter this time, no caution or anger now, in his voice. Something else again. She wished she knew him better, knew how to read his silences as well as his voice.

"When I last saw you there was nothing decided on Mupata. We were simply one of several companies who put in a bid for the work. No one knew when, if ever, a decision would be made about the dam. It's been on the cards for years, either there or somewhere else on the Zambezi. Unfolding history at the time made any plans or predictions a bit of a thumb-suck. Peta, it could just as easily have been one of the other companies who got the contract."

"But you got it! Sir Courteney Hutton of Hutrhon Limited managed to pull the deal off. Before the country has even got full independence, you've managed to get both feet in the door. How did you do it, Dad? That little fishing trip you spoke about up on Kariba, with the governor, was that where you mixed your bit of politics and business? Was that where you mixed one of your special Hutrhon cocktails? Is that shooting wild, or am I close?"

Despite the miles and the silence, she felt that she had hit home.

"Peta, I find this unsatisfactory, discussing such a subject over an open line. I had planned to be in Zimbabwe next week. However, it would seem a good idea to get there sooner. I'll re-schedule a few things here and have my aircraft made ready to leave first thing tomorrow. Will you meet me for dinner tomorrow night, at the same place?"

She had it pinned now. He sounded apprehensive. No doubt Sir Courteney Hutton was worried that his project was out of the bag too soon.

"So I can listen to more of your blarney, more tycoon double-speak? No, I don't think so, Dad. The only reason I went to the trouble of tracking you down and making this call was so I had a chance to tell you what a worm I think you are."

"Please be there, Peta. And please bring Harry. It isn't the most opportune time to finally meet him, but I would like to discuss this face-to-face."

"Harry is quite prepared to shoot you on sight, Sir Courteney Hutton. So am I, for that matter. Watch the press for details, by the way. We might not be able to stop you, but we will sure as hell show the world what a duplicitous bastard you are!"

Peta put the receiver back on its cradle and let out a long shuddering sigh. And that's that, I suppose. The lines drawn and the battle joined. She realised she was crying.

****

If I sold the tusk, would the money be enough to pay for a full-page advertisement in the likes of *National Geographic?* Harry ran his hand over the long curve of the ivory again. Perhaps with the other loot I have stashed, the blood money I made so long ago from shooting elephants and crocodiles, a small campaign could be financed. Use the money I got from the ivory way back to help the elephants and wildlife today. Seems a fair trade-off to me. At least it would get the ball rolling, initiate some kind of action. *Action?* Did the man say action? There is a box of goodies still hidden near a certain pan in the valley. In which there is an RPG 7 with rockets, a handful of automatic rifles with plenty of ammo. Enough for a private little war. A last stand. Now that's action, Harry Kenyon! Now you're talking sense. Fight fire with fire, it's the only thing the bastards will understand! What about unearthing that little treasure and making a safari to the bright lights? Yes, indeed. Carry out a little judicious culling there, commencing with one Courteney Hutton, forget the 'Sir', and whichever governmental types are tied up in this. Hell, start at the top, why don't you? Never mind the consequences, give the cat another goldfish. Thoughts skittered around his brain, flickering erratically, like a campfire in an errant river breeze. Harry Kenyon starting to go coldly and quietly berserk, beginning to turn on the 20th

Century. He began to pace his office. Five paces, turn. Five paces and a hand reaching out to touch the tusk again. Turn. He wondered where Peta was. She had been away in Salisbury for two days now, which was unusual for her. She was always keen to get out of the city. Hope she's all right, and gets back in time to come down to Nemana with me tomorrow. Five paces, turn.

He heard the vehicles whilst he was in the radio room. Heard them growling up the hill to the base as he listened to the end-of-day reports being sent. Monitored the messages for a few moments longer, jotting down notes for the day visit to Nemana on the morrow. Then he went out on to the verandah to meet Peta, wondering at the identity of the second car he had heard along with the Landrover. Stopped on the edge of the verandah, his gaze switching from her to the person climbing out of the Jaguar. Took in the knife-sharp creases on the green cotton-twill safari suit, the thick-soled boots and the splash of colour that was a scarf. Knew instinctively who it was. Did not want this, not at all. Saw the unease sitting heavily on the man, in his body language and in his eyes. Just as he saw the appeal in his wife's stare, knew what she was thinking. Please, Harry, don't do anything rash. *Like what, for instance? Shoot him, you mean?* Or just take him apart as he stands, right now, this instant.
He was speaking. Peta's father.
"How do you do, Courteney Hutton."
He held out his hand, stood thus. Harry nodded briefly at him, went past the man to help Peta with her bag. She was pale, he noticed, her eyes seeming even bluer against the pallor. Hutton's voice pursued him.
"I realise that I am probably public enemy number one, as far as you are concerned Mr Kenyon, and that I might be treading on dangerous ground. Peta left me in no doubt as to what to expect from you, and was most reluctant that I make this effort

to meet you. However, I believe in sorting out differences man-to-man, hence my presence here."

Harry stopped, switched his attention from Peta to him.

"How very noble of you, Hutton. What differences do you envisage 'sorting out'? Have you pulled your team out of Mupata, perhaps? Maybe you've taken this ride out into the country to tell me that the dam is no go, that the valley is no longer under threat. But I doubt it, somehow."

"I'm afraid that what is in place at Mupata Gorge is almost impossible to stop at this stage, for the simple reason that ..."

He paused, halted by Harry's upraised palm.

"Then you and I have nothing to talk about, Hutton. So I suggest you turn around, squeeze yourself back into your Jaguar and get out of my sight. Because I am already finding it very difficult not to ease over to you and re-arrange parts of your anatomy. You are not in one of your boardrooms here, and there is no captive audience hanging on your words. So get the hell out of here!"

Peta spoke then, her voice tired and unemotional.

"He insisted on seeing you, Harry. To talk. Which we did, a lot, last night. There's nothing to get excited or hopeful about, I'm afraid."

Harry studied her, concerned about her lack of colour.

"Never mind him," he said quietly. "I'm worried about you. You look terrible."

She forced a smile.

"I'm okay, really. It's just that so-called civilisation drains me almost as much as it does you, these days." She nodded at her father who stood silently now, watching them. "Plus there was a lot of acrimonious discussion last night, from my side mostly. I don't know why I decided to stay and see him. Sorry to land this on you out of a clear blue sky, lover, but he wore me down eventually, wanting to see you. One thing he said that was new, was that he was prepared to contribute a lot of money to a game rescue and translocation programme in Nemana. I told him to shove it, that you would probably do the same, perhaps physically."

Harry forced a smile at her before shaking his head.

"They have no idea, do they? The smooth men? They just do not realise what is at stake, how important that region is."

He uttered a soft curse, looked at Hutton again.

"Have you ever been down into that valley? Have you ever bothered to go to Nemana or its surrounding areas? Do you know what kind of wilderness you intend wiping out? Don't those considerations ever give you pause, in your ivory towers?"

The chairman of Hutrhon Limited met the hard, angry stare of the game warden.

"No, I have not been to that part of the Zambezi Valley. However, I did tell Peta last night that Hutrhon would fund a rescue mission for the wild animals ..."

Harry's brittle grin stopped him, and he eyed him warily. Saw the man's anger and disgust mirrored in his daughter's eyes. Winced inwardly at that. Stepped back a hurried pace when Harry suddenly closed the distance between them, thought for a moment that the violence he had seen swirling in the other man's eyes was about to erupt.

"You think that absolves you? Do you really believe absolution comes that easy, that cheap?"

Harry's voice had become ragged. Hutton saw that he was close to losing control. Wondered if he had been wise to push his daughter into bringing him out here. Several long seconds went past before Harry spoke again, his voice under control, at least.

"Tell you what, Hutton. You *should* see it. You *will* see it. You say you want to talk? Okay, we shall talk, but it will be in my boardroom. It's somewhat bigger than your one, I'd guess, though probably not as smart. But it has a hell of a view. For the time being, anyway. Tomorrow I have to go down to Nemana, on a day visit only, and I'm taking you along for the ride. So you can see what you have plans to destroy. Now, I want you to know that I consider a day, five minutes, in your

company as purgatory. But I'll do it, just this once. So that I can say I tried, later, when we draw the line in the sand."
Harry raised his eyebrows, flicked a wolf-smile on and off.
Because you should have one chance to change things. So I won't have to kill you.
Hutton stood, returning the warden's stare, not liking the corner he had been pushed into. Was aware of Peta's scrutiny. Nodded at last.
"Good," said Harry levelly. "It means an early start, well before sun-up tomorrow. There will just be you, Peta and me. For tonight I will have one of my staff show you the guest quarters, and a meal will be sent over to you later. I'm not sure I could handle a whole evening in your company, as well as a full day tomorrow, so please excuse me for now."

CHAPTER FORTY-NINE

The sun came up as they snaked their way slowly downwards around the curves and twists of the escarpment road. They had stopped at the first lay-by, as he had done a hundred times in the past, and watched the light change over the valley. Peta remembered when she had first stopped here, with Harry, on her way to Nemana for the first time. She found it as beautiful now as she had then, staring out over the grey-green ocean of bush that stretched away into infinity, the heat haze already forming despite the early hour. December again, with its accompanying humidity and little sign of rain, just distant puffs of cloud, like smoke, on the horizon. No hint yet of the summer squalls to come. She had a lump in her throat, which was not unusual. Peta had tried to capture the vista on film several times in the past, but had failed. It was just too big. She could see the baobabs, even from up here, and the elephant trails. They looked as if they had been there forever. She looked at her husband, knew he was thinking the same thing. Looked past him at her father, and wondered if it moved him at all. He was standing on the edge of the lay-by, the valley falling away at his feet. His face was expressionless.

The road to Nemana had been alive with animals. Near Chawoyo Gate they had had to wait for a rhino and her calf to give them the road, and at the gate itself a pride of nine lions had been resting in the riverbank shade, just a stone's throw away from the boom. Near them two elephants were digging resolutely in the sand of the riverbed. After, in the dry shadeless mopane belt, where few animals could survive at this time of year, a leopard sauntered across their front in the hot brightness of mid morning, paused to flick its tail at them, and moved on. Harry had smiled. Four of the Big Five, just on the way in, he mused. It's as if they're all putting on a special show for friend Hutton. He glanced past Peta at the man, noting that he seemed to be taking the heat and dust in his stride. The warden had been grudgingly impressed earlier, when he had found the Hutrhon chairman shaved and dressed at four, ready to go. One of Harry's yardsticks in judging people was how ready and well turned out they were at the start of a new day, whatever the hour. And he passed that test, he reflected now. If no others.

When they came down out of the mopane and the jesse on to the flood plain they had to detour around a herd of buffalo that had settled down for the hot hours. The animals stared at their vehicle with mild curiosity, made no attempt to move off. Harry studied them, letting his gaze sweep over the mass of dark forms. One of the summer aggregations, he judged. There's over a thousand of them. He eased the Landrover off the gravel road and swung away, giving the beasts plenty of room. When they regained the road, he flicked another glance at Hutton, was pleased to see that the huge herd of buffalo had made an impression on him. They drove slowly across the last kilometres to Shingela base, and once again Harry noted trees and shrubs, termite mounds and quiet shaded nooks where he had seen some extra special event in the past.

505

The place where the young leopard had caught a bushbuck, had retreated when a lone hyena had come bounding in – and literally tripped over the bushbuck carcass in the grass, tumbling head-over-heels. The termite mound, on top of which he had seen the biggest kudu bull in his life poised relaxedly, watching the warden staring at him. The acacia where he had watched the big male lion climb, straight up the trunk and into the middle branches, to the warthog stored there by a leopard. Near the tree was where he had seen the albino waterbuck. And there was the glade where he and Kashili had watched the wild dogs finally stop a zebra stallion and pull it down. So many memories. So many years watching life and death in paradise. He slowed the Landrover to a crawl as a pair of francolins scurried across the track, running on quick jaunty legs, lifting off to flicker into the long grass. Ahead was Shingela.

He was irritated to find the senior ranger ensconced on the verandah of his bungalow reading *The Green Hills of Africa*. Was doubly irritated that the ranger had allowed himself to be caught with his feet up, knowing full well that the provincial warden was due in Shingela in the late morning. Further, he had not shaved. That the tourist season had ended a few weeks ago, with Christmas around the corner, was no reason for anyone to slide into holiday mode, Harry had pointed out in clipped, measured tones. And there was no need to look like a bloody hippie. Had swept a jaundiced eye over the ranger then, before walking back to the offices. Stood on the verandah for long minutes, drinking in the river vista. He had only been out of Nemana for ten months, and he missed it already. Badly. He pushed his thoughts aside as Peta and Hutton joined him. Smiled at her. She certainly looked well today, he thought. It's Nemana. The valley. A cure for all ills. Except for the one Hutton intends to inflict upon it.
"My business here with Ed should take me a couple of hours. Why don't you take your father for a long therapeutic stroll

along the river. Show him some more of what we find so special." He grinned crookedly. "Perhaps it would be an idea to take a couple of photos of Sir Courteney Hutton standing beside the Zambezi. They may come in useful, at some time in the future."

Hutton had allowed a small, dry smile to cross his features, acknowledging Harry's thrust. The warden continued. "I would suggest that we stop on the way back and have something to eat. Have a late picnic lunch out, instead of here as we originally planned. We can pick a fine shady tree and have our sandwiches there. I see the Stanley flasks have kept the lime juice nice and cooled. It won't be Meikles, but it will be close."

The business of the day had, in fact, taken less time than Harry anticipated. There had not been much small talk, not after his broadside delivered earlier. Edward Rogers had escorted Harry out to his vehicle afterwards. They could see Peta and her father out on the edge of the river. He put his canvas briefcase and the worn rifle case into the recess behind the seats, before turning to the ranger.

"When was the last time you saw Kabakwe?"

Rogers grinned.

"A couple of days ago, as a matter of fact. Upriver, on the Kabwatu road. The bugger chased my vehicle very determinedly. I think he was in the last stage of musth, judging by his condition. He's not usually as aggressive."

Harry chuckled.

"I'll keep an eye out for him. I've decided to take the river track, going back, as far as Kabwatu, and then I'll cut across to the main road. It will give Hutton another opportunity to take a look at more of the region he plans to drown, as well as giving me a chance to take a ride through one of my most favourite stretches of country."

The track wound its way beside the river, which they could nearly always see on their right, sparkling in the afternoon sun.

The amount of game, even in this hot period of the day, was staggering. Everywhere they looked, there were animals. Until the rains, Harry knew. Then they would disappear overnight. Which sure as anything are well overdue now, he thought again. They haven't been this late for a long time. The riverine vegetation is taking a hammering, especially from the elephants. He stopped the Landrover suddenly.

"Look."

Peta stared around them, wondering what had particularly caught his attention. Hutton had been dozing upright, bracing himself against the gentle lurching passage of the vehicle. Now he peered vaguely around at the bush. Peta glanced questioningly at her husband. He grinned and nodded at a tree a few paces away.

"There. That pink jacaranda. Beautiful, isn't it? It's flowering very late. Maybe that's why the blooms stand out so well now."

It was true. The pink bell-shaped flowers were a striking contrast against the background of sere parched bush. Harry got out and picked a small spray of the delicate blooms. Came back and held them out to Peta.

"They should press nicely, between the pages of your book."

She blew him a kiss.

"Thank you, kind sir."

Sir Courteney Hutton watched them impassively.

Harry climbed back in.

"The Nyamawari is just ahead. We'll cross it and stop for a rest. Have our picnic. The tsetses are a little aggressive, but we won't be staying long. There's a way to go yet."

In the quiet coolth of the evergreens that crowded the wide sand river they stretched cramped muscles. Harry rested his rifle across the seats and unlimbered the wooden safari box from the back of the Landrover. As he had predicted, the tsetse flies found them quickly. He grinned as Hutton swatted angrily at them.

"The more you flap around, the more they'll zone in on you. Try to ignore them."

Hutton muttered an epithet, giving the warden a rueful grin.

"Easier said than done, Harry. They seem attracted to me. Perhaps I'm more blue-blooded than I thought."

Harry carried the day box into the shade of the mahogany, and then watched Peta hold the canvas jossak up to pour water over her face. Saw it spill down her front, the suddenly wet shirt moulding to her skin. She saw him looking at her. Smiled. He changed the direction of his thoughts.

"I saw a couple of places where jumbo have dug holes in the river bed. I'll take the jossak and the spare jerry can and top them up. The temperature gauge is running a little high, and we still have the escarpment to climb. Perhaps you can unpack lunch, Mrs Kenyon."

"Sure, lover."

"Need a hand, Harry?"

Sir Courteney Hutton was trying. Harry had to give him that, he supposed. But it wasn't enough. *Not nearly so.* He shook his head.

"No, thanks. It won't take long. Don't wander off. This area is crawling with rhino and most of the other big stuff. Never know what's dozing the hot hours away nearby." Harry gave his father-in-law a half grin.

"Hate anything to do you in, not right now. That's my prerogative."

Let the grin widen at the expression on Hutton's face.

He shucked the .375 out of its case and checked the magazine, then drew back the bolt and chambered a round. It's nice to be able to get back to the precision sporting weapons, he reflected. Instead of the FN. He sniffed at the faint smell of gun oil. Ah yes. Shouldered the .375 and picked up the jossak and the jerry can, hooked a plastic cup from the dash of the Landrover as he went past it. Stepped out of the deep cool shade into the solid heat of the valley sun. Began sweating anew. Knew he would be sweating a lot more by the time he had taken the water he needed from the miniature carefully sculpted wells out in the middle of the dry river bed.

The jerry can was almost full when he heard the scream.
Knew it was trouble of the direst kind, even before he had jumped to his feet, seized the rifle from where it leaned against a piece of driftwood. Eyes searching in the direction of the scream, moving, breaking into a trot, feeling the sand grind under his feet. No tsetses out here in the sun, just the mopane flies swarming. Stopped, as the man burst out of the scrub on the edge of the dry river. Saw, even over the distance that separated them, the terror etched on his face. What, thought Harry, is chasing him? Why the hell did he go off on his own? Why don't people listen? Hutton tripped, scrambled up in an instant, threw a frantic glance over his shoulder. Whatever he saw caused him to run even harder, his mouth wide in a soundless scream. Harry saw it then, saw the elephant appear behind the man. Saw the long sweeping tusks, saw the ears flapping like loose sails, saw the dark wet streak running down the side of Kabakwe's face. The elephant was very close behind Sir Courteney Hutton. *Damn.* Harry lifted his rifle, found the tycoon and the elephant over his sights, enmeshed. Grinned savagely as the ivory bead centred on Hutton, stayed on him as he made his panic-stricken run from the elephant. So easy, thought the warden, such a nice clean shot. *Boom!* So sorry, old chap, I was trying to shoot the elephant. Didn't mean to drop you in your tracks. The seconds ricocheting past. The grin became a grimace. The elephant was on top of the running man, loomed mightily over him. *Jesus.* The ivory bead on Kabakwe now, right there steady on his lower forehead, just a tad higher than the human in front of him. *Noooo.* Not Kabakwe. Not to save the bastard who plans to kill the whole valley. The only one of the Big Four still alive and I've got to kill him, before he kills Hutton. Sod it. Let the elephant have him, let Kabakwe kill the son-of-a-bitch. He deserves it. Oh Jesus! He fired, shifted his aim and fired again. Saw Kabakwe

stop, pull up as if he had run into an invisible wall, as Hutton
went down. Walked quickly forward, seeing the dust billow up.
Saw Kabakwe standing tall, searching for the new disturbance,
ears wide. Harry could see the neat round holes his bullets had
made, one in each ear. Hutton was moving, having trouble
getting up.
"Stay down, Hutton. Freeze where you are. Don't move, not
one muscle."
Harry shouted loudly. So the man could hear. So the elephant
could locate him. So Kabakwe could focus his attention on the
warden. Yet again, Harry's brain reminded him. Just like
Scratch Peters. Come on, elephant, look at me. Find me.
Leave that idiot alone, he's not worth the trouble. You know
me, we've been through this before. Been there, done that.
Only that time you weren't in musth. Your mind wasn't
scrambled with testosterone. And we both went our separate
ways. Please let it be the same this time.
 The elephant, he could see, had picked up Hutton's scent
on the ground, even though he couldn't see the motionless
human in the dust. Had begun to focus anew on his original
quarry. Harry trotted forward a last dozen paces. Stopped and
called his name.
"Kabakwe!"
The elephant's head jerked up. Harry saw his eyes find him, his
great body stiffening in tandem.
"Yep, me again. We've got to stop meeting like this. That's
good, there's a good chap. Keep on coming."
Kabakwe had stalked forward a few paces, his gaze riveted on
the warden. Hutton was now to the elephant's left, behind his
line of vision. Harry flicked a glance at the man, saw the terror
still scrawled across his face, his eyes wide as he cowered,
staring up at the bull elephant beside him. Stay there, mister.
Don't move a muscle, not even an eyelash. And you might just
get out of this mess alive. On the periphery of his vision Harry
caught movement. Checked swiftly. Saw Peta standing very
still, further along the river bank. Concentrated on Kabakwe

again. Knew, suddenly, that he was going to charge. The elephant had had enough of this. *No, dammit. Damn, damn, damn.* The bull came at him. Head down, tusks scything just above the ground, ears swept back. Hutton behind the elephant now, scrambling, lurching up, running away. Harry lifted the rifle. Smiled. Come on! Stood waiting. Do it! *Africa, bloody Africa,* his mind sang.

He saw himself as if from afar. Saw the man lying broken and bloody in the sand of the river bed. As the vultures would see him. Tried to squint through the blood and the sand up at himself. Up at the sky. Looking for the vultures. Could not see any because the sun was too bright in his eyes. So bright. But they were there, the birds, he knew. They were always ...

CHAPTER FIFTY

T he tantara of warm African rain on a corrugated iron roof. Blue-white flashes of lightning, not so threatening now, illuminating the game-cropped lawn and the space that there is across it. Peta Kenyon sitting far back on the verandah, close to the French doors that are open, where the light from the lounge can fall on the book and the letter she has finished re-reading. Half listening to the rain, her thoughts lingering on the letter from her father, on the enormity of what he had told her. And what he had not. She shook her head softly. So, he did it, in the end. He stopped the dam, together with Kabakwe. Squeezed her eyes shut to keep the tears back. *But what a price, Harry.* It cost us both dear. She let her thoughts go back to that day. Did not let them wander too freely, she was not ready for that, not yet. They skirted away from the image of Harry lying on the sand, the elephant, frozen, after ... after... a red smear on one tusk, wheeling quickly and running away, tail curled high in sudden panic. Focused on her father, ashen-faced and trembling, staring at Harry's broken inert form, his silence that had persisted for days after Harry ... after he ... no. He had been at her side through all of the aftermath, moving sometimes like an automaton, but there. Then he had gone. And yesterday she received his letter with the London postmark.

He had, he told her, been forced to terminate Hutrhon's operations at Mupata, had advised the interim government of the re-evaluated findings by the Department of Research, Study, Geo-Mapping and Sample Analysis at Watford. The core samples were not, after all, conducive to the weight and impact of a dam wall being built across Mupata Gorge. How such elemental mistakes had been made in the results of the preliminary tests no one could, or would, say. It was indeed fortunate that the current analyses had prevented further money wasted and perhaps even, eventually, loss of life.

Peta put the letter down again. What did that cost you, Dad? How did you manage to swing that? Because I have no doubt that you did. That you pulled some strings, made heavy contributions to some fund or other. I should thank you, I suppose. But I can't. Not yet. Harry would be pleased, I know that. So I will thank you for him. A dam, the drowning of Nemana and the valley, would have killed him, one way or another. Just as surely as the elephant. So where does that leave us? She opened the book, *Vanishing Eden*, where the pressed pink flowers were, stared unseeingly at them. Felt the stirrings in her belly again, smiled through the tears that had come. The rain had almost stopped.

POSTSCRIPT

The surviving public figures that appear in this story continue to appear in the media of Zimbabwe, and, occasionally, the world.

General Hugo Winters left Rhodesia on 5 January 1980. He now lives at Cape Maclear on the edge of Lake Malawi, where he has a thriving fish business.

Jack Breen holds a position with the Ministry of Interior, Bahrain, where he has lived since April 1981.

Whispering Jim Lannigan went on to serve with various military organisations in Africa, being severely wounded in Angola. He is, at this time of writing, in Sierra Leone.

Obert Hadebe returned to Rhodesia on 26 December 1979 with other top nationalist military commanders in time for the cease-fire negotiated at Lancaster House. He was killed shortly thereafter in a vehicle accident.

Dr Alistair Drummond left his post in Zimbabwe in 1983 to take up a position with World Wildlife Fund. He now lives in Knysna, in the Cape region of South Africa.

Garnet Clayton took early retirement in January 1981 and lives in the Eastern Highlands of Zimbabwe, augmenting his pension producing trout flies and growing antheriums.

Roscoe Daniels is now a professional hunter in Tanzania.

Sir Courteney Hutton died in 1995 at his home in Berkshire, England. His book *Whose Turn to Wear the White Hat Today*, published in 1989, about business and politics in Africa, became a controversial best seller.

Shadrek, son of Kashili, continues to live adjacent to Gona re Zhou National Park, doing what he does best, supported by certain key figures of the Zimbabwean hierarchy.

Peta Kenyon lives with her son, Harry Jnr, in the Karen suburb of Nairobi. She has not re-married. Harry is apprenticed to legendary hunter and guide, Bongo Fletcher.